Let's Begin Again

***Also by Debra White Smith
in Large Print:***

The Awakening
For Your Heart Only
Second Chances
A Shelter in the Storm
This Time Around
To Rome with Love

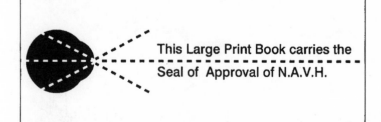

This Large Print Book carries the
Seal of Approval of N.A.V.H.

Let's Begin Again

Debra White Smith

Thorndike Press • Waterville, Maine

Published in 2006 by arrangement with Harvest House Publishers.

Thorndike Press® Large Print Christian Fiction.

The tree indicium is a trademark of Thorndike Press.

The text of this Large Print edition is unabridged.
Other aspects of the book may vary from the original edition.

Set in 16 pt. Plantin by Al Chase.

Printed in the United States on permanent paper.

Library of Congress Cataloging-in-Publication Data

Smith, Debra White.
    Let's begin again / by Debra White Smith.
      p. cm. — (Seven sisters ; #7) (Thorndike Press large print Christian fiction)
    ISBN 0-7862-8746-2 (lg. print : hc : alk. paper)
    1. Pregnant women — Fiction. 2. Married women — Fiction. 3. Florida — Fiction. 4. Large type books.
I. Title. II. Thorndike Press large print Christian fiction series.
PS3569.M5178L48 2006
  813′.6—dc22   2006008690

*To Harvest House editor Betty Fletcher
for her undying patience with me as I'm
forever juggling my deadlines.*

Acknowledgments

Special thanks to my critique partner, Dr. Bob Osborne, who stepped in at the last minute and saved me from drowning in a sea of words. Bob served as general editor, literary advisor, outline magician, and special friend as I strove to complete this book. Thanks Bob for being willing to offer your wisdom and counsel. I will forever be grateful!

Also, thanks to the Jacksonville, TX fire department for their willing help and insight — especially Kevin McKinney and Joe McLane.

The Seven Sisters

Jacquelyn Lightfoot Franklin: An expert in martial arts, Jac has seen plenty of action in her work as a private detective. Part African American, Native American, and Caucasian, Jac is married to Lawton Franklin, and they reside in Denver, Colorado.

Kim Lan Lowery O'Donnel: Tall, lithe, and half Vietnamese/half Caucasian, Kim is a much-sought-after supermodel. She and her missions-coordinator husband, Mick, adopted a son with special needs from an orphanage in Vietnam.

Marilyn Douglas Langham: Joshua and Marilyn, along with Marilyn's daughter, Brooke, live in Arkansas. Marilyn works as an office manager for a veterinarian; Joshua is a minister.

Melissa Moore Franklin: After a stormy reconciliation and an eventful Mediterranean cruise, Melissa married Kinkaide, a well-known Christian musician. An M.D.,

Melissa runs a small medical clinic in Nashville.

Sammie Jones Butler: An award-winning writer/editor for *Romantic Living* magazine, Sammie also is building a writing career as a Christian novelist. After marrying R.J. Butler she and her son, Brett, moved to R.J.'s boys ranch in Mena, Arkansas.

Sonsee LeBlanc Delaney: A passionate veterinarian known for her wit, Sonsee grew up in a Southern mansion outside New Orleans. Sonsee and Taylor, a Texas rancher, have an eighteen-month-old son, Donny.

Victoria Roberts: Cohost of "Extraordinary Homes," Victoria is a charming, softspoken domestic "genius" who loves to cook, work on crafts, and sew. She has been married to Tony for six years, and they live in Destin, Florida.

Let's Begin Again Cast

Brandon Quinn: Brother-in-law to Eddy Graham, Brandon works in the attorney general's office for the state of Florida.

Buster Shae: A part of the mafia, Buster loves both money and murder.

Coty Norris: Toddler of Kevin and Rhonda Norris.

Calvin Sinclaire: Adoptive father of Evelyn Toni Sinclaire.

Darnell Hopkins: Long-time chief of police in Destin, Florida.

Eddy Graham: Best friend and firefighting partner of Tony Roberts. Eddy backs up Tony during firefighting and through the traumas of life.

Evelyn Toni Sinclaire: Nicknamed E.T., Evelyn is the daughter of Calvin and Macy Sinclaire and the birth daughter of Tony Roberts.

Johnna Blackwell: E.T.'s best friend.

Kevin Norris: A bank vice president, Kevin discovers his illegal dealings are leading to his own destruction. He is married to Rhonda.

Matt Leavey: College basketball player and friend of E.T.

Macy Sinclaire: Adoptive mother of Evelyn Toni Sinclaire.

Rhonda Norris: Married to Kevin Norris. Rhonda hides a shameful past and believes her husband is more honorable than she.

Sal: Secretary at the fire station where Eddy and Tony are employed.

Tony Roberts: An acclaimed firefighter, Tony has been married to Victoria for six years. His heroic tendencies often land him in the middle of danger.

One

Tony Roberts crawled up the stairway ravaged by the fire that threatened the lives of the mother and son trapped inside the inferno. The boiling smoke erupted around him like a churning wall of molten lava. The only evidence that his partner, Eddy Graham, was still with him was the presence of his gloved hand gripping the water nozzle they'd dragged into the blazing beach house. Eddy systematically blasted the water at regular intervals in an attempt to keep the path clear of fire. The knees of Tony's bunker pants ground against the heavy layer of soot that clung to the steps like a woolen blanket. The snapping flames in the depths of billowing smoke devoured the immaculate two-story home, and spit forth more soot. The fire's crackle and roar nearly drowned out the sound of Tony's controlled breathing into the self-contained breathing apparatus. The cool oxygen from the air pack bathed his face and offered relief from the heat's intensity.

Neither he nor Eddy knew what the next few minutes might hold. In a matter of seconds they would either become heroes or a pair of statistics in the daily newspaper. A surge of adrenaline insisted Tony take the chance. According to the frantic neighbor, a woman and her son were trapped upstairs. Tony refused to bow to the unrelenting flames.

A river of sweat prickled his spine, and the smoke swirled around his mask as if to taunt him. Tony's damp fingers, covered in heat-resistant gloves, flexed against the handle of the ax he dragged alongside him. At last he and Eddy topped the final stair, and a flaming doorway loomed within ten feet of them. Tony nudged Eddy and pointed toward the doorway. Like divers in the inky deep, the two men moved closer, and through the dense smoke, made eye contact. Eddy gave the nod, and his black eyes shone with the assurance that they were in together and Tony was covered.

Tony had no guarantee that the woman was in that particular room, yet a strong hunch bade him take his chances and plunge through the doorway veiled in devilish flames. There were no promises on the other side. Jumping through the flames might land him in the center of an air pocket, free of fire. Then again he might land in the bowels of Hades. Last year they had lost a crew member in a similar situation when a ball of fire ate him alive.

A high-pitched noise, vague yet recognizable, penetrated the steady whisper of Tony's breathing — a noise he would have sworn was a baby's shriek on the other side of the room's doorway. As Tony struggled to his feet he was fully aware of the extra 100 pounds of weight his turnout gear and air pack added. His whole body, now drenched in sweat, begged for water and the coast's refreshing breeze. Yet Tony ventured forward, driven by the champion within who pushed him to the brink of endurance.

He spoke into the receiver strapped inside his mask, "We think we've found them. We're going deeper!" As if punctuating Tony's words Eddy shot a blast of water along the blazing doorway.

Tony surged forth to the mission that proved his life's calling — a calling to rescue those in need. His heart pounding in his throat, he and Eddy stepped through a wall of rolling smoke, stomped toward the room, and lurched through what Tony hoped wasn't the gateway to death.

After the blare of orange, the flash of heat rushed upon Tony; then the firm floor beneath his boots. He absorbed the jolt with bent knees and was thankful that going with his gut instinct had paid off once again. Eddy bumped into him as he gazed around the room filled with a crib, toy box, and a menagerie of stuffed animals. This room reminded him of the decor his wife, Victoria, had begun the minute she learned of her pregnancy.

Before Tony had time to register the victims' locale, a woman fell headlong against him. Her lips moved but Tony's headgear prevented him from full comprehension. Nevertheless, the little boy in her arms squealed with an intensity that might have pierced Tony's temples like an ice pick if not for the helmet and nomex hood.

"It's going to be okay," Tony hollered and gripped her shoulder. He scanned the room for something in which to wrap the trembling woman and her child. He spied a blanket draped across the crib's rail about the time Eddy stepped forth to grab it. Tony steadied the coughing woman with a firm grip on her upper arm as Eddy settled the blanket over her head and shoulders.

Tony and Eddy exchanged a brief glance that said, "Let's run!" Tony peered into the woman's rich-brown eyes, drenched in tears, and pointed. Her head bobbed in agreement, and she reminded Tony of an Indian woman ensconced in tribal draping.

Gripping her arm he urged her forward as Eddy blasted the doorway with water. Head ducked, the lady braved the blazing doorway, and Tony followed in her wake. Yet as he passed the child's dresser, a petite book, bound in leather, caught his eye. A lock, flat and brassy, claimed the book's side, and a pen protruded from the center. Undoubtedly, a diary. More than once Tony had snatched up cherished treasures such as photos or a baby's bronzed shoes on his way out of an inferno. Usually, the victims clutched the valued possessions as if they were their lifelines. He figured the forgotten diary must hold a wealth of memories the brown-eyed woman would be loath to lose. Tony scooted the diary into his gloved hand and braved the flames once more.

As soon as he and Eddy emerged after the woman, a sickening swoosh and knee-shaking crash accompanied a cloud of heat from behind — heat extending blistering arms that threatened to pull Tony into the inferno. Usual survival techniques insisted they crawl out of a burning building, but a knot of terror in his belly urged Tony to take his chances on running for his life. As Eddy moved forward, spraying water in their path, Tony hunched his shoulders and didn't look back. The baby screamed. The lady swiveled. Her hollow eyes, smudged beneath, widened as raw terror ripped across her face.

He shoved the diary into a pocket of his fire-resistant suit and wrapped an arm around the woman. *"The stairway — now!"* he screamed, and the captain's urgent voice crackled across the receiver near his ear. "Get out! *Get out now!"*

As the woman leaned into him and fought an onslaught of coughs, Tony battled a surge of panic blazing through his veins. In all his years of service, he never wagered a fire would take him down — until now.

Nevertheless, he surged forward and scrutinized the smoke-ensconced stairs, where tongues of fire now licked along the east railing. Through a swirl of smoke he caught a glimpse of Eddy's yellow coat, and Tony couldn't deny that the band of flames racing the stairway was forcing Eddy down the steps. Tony's pulse pounded, and he didn't know whether he was feeling his own terror or sensing his partner's desperation. Eddy never moved so far ahead — especially when he was covering Tony.

Stretching his lips into a grim line, Tony refused to look behind. Instead, he shoved the woman toward the far wall and hoped they escaped before the stairs collapsed. The creak and groan of tormented wood reverberated through the soles of his boots as they scrambled past one step, then the next. The smoke's intensity increased with every step. The woman's body shook with ravaged coughing; the baby's shrieks had long stopped. Tony growled when he caught sight of the woman clutching the limp form of the dark-haired toddler. She leaned heavily into him, and without another thought Tony swung the lady into his arms. The toddler toppled against his chest like a rag doll.

The woman's distressed coughs vibrated through Tony's suit, against his heart. And he wondered how he would feel if this were *his* wife and *his* child trapped with a fireman as her only means of survival.

An all-too-familiar groan and crack rumbled from behind. "She's coming down!" Eddy's distraught scream garbled over the radio receiver strapped inside his hood. The captain's oath followed. A blast of rushing water cut through the smoke and barely missed knocking Tony to his knees. He ground his teeth and raced down the rest of the stairway. Eddy loomed at the smoky base, crouched, as if ready to catch Tony . . . or run. Only a dozen steps now separated

Tony from his partner.

A groan ripped through the disintegrating home like the primeval protest of a prehistoric beast. The stairs rumbled. Eddy stumbled back toward the gaping hole that once served as dining room. "Jump!" his bellow ricocheted through the receiver.

A flash of yellow from behind validated the terror in Eddy's voice. The moan of the collapsing stairs reverberated through him like the final chords of a dirge. He gripped the hacking mother and unconscious child, flung himself into midair, and hoped he would get out alive.

Two

The abdominal pain began that morning as a fluttering ache, vague yet irritating. Three hours ago, Victoria Roberts had equated the pain with the intestinal bug she had endured a couple of days before. Now, she wasn't so sure. Victoria shifted in one of the production set's plush leather chairs. She knitted her brows and touched her lower abdomen.

A commercial's upbeat music trotted around the TV set. "Are you okay?" her cohost Gaylord Rodriguez prompted. "You seemed a little quiet during the interview."

Victoria rose from her seat and cast a vague smile toward the weekly show's well-tanned female guest. She then glanced toward Gaylord, who had helped her make "Extraordinary Homes" a huge hit. His dark eyebrows, lined by years of laughter, peaked above sepia eyes. A full 25 years her senior, Gaylord had acted the part of doting uncle from the time he and Victoria began working together three years ago. But in light of her pregnancy and recent marital separation, Gaylord had metamorphosed into nothing short of a mother hen.

"I'll be fine." Victoria fumbled with her lapel mic, unclipped it, and extended it to their energetic producer, Simon. "I think my lunch isn't agreeing with me. That's all." Her claim held no conviction; Victoria reached for the high-backed chair to steady herself against a dizzy wave that left as quickly as it arrived.

The crease between Gaylord's brows deepened. He examined Victoria's face until she was certain she must look like death.

"Kitchen segment!" Simon announced in a tone that suggested Victoria should move along.

Gaylord stood and extended a hand to their guest, a gardening expert who had just shared the latest techniques for growing vegetables organically.

Leaving the two to their amiable chatting, Victoria stepped from the living room setup and moved toward the brightly lit kitchen. She wiggled her fingers at the blonde who sat in a director's chair near the vacant newsroom set.

Marilyn Langham waved back and called, "Break a leg!"

"Don't tell her to do that," Simon shot toward Victoria's friend, "she just happens to be the best hostess in western Florida."

"Here, here," Victoria chanted.

"Besides, we don't want anything to stop her from showing up next Friday," he said with a loud whoop of laughter.

"Oh, you!" Victoria chuckled at the young man who looked like he just stepped out of the halls of high school. Nevertheless, Simon was a 26-year-old whiz of a director and cameraman. And her temporary concern over the abdominal discomfort faded as she moved toward the kitchen where a row of white ducks around the border beckoned her to cheer up. Victoria squared her shoulders and hoped for the best. Perhaps the abdominal pain was but a passing annoyance.

The routine was the same every Friday. She and her cohost interviewed a guest during the first of three segments that made up "Extraordinary Homes." The second segment unfolded in the kitchen where Victoria's culinary abilities captured the fancy of thousands of weekly viewers. The third segment featured Gaylord's remodeling talents. The two of them always wound up the final moments with a money-saving tip — a segment that had proven to be one of the show's most popular features.

"Okay, we've got one minute, Vickie," Simon called.

Inside, Victoria frowned at the nickname. *My name is Victoria,* she wanted to counter in a no-nonsense tone that would exterminate all chances of his ever calling her Vickie again. Instead, she feigned a winning smile, waved at Simon, then extended the thumbs-up sign to Marilyn Langham who responded with a double thumbs up. Marilyn, one of Victoria's six "sisters" from college, had called earlier in the week and asked if she could come for a weekend visit. Marilyn's husband, Joshua, was away on a mission trip to Los Angeles' inner city. Her daughter, Brooke, was spending the weekend with Marilyn's ex-husband, Brooke's biological father. Victoria had readily agreed to Marilyn's visit. Since she and Tony separated a month ago, the weekends seemed to be getting longer and lonelier.

As the seconds ticked on, Victoria dashed aside thoughts of Marilyn and her own tattered marriage and focused on the task at hand. She meticulously adjusted the mincing knife so that it was in perfect alignment with the cutting board. Next, Victoria pulled a hand mirror from a drawer, ran smoothing fingers along the side-slung ponytail that hung across her shoulder, and examined her makeup. She touched the corner of her lips and removed a minuscule smudge of peach-colored gloss that perfectly matched the hue of her lightweight cotton sweater. Victoria frowned at the dark circles under her hazel eyes. Either the concealer wasn't doing its job or her pregnancy was demanding more rest.

"Twenty seconds!" Simon chimed.

With the smell of a freshly baked Mexican casserole teasing her senses, she plopped the mirror back into the drawer, snapped it shut, laid her manicured hands atop the counter, schooled her features into a serene mask, and smiled into the camera. The lights gradually dimmed. A classic Mexican tune frolicked around the set. Simon held up fingers and silently counted down to three. The lights slowly brightened. Simon's index finger pointed upward then straight at Victoria.

She opened her mouth to greet her loyal audience, and the fluttering pain returned like needles in her womb. Victoria's eye twitched. Her fingers curled around the knife handle. Impish thoughts whispered all sorts of alarming possibilities — each regarding her pregnancy. Once again the pain vanished.

Victoria wrapped clammy fingers around the top of an onion and forced a smile that usually sprang from genuine enjoyment with the task at hand.

"Welcome back," she purred into the camera. "Today, I'm going to be creating a dish that's as delicious as it is easy. It's called Chicken Enchiladas, but we'll be using tortilla *chips* in the bottom of the dish rather than traditional flour or corn tortillas." She touched the top of a bag of chips, strategically propped against a large, wooden bowel. Her damp fingertips quivered against the cool, yellow wrap as another dizzy flash sent the set's glistening black appliances into a momentary spin. "That way —" She cleared her throat, blinked, and pasted a fresh grin across her stiff face. "That way, you can cut out the time it takes to stuff and roll the tortillas, but you still get the same delicious effect — or maybe even better, in my opinion anyway," she added with a chuckle. "This just happens to be my hus— my husband's favorite dish."

Victoria diverted her gaze from the camera as another ache attacked her. This time, the ache involved her heart. She hadn't seen her husband Tony in a month — not since that big fight when he slung his clothing into a suitcase and stomped out. He'd been in permanent residence at the fire station ever since. They'd talked a few times since then — the last time only yesterday when he'd called to see how she was doing. As with the previous call their talking turned to accusations that only broadened the chasm between them.

She reached for the butter, lying in a saucer by the chips. "First, you start with a stick of butter or margarine. And all of you regular viewers know that I'm using butter, not margarine. I always prefer the real thing." *And that's what I thought Tony and I had — the real thing.* Her knees quivered as Tony's words from yesterday crashed through her mind. *It's like you think I'm supposed to be some sort of impossibly perfect man, Victoria! I'm not perfect and I never will be! I don't even know why I keep trying.*

Victoria dropped the butter into the saucepan and turned on the electric burner. "Now, while that's melting," she cooed in a tone that belied her emotional turbulence, "let's mince our onion." Victoria retrieved the white onion and held it up. Another flash of dizziness spun through her head, and she struggled against dropping the onion. "I'm using a white onion because they always add a milder, more mellow flavor to my cooked dishes. When a recipe requires the onion remain raw, then I always choose purple." In order to avoid the inevitable rush of onion-tears, Victoria sliced the onion only once and forced herself to amiably chat about the versatility of their chosen dish.

At last the butter's faint, telltale sizzle cued her to action. "And as always . . ." She attempted a mischievous grin toward the camera, but the smile felt more like a grimace. ". . . the cooking elves have visited me again. I just happen to have an onion already minced." She picked up the glass bowl containing the onion. It trembled in her hand. She managed to dump the prepared onion into the saucepan, grab a flat wooden spoon from the crockery urn, and stir.

"Next, we will be adding a small can of chopped green chili peppers." Victoria's fingers grew clammier as she touched the top of an unopened can of chilies; then she picked up a miniature bowl full of the chopped peppers.

The instant she dumped the peppers into the onion mixture the needles in her womb erupted with greater persistence. A moist warmth crept up her neck, and Victoria swallowed against a wave of nausea. The smell of simmering onions, peppers, and butter invaded her senses and threatened to hurl her into a violent heave. The warmth from her neck crept over her lips and into her mouth.

She forced a swallow and snatched up a larger bowl containing cream of chicken soup. "Sauté the green chilies and onions until the onions are clear," she choked out and hoped she didn't sound as strained to the viewers as she did to herself. "Next, we add three cans of cream of chicken soup." Victoria dumped the soup into the onion mixture and wasted no time shoving the pan with its offending odor to the far corner of the stove.

She gulped in a breath and touched the top of her forehead, which was covered in a thin film of sweat. Victoria composed her features and prayed that Simon would run an early commercial. A movement on the set's far parameter caught her eye. She leaned against the counter, reached for a second saucepan, and cast a discreet glimpse toward the movement. Marilyn hovered in the shadows as if she were ready to bolt forward. The appliances whirled once more, and her grip on the pan diminished with the room's every rotation. She dropped the pan to the counter, steadied herself, and looked up. Marilyn strode toward her, a bright smile plastered all over her face. Victoria gazed into the camera and warbled out a gracious, "Today, we have a surprise guest — my friend, Marilyn Langham. Marilyn is the one who gave me this recipe."

"It's been in my family for years," Marilyn said as if she were a seasoned TV professional. She stopped beside Victoria, grinned into the camera, and slipped a supportive arm around her friend.

Victoria leaned into Marilyn and stiffened her wobbling legs. Something was wrong — desperately wrong. Victoria blinked against the sting of tears. *If I lose this baby, I don't know what I'll do.* She had harbored a tiny hope that the baby would awaken Tony to his failings and restore their marriage. So far the pregnancy had not wavered Tony's claims that Victoria was also a major element in their marital problems. Even if her marriage never recovered, Victoria had clung to the possibility of the fulfillment she had longed for her whole adult life — the fulfillment of motherhood.

"The next step in this easy recipe," Marilyn said, "is simply to add the cubed, cooked chicken to the mixture and then pour it into a dish lined with tortilla chips." She pointed toward the bag of chips propped against the wooden bowl. With her free hand, Marilyn reached for the baking dish containing a small bag of chips, and maintained a firm grip on Victoria's waist with her other hand.

Feeling as if she were moving in a time warp, Victoria reached for the dish and assisted Marilyn in setting it closer. The smell of the soup mixture now filling the set sent another bulge of nausea up her throat. She leaned into Marilyn and conjured all her strength to fight the discomfort. This time the nausea subsided more readily.

The next few minutes blurred into a swirl of bright lights and Marilyn's cheerful chatting as if she and Victoria didn't have a care in the world. At last, she and Marilyn managed to top the casserole with shredded cheddar cheese, slide the dish into the oven, and retrieve an identical dish containing the fully prepared and cooked casserole. The camera zoomed in for a final focus on the delicious dish, and the delightful Mexican tune that ushered in the segment cued the end of Victoria's on-camera plight.

As if awaiting the moment of release, her body went limp. Her arms seemed to weigh a ton and her knees buckled. Without a word, Victoria slumped against Marilyn.

"She's in trouble!" Marilyn hollered.

The two stumbled toward the set's glass-topped dining table, and the smell of Marilyn's jasmine perfume triggered Victoria's gag reflex.

"I'm not feeling well," she coughed out as she plopped into the dining chair. As if to underscore her words, her abdomen protested with a spasm that reverberated into her back and sent spikes down her legs.

"I had a hunch she wasn't going to make it through that segment," Gaylord's voice, deep and concerned, vibrated from a far land.

Victoria placed her arms upon the table's glass surface, propped her head atop her sweater-clad arms, and squeezed her eyes against the sting that refused to go away.

"She turned almost gray," Simon said. "I was going to cut to an early commercial when her friend came on the set. I'm sorry — your name escapes me," Simon said upon an urgent tremor.

"My name is escaping even *me* right now." Marilyn's grim undertones heightened Victoria's concern — a concern that threatened to explode into panic. "I thought I was helping when I came onto the set," Marilyn continued. "But it sounds like I just prolonged her misery." A gentle hand descended upon Victoria's shoulder.

"I'll go for a bottle of water," Gaylord said.

"Water would be nice," Victoria said hoarsely. Her warm breath ricocheted off the tabletop and back onto her face. No matter how tightly she squeezed her eyes the spinning sensation only increased, which produced the odd impression of weightlessness in a dark chasm.

The waft of jasmine accompanied someone leaning near, and Victoria tightened her throat against another gag.

"Want me to take you to the doctor?" Marilyn asked.

Her friend's very words held the hint of a storm on the horizon, a storm Victoria dreaded even acknowledging. She had heard of women having miscarriages her whole life. Somehow, she never considered that she might become one of them. The agony in her womb pierced Victoria's heart, and she sniffled against the flood of tears that threatened to explode like a hot geyser.

"Y–yes. I'm — I'm cramping," she whispered in hopes that no one else heard.

As Marilyn tightened her grip on her hand Victoria opened her eyes and stared through the glass table at her short-topped leather boots. She thanked heaven that the spinning sensation seemed to be abating.

"Water — here's the water," Gaylord's breathless announcement echoed around the set.

"Might be best to go to the emergency clinic," Simon suggested, and his voice held the same hint of a storm as Marilyn's.

A gentle, cool nudge against Victoria's fingers prompted her to ease up her head and wrap her fingers around the cold bottle that Marilyn proffered. Bucketsful of concern poured from Marilyn's soft brown eyes, and Victoria wanted to speak her thanks but couldn't produce a word. She tilted the bottle against her lips and gulped a generous swallow. The frigid liquid hit the back of her mouth and trailed an icy path into her tense stomach.

"One minute!" a cameraman's urgent voice beckoned from across the room.

"That's you, Gaylord!" Simon urged. "Home improvement is next."

Gaylord gripped Victoria's hand. "Somebody needs to call Tony and let *him* take her to the doctor," he ground out. "Or at least meet her at the clinic. How any man can leave a pregnant woman is beyond me." The bitter words darted around the set like the fire of a machine gun and confirmed what Victoria had long suspected about Gaylord's opinion of Tony. "It's time for him to take some responsibility in all this —"

"But —" Victoria began.

"Thirty seconds!" Simon's urgent call prompted Gaylord to loosen his clasp on her hand and sprint toward the other side of the studio.

"It isn't like that," Victoria whispered to Gaylord's retreating form. *He's offered to come back home* she added to herself, *but we always wound up fighting.*

"Can you make it to the car?" Marilyn asked.

"I — I think," Victoria croaked. "If I can lean on you."

"Want me to call Tony?" Marilyn asked. "We can use my cell phone."

After studying the top of her water bottle, Victoria took another slow swallow. Yesterday's heated argument toppled through her memory along with tons of aggravation. And with the remembrance of each word, Victoria marveled that she had defended Tony in the face of Gaylord's accusations.

"You put more energy into your church work and crafts than you ever have into our marriage," Tony had accused. "Then you expect me to be some sort of perfect lover I can never be!"

"Well, you act like you couldn't care less

about me most of the time, Tony!" Victoria had replied.

She relived the receiver's click in her ear. The last person she wanted to have to deal with right now was Tony Roberts.

"No, let's *don't* call Tony," she replied.

Marilyn's thinly penciled brows peaked under her wispy bangs as if that were the last decision she expected Victoria to make. Her brown eyes, normally soft and reassuring, took on a penetrating edge that raised Victoria's defenses.

A new onslaught of warmth crept up her cheeks, and Victoria wasn't sure this warm rush had anything to do with her physical problems. She averted her gaze to the tan suede pants she had declared her bargain of the year. No matter what Marilyn thought, she wouldn't budge on her decision. This baby was in *her* body, and she would deal with the problems herself.

Three

Tony's boots crashed against the smoking carpet as the burning staircase thundered to a fiery end. The house shook as if it were a toy being tossed about in a merciless earthquake. Hurled forth by the momentum that had propelled him through the air, Tony toppled forward and stumbled to regain his equilibrium. The combined burden of the woman and child ensured his fall. His knees pounded into the floor with a jar that rattled his teeth. His breath exploded from tight lungs on a powerful swoosh. Despite the fall, the rumble and heat of the inferno fueled Tony with the resolve to struggle back to his feet. The toddler's limp head jostled against his chest, and the woman's eyes slid shut. She fought to reopen them and struggled against a series of coughs.

Eddy, his hood still in place, emerged through a swirl of smoke and plucked the child from Tony. The sizzle and pop of flames promised the house was coming down. His burden now lightened, Tony ran in Eddy's wake toward the gaping hole that was once the elegant dining room's outside wall. A new round of coughs absorbed the woman's ragged breathing as Tony emerged into the Florida morning's February sunlight. The sounds of roaring water pounding into the inferno confirmed the presence of stout fire trucks that served the Destin community. The ladders going up announced that the walls would soon go down.

A knot of EMTs ran from the ambulance parked at curbside. Showers of soot raining upon him, Tony staggered toward the gurney the medical technicians hauled across the yard. Amid the haze of smoke the EMTs raced to Tony's side, secured the gurney on its wheels, and assisted him in settling the troubled woman against the taut black surface.

Once his burden was released Tony clawed at the clasp holding his helmet in place. He ripped it off and welcomed the ocean-side air that bathed his sweating face in a blast much cooler than the home's blazing interior.

"My baby . . ." The woman's groan was nearly drowned out by the water's deafening rush, yet Tony would have read her parched lips even if he were unable to understand a word she said. For the words were forever emblazoned upon his own heart. They were the words he had repeated over and over again at the age of 17 when wrong choices had landed him and his girl-friend in roles neither of them were able to embrace.

"My baby . . ." The brunette's tousled hair flipped against the gurney as she tossed her head from side to side. The fine lines around her eyes, accented by soot, revealed a woman in her early 40s.

"My partner has him," Tony hollered over the barrage of water and flames. "The EMTs will make sure he's okay," he added and hoped the little boy suffered only minor injuries.

The woman lifted her hand toward her throat and barked out a barrage of rough coughs. Copious mucous flowed from stressed tissue. Her T-shirt, singed along the sleeve, did little to hide the scarlet burns marring her left arm. Tony winced and clawed at the coat that had helped preserve his life. As the knot of medical professionals secured the woman on the gurney another EMT moved to Tony's side and began the process of removing the weighty bunker suit and oxygen bottle.

Tony's body screamed for water. He sucked in great gulps of air and wobbled. Like a warrior in raging battle he fought against collapsing to his knees. Just as he thought he might go down, the woman's face turned toward him, her deep brown eyes drooped open, and she gazed up at Tony. Time stood still, and a spark of unfathomable appreciation glistened from her soul to his. Yet mingled with the appreciation Tony detected a flicker of some intangible essence that defied definition — something that left him at ease and made him feel accepted, despite the fact that his rescue had been far from perfect. He observed the woman's burns once more and wished he could have prevented her injury. Yet her appraisal assured him she would never blame him for the pain.

The EMTs crowded nearer. Tony could hold himself up no longer. He crashed to the ground, hunkered over, and braced himself against falling face first onto the spongy earth.

The EMTs whisked the victim toward the ambulance, and another member of the rehabilitation crew joined the man who assisted Tony. The two of them succeeded in removing the oxygen tank from his back and assisting him in escaping the confines of the protective clothes. One of them shoved a bottle of water into his hands, and Tony poured the liquid down his parched throat.

The cold fluid spilled from the corners of his mouth, trickled down his neck, and soaked his damp T-shirt. The icy trail down his throat and neck only made Tony long for more. At last he managed to struggle to his feet and step free of the gear.

He rubbed his face with the hands that had rescued more lives than he could remember and caught a glimpse of a book lying at his feet. *The diary,* he thought and bent to retrieve the worn book. But on his way up, he staggered and nearly crashed back to the ground.

"It's rehab for you," one of the EMTs insisted and tried to pull him toward a second ambulance parked nearby.

"N–no." Tony shook his head. "I — I'm okay. I just need more water."

"Oh boy, here we go again," one of them drawled. "This is not the time to be tough," he added.

For the first time Tony looked at the two men dressed in blue. One of them was over six feet tall — nearly as tall as Tony — and the other looked like he should be tackling oxen rather than serving the medical field. Both of them peered at him with a steely glint in their eyes that reminded him of pit bulldogs — a glint that silently challenged him to resist rehab. The truth was, no self-respecting fireman ever went to rehab without a fight — unless he was so far gone he had no strength to resist.

Tony cut a glance toward Eddy who was downing a bottle of water with his own pair of EMTs looking on. Tony figured he'd land in rehab whether he wanted to or not, right alongside his partner. In the meantime he clutched the diary, evaded the team of bulldogs, and glanced over his shoulder toward the disintegrating home that claimed a scenic stretch of beach along the Gulf of Mexico. One of the second floor's expansive windows exploded in a shattering spray whose boom competed with the water's pounding.

Tony gripped the back of his neck and stayed himself against the tremors that started in the center of his soul and reverberated to his extremities.

"That one was close," he whispered, "too close."

A heavy hand descended upon Tony's shoulder, and he figured the bulldogs were about to drag him to the ambulance. When he looked up he encountered Eddy's fraternal approval. Tony pivoted to face his partner and best friend whose dark eyes shone with respect.

In a flash Tony gazed past Eddy to the

team of medical professionals who gingerly placed a red-faced, screaming toddler near his mother. The brunette struggled to sit up on the gurney. A firm-faced woman placed a hand on the victim's shoulder and pressured her to remain horizontal. The baby snuggled beside his mother, who cradled him in her arm.

"You're the hero, man!" Eddy underscored his jubilant claim with a slap on the back that threatened to knock Tony flat.

"Now if I can just survive your beating," Tony complained and grappled to maintain his grip on the diary. The book toppled to his feet.

"This time I was worried you weren't going to make it," Eddy said and placed one hand on his hip. He leaned onto one leg in a gesture Tony recognized well. Eddy was as close to collapsing as he was; but neither of them would ever admit it.

"What do you mean?" Tony bent to pick up the diary whose pages had flopped open to release the pen onto the lawn. "I always make it." His words sounded as weak as his knees. Tony scooped up the diary and pen, straightened, and glanced over his shoulder. He eyed the steady stream of water that spewed onto the American dream now ensconced in ravenous flames. Then, he observed the knot of four EMTs who had decided to come after him and Eddy.

"Looks like we're headin' for rehab," Tony mumbled. "They're after us."

"Happens to the best of us," Eddy admitted and tossed aside his empty bottle of water. "I could use more water, that's for sure." A stream of sweat trickled down Ed's temple and added to the sheen upon his dark skin.

Eddy grabbed Tony's shoulder again and repeated his claim. "You're the hero of the hour, man!"

"If only my wife would figure that out," Tony mumbled.

" 'Scuse me?"

"Oh, nothing," Tony replied as yesterday's argument exploded through his mind like an internal version of the inferno behind him.

"When are you going to understand that I'm not like one of your emergencies you can just run in and throw a bucket of water on and keep me happy? I have needs, Tony!" Victoria had yelled into the phone.

"Needs! You want to know about needs?" he had countered. "I can't even *remember* the last time you acted like you gave *one* flip about *my* needs! All it seems you ever focus on is my faults. So I've got a few faults, Victoria! I'm not perfect! Somebody sue me!"

"And to think I actually thought I could move back," Tony mumbled under his breath. *Right now I don't have one clue about how to go about repairing this mess of a marriage — or even if it can be repaired.*

Tony tucked the pen back into the diary, closed it, and examined the leather cover, worn from years of use. The lower corner bore the name Rhonda Black. Only the tinge of gold along the letters' edges suggested that the fading name's presence had started as an elegant engraving.

"I found this on the way out." Tony lifted the diary. "I'm going to take it to the lady — I guess her name's Rhonda."

"Okay, guys," the linebacker EMT growled. "You're headin' for rehab whether you like it or not. We have orders to take care of you."

With a shrug Eddy nodded. Head hanging he fell in beside the pair that had assisted him. Tony backed away from his watchdogs.

"Give me a minute," he demanded, yet the words came out on a dry squeak that did little to hide the quiver in his knees. He sucked in a lung full of cool air that smelled like singed salt with a carbon coating. The piercing Destin sunshine felt like twin spikes in his stinging eyes. Tony rubbed his forefinger and thumb across his eyes and tried to shake the furious flames from his memory.

"This one might need a gurney," the tall guy said.

"I can walk!" Tony claimed.

"Okay, show us," the stocky man challenged and nudged him toward the rehab ambulance. The guy's name tag said his last name was Grouse, and Tony figured the name fit. Grouse didn't look like he would take a thing off anybody.

"No!" Tony stumbled away from them. "I'll go — but first let me give this to the lady." He raised the diary.

"We'll see she gets it." The tall guy reached for the book, and Tony moved toward the ambulance crew tending Rhonda.

"*I'm* going to give it to her," Tony insisted and glared at the two.

"Okay, okay." Grouse held up his hands. "But then you're going with us, and I don't care if we have to drag you. Understand?"

"Yeah." Tony nodded. The truth was the ice packs, cold towels, and chilling water awaiting him in rehab would be a welcomed reprieve.

Tony had barely taken three steps when a silver sedan skidded to a halt at the curb. A frantic man dressed in a suit scrambled out of the vehicle. In his haste he left the door ajar and raced toward the woman and child. Tony slowed his step as the man stopped by the gurney and grabbed the victim's hand. The baby's crumpled face and outstretched arms testified to his adoration of his father. As Tony neared the gurney, the man gathered the child to his chest and covered his smudged forehead in kisses. Like the woman, the man looked to be in his forties, if the gray-streaked hair was anything to go by. Tony figured this couple must be one who most likely married later in life or waited a while to have children.

Tony cast another glance toward the impatient duo and decided he'd better take care of his business before they dragged him off. As he resumed his approach, the brunette attempted to sit up once more, yet the persistent EMT nudged her back onto the gurney. With every step the house's crack and roar diminished. Like a man who awakens from a nightmare to find all is normal, Tony welcomed the sounds of ordinary existence. The baby's cries. The father's soothing overtures. The lone bark of a dog down the stretch of beach. He paused within a few feet of the family reunion.

"That's the man who rescued me," the brunette claimed.

"Thank you! Thank you so much." The shorter man extended his free hand and pumped Tony's hand until he was sure his arm might fall off.

"That's my job," he answered as a warm satisfaction oozed through his wavering spirit.

"Well, this is one husband and father who's glad you do your job," the man continued. His keen gray eyes misted as he stroked his son's tousled dark hair. "I'm Kevin, by the way, Kevin Norris." He shifted the child into the crook of his left arm and extended his hand for another round of pumping.

"Tony Roberts," he said and braced himself against collapsing. A wave of dizziness underscored his need of more fluid, and Tony wondered which hand the IV would go into this time.

"I can never tell you how much I appreciate what you've done for Coty and Rhonda," the man continued. "When they called me at work about the fire, I almost lost it."

A plump EMT bumped into Kevin. "Oh, excuse me," he said. "But we're ready to load your wife into the ambulance. Can you step aside?"

"Oh, sure," Kevin said. "Will I be able to ride to the hospital with you?"

"Not a problem with me," the EMT countered. "Might be for the best, since you've got the little guy there. We're taking them on to West Florida Regional in Pensacola. They'll both be admitted for observation, and your wife has burns on her arm."

"Okay. I'll go turn off my car and lock the door."

As Kevin whirled to his mission, a whiff of sporty men's cologne tinged the acrid air, and Tony figured the stuff probably cost a mint. He never had cared for what he called froufrou men's products, but he fleetingly wondered if a dash of that stuff might positively influence Victoria. Right now, Tony was ready to try about anything to raise her opinion of him, but he was at a loss to determine exactly where to begin. After all, they had a baby on the way. Tony's baby. And he had decided one lonely winter's evening 18 years ago that he would never — absolutely never — release another child that he had fathered. Tony was going to be there for this baby, be close to this baby no matter what. He wasn't prepared to be a long-distance father — even if it meant living with a wife who didn't love him.

His foggy mind meandered back to the problem at hand. Tony eyed the diary whose threadbare edges bespoke years of use and wondered what hidden secrets the pages must have captured. The knot of EMTs prepared to lift the gurney into the ambulance, and Tony motioned for them to stop. He stepped toward the side of the gurney, lifted one corner of his mouth, and extended the diary to Rhonda. "I found this on the way out," he said. "Thought you might like to have it."

Her soft brown gaze landed on the book with a glimmer of recognition. She cradled her injured arm against her abdomen and reached to take the diary. Then, Coty's worried whimpers accompanied the crunch of loafers on pavement. "Okay, the car's locked," Kevin called. "I'm ready."

Rhonda's hand dropped from the diary. Her eyes clouded. Her brow wrinkled as a thread of indecision marred her features. She shook her head. "It's not mine," she denied and cast a furtive look toward Kevin, who was consumed with consoling the toddler.

Tony's eyes narrowed. He glanced from Rhonda to her husband and back to

Rhonda. "Was your maiden name . . ."

She shook her head, and a silent yet forceful *Stop!* reverberated between them.

Tony glanced back at Kevin, who consoled his whimpering son. He discreetly slipped his fingers around the diary and stepped away from the ambulance.

The mysterious book seemed to warm in Tony's grasp as the click and snap of the gurney's collapsing legs accompanied the ambulance's cranking engine. Within seconds, Kevin scrambled into the ambulance, his son in his arms. The doors banged shut, and Tony was left with the impression that Rhonda Black Norris hid a secretive past from her husband.

"Okay, champ, that's it." Tony's tall EMT grabbed him by the arm and Grouse gripped his other arm.

Shaking his head Tony allowed the two to usher him toward the waiting ambulance. He stumbled and slumped against Grouse. The ambulance wobbled into a blur of white and blue and red.

"He's going down," Grouse claimed.

"We should have slammed his rear in here the second he came out."

"No I'm not. I'm n–not going down!" Tony protested and forced himself to stay strong. The last thing he wanted was for any of the crew to see him faint like a wilty old woman. "I'm — I'm just tired," Tony admitted and somehow shoved the mysterious diary into the back pocket of his worn jeans. "I don't think I got three hours sleep last night."

He cast one last glance toward the disintegrating home that must have cost a small fortune. Interestingly enough Kevin Norris hadn't said a word about the loss of his possessions. His whole focus had been on his wife and child.

Tony narrowed his eyes. Despite his body's raging need to collapse, his own troubled marriage flitted through his mind. Rather than fire, he figured a wall of ice had invaded Victoria's heart and was gradually destroying their union just as sure as the flames were demolishing the Norris home. And while Tony knew exactly what to do to rescue Rhonda and her son, he held no clue about how to free Victoria from her disillusionment. Indeed, he was afraid that if she remained in her cold resolve much longer she might very well turn into an ice goddess, unreachable and unloving. Unloving and lost. Lost and lonely.

Four

Marilyn Langham stepped into the hospital hallway and released the unshed tears she had held at bay for the last three hours. For three hours she had been strong for Victoria. For three hours she held Victoria's hand and assured her that God was in control. But despite the doctor's attempts to stop the miscarriage with intravenous medications, Victoria's baby was no more.

After an agonizing morning Victoria now rested peacefully, and it was Marilyn's turn to mourn. She sponged her eyes with a wad of tissue and maneuvered through a maze of medical carts, housekeeping bins, and the occasional visitor. The smells of coffee and antiseptic and a whiff of baby powder all mingled together to create the essence of a memory — Marilyn's own hospital stay after giving birth to her daughter, Brooke.

But Victoria won't be carrying home a bundle of joy, Marilyn thought and pressed her knuckles against her lips to stay the sob tightening her throat.

After a series of sniffles and discreet coughs, Marilyn spied the O.B. visitor's lounge near the nursery. She inhaled a steadying breath. Her loafers squeaked against the polished floor as she rounded the corner toward the lobby. Marilyn hoped to find a private alcove in which to call one of the friends whom she and Victoria had remained close to since college: Sammie Butler, Jacquelyn Franklin, Sonsee Delaney, Kim Lan O'Donnel, or Melissa Franklin. Sammie Butler often referred to the group as "The Sassy Seven," but they mostly called themselves the Seven Sisters. The seven of them had stuck together through many of life's toughest turns. They had stood beside Marilyn through a nasty divorce five years before. Marilyn in turn had been there for each sister as she grappled with disappointments and triumphs. She knew beyond doubt that all the sisters would comfort and support Victoria during this trying hour. As a matter of fact, Marilyn figured a mammoth bouquet bearing each of their names would arrive by dinner.

As she passed the nursery Marilyn slowed and glanced through the large windows. Crib upon crib held infants of all races and sizes. But the tiny faces, feet, and hands that usually evoked awe only increased Marilyn's flow of tears. She gripped the edge of the narrow windowsill and lowered her head. With the smell of baby powder awakening her senses once more, Marilyn propped her forehead against the cool windowpane.

A smiling nurse walked from the back of the nursery and picked up an infant from a crib with a blue ID card. Flailing arms accompanied screams that penetrated the nursery walls. A low chuckle beside Marilyn prompted her to glance at the short, stocky man standing next to her. His black eyes sparkled with glee as his fingers rested against the window. He cut a look at Marilyn and proudly stabbed his chest twice with his index finger. His full lips stretched into a smile about as broad as the Grand Canyon.

"He's our third," the man said, "and it's just as exciting as the first." A trickle of moisture seeped from his eye onto a cheek the color of rich coffee.

Marilyn fiddled with the hem of her cotton sweater and tried to smile.

"Congratulations."

"Thanks." The man nodded toward the nursery. "And which one are you here for?" he asked.

"Uh . . ." Marilyn hedged and swallowed a lump in her throat. "Actually, I'm here for a friend. There's no —" she coughed, "—

no baby." And Marilyn was once again relieved she hadn't told Victoria that she and Joshua had decided for sure that they would adopt.

"Oh, I understand." The man's soft words revealed a wealth of insight, and Marilyn took advantage of his silence to make her exit.

"Well, good luck," she said and lightly touched his arm.

He nodded his appreciation, and the newborn riveted his attention once more.

Marilyn took several steps toward the lounge then stopped in her tracks. She pivoted to face the new father again.

Something in the man's demeanor caused a dash of chills up her spine that spread down her arms. He reminded her of a friend who expected to be a new father in a few months — Tony Roberts. Victoria had told Marilyn not to call him, but from the start of that request Marilyn had doubted the wisdom of Tony's not knowing. After all, he *was* the father of that baby, and by Victoria's own admission he still deeply cared about her pregnancy. *He should be the first to know about the miscarriage.*

In a private e-mail the other day, one of Marilyn's "sisters," Sammie Butler, had hinted that she believed Victoria was as much a contributor to her marital upheaval as was Tony. But being the loyal sort, Marilyn had resisted believing Sammie, even though Sam had spent more time talking to Victoria during the split than Marilyn had. After reading Sam's e-mail Marilyn was hard-pressed to picture the serene, ladylike Victoria as anything other than a gracious and loving wife who had been severely wronged. Nevertheless, the obstinate glint in her eyes when she told Marilyn not to call Tony posed itself as the antithesis of grace.

The young father motioned to the rosy-cheeked nurse who tended the crying infant. With an understanding smile, the white-capped lady neared the nursery window and held the squirming infant at best vantage for the father to see. A spontaneous gurgle of laughter oozed from the father as he rested open palms against the glass. An older gentleman joined him.

"He's my first son," the new father explained. "I have two girls, but this is my boy."

"Looks like a ball player to me." The grandpa nodded. "My son got *two* ball players." He pointed across the nursery and beamed. "Twins."

And Marilyn wondered for the hundredth time if Victoria's baby would have been a boy or a girl, or maybe even twins. At the early stage of only ten weeks into her pregnancy, Victoria hadn't yet discovered the gender of her baby. Marilyn imagined Tony, tall and fair, standing between the new father and grandfather. A guilty twinge squirmed through her midsection.

"I've got to call him," she muttered as she turned toward the lobby again. "It's the only decent thing to do."

Marilyn blotted the last vestiges of tears, reached inside her denim purse, and pulled the cell phone from the inside pocket. She glimpsed a vacant corner in the lounge and directed her steps toward an unoccupied seat near a silk palm. By the time Marilyn settled into the upholstered chair, she had the cell phone poised to dial Tony's work number. When she first got the phone she had programmed all her sisters' home and work numbers as well as the work numbers of their husbands. At the time she wondered if perhaps the task had been a waste of effort. In spite of rarely calling one of the sisters' husbands, she clung to the belief that she'd be glad of the effort if ever there was an emergency. Looking back she viewed the decision as a God thing.

Her thumb hovered over the phone's "send" button, and she wrinkled her brow.

A flash of doubt assaulted her, and Marilyn wondered if going against Victoria's wishes would reap her wrath. She thought about each of the sisters and weighed her decision.

"Melissa would have already called all the sisters as well as Tony," she mused with a smile and recalled Mel's self-appointed nickname, "mouth of the south." Marilyn pondered Jacquelyn, that feisty private eye who at times had aggravated all the sisters with her independent streak. "She probably wouldn't even call any of the sisters, let alone Tony." Marilyn pressed her index finger against the back of the phone and ran her free hand down the front of her corduroy slacks. *That leaves Kim Lan, Sonsee, and Sammie. Sam would call Tony,* she thought without reservation and considered the implications of her e-mail that hinted at who-knows-what about Victoria's part in her rocky marriage. "And I have no idea what Kim Lan and Sonsee would do," Marilyn whispered. *Kim Lan would probably call Sonsee for advice.*

The jubilant father walked into the waiting room, now accompanied by a tall, thin man wearing a black suit with a white clerical collar. The new father nodded toward Marilyn in brief acknowledgment then focused on the minister.

His very presence underscored her commitment to contact Tony. Marilyn curled her toes, gripped the chair's armrest with her free hand, and pressed the phone's "send" button.

Five

Tony settled onto the worn sofa that the fire station's secretary wanted to replace a year ago. Problem was, none of the guys agreed with Sal. And Tony was glad. The sofa, although threadbare around the edges, fit his form like a glove. He closed his eyes, rested his head against the sofa's back, and allowed the solitude to penetrate his soul. The only noises that marred the silence were the whir of the ceiling fan overhead and the hum of the VCR. The machine was rewinding the video Tony taped every Friday morning at 9:00 — "Extraordinary Homes."

The VCR's click prompted Tony's opening his eyes, raising his head, and pointing the remote control at the TV, housed in an eclectic entertainment center. He pressed a button, and the word "play" appeared white against the screen's blue background. He caught the first glimpse of Victoria, and Tony's gut tightened. This morning while he was fighting that horrible fire she had sat across from Gaylord Rodriguez and interviewed someone about gardening. Tony scowled at Gaylord and honed his focus on Victoria. The peach-colored cotton sweater he had given her for her birthday usually added the flush of spring to Victoria's features. The color did nothing for her today. Indeed, her eyes looked hollow, her skin, ashen.

Tony frowned, leaned forward, placed elbows on knees, and scrutinized the set. There had been a few times when his wife had gone to the studio even though she was suffering from a cold or just recovering from the flu. On those occasions Tony had marveled at what a good job the makeup artist did to cover her pallid state. But this time, there was no denying that Victoria had felt less than chipper this morning. On second consideration Tony speculated that most viewers wouldn't notice Victoria's plight. But Tony noticed. He noticed because his lips had touched every inch of that classic face.

"Sometimes I wonder if I know her *too* well." He considered the early days of their marriage. Bit by bit the fire had worn off of their attraction. It was almost as if the more Victoria got to know Tony the less she valued him.

And Tony cringed at the thought of her ever learning he had fathered a child out of wedlock when he was a 17-year-old kid. Before they got married he had known Victoria was a virgin and lied about his own virginity. Since he never righted the wrong, the falsehood created a chasm between them. Nevertheless, the idea of actually telling Victoria the truth presented itself as an impossibility. Tony was sure from the start of their marriage that Victoria was so infernally proper she would probably never forgive him for his misdeed. Indeed, as a newlywed he feared he might forever lose her respect. Ironically, he somehow managed to do that anyway.

Looking back over that youthful season of his life when he had made wrong choices with the wrong girl, Tony wondered why the girl's father hadn't kicked him in the seat of the pants.

"I deserved it," he groused and for the millionth time wondered about the details of his daughter's life. The questions he had endeavored to bury resurrected themselves anew, and he was bombarded by those brief moments when the nurse allowed him to hold his baby after he'd signed the adoption release papers.

Is her hair as blond now as it was when she was born? That alone made her look like me. And her eyes — did they turn out gray like mine or blue like her mother's? Is she tall like me? She graduates from high school this year. Will she graduate with honors like I should have or did she bum her way through?

Tony reached for the icy bottle of cola beaded in droplets of dew. He touched the drink to his lips, allowed the cold liquid to slip down his throat and winced against the welcome sting of carbonation. With iron determination he dashed aside the memories of his daughter and forced himself to focus upon Victoria.

She and Gaylord laughed at something the gardener said. For a snatch in time the brief glimmer of joy seemed to erase the dark circles under Victoria's eyes. Tony grimaced at Gaylord, grabbed the remote control, and pressed the fast forward button. After a series of short commercials Victoria's face appeared upon the screen. Tony pressed the play button.

Her calm voice floated into the fire station. Tony could have sworn the pool table's balls clacked together, resonating the melody of her tones. "That way, you can cut out the time it takes to stuff and roll the tortillas, but you still get the same delicious effect — or maybe even better, in my opinion anyway," she added with a chuckle.

"This just happens to be my hus— my husband's favorite dish."

Victoria's step-by-step instructions mingled into a verbal blur as Tony inspected her eyes for any sign of emotion. Love, for instance. He discovered nothing except the cool countenance of a television cook, intent upon the task at hand. And he wondered if there was anything left in that heart of hers but walls of ice. Tony yanked on the neck of his worn T-shirt, pointed the remote at the television, and prepared to press the stop button.

But when Victoria darted a cautious gaze to her left, and leaned against the stove, Tony's finger hovered over the button. She dropped the saucepan she was holding and her face drained of all natural color. Only twin blotches of peach-colored rouge remained on the apples of her cheeks. Tony released the remote control onto the coffee table that had been chewed around the edges by their station pup. He studied his wife, and an uneasy dread settled in his gut like a sack of cold rocks.

Finally, Victoria conjured a bright smile that smacked of fake as a blond stepped onto the set — a blond Tony recognized as one of Victoria's six friends from college. Momentarily her name escaped him, and he

65

silently ticked through the friends' names until he stopped on Marilyn — only one second before Victoria looked into the camera. "Today, we have a surprise guest," she said, "my friend, Marilyn Langham. Marilyn is actually the one who gave me this recipe."

"It's been in my family for years." Marilyn beamed into the camera, and Tony wondered if that grin looked as alarmed to the rest of the viewers as it did to him. Or, if anyone else in TV land noticed that when Marilyn slipped a supportive arm around her friend, Victoria leaned against her a little too heavily. He stepped toward the TV and stopped mere inches from the screen.

Tony's fingers dug against the sides of the TV, and he scrutinized his wife as she appeared to gradually pale from existence. At last, Marilyn was the only one talking while Victoria made a monumental task of repeatedly swallowing. A mountainous fear emerged from the pit in his mind — a fear that he just might lose another baby. Tony ground his teeth together and focused solely upon Victoria, as if the harder he looked at her the greater the possibility of reading what was going on in her mind . . . and in her body. But that only resulted in renewed anxiety as the word "miscarriage" reverberated through his being and shook him to his core.

"No," Tony mumbled and shook his head. "No . . . no . . ." He glanced at his trusty wristwatch — a leather-banded timepiece his father had worn until the day he died. Twelve-thirty swiftly approached. *Victoria taped the program about three hours ago,* he calculated. *If there were problems, wouldn't she have called?* He released his death grip on the TV and stepped back.

Yet the moment of ease was short-lived. For the very act of stepping away from Victoria's image hurled him back in time to that agonizing afternoon when he bid adieu to his newborn daughter. No one had been there with Tony in that empty hospital room. No one. By the time the baby was born he and his girlfriend had broken up by their parents' design. Even though his parents had offered to go with him, Tony refused. He knew in his 17-year-old heart that this was something he had to do alone. That 15 minutes of solitude with his daughter had shaken him as he never imagined. After all, guys weren't supposed to be the ones who hurt in situations like this. Everyone had focused upon his girlfriend. Tony figured that was for good reason. Still, he had wanted to at least *see* his baby.

The nurse had cast him a scornful glance when she placed the sleeping newborn in his arms. Tony chose to ignore her chilled reception and focused instead upon his daughter — a little girl he had named Toni. The second the hospital room's door closed he pulled a sterling silver rattle from his jeans pocket and tucked it out of sight under the folds of the baby's blanket. The thing had cost him every penny he could scrape together, but Tony had bought it the day before and had the jeweler engrave the keepsake, "I love you. Dad." He fully understood that there were no guarantees that the birth parents would keep the gift, but once again, this was something Tony had to do.

After making certain the rattle was in place, Tony awkwardly cradled the little doll with one arm and pulled a handwritten note from his hip pocket. He slid the note under the rattle and hoped the adoptive parents wouldn't toss them both. He had called her Toni in the letter because he hated the impersonal tones of "To my daughter."

Tony spent the next few minutes doing what most every new father has done through the generations. He picked up her tiny hands and marveled at each of her ten fingers. He brushed his fingers along the top of her velvet-like blond hair. He inhaled the smell of baby lotion and rubbed his cheek against her satiny forehead. And for a moment in time Tony fooled himself into believing that he could take this baby and raise her. Even if his girlfriend cared nothing for her, Tony wanted her. He desperately wanted her. For she was a part of him — a part he would never regain if he let her go.

He remembered those adoption papers already signed. An icy dash of reality chilled him to the bottom of his feet. A wild voice deep within urged him to run with his daughter. Run and hide. Hide in a place where he'd never be found. The hospital's antiseptic, sterile smell nearly overtook him.

He cradled his baby closer, and his legs threatened to buckle. Tony collapsed into a nearby chair, placed his face against Toni's fragrant blanket, and allowed the tears to silently seep into the cotton-soft fabric. The tears themselves seemed to whisper that he had made the right choice, that Toni's adoptive parents could provide for her better than a single father ever could, that if he *really* loved his daughter he would stick with doing what was best for her. In that moment he felt as if half his heart were being ripped from his body.

Nobody ever knew. Nobody. By the time the nurse came back Tony managed to pull himself under tight control. Without a word he placed his Toni in the nurse's arms. That stone-faced professional observed him as if he were the scum of the earth. In the passion of youth he was tempted to smear that expression off her face. Instead, he walked from the room, down the hallway, and out of the hospital.

That day, sitting in his sporty Jeep, Tony dug a pit in his mind and shoved all those haunting images to the bottom. By the time he got home his invisible shield was firmly in place. He didn't talk about the visit to anyone. Not his parents. Not God. And certainly, not when he met Victoria.

"Yeoweee! You little she-devil!" Tony's reverie was broken by Eddy's cry echoing up the hallway.

Tony snapped his attention toward the game room's entrance where his partner came in carrying the latest addition to the station — a golden lab puppy. The pup had latched onto Eddy's hand and wasn't offering to let go.

"This dog is a real tiger," Eddy said.

Still distracted by the phantoms of his mind, Tony nodded toward Eddy and refocused on the TV. The final seconds of the shoot were rolling, and Victoria still leaned on Marilyn. As Tony continued to watch, Victoria's eyes lost all glimmer. Indeed, he was overcome with an irrational terror that perhaps the last vestiges of life were draining from his wife . . . or, more likely, from their baby.

She would have called, he reminded himself and awaited the calming effects of logic. But this time the logic seemed far from faultless.

"Blast it!" he yelled and snatched up the remote from the end table. He ground his index finger against the remote's stop button and flung the remote back at the table. The instrument hit the side of the table and spun across the indoor-outdoor carpet.

"What's the matter with you?" Eddy demanded as he dropped onto the worn couch. "Should I duck?"

"No — nothing's the matter!" Tony mumbled and snatched his cell phone from his belt loop.

"Have you been talking to Victoria again?"

"No." Tony scrolled to the screen where Victoria's cell number was programmed. Before he could press the send button, the secretary's voice popped over the intercom,

"Tony, line one. Tony, line one."

He looked up and held Eddy's intense gaze for a full ten seconds. Tony knew something was indeed wrong — desperately wrong.

"What in the world is the matter with you?" Eddy's brow wrinkled as the puppy wobbled onto the sofa and tore into the edge of an olive-colored cushion.

"I can't talk right now." Tony dashed toward the wall phone hanging near the bunk room entryway. He snatched up the receiver and turned the corner into the bunk room filled with a dozen cots and a bookcase across one wall.

"Victoria!" Tony blurted into the receiver.

"No, this is her friend Marilyn." The hesitant feminine voice that floated over the line matched the one on TV.

The silence that seized Tony belied the turbulence that tortured his mind. "I just watched the video," he shot out.

"Video?"

"Of 'Extraordinary Homes.' I tape it every Friday. Where's Victoria? She looked awful on the set. Is she okay? Can I — can I talk to her? And the — the baby — is the baby okay?" A sound like that of his own crying newborn assaulted him from within.

Tony scrubbed the heel of his palm against his ear to wipe away the memory.

Silence was Marilyn's only answer. Silence and a telltale sniffle.

Tony slammed his back against the wall, squeezed his eyes tight, and with stony resolve forced himself to breathe evenly. "She had a miscarriage, didn't she?" he asked in an even voice. A film of sweat bathed his spine and crept to his upper lip. In the last two years five of the firemen had experienced the same. They'd even debated whether or not the toxins they were exposed to perhaps triggered the spontaneous abortions. As Marilyn's silence stretched into infinity, a shroud of guilt penetrated Tony to the bone.

Another round of sniffles proceeded Marilyn's wobbly voice. "Y–yes. She *did* have a miscarriage — this morning after the filming."

"How is she?" he croaked.

"Fine. She's fine. She's resting now."

"And she's . . . at the hospital?" He squeezed his eyes tight and with an iron will forced himself not to reveal the sting in his eyes.

"Yes. We're here at West Florida Regional."

"Why haven't you called before now?" He moved away from the wall and stood with his feet apart, his spine rigid as if he were preparing to lurch into battle.

Only the sound of the puppy's yelp and Eddy's playful growl split the silence. The faint whiff of pizza attested to Sal's lunch-time weakness. The smell that often tanta-lized now sent a revolting twist through his stomach.

"She didn't want you to call me, did she?" Tony demanded and wondered if his gruff tone hid the agony that boiled through his veins.

"N–no," Marilyn replied. "I'm sorry, but I — I just couldn't let you know sooner."

"So do you think I should come up there?"

"I think that baby was as much yours as hers," Marilyn said.

"Yes, I know." *How well do I know,* Tony continued to himself and wondered if this would be the final blow to his marriage. No matter what he did he couldn't make Victoria happy. Now they didn't even have the promise of a child to encourage them to mend their marriage. Nevertheless, Tony was ob-sessed by the urge to at least go see his wife. At one time they had something special. Maybe, just maybe, they could begin again.

"I'm coming up there," he blurted. "What room is she in?"

Six

Evelyn T. Sinclaire pounded the basketball along the court. The rhythm of her heart thumped as one with the tattoo of the ball against the polished wooden floor. The squeak of the team's high tops along the court, the smell of perspiration, the steel glint in the opposing guard's eyes all fueled the fire in Evelyn's belly — a fire that insisted she win, even if this *was* just a practice game.

Her best friend, Johnna Blackwell, lunged at her in an attempt to snatch the ball. Evelyn skillfully bounced it between her legs and orchestrated a smooth side step. She darted a devil-may-dare glance at her friend and continued on her journey toward the goal. This was no time to let personal affiliations cloud her focus. For now, Johnna was the enemy.

Evelyn ducked to the right as another guard lunged toward her. A swoosh of air escaped her lanky counterpart, and Evelyn was sure she evoked a low groan. She paused but a second to size up the scene. Her gut urged her to go for a lay-up. She glanced at the clock, counting down from five seconds. Evelyn could almost hear the crowd from last Tuesday's game chanting, "E.T. E.T. E.T."

"E.T. is my name, and basketball is my game," she muttered under her breath.

She glanced at the clock again, and the competitive juices wouldn't let her pass up the chance for a last minute score. Evelyn slipped through the maze of gyrating players to perform the lay-up her admirers said revealed the years her mother had insisted she take ballet. But E.T. had only tolerated ballet while she ate, drank, and slept basketball. The six-foot-two-inch senior slammed the ball into the net and hung onto the ring for a quick, triumphant swing.

The buzzer sounded. She dropped to the court. Sweat seeping into her eyes delivered the delightful sting of victory. And her teammates began the chant that filled the halls of the Orlando Christian Academy after every game she drove the team to victory.

"E.T. E.T. E.T. . . ."

A warm glow radiated through her perspiring torso, and she mopped the sweat off her forehead.

Johnna neared and smacked her on the behind.

"You're awesome, girlfriend," she admitted while shaking her head.

Evelyn winked at her friend and feigned a long shot from the sideline. The coach observed her from across the court and gave her a double thumbs up. His eyes shone with an extra measure of joy and pride. The man she called coach was her father.

"Okay, people!" the dark-haired coach hollered through cupped hands. "Hit the showers!"

The team trotted toward the dressing rooms, but Evelyn hung back to talk with her pop.

"So, whazup after school?" she asked and grabbed a towel hanging on the side of a ball bin.

His brown eyes danced as he looked up at his daughter. Calvin Sinclaire tugged on her long, blond ponytail and winked.

"Your mom mentioned taking you to the ballet tonight."

"Oh, no," Evelyn groaned. "Dad, do I have to? I —"

He winked again.

"Or maybe you'd prefer going to an Orlando Magics game with me."

"What?" Evelyn stopped and whirled to face her father. "Get outta here! You're kidding, right?"

He shook his head and the corners of his eyes crinkled as indulgent laughter spilled from him.

"Would I joke about something so important?"

"No way," Evelyn admitted.

"Well, tonight it's just you and me, kid." Calvin reached up for a light tap of his fist against her chin. "We can scream all we want."

"Oh, *yes!*" Evelyn shoved her fist into the air.

"Hit the showers," Calvin encouraged. "You don't want to be late for English."

"You're the best, Dad!" she called over her shoulder and really meant it. More than one friend told her she had the best parents in the world. And Evelyn had often wondered about the circumstances that placed her in their care . . . about the birth parents who had released her into the arms of Calvin and Macy Sinclaire.

Evelyn trotted into the locker room that smelled of leather balls and deodorant soap. Metal doors banged. Teammates hurried to shower and change. Evelyn rummaged through her cluttered locker until she dug out her jeans and T-shirt from beneath her backpack. The pack crashed to the concrete floor, and books tumbled in all directions.

"Oh, great!" Evelyn sputtered as she dropped to her knees and snatched up papers and books and a scattering of pens. She righted her backpack and unceremoniously shoved the escapees inside.

"Oh, dude," Johnna said and flung open her locker. "You've got a mess."

"I'm *not* a dude," Evelyn growled and looked up at the tall brunette who was probably going to be voted most beautiful by her senior class.

"You can say that again," Johnna said with a giggle. "At least Ray-Ray Mancioni would agree to that one."

"Oh, puh-leeze," Evelyn said and decided that actually zipping her backpack this time might be the best move. "Lay off him."

"But he wuvs you, girlfriend!"

"He's in the *ninth grade!*"

"Young and tender." Johnna pulled the towel from her hair and began brushing through the damp mop that would dry into a cascade of natural curls — the antithesis of Evelyn's straight locks.

"Get outta here," Evelyn chided.

"I'm trying!" Johnna claimed and waved her brush as if she were the queen of England. "You need to get showered or you're gonna be late."

"I'm going! I'm going!" Evelyn claimed

and shoved the backpack into the top of her locker's matted contents.

"There's probably fungus growing at the bottom of all that!"

Evelyn slammed the door and grimaced, but the sour face was lost on Johnna, who bent over to retrieve a small silver object from the floor.

"Whose is this?" she asked and held up a silver baby rattle.

"That's mine." Evelyn grabbed the keepsake and averted her face. She reopened her locker and slipped the newly polished rattle into her backpack's pocket.

Only the sounds of spraying water, a slamming door, and seniors rummaging through overstuffed lockers filtered through the friends' silence.

"Whazup?" Johnna asked, and the caution in her voice sent an alarm through Evelyn.

She gave her backpack a final shove and whacked her locker shut. Evelyn glanced at Johnna who had stopped brushing her hair and was observing Evelyn as if she were about to announce the earth-shattering news that she was pregnant.

"Nothing's up!" Evelyn scowled. "You know me better than that! It's just a keepsake. That's all."

"Okay . . ." Johnna hesitated, yet her candid gaze felt as if it pierced E.T. to the bone.

She shrugged. "If you must know, it's from my birth father." Evelyn pulled her T-shirt away from her sweating torso and eyed the jeans and shirt she held. A melancholic tendril wrapped her spirit, and she experienced the uncanny sensation of being so close to her birth father — so close, yet so far away. "I found it when we were cleaning out the attic a couple of months ago. There was a letter, too." She coughed and slipped off her gym shoes. "He called me Toni."

"No way." Johnna gripped Evelyn's forearm. "But — but that's your middle name, isn't it?"

"Yeah. Mom told me that's why they chose that name. They just felt like it was the right thing to do." Evelyn bent to remove her socks and wiggled her toes as the cool air refreshed her perspiring feet. "She said the rattle and letter were inside my blanket when they got me home from the hospital. She wanted to give them to me before now but didn't quite know how." Evelyn shrugged. "At first, I was a little aggravated. I mean, they've had the note and rattle all these years —"

"But —"

"But then I figured it was just hard for them. It seems like they thought the note and all might make me want to contact my birth parents — my father anyway."

"Did your birth mother send anything?"

Evelyn swallowed a lump in her throat. "No," she said and was pleased her answer revealed no sadness. "I don't know if that means that my father cared more than she did or —"

"Oh, Evelyn," Johnna whispered, "I'm sure it was probably just all too painful." Evelyn nodded and looked at her friend, whose teary eyes now shimmered like the vivid blue waters off the Florida coastline. "Imagine how you would feel."

"Awful," Evelyn admitted and leaned against the lockers. Her gaze trailed to the doorway where a knot of team members loaded with books and purses bounded toward their next class.

"So, what did the letter say?" Johnna asked.

"Oh, you know, this and that." Evelyn conjured a casual shrug and decided she'd talked about this as much as she could stand for one day. The last thing she ever wanted to do was break down and sob in front of her friend. After all, Evelyn had an image to uphold. Winners didn't cry by her estimation.

She surged toward the showers and cast a final glance over her shoulder. Johnna's rapid blinking and piteous expression only confirmed Evelyn needed some time away from her high-strung friend.

And what I really need, she added as a heavenward plea, *is somebody I can talk to — anybody who'll understand and not bawl their brains out.* "I've got to hit the showers or Mrs. Tinsley is going to slam dunk me all the way to South America," she called.

"But — but — are you going to try to get in contact with him?" The rapid tap of Johnna's loafers from behind made Evelyn want to hurl herself into the shower and slam the door.

"I'm thinking about it," she shot back, and this time the words oozed from a heart laden with emotion. For the truth was, E.T. Sinclaire now believed she had little choice but to find the father who cared enough to buy a silver rattle and engrave it with his love. A father who had written his heart in a letter, yellowed with time and spotted with tears. A father who pledged to never forget her as long as he lived.

Seven

A thud penetrated Victoria's sleep, and her torso twitched. She opened her eyes, peered around an unfamiliar room, and attempted to remember where she was and why she was there. The faint click of a machine next to her bed prompted her to glance up at a bag hanging from a stand. Victoria lifted her right hand and recognized the IV equipment.

Then she remembered. She remembered the harried morning . . . the swift drive from the TV station, the ER admission, the nurses and doctor's frantic attempts to save her baby — a baby that was no more. The pain that formerly wracked her womb now assaulted her heart. Victoria blinked against the rapid influx of tears and wished for the balm of sleep.

Footfalls neared from the doorway. Victoria connected the steps of the approaching person with the thud. Undoubtedly, someone had just entered her room. She strained to see around the corner and soon encountered the towering image of her six-foot-four husband.

Without a word Tony eased toward her bed. He set a bouquet of mixed flowers atop the service tray and neared her side. Victoria, uncertain what to say, peered up into gray eyes — eyes as difficult to read as ever.

"Marilyn called me," he said, and his words held no hint of compassion. "Seems like you told her not to."

"She told you that?" Victoria asked and wondered whose side Marilyn was on.

"No, I guessed it," Tony admitted. He shifted his position and looked past her.

The effect was the same as it always had been — as if Tony were with her but not *really* with her. The first few years of their marriage Victoria believed she would one day break through that wall of his, but during the last year she had almost given up hope. The only time Tony seemed close to really being *with* Victoria was during their physical union. But even then, there was something, an elusive "unspoken" that held them apart.

Victoria wadded the edge of the cool sheet against clammy palms. Her neck tensed, and she wondered exactly why Tony was here. Obviously he knew about the miscarriage, but he looked like he really couldn't care less. Something inside Victoria urged her to reach out to him and weep against his shoulder. Three years ago, that would have been the natural reaction. But now . . . now . . . Victoria doubted her every move in his presence. Indeed, one of the reasons she hadn't wanted Marilyn to call him was her uncertainties about him. The other reason involved leftover irritation after yesterday's heated encounter. The last thing Victoria needed was for Tony Roberts to level another load of verbal antagonism against her. She rubbed one foot against the other and wished she could run.

"So . . ." Tony said and took one step closer. "How are you?"

"Fine." Victoria eyed the TV and wondered where the remote was. Any break in the stifling atmosphere would be welcomed. Fleetingly, she speculated if the miscarriage would prove to be the final blow to their marriage. Until this morning the two of them had at least one thing left in common — their expected child. Now that child was gone.

Her eyes blurred, and the negative wave of emotion from the morning threatened to suck her under. Victoria turned her head away from Tony and clamped her teeth in an attempt to stay the tide. If he didn't care enough to reach out to her on his own she certainly didn't want him to feel obligated because she was weak enough to start crying.

"I'm sorry," Tony said, yet the words held about as much feeling as a bag of rocks.

"Me, too," Victoria strained out, and the smell of his wild flower bouquet titillated her nose.

"Is there anything I can do?" he asked, and for a wrinkle in time Victoria thought he might be moved more than she perceived.

She darted a swift glance his way. One look at his impassive face was all the evidence she needed. Tony Roberts cared about as little for their child as he did for her. The agony of the last few years rushed upon Victoria. She had felt so isolated and unappreciated recently she had even been attracted to their church choir director, Ricky Christopher. She lowered her eyelids, stared at her toes protruding under the white coverlet, and wondered what her husband might think if he knew she had fallen to such shameful temptations. As the disgraceful memory threatened to smother her, Victoria closed her eyes in an attempt to shield herself against Tony's perceiving her thoughts. . . .

That balmy day six weeks ago she had

stood on the porch of Ricky Christopher's tiny brick home.

The languid melody of a Kenny G saxophone solo floated from inside the home, and Victoria recalled the sacred solo Ricky played during the Sunday evening service. Her stomach lurched with a delicious, delightful quiver as she pondered his dark hair and striking blue eyes gleaming beneath the sanctuary's lighting, mild and worshipful.

Now, the minister of music was inside, awaiting Victoria's arrival, expecting her to share the domestic expertise he so needed before his mother's visit. She reached for the illuminated doorbell, stopped, and contemplated her deepest motives — motives that weren't exactly pure. A seagull's distant call seemed to echo a truth that left Victoria far from comfortable: *You're married! You're married! You're married!*

The ocean breeze lifted wispy tendrils of hair that escaped the saggy bun into which she had twisted her wavy locks. The smells of sea and salt enlivened her senses, even though the Destin shoreline was blocks away. She shifted her feet, swallowed, and gazed toward the southern horizon where a band of dark clouds attested to a squall blowing in. Victoria glanced down at her ankle-length denim dress and laid her palm against her lower abdomen. The decent thing to do was make this a quick visit where she fulfilled Ricky's request of helping him with some decorating suggestions. *Yes, quick and professional,* she thought. *Professional and instructive. Nothing more. Nothing less.*

She straightened her shoulders and pressed the doorbell. By a count of three, the door whipped open. Ricky Christopher flashed a white-toothed beam as if Victoria were the most important woman on the planet. "You're here!" he exclaimed, and his eyes glistened appreciatively.

"Well, you — you said 9:30," she claimed and shifted her handbag from one sweaty palm to the other. *Good grief! He's just too good-looking for his own good,* she thought, and her former resolve to keep this encounter brief blurred in the face of his magnetism — a magnetism to which he seemed oblivious — and that only heightened his appeal.

"Yes! Come on in!" Ricky opened the door wide and allowed Victoria to step inside. As she passed him, she picked up a citruslike, carefree scent that reminded her of a cologne her youngest brother wore.

Victoria's open-toed sandals padded against the short pile carpet as she strode into a bachelor's home, neatly kept but void of any flair. The smell of cinnamon tea, warm and inviting, wafted from the kitchen. And Victoria gazed around a room full of furniture she would have passed over at a yard sale.

"See what I mean?" Ricky despaired, referring to his former request for her decorating assistance. "I need help. This place is the pits! Do you think there's any hope?"

"Well . . ." Victoria hedged as she took in the metallic blinds, tweed sofa, and "yuck brown" carpet. When she observed the petite brick home that sported a neat, cheerful exterior with bushes and ferns, she had wondered if Ricky might be exaggerating. But the place actually looked more like a refugee camp for dorm-room rejects than the home of a church staff member.

The room's only salvation was the corner devoted to musical pursuits. A black lacquer electronic piano glistened beneath a brass floor lamp. A guitar sat in a stand near the piano and gleamed in the lamplight. A saxophone lay atop the piano and attested to the tune she'd heard while standing outside. Above the piano hung a poster-sized print of an ebony grand piano with a rose lying atop the keys.

Fifteen minutes later Victoria had taken

in the full implications of Ricky's domestic needs, and she agreed that the man needed help — a lot of help.

"So do you think there's any hope at all?" Ricky implored.

"Okay," she paused at the end of the tired sofa and placed a hand on one hip. "There is hope," she began. "There's always hope. The question is, how much time do you have to put into this? One month is not very long to pull off a major overhaul."

"I can give it as much time as I need." He lifted both hands. "I'm free nearly every evening from five until midnight. And I've got a couple of friends in Pensacola who just might come down and help. Just tell me what to do!"

Victoria pivoted and gazed around the room whose paneling matched the yuck brown carpet. "Okay, the first thing we need to do is paint." She shook her head. "Problem is . . . I'm expecting," she blurted and faced him. "So I can't help you there. I'm not supposed to breathe any kind of fumes like that."

Ricky slapped his forehead. "Oh no! I didn't know! How could I have even asked your help when . . . when . . ." He waved toward her midsection then gave her a blank stare that bespoke his sudden attack of verbal helplessness. "I'm so sorry. I feel like a total cad, here." His hands moved in nervous twitters, and Victoria was reminded of a 1920s hero from a black-and-white movie. "You should be at home, propping up your feet, and — and —"

"It's okay. Really." Victoria managed an assuring grin, despite the fact that her betraying heart leaped once more. Tony had been far more low key about her welfare. "I'm just now adjusting to it, and I feel fine." She raised her hands to assure him.

"Look . . ." Ricky raced toward the kitchen. "I made tea," his voice rose as he entered the other room, and Victoria was reminded of the honey-smooth solos the high-energy musician bestowed upon their enraptured congregation. "I'll pour some tea, and we can sit down and discuss this at the table. I'm sure you've been on your feet too long now!"

Chuckling, Victoria followed him.

"Really," she insisted. "I'm quite all right. The early stages often go like a breeze for many. As a matter of fact, I can barely even tell." Victoria, forever sensitive about propriety, stopped short of more commentary. Instead, she settled at the table and reached for the mug of fragrant tea he offered.

A shrill ring erupted from the living room,

and Ricky glanced at his sporty wristwatch. "I'm expecting a call from one of my friends," he said and rushed toward the phone. "If this is who I think it is, he's one of the guys from Pensacola, and he owes me big. I'm sure I can get him to help with the painting."

Victoria nodded then inspected her French manicure as a hint of nausea flitted through her tummy. She took several sips of the tea in hopes that the warm liquid would wash away the momentary discomfort. The cinnamon beverage increased the queasiness. She scowled at the tea and marveled that a flavor that once brought her pleasure was now inflicting discomfort. *Could it be my pregnancy?* she wondered as a new awareness of the life within was followed by a hot wave of renewed guilt regarding her motive. I have no business staying here a minute longer, she scolded herself then abruptly stood and snatched her purse.

"Oh hi, Francine!" Ricky's pleasure-filled voice sliced through Victoria's quandary. "Okay . . ." he hesitated. "Well, what about Saturday night, then? Are you available?" The anxious hope in his voice bespoke more to Victoria than she wanted to hear. This Francine might very well be a significant other for Ricky. "Great!" he continued on a relieved note as Victoria eased toward the front door.

"Oh, I forgot!" Ricky stopped and slammed his palm against his forehead as an uncertain silence cloaked the room. "My mom is coming for a visit soon, and I have got to do some work on my house! This place is a disgrace. I have an interior consultant here right now. I might be up to my eyeballs in paint Saturday night."

Ricky darted a glance toward Victoria, held up his finger, and enveloped her in one of those heart-stopping smiles that Victoria was certain had not been lost on Francine. A splash of jealousy erupted from the pit of her stomach, and a new wave of mortification followed in its wake. *These emotions are beyond ridiculous,* she affirmed. Indeed, the potency of these foreign feelings both astonished and appalled her. *I have to get out of here and get a grip!* she continued. *I have never experienced anything like this!*

Her eyes stung; she clutched the doorknob and pondered the unraveling fabric of her life. Compared to several of her "sisters," Victoria's existence had been almost boring. She had been raised and adored by functional parents who loved the Lord, were nuts about each other, and still provided ample support and security for their three grown sons and Victoria. Being the only girl, Victoria had borne the brunt of her brothers' teasing as well as the bounty of her parents' doting. She rarely missed a church service growing up and continued that habit into her adult years. Victoria had never smoked or drank or even thought about doing drugs. She guarded her virginity until marriage, and through the years she thanked the Lord for her choices and His protection. Indeed, she had even refused to sneak out at church camp and spray shaving cream all over their counselor's car. Victoria had been dubbed "goody-two-shoes" by both her school and church friends, and she hadn't even cared.

They certainly wouldn't think I was a goody-two-shoes today, she thought, and her fingers flexed against the knob. The nausea bulged up the back of her throat. A clammy chill burst upon her body. Victoria twisted the knob and decided she could call and explain her hasty departure. Ricky would understand. . . . She made it to her Volkswagen. Somehow she managed to maneuver the vehicle home, drag herself through the front door, and plop onto the sofa's cool cotton cushions. She closed her eyes and lay perfectly still. Still and rigid. Rigid and distraught. The shame that ravaged her soul like a rampaging hurricane made the physical nausea seem minuscule.

Something's got to change in my marriage, Victoria thought. *It's Tony. Tony has got to change.*

Victoria stirred beneath the covers. The tension eased from her limbs as that horrid memory flitted from her mind as quickly as it had intruded. Yet her spine stiffened; she dreaded having to make small talk with the man who had promised to cherish her and failed.

Nevertheless, Victoria opened her eyes in the same instant the door produced a faint click. Tony no longer stood beside her bed. She glanced around the room to discover she was alone. Victoria struggled to sit up and nearly gave in to her first instinct to call out to her husband, to reach for him, to beg him not to go.

But it was too late.

Victoria's elbow pressed into the firm mattress, and she rested her weight upon it. She peered toward the bouquet of mixed wildflowers and remembered a similar gift Tony bought for their first anniversary. The very presence of the flowers suggested that

Tony had put some thought into his visit . . . that perhaps he did indeed still care . . . that maybe Victoria had jumped to the wrong conclusion.

Then there was that steel mask she collided into every time she tried to look into Tony's soul. A swirl of confusion and heartache and leftover love twisted Victoria into a bout of what-might-have-beens. She flopped back onto the pillow, ran a trembling hand across her forehead, and wondered what she would do without Tony Roberts in her life. All these years her focus had been upon making a home and hopefully having a family. If Tony were no longer in her life, Victoria would have no one to make a home for . . . except herself.

She pressed her forefinger and thumb together and began clicking the tips of the fingernails against each other. *But maybe I've been making a home mostly for my own benefit anyway.* The wayward thought challenged her to examine her motives. She shrank from the tiresome task.

"Oh, who knows!" she whispered instead.

Victoria looked back at the flowers, and for the first time noticed a card attached to a ribbon. She sat up, snagged the edge of the service table, and tugged it closer. The thin vase wobbled, she steadied it, and then fumbled with removing the pin holding the card to the ribbon. At last Victoria extracted the note from the envelope and winced as the edge sliced a thin cut along the top of her ring finger. She put the end of her stinging finger against her tongue and prepared to read the note. The card bore no message. No pledges of undying devotion. No heartfelt sympathy. Nothing. Not even a signature.

Victoria crumpled the paper. Her brow wrinkled as another disillusionment slammed into her mind. Perhaps, the flowers were nothing more than the obligatory act of an estranged husband rather than the heartfelt gift of one who truly cares.

All at once Victoria didn't want to be separated anymore. She longed for things the way they were on their honeymoon and even during the first year they were married. But even then she couldn't recall a time when Tony had let her see all the way to the bottom of himself. She examined the cut on her ring finger and figured that many gifts from Tony had come with pain.

A new longing overtook Victoria — a longing to see the real Tony, to know the real Tony. If only . . . if only it wasn't too late . . . if only she could reach him . . . if only she knew *how* to reach him.

She turned her head into her pillow, curled into a ball, and shook with the silent sobs that wracked her soul.

Eight

Tony stepped outside the hospital room and hovered in the hallway, abuzz with nurses, visitors, and the occasional housekeeping professional. He reluctantly released the door's handle and debated about the wisdom of leaving Victoria. Obviously, she was so exhausted she had eased into a light sleep with him right in the room. So Tony decided his best bet was to make a gracious exit and let her sleep. *But perhaps I should hang out a while longer and check on her in about an hour.* Despite their strained relationship, Tony was still her husband. He couldn't deny the near primeval need to protect her, to make certain she was well-cared for.

By the time he arrived he had already given into a cry but managed to firmly contain himself in her presence. However, Tony felt as if he still didn't measure up to her expectations. So, he didn't quite know whether to hold her hand, kiss her cheek, or just keep his distance. After all, the last time they spoke he'd hung up on her. The sight of her hollow eyes and pallid skin had done little to encourage him to maintain his equilibrium. Just about the time he almost let down his guard Tony reminded himself that Victoria didn't really know everything. She didn't seem to like him much *without* a flawed past. If she ever learned the truth, he figured he'd lose every scrap of what little respect she had left for him.

Tony expelled a tired sigh and shoved his hands into his twill pants. He checked his watch and decided he would indeed hang around a while. He might give Victoria time for her nap and pop back in for another visit. Maybe this time Tony could say more . . . what, he didn't know.

He began the slow trek toward the elevators and pondered the woman he'd married. *The problem with you, Victoria, is that everything you do is perfect. You follow all the rules, and you always have. There doesn't seem to be room for anyone who's blown it.* Tony scratched the side of his face and rubbed his jaw. He wondered what she would think of him if he just blurted his thoughts. *She'd probably ask exactly how you've blown it, you idiot.*

After pressing the down arrow Tony decided his best bet was to forget trying to figure out his wife. He'd tried for six years. He wasn't sure he'd accomplish that feat in *sixty* years.

"Tony?" the slightly familiar feminine voice mingled with the elevator bell's ring.

He swiveled to face the blond who was on TV with Victoria.

"Oh, hi, Marilyn." He extended his hand and the two exchanged a warm shake. With the smell of her jasmine perfume meeting his senses, Tony purposed to show her his best image. "Listen, thanks so much for taking the time to call me. I really appreciate it." He infused each word with the essence of an appreciative smile.

"Oh, you're quite welcome." Marilyn's welcoming brown gaze bespoke a hint of caution. "Did Victoria figure out I was the one who called you?"

"Yes." The elevator door hissed open and Tony stepped away so others could board.

"And?"

"I don't think you're in the dog house *too* bad," he said.

"Oh, good." Marilyn laid her hand over her heart and then picked at the weave of her cotton sweater. "I didn't want to anger her, but you know . . ." she shrugged, "I figured you had every right to be up here."

"I was just in to see her," Tony claimed, "but she dozed off on me. Actually," he pointed to the elevator, "I was going down to find a soda. Care to join me?"

The faint notes of "The Star Spangled Banner" began to play from somewhere nearby. "Oh, nuts," Marilyn said. "That's my cell. It's probably another one of the sisters. I called one of them — Sonsee DeLaney — and asked her to call around with news about Victoria and now they're all calling in one at a time."

She fished her phone from the folds of her denim purse, read the tiny screen, pressed a button, and held it to her ear. "Just a minute, Melissa," Marilyn said into the receiver. "I'm talking with Tony." Without waiting for her friend's reply Marilyn covered the mouthpiece. "It's Melissa. This is probably going to take awhile. She likes to talk. We call her the 'mouth of the south.' " Marilyn's girl-next-door face brightened with a mischievous smile. Nevertheless, her swollen eyes attested that the miscarriage had affected her deeply.

Tony rubbed his index finger across his eyes and wondered if Victoria could tell that he, too, had been forced to release his emotions. He didn't think he'd cried so hard since he'd placed Toni for adoption.

"Actually, I just finished a soda," Marilyn said, "so I'll sit in the waiting room a while."

"Okay, not a problem. I'll be back up in a few," he called as she walked toward the visitor lobby. *She's nice,* he thought. Much to Tony's surprise there was no animosity in her eyes — only the essence of acceptance. He'd figured by now that Victoria had informed her friends of all his shortcomings. In Tony's experience that group of seven women were thicker than thieves. More than once he'd found himself wishing that Victoria would put as much energy into their marriage as she did into her girlfriends.

The elevator doors sighed open, and a knot of people flowed out. Tony awaited his turn and stepped into the car. On a whim he decided to see if he could visit Rhonda Norris. Tony recalled the paramedic mentioning West Florida Regional. The burns on her arm did look nasty and the child was still struggling to breathe when they'd been taken away. An indescribable something in her eyes had seemed to communicate with Tony in a way few people ever did. The whole thing was odd, but looking back Tony sensed he and that woman somehow spoke the same language. "Not like an attraction or anything," he mumbled and figured she was a good ten years his senior. But there was something in that woman he seldom saw, something he couldn't pinpoint. Whatever that elusive something was, he was sure he also saw a hint of it in

Marilyn's eyes. He only wished he could see the same in Victoria.

Within a matter of minutes Tony had grabbed a bottled soda and inquired if Rhonda Norris had been admitted. Sure enough, she was being held in the outpatient care unit until the evening. Tony decided to trot up the flight of stairs to the fourth floor rather than take the elevator. He needed to increase his exercise regime; otherwise, the 10 pounds he'd gained would increase to 20.

He found room 423 and lightly tapped on the door.

"Come in." Rhonda's serene yet raspy voice beckoned him to enter.

As soon as Tony stepped into the cheery room spotted with flowers, he recalled the diary. *I should have brought it with me,* he thought and then realized that such a task would have required coherent thoughts of the immediate future — something Tony had been incapable of when he left the fire station. He'd been too consumed with thoughts of Victoria and their baby.

The pain of his loss swelled upon Tony anew, and he was tempted to bolt from the room, to run and not stop running until he outran the pain. Instead, he slammed the traumatic facts into that pit in his mind.

The last thing Tony needed was to be anything but brave. *Rhonda Norris doesn't need a neurotic fireman on her hands,* he admonished himself.

Tony stepped into the second hospital room of the day and tapped the door closed behind him. As in Victoria's room the narrow entryway blocked the view of the patient except her feet protruding from under the covers. After passing the restroom, Tony saw her.

Rhonda sat up in the midst of a crumpled collection of pillows and sheets. Her bandaged arm rested on one of the pillows; her head rested against another. The second Rhonda saw Tony she blossomed into an appreciative smile that brightened her face, currently void of makeup.

"Hi!" she said, and her voice cracked on the upbeat note.

Tony nodded and neared her bedside.

"Hi, yourself," he said while passing a huge bouquet of red roses perched atop a shelf. He glanced at the card, covered in masculine script — most likely her husband's. A horrid thought struck Tony between the eyes, and he nearly stopped in his tracks. *You idiot!* he blasted himself. *You forgot to sign the card on Victoria's flowers!* He pinched one of the buttons on his oxford shirt until the thing dug into his fingertip. *Maybe I can sneak in while she's asleep and write something on the card.* For the life of him, he couldn't figure out what to write. Nothing seemed right.

"I'm sorry" was lame.

"I love you" seemed questionable in light of their recent rounds of bitter arguing. Tony had to admit that Victoria *and* he had seemed more interested in pointing out the other's faults than listening.

The phrase "let's begin again" crashed into his thoughts, and Tony paused to savor the implications. The truth was he *did* wish he and Victoria could somehow start over; he just wasn't sure how to make that happen. Furthermore, he wasn't so certain that if he and Victoria *did* begin again they wouldn't wind up exactly where they were now — especially if he didn't tell her the truth about his past. But Tony figured he'd rather face a firing squad than confess his lie. If there was one thing Tony was certain of it was that his prim wife would be anything *but* understanding about his having an illegitimate daughter.

Rhonda Norris' voice broke into his reverie, and Tony grappled to piece together the part of her message he had missed.

". . . really wish Kevin were here. He just

stepped out a few minutes ago to get a bite to eat and go to Coty's room. Kevin's mom has been sitting with him," Rhonda explained. "Kevin's family has been so good to us and so gracious when we moved back to Destin. I don't know what I'd do without them." Rhonda propped her head against the pillow. Her gaze drifted past Tony, to the bouquet of roses, and back to him. Her eyes reminded Tony of the richest of chocolate mingled with a dash of remorse. Remorse and caution. Caution and a hint of that intangible something Tony had seen in Marilyn's eyes as well.

A tense silence settled between them. Tony wiggled his toes in his loafers and wondered what to say next. The air conditioner's faint hiss mingled with the sound of a cart being pushed down the hallway. Tony perceived the scent of antibiotic ointment and eyed Rhonda's arm. He figured he detected the medication with which they were treating her.

"Did you bring my diary?" she finally asked.

The mention of that mysterious book jolted Tony to meet her gaze. The candid tilt of her wide mouth bespoke her determination to cut through the former pretense. "No — no, I didn't," he answered. "I didn't even think of it when I came up here. I was — was distracted." *No sense in burdening her with my problems,* he thought.

"I — I know you thought it was a little odd that I didn't want my husband to see it."

"Actually . . ." Tony began and pondered the pit in his mind where his own secrets lay buried. "I figure that's between you and — you and — and God," he finished and considered why he of all people had referenced the Almighty.

While Victoria had always faithfully attended church his dedication to the holy had waned through the years. Essentially, Tony had never really connected with Christ the way Victoria or his parents professed. Even though he had attended church before meeting Victoria and after, Tony had never confessed to the life-changing encounter he had heard others refer to. If the truth were known, he had attended that singles Sunday school class where he met Victoria more as a means to meet a decent woman than as a statement of spiritual experience. After learning that religion played such a big part in Victoria's world, Tony had allowed her to assume he was "dedicated to the Lord." He simply never told her any different. Looking back

Tony wondered if that issue had also added to the heap of their mounting marital problems.

"Do you — you think you could bring it back up here soon . . . by tomorrow maybe, before I'm released. I — I hate to be a bother, and I know it might be a lot of driving, but it's terribly important." She lifted her arm a fraction. "My husband won't be back until about seven or so tonight . . ."

"Oh, sure. I don't mind bringing the diary back up here."

"I can slip it into my duffel bag . . ." She darted her gaze toward the scarlet bag lying in the chair behind Tony. ". . . so he'll never notice it."

Tony's brow rose and wondered what dark secrets lay in that diary. Adultery? Addictions? Gambling?

Rhonda observed the covers as a wash of red crept up her cheeks. "I guess I've really left you wondering, haven't I?" she asked, and Tony wondered if his thoughts were really that transparent.

She sucked in a quick breath. "I had an abortion 20 years ago — before he and I met," she blurted. "He doesn't know, and I don't want him to know."

"You don't have to explain." Tony held up his hand.

"No, I *want* to," she continued and shook her head. Her curly locks rustled against the starched pillowcase. "It doesn't matter that *you* know. You're a —"

"Stranger?" Tony inserted and marveled that he felt nearly the same way Rhonda did. He recalled a plane trip two years ago when he actually told the person sitting next to him about Toni. But that person had been a stranger. He had never seen him before or since. Tony didn't care what the stranger thought. The very fact that he didn't care had imparted a freedom to share that Tony seldom experienced.

Rhonda glanced toward the large window as a sad smile claimed her face. "It's odd that I feel more at ease telling you about it than I do my own husband. I guess I'm — I'm afraid that he'll think . . . well, you know." She shrugged and looked toward Tony. This time, her red-rimmed gaze slid past him.

"I understand." Tony lightly touched her arm for added assurance. *You don't know how much I really* do *understand.*

"That diary is what I wrote in after — after the abortion. It was so awful, I almost killed myself. I — I still write in the diary some. Kevin doesn't even know I have it. I didn't want him to even see it. He might ask

111

questions. Or even worse, find it and read it." She flicked her attention back to him for a second and peered over his shoulder once more. "Kevin is so respected in church and — and at the bank. He's a vice president with Continental Bank. Did you know?" She lifted her chin a fraction and Tony detected the sparkle of pride in Rhonda's eyes. "We transferred here 18 months ago."

"No, I didn't know," Tony answered.

"I just don't want to release any information that might hurt his image or his career or — or his respect for me." The last few words, gentle yet dark, reminded Tony of the faintest summer breeze that ushered in the blackest of storms.

He crossed his arms. "Don't you think that if he really loved you he'd forgive you?" he asked and felt like the most two-faced cad of the century. After all, he wasn't in any way interested in taking his own advice. By the same token Tony had never felt that Victoria's love was the unconditional variety either.

Well, what about your love for her? The disturbing question posed itself as one of those best ignored.

"You're right, I know," Rhonda admitted, "but somehow it's easier to keep things like they've always been." She stirred under the covers and her arm shifted against the pillow. "I had decided that you'd probably throw it away, and I'd lost it forever. But I would like to have it back. Somehow having those pages that I wrote after the procedure helps me feel close to the child I never had." She waved her free hand. "I know that's crazy, but it's the truth."

He nodded. "That's fine. I'll drive back to the station and get it." Tony checked his watch and calculated that by the time he got back Victoria would be better rested. "I've got time now."

"Thanks." Rhonda stifled a yawn. "And let's keep this conversation private, shall we?"

"Okay." Tony nodded. "Just between you and me."

Her eyelids drooped, and Tony wondered if his main task of the day was lulling damsels in distress to sleep.

"I'll be back soon," he said and eased toward the door.

"Okay, thanks," she agreed.

Tony left the room, cast a longing glance toward the elevator, and decided the stairs would once again be his wisest choice. He broke into a brisk gait and hit the stairwell with the determination to trot down, despite the moans of his lazy streak. When

Tony neared the fire escape doorway, a thud indicated that perhaps someone was trapped outside and attempting to get in. Another thud rattled the doorknob, and Tony leveled his gaze with the narrow window that offered a view of the alley behind the hospital.

Looking through the window he saw two men locked in combat, both dressed in suits. As the two struggled against each other, Tony was hard pressed to view their faces. He caught only a glimpse of dark hair, tightened fists, and the flash of a blunt barrel.

Tony gripped the door handle and stayed the urge to whip open the thick metal partition. If he did the man with the gun might very well pull the trigger on *him*. His pulse hammered against his neck, and Tony went rigid. If he didn't barge in soon the shorter man might lose his life.

The victim struggled against the hold of the adversary until at last brute strength won out. The tall man twisted the other man's arm behind him and shoved the gun into his back. Now, Tony got a full view of the shorter man — a man he had seen only that morning: Kevin Norris. Tony's brow's rose. His fingers flexed against the handle.

The taller man placed his lips against

Kevin's ear and began to mumble something that must have been sinister, considering the wicked slit of his lips.

Kevin's panicked gaze collided with Tony's. The flair of recognition blazed between them.

"Help me," Kevin mouthed.

Nine

Marilyn pressed her cell phone's end button and checked the time on the instrument's face. Nearly 30 minutes had lapsed since Tony went downstairs. She'd been on the phone with Melissa most of the time. But Kim Lan had beeped in on Mel. So by now Marilyn had talked to all the sisters except Jacquelyn. With a shake of her head, she figured Jac might get around to e-mailing tonight. Since Jackie had married Lawton, and he moved into her apartment in Colorado Springs, the sisters seemed to be able to keep better track of her. More than once Jac had mentioned that Lawton reminded her to return a call that probably would have slipped her mind a few years back.

Before putting up her cell, Marilyn checked her used minutes for the month. According to the timer she was ten minutes over her free minutes limit. Marilyn grimaced. This billing cycle still had six days left. Her husband, Joshua, had jokingly told her he was going to start dividing their phone bill by seven and send each of her six friends their portion. Since they all had cell phones now they *did* keep the phone lines hot some days.

Interestingly enough Marilyn's first husband, Gregory, was far less understanding about such matters. She recalled one afternoon when he had thrown a raging fit over a telephone bill with "too many" long distance calls to her mother. Of course, that was only a few months before Marilyn found out he was having an affair with his secretary and was already planning a divorce. Despite Marilyn's pleas for a reconciliation and her volunteering to attend counseling, Greg had chosen the pathway of sin, even though he had been a respected pastor.

Marilyn pressed her index finger between her drawn brows and reminded herself that those horrid years were behind her. Indeed, God had given her a second chance with a husband who truly loved her with God's love. And in their nearly three years of marriage Marilyn couldn't recall one time when Joshua Langham had intentionally hurt her. Oh, they each had to say I'm sorry for various shortcomings, but for the first time in her life, Marilyn was understanding what it meant to be cherished by a husband who would give his life for her.

If only Victoria and Tony could get to that

point, Marilyn thought and wondered how his brief visit *really* went.

She pressed the phone's antenna against her palm, eased it back into the shaft, and slipped the cell into her purse's side pocket. Marilyn stood, stretched, and crooked her neck to gaze down the hallway toward the elevators. Still no Tony. On a hunch she decided to check in on Victoria. If her friend seemed okay Marilyn planned to go back to Victoria's beach house for a nap. She had managed to squeak together enough money to fly down to Victoria's and had arrived on last night's late flight. She and Victoria sat up until the wee hours talking. Her lack of sleep plus the morning's pressure had taken their toll.

A yawn crept up her throat as the "Star Spangled Banner" beeped forth from her purse. "Who could *that* be?" she mumbled through the yawn. Marilyn pulled her cell phone from her purse and examined the minute screen to see the name "Joshua Langham" displayed.

She pressed the send button and didn't get a chance to even speak her greeting.

"Mar, it's me — Josh."

"Yes, I saw your name on my screen," she cooed. Nobody else but Josh had ever called her Mar, and she never ceased loving the endearment. "I wasn't expecting you to call again so soon," she continued. The mission group had arrived in Los Angeles a week ago, and Josh had chatted with her last night. "It's great to hear your voice again. What are you up to?"

"I . . . uh . . . I . . . have something I want to discuss with you."

"Oh?" Marilyn queried and lowered herself back into the chair she'd just vacated. His voice's hesitant chord reminded Marilyn of his tone last year when he informed her that the loud blast in the front yard was coming from the elephant he arranged to attend Brooke's birthday party. The first news Marilyn had of the elephant was when the thing proclaimed its presence; she nearly dropped her daughter's birthday cake. Josh thought having the beast in the front yard was the grandest thing ever. All the kids loved the rides the elephant's master proffered. The whole ordeal had proven a huge success, but Marilyn possessed her share of doubts at the onset.

"Uh . . . I know we have talked about adopting and decided that it's where the Lord is leading us in the future. But . . ."

"But?" Marilyn squeezed the cell phone and concentrated on the nurse who whipped around the corner pushing an IV pole. While she and Josh had certainly *de-*

cided to adopt they had yet to start the paperwork or even begin saving money for the addition to their family. Right now Marilyn's daughter, Brooke, was seven. Marilyn figured she had one year, maybe two before the arrival of the new child.

"You know we're working with the inner city street people."

"Yes."

"Well, uh, there's a — a young woman here, Marilyn. She and her little girl have been living on the streets. The baby is only two . . ."

"Okay . . ." Marilyn said as her mind whirled with Joshua's direction.

"She told me last night she's decided to place her baby for adoption." The words tumbled out so fast Marilyn struggled to keep up with him. "She can't take care of the baby. The baby's name is Abigail. She's sick a lot because she's on the streets. She needs a stable home, Marilyn."

A mixture of panic and anticipation zipped through Marilyn. She stood and pivoted to face the row of wall-to-wall windows that offered a breathtaking view of palm trees against a shocking blue sky. Indeed, the Florida sunshine seemed to glisten with stardust as Marilyn caught her breath.

"I think maybe this baby's the one, Mar,"

Josh said, and his voice cracked over the words.

"Really?" Marilyn gasped. Her eyes stung. Her knees wobbled. She gripped the back of her neck and sat back down. The smell of tile wax accompanied the whir of a floor buffer just out of sight. Marilyn considered her job as office manager for the only vet in Mena, Arkansas. She loved her job and it provided a much-needed addition to Joshua's modest pastor's salary. But having a troubled two-year-old would certainly force Marilyn to evaluate whether or not she should continue working. Besides, they had zero dollars set aside for adoption. Marilyn's mind spun with exactly how much this adoption would cost.

"Okay, why all the silence?" Josh asked. "Is it surprise or are you trying to figure out how to let me down easy?"

"Oh, Josh, no! If you've prayed about this and you really believe —"

"I *do,* Marilyn. I do! She's beautiful. But she has an — an imperfection that will make her hard to place if the lady releases her to the department of human services. The workers here at the mission say she'll be classified as a special-needs child."

Marilyn's eyes widened as she imagined all sorts of disabilities that might involve major medical expenses they simply weren't in financial shape to absorb. While Marilyn's big heart ensured she would *never* reject a child because it was disabled, she also couldn't deny that they wouldn't be doing the child a favor if they didn't have the money to provide for her.

"I don't think you've ever been so quiet, Mar," Josh commented. "Are you okay?"

"Uh . . ." She fumbled with the crease in her slacks as the stress of the last 24 hours seemed to double. "I'm — I'm fine. It's just that . . . Josh, we can't afford this! I know because I just balanced our checking account! We're not in the red or anything, but we don't have an extra 10,000 dollars lying around right now to pay a lawyer. And besides all that, if this child has extensive medical problems —"

"Oh no — no! She doesn't have extensive problems — just — just an imperfection. She's blind in her left eye."

"Oh. That's all?"

"Yes, that's all."

"And they say she's special needs?"

"It seems many adoptive parents want, well, unflawed children, so the ones with the problems are usually more difficult to place. The blind eye causes her to be labeled special needs."

"Go figure," Marilyn said, and the initial anticipation bubbled forth anew. She stood and once again encountered that glorious tropical scenery.

"The way I see it, since you and I can actually *have* children I would prefer to give a home to a child who might not find a permanent home, rather than stand in line for one that others are in line for. From what I can gather, most adoptive parents want newborns — not toddlers who've been living on the streets."

As Josh continued a faint hint of warmth sprouted in the center of Marilyn's heart. "And . . . uh . . ." Joshua hesitated. "I debated whether or not to bring this up, but I might as well ask. Doesn't your friend Kim Lan have some sort of adoption fund or grant system set up or something?"

"Has Mick mentioned helping us?"

"No."

"Well that makes sense because I don't think you could call it an official grant. She has funded a few adoptions for couples in her church." Marilyn paced toward the coffee pot in the corner. She picked up a Styrofoam cup and marked the edge with her short thumbnail. "But . . ."

"But?"

Marilyn deposited the cup beside the pot

and poured a cup of the steaming brew whose mellow aroma, although inviting, reminded her she really didn't want another cup of coffee. "I hate to call her up and blurt something like, 'Okay . . . we've found the child, now hand over the cash.' " She gripped the cup and gazed at the ceiling's recessed lighting as a barrage of conflicting thoughts prickled her from all sides. "One of the things that I — well, all the sisters, for that matter — have tried to do is treat Kim Lan exactly like we did before she got to be Kim Lan Lowery, supermodel extraordinaire. We've even had a conversation or two without her where we made a pact *never* to ask her for money."

"Okay, yes, I understand," Josh said. "I guess I misunderstood. I thought she actually had some grant fund set up. I even came close to asking Mick. Now I'm glad I didn't."

"She *did* mention in passing a few weeks ago that if and when we find our child to let her know, but —"

"But I don't think we need to go there," Josh said.

"Good. We're on the same page." Marilyn took a tiny sip of black coffee. "I guess I'd even hesitate if she did have a grant system set up. I mean, it's only been about four years ago that Kim Lan popped in and left me a check for 5,000 dollars. That happened right after you and I first met. I was really struggling financially, and she knew it."

"Yes, I know. You said you kept it because of Brooke."

"That's right. I wouldn't have otherwise."

"I'm with you, babe," Josh said. "We'll figure this out from another angle."

"Have you even checked into the prices of lawyers and what all is involved?" Marilyn swallowed a larger portion of coffee and the bitter liquid scalded all the way to her stomach.

"No, not yet," Josh said. "I — I guess I just wanted to see what you think first. Actually, the young woman — her name's Camille — is 19. She's been on the streets for only six months. She just came in yesterday and started talking to Mick about releasing her daughter."

"Oh, Josh." Marilyn shook her head and her eyes watered. She imagined herself being in such a desperate situation. "Isn't there anything we could do to help the mother, too?"

"I don't know, Mar," Josh said.

"I mean, what if we took them both into

our home or something?"

Thoughtful silence permeated the line, and the elevator bell dinged in the distance.

"I can't imagine releasing Brooke for adoption." Marilyn covered her heart with her flattened palm. "Isn't there more we can do?"

"You know, Marilyn, I love you." Joshua's words held a hint of awe. "I love your heart. I love your vision. I didn't even think about the mother. All I could think about was the little girl and our wanting to adopt."

"Well, at least this time your plan didn't involve elephants," Marilyn teased.

A low-key chuckle rumbled over the line. "But the guy offered for free! How could I resist!"

"Oh, dear." Marilyn rolled her eyes. "Here we go again."

"Listen, let me talk some more with Mick, and I'll talk to the mother as well. Maybe we can come up with a plan that will help everyone."

"Right." Marilyn nodded, closed her eyes, and tried to maintain her equilibrium. Thirty minutes ago, her focus was upon trying to assist Victoria through this difficult time. Yet within minutes she was faced with a potential adoption or taking in a mother and her toddler. This was all going so fast, she felt as if she were spinning.

"Okay, okay . . . I hear ya," Josh said in response to a man's muffled voice. "Sorry, Mar, that was Mick. He says we need to hit the road. We're working in one of the soup kitchens today. I'm exhausted, but it's the best tired I think I've ever enjoyed."

"I understand," Marilyn said.

" 'Bye, honey." Joshua's voice caressed her taut nerves. Marilyn couldn't resist memories of the last night before his departure. Brooke had spent the night with Marilyn's parents. She and Josh had watched the sun set and spent the rest of the evening in each other's arms. A shiver of delight danced along her spine.

"I miss you," she said.

"Mmm." Joshua paused. "I miss you, too."

"I love you," she breathed and wondered how much their intimate existence would be interrupted if Josh brought home a destitute mother and her child.

"Okay, Mick!" Joshua said. "Hang onto your hat, will you? I'm on the phone with my *wife!* You have one of those too, remember?"

Marilyn giggled. "You two seem to be getting along quite well."

Josh snorted. "I guess you could say that. He snores all night and works like a dog all day. What more could I want?"

"Don't believe a word he says, Marilyn!" Mick's faint claim resounded over the line.

"I guess I really *do* need to go," Josh admitted. "Keep us in your prayers today, will ya?"

"I will, I will," Marilyn agreed. "And pray for Victoria and Tony. They had a miscarriage today."

"Oh man that's awful," Josh said. "Is Victoria okay?"

"She's going to be fine — physically."

"We'll be praying."

"Thanks, I knew you would. I know you have . . ."

"Mar — I really have to go."

" 'Bye. I love you!"

"Love you too," Josh responded and hung up.

She collapsed back into the chair. This time the hot coffee sloshed all over her pants and sent a searing path along her thigh. With a growl, she stood, tossed the cup into the trash can, and tried to convince herself that she hadn't just volunteered to take in a desperate mother and her daughter. Yet the truth wouldn't allow her to delude herself. Marilyn considered their cottage-of-a-parsonage and its two small bedrooms. The next few weeks could indeed become interesting.

Ten

Kevin Norris mouthed those piteous words once more, "Help me!" Beads of sweat popped out along his forehead, and his face grew redder by the second.

Tony Roberts pushed the handle to the hospital's fire escape exit. He hesitated as his brain rushed with the options and the consequences of each. If he flung open the door, the villain might shoot. If he bounded out upon the gunman, Tony would have the element of surprise on his side. The other option involved Tony's turning a blind eye to the whole scene. But he had never lived by that rule — not Tony Roberts, the man who had jumped through more fires than he could remember.

Just as he was ready to hurl open the door Kevin somehow broke free of the enemy's grasp. In an attempt to secure Kevin once more, the gunman moved in direct alignment with the metal door.

Simultaneously, Tony seized the moment and shoved open the metal door with all the force he could muster. It door smacked the man. A series of thumps followed. With a battle roar surging from his throat, Tony hastened through the doorway only seconds before Kevin Norris hurled himself into the hospital stairwell.

The sound of footsteps pounding down the stairs mingled with moans as the gunman staggered from behind the door. He held the front of his head and glared at Tony as if he were the devil himself. Tony prepared to lunge at the pimple-scarred ruffian, but found himself looking into the end of a revolver instead. The owner of that gun was predicting Tony's death through a tirade.

As if he'd slammed into an invisible wall, Tony halted his progress and held his breath. He looked into the eyes of that inky-orbed devil and felt as if he were being sucked into the vindictive soul of a black mamba. His ears roared with the rush of pounding pulse. A quiver starting in his knees slithered up his thighs and wrapped around his spine.

The distant squawk of a seagull mingled with a lone cat's sorrowful meow. Tony longed to glance up and down the alley to see if anyone might be available for help, but he was afraid to break the man's eye contact.

The smells of exhaust upon the balmy

ocean breeze attested to the traffic zipping up the streets on each side of the hospital. Tony detected the slightest whiff of hamburgers. The gunman's nostrils widened. He panted, and the bitter aroma of cigars tainted the air.

"Security!" a masculine voice declared. The crunch of pounding footsteps neared the fire escape from the east street.

The gunman cut a wicked glance toward the voice. The gun's barrel angled off Tony as the black mamba edged toward the stairs. Tony, muscles taut and ready to spring, decided to assist him on his journey. Holding his breath, he shoved the rascal. The rogue's gun hand flailed as he fought to regain equilibrium before he tumbled down one flight of metal stairs. Accompanied by a series of thumps and mutterings, he crashed to a crumpled heap on the next landing but managed to regain his footing. The revolver clattered through the steps and tumbled to the pavement below.

"Stop right there!" The security officer hollered, his voice jolting with his swift gait.

The black mamba cast a last glance at Tony — a glance that said, "You haven't seen the last of me!" He grabbed the handrail, struggled atop it, squatted, gained his balance, and jumped the two stories down to the alley. Tony clutched the handrail and leaned over for a better view of the gunman. After recovering from his daredevil antics, the knave retrieved his gun and hurried toward an ebony sedan parked near the stairwell. Without a backward glance, the invader clambered into the vehicle, cranked the engine, and roared up the alley.

The security guard pointed his gun low at the retreating vehicle and aimed at one of the tires. When he pulled the trigger the bullet bit the pavement just behind the Buick, and the gun's explosive bang slammed into Tony's ears like a blow with a baseball bat.

The black car, glistening in the sunlight, skidded around the corner into the flow of traffic on Driftwood Avenue. The tires squealed. Gravel scattered with a patter and ping as the vehicle surged into traffic. Bellowing vehicle horns filled the alley with a cacophony of protests. The sedan, fishtailing in front of a white van, screeched its way out of sight. Within a dozen beats of Tony's racing heart the city's cadence ensconced the alley once more. All was peaceful.

The security guard halted and eyed the exit but a second. His tanned faced stony he snatched a cell phone from his belt loop, pressed one button, and blurted a curt message, "He got away. He's in a black Buick heading north on Driftwood. License plate number BDS 59L."

The guard then looked up at Tony. "You okay?"

"Yeah." Tony hung onto the side of the rail and felt like he did this morning when he exited that blazing beach house. This was definitely turning into a day to remember.

"Are you the one who called?"

"C–called?" Tony stuttered.

"We got an alert from the police station. Somebody called 911 from his cell phone, and they forwarded the call to us."

"That would probably have been . . ." Tony glanced over his shoulder. The ajar door revealed no sign of Kevin Norris.

"We'll need a statement from you. The police will probably be here in a few minutes as well. May I see some identification?"

"Of course." Tony nodded. He pulled out his wallet, retrieved his driver's license, and stepped toward the third-story stairwell.

"Meet me at the front of the hospital in a minute, will ya?" the guard requested. "I'll take your information then."

"I'll be there." Tony snatched a steadying breath, slipped back into the stairwell, and snapped the door behind him. He paused to absorb the hospital's cool air and swiped his forehead with trembling fingers. After another steadying breath, Tony pivoted to descend the stairs, and Kevin Norris hovered at the bottom of the flight.

Tony stopped. Kevin's desperate gray eyes glistened like twin points of light. Without a word Kevin took the stairs two at a time and halted beside Tony.

"You can't tell anyone I was involved in this." His right eye twitched beneath a trimmed brow.

"Excuse me?" Tony asked.

"They set fire to my house this morning." He twined his fingers together then maneuvered them against each other. "They'll kill Rhonda and Coty if I don't cooperate."

"Cooperate?" Tony echoed.

"Rhonda doesn't know. She doesn't know!" Kevin rammed a hand into graying hair and wadded it against his scalp. He yanked at the knot of his striped tie, unfastened the top button of his white shirt, and maneuvered the tie's knot lower.

Tony felt as if he'd been dropped into the Twilight Zone. He grappled for some clue that might hint at Kevin Norris' dilemma but deduced nothing. All he could piece together was that Rhonda Norris held a high opinion of her "honorable" husband, who was obviously involved in something less than ethical.

"What was that all about?" Tony swiped at the sweat that trickled to the corner of his eye, producing a nagging sting.

"I can't tell you." Kevin cracked his knuckles one after the other. "I can't. I can't. If they find out I talked to anyone, they'll kill Rhonda and Coty." He grabbed Tony's forearm. "Promise me you won't mention my name!"

"How can I not?" Tony demanded. "I just told the security guard I'd meet him downstairs and give him and the police a statement. I hinted that another man had called security. I'm assuming that was you?"

"Yes — yes, that was me." Kevin nodded. "I called from my cell phone. Actually, I called 911, and they alerted the hospital."

"That's what the security guard said."

Tony gazed down the stairwell. How in the world he managed to get himself tangled in some of these situations was beyond his wildest imagination. Only two years ago, Tony had stumbled upon a convenience store robbery in Pensacola. Before the whole thing was over he tripped the robber and sat on him until the police arrived. Nothing glamorous about his methods, that was certain, but the local paper had treated him like some sort of hero. At times Tony wondered what all he would have to do to convince Victoria that he was *her* hero. Thoughts of Victoria reminded him that he'd just lost his very own bundle of joy.

Enough of that, he scolded, and centered his thoughts back upon the problem at hand.

"So . . ." Tony toyed with his driver's license. "What exactly do you want me to tell them?" He leveled a hard gaze at Kevin. "I won't lie to the police. If they find out I lied, I'd be in big trouble. My job could be put in jeopardy." Tony pressed his fingers against his chest. "I'm a public servant, for pity's sake," he stressed, as if Kevin didn't already know. "I have a duty to protect people. The fire department doesn't exactly smile on its employees lying to the police!"

"Listen to me!" Kevin grabbed Tony's arms, and his fingers ate into taut biceps. He looked up at Tony and his eyes glazed with an urgency that couldn't be denied — an urgency that sent a chill through Tony's bones. Whatever Kevin was involved in, it was serious. Serious and illegal. Illegal and deadly.

"If the police hear one hint of my name, my wife and my son will be killed." Tears reddened his intense eyes. A rash of sweat erupted along Kevin's cheekbones that were marred by tanned laugh lines.

"The police?" Tony questioned and wondered if Kevin was implying the local authorities were involved in his insidious game.

"Do you have a child?" Kevin demanded in a tight voice of controlled hysteria.

Yes, her name's Toni, his mind responded, *and I haven't seen her in 18 years.* Instead of voicing his thoughts Tony said, "My wife and I have never had children. She just miscarried. That's why I'm here."

Kevin's gaze faltered. "I'm sorry." Yet his hollow voice resonated his own stress rather than true remorse for Tony's loss. He released his iron grip on Tony's arms and rubbed his opened palms against his face. As if the act granted him more resolve, he directed another determined gaze toward Tony. "Have you ever gotten sucked into something that seemed so easy and harmless at the time but turned out to be way bigger and way uglier and way more illegal than you ever imagined?" Regret tainted his every word.

"No, I haven't," Tony answered without a pause. "Somehow I've always managed to stay on the right side of the law."

"Believe me, the law isn't always in the right." A drop of sweat trickled down Kevin's temple.

Tony's brows quirked as his previous suspicions were confirmed.

"And I'm not lying to you when I tell you — if you even so much as peep the wrong information, my wife and son are history. And there's nobody who will do anything about it because the people who are supposed to investigate murder are the ones who will have the blood on their hands." Kevin's words pounded into Tony one at a time like well-aimed bricks. But whether they were absolute truth or not was anybody's guess. In Tony's experience, people who would stoop to breaking the law wouldn't blink at lying.

"And . . ." Kevin added with a manipulative gleam in his eyes, ". . . if I were you, I'd watch my back for a while. Be careful what you say to that security guard. Do you *understand?*" The clap of a door several flights up underscored Kevin's last word.

Tony nodded as a grave realization hit him. In his willingness to assist Kevin he might very well have stepped into a nasty scheme that could prove more life-threatening than any convenience store robbery. Memories of the look in the eyes of that inky-orbed black mamba laced Tony's heart with a dreadful chill that crept into the pit of his stomach.

"I'm telling you," Kevin insisted, "if you play your cards right you can go home and no one will bother you. But if they decide you know too much . . ." Kevin's brows lowered and he shook his head, ". . . they'll kill you." The final words rasped out like the whisper of the death angel himself.

The tap of shoes against steps announced that the same person who slammed the door was steadily descending the stairs. Kevin glanced over his shoulder, but Tony figured the person was still probably two floors up. Without another word, Norris spun and raced down the stairs.

The footsteps sounded closer. And the firm, steady tattoo hinted that the shoes were flat and masculine. Tony had no clue who might be nearing but a burning hint of panic spiraling his gut insisted he not hang around to find out. Most likely the person was a hospital employee or visitor. *But what if he's the evil one's cohort?*

Tony dashed down the stairs in Kevin's wake, yet when he rounded the first landing no sign of Kevin remained. With Norris' claims storming his mind, Tony sprinted to the first floor. Before opening the door that would admit him into the main lobby, he toyed with the idea of taking the back exit and sneaking out to his vehicle. There was no reason he absolutely had to come back today. He could very easily call Rhonda and arrange to deliver the diary at another time and place. And as for Victoria, Tony could call her as well and offer to drive her home tomorrow. The solid footsteps slowed one story up. A door slammed and silence seized the stairwell.

He whipped open the door and pressed his lips into a firm line. *Running is not an option,* Tony decided. *I might have my share of faults but I'm not a coward.* "And I don't lie to the police," he mumbled, *"ever."*

After stepping into the hallway beside the elevators, Tony turned toward the front entryway and strode past a knot of people awaiting the elevator's descent. He had no clue how he would handle the statement to the security guard.

He passed the gift and coffee shop, and the smell of cappuccinos trailed him toward the glass entryway where the stone-faced security guard stood. The guard folded his arms as his keen gaze shot across the lobby, toward the elevators, and darted back to Tony. With a nod, he stepped forward, and Tony strode into the inevitable meeting.

Eleven

Darnell Hopkins eyed the hulking man who entered the hotel room near the West Florida Regional Hospital. The door snapped shut, blotting out the hum of traffic and the eye-piercing sunshine typical of a day in Pensacola. Darnell, thin and tense, strutted around the room's desk and snatched up a packet of Camels. He placed one between drawn lips, snatched up the disposable lighter, and ignited the cigarette's end. After one puff his drive for nicotine subsided enough for him to focus upon the task at hand.

He exhaled a cloud of smoke and eyed the man in front of him — a man whose eyes chilled the soul. Buster Shae observed the end of Darnell's cigarette and chewed a smoldering cigar between clamped teeth. "I made the connection, like we planned." His words held but a hint of the years he'd spent in New York.

"And?" Darnell stepped back and leaned against the wall behind him. He drew deeply on his cigarette and relished the uncoiling of the nicotine need.

"He got the message." Buster unbuttoned his sports coat and slid into the rolling chair near the desk.

"Is he still in?"

"Of course." Buster's assured smile bordered on cocky. As usual Darnell suppressed the urge to smear that smile all over the jackal's face. He hid every vestige of the thought.

"We had our . . . conversation at the hospital on the third-floor emergency exit landing — facing the alley — just like we planned." Buster's attention trailed across the room decked in typical Holiday Inn decor. "But some blond-headed maniac busted in on us."

The Destin chief of police tensed and restrained himself from grabbing Buster's chin and forcing the ruffian to look him in the eye. He *hated* it when Buster broke eye contact. There was usually bad news in the offing. Darnell locked his knees, gritted his teeth, and waited for the other piece of information that undoubtedly involved the blond guy.

"Before it was over, I was running, and a security guard was on my trail," Buster admitted.

"What?" Darnell rounded the desk and stopped three feet from Buster's chair. In the past the chief had played his hand at bullying his criminal conspirators. But this guy wasn't the sort you could domineer, especially since he was a good inch taller and probably 80 pounds heavier than Darnell. Furthermore, Shae's network had approached Darnell about the joint endeavor, so he wasn't the one on top here. Nevertheless, Hopkins refused to allow Shae to think he was intimidated.

"If I were you," Buster's wayward gaze flitted back to Darnell, "I'd call hospital security and tell them I'm in custody. Otherwise, there's going to be a report and things could look suspicious."

The chief snatched up the phone book from the desk's edge and fidgeted with the pages until he arrived at the number for West Florida Regional Hospital.

Within two puffs of his cigarette, he was interacting with a familiar voice. "Zulick here."

"Zulick, it's Hopkins."

"Yes."

"The Pensacola Police Department just called my office. It seems they've picked up a man who's wanted in Destin for all sorts of trouble. They arrested him for speeding and found out he's got a record a mile long. They said he came out of the alley behind

143

the hospital. I'm assuming there must have been an . . . altercation." Hopkins tapped the end of his cigarette against the glass ash tray. The acrid smell of tobacco nearly blotted out the scent of bathroom cleanser.

"You guessed it. Gilley's on it. He's questioning a witness now."

"Tell him the suspect is in custody in Pensacola, and we're sending a man to pick him up. We'll call if we need any more details. But right now, he's got so many charges on him we can keep him in jail awhile."

Nothing but silence permeated the line, and Darnell squinted as he drew deeply upon the cigarette.

"How much are you offering this time, Hopkins?" Zulick finally asked.

Darnell bit into the cigarette and glared at Shae. He covered the receiver and hissed, "He wants to be paid off."

"So promise him a thousand." Shae shrugged. "It's the cost of doing business. We've done it before; we'll do it again."

"And nobody's going to come down on me?" Hopkins recalled the one and only meeting he had endured with the boss in Chicago during the setup of this whole scheme. That evil man might even top Shae's wickedness. Darnell resisted the quiver in his belly.

Twin lines formed from Buster's nose to the corners of his mouth. The smile was far from kind. "I didn't say that," he said. "But a thousand is nothing compared to the millions we're handling. Besides, a wrist slap from Chicago will sure beat a prison cell any day. Don't you think?" Shae's bushy brows arched.

Darnell crammed the receiver to his ear. "Okay, a thousand," he barked into the phone. The chief rested his hand against the desk top. Zulick had proven himself an idiot on more than one occasion, but he never failed to smell the potential for money.

"Let's see, this is the second time in six months, Hopkins," Zulick reminded. "Make it two, and we didn't see a thing."

"It's a deal," Darnell agreed. "We'll take care of the electronic transfer within 24 hours. Is your account number the same?"

"Haven't changed a thing," Zulick purred.

Growling under his breath Darnell dropped the receiver into the cradle. "He asked for two."

"Figures." Shae shifted in his seat. "One down, one to go."

Hopkins left his cigarette in the ash tray and methodically rolled up the sleeves of his cotton shirt. "I guess you're talking about the blond guy?"

"Of course," Shae answered with a slight nod. He rubbed blunt fingers along a cheek scarred by adolescence. "I made sure I got a good look." His inky eyes narrowed. "A really good look."

"And you think he'd recognize you?"

"Most likely. At least when I'm dressed like this." Buster placed elbows on the chair's arms, made a tent of his fingers, and rested his chin on the tips. "So I'll start with Norris and force him to tell us what he knows about him. From there, I'll just take out the blond nut the first chance I get."

Darnell reached for his Camel and his index finger trembled against the source of his need. While Hopkins had covered innumerable descrepancies throughout his ten years as police chief, this money laundering scheme was his first venture into the big leagues. Murder had never crossed his mind when he allowed his name to be used as the owner of "Hopkins International Arts." The business that claimed to buy and resell priceless paintings didn't exist, except on paper. Indeed, it was nothing more than a funnel for dirty money processed through the Cayman Islands and back into the U.S.

Darnell sucked on the Camel and expelled the smoke. He ground the finished cigarette in the center of the ashtray, rocked back on his heels, and crossed his arms. He hoped the stance spoke a calm he was far from feeling. In a matter of minutes a representative from the FBI would be meeting them. The agent had promised to deliver all the paper evidence of their endeavor the FBI had amassed in exchange for a hundred grand. He hoped Shae wasn't planning to kill that poor devil, too.

The chief eyed his freckled forearms, exposed by the tan shirt's rolled-up sleeves. The thatch of sandy-red hair covering his arms was now as much gray as red. He studied the short-piled carpet and imagined himself sailing into the Gulf of Mexico with a cool ten million to his name. Darnell would have a good 20 years left to enjoy it. Perhaps a few murders would be well worth the luxury of early retirement.

As Tony neared the security guard he noted his name tag. F. Gilley, claimed the sliver of metal against the navy uniform. Tony paused a few feet from him and extended his hand.

"Tony Roberts."

"Name's Gilley." The guard's sun-worn face didn't offer the hint of a smile. "Let's take this to the security office." He darted a sharp gaze toward the waiting room, the elevator, and then the gift shop. "The police should be here soon."

Tony took in their surroundings. The smells of floor polish and fresh flowers . . . the sight of the pink-clad ladies behind the welcome desk . . . the bustle and whir of visitors and professionals intent upon their missions suggested business as usual. No one would have ever guessed that a brush with death had just occurred in the alley.

Gilley took several steps to the right, and Tony followed. They had barely progressed six feet when Gilley stopped and pivoted to face Tony.

"Wait a minute," he said. "Earlier you indicated you might know the other witness — the guy who called the police."

Tony looked down at the stocky guard and groped for the right words. Despite his doubts about Kevin Norris, the desperate gleam in the man's teary eyes had suggested that he might very well believe what he said. *What if the authorities really* are *involved?* The thought splashed Tony with a tidal wave of doubts.

"Uh . . ." He hesitated. Before he got another word out Gilley's cell phone emitted a series of short beeps.

The guard snatched the phone, pressed a button, and snapped the receiver to his ear.

"Gilley here," he growled as if he were planning a defense against World War III. Tony decided the guy needed to join the FBI or CIA as an international spy.

"Yes . . . yes . . ." he said. "I see." His bushy brows lowered over keen brown eyes, and the lines around his mouth deepened. "But —" He placed his free arm across his chest and tucked his fingers around his torso. "I don't think —" A scarlet veil crept up his tanned face. "Yes, Mr. Zulick," he agreed, yet a tinge of belligerence twisted his lips. Gilley ended the call, shoved the cell into the side holster, and observed Tony as if *he* were the criminal.

Tony didn't flinch away from his intense gaze. The last thing he needed was for this "CIA spy" to think he had anything to hide.

"That was the head of security." Gilley's words shot out like the rhythmic pound of a hammer. "He said the police station called. They have the suspect in custody. He's supposed to have several outstanding warrants for his arrest. They won't be requiring a statement on this incident." The frustration in Gilley's eyes bore witness to his opinion.

Narrowing his eyes, Tony evaluated what he knew of police procedure. He was almost certain that a criminal's past record didn't delete the need for a report on a current offense. Something was strange about all this. Something that underscored Frank Norris' final warning as worth heeding.

And I'm not lying when I tell you — if you even so much as peep the wrong information, my wife and son are history. And there's nobody who will do anything about it because the people who are supposed to investigate murder are the ones who will have the blood on their hands. . . . If I were you, I'd watch my back for a while. Be careful what you say to that security guard. Do you understand?

Then Tony recalled the look in that gangster's eyes. The look that promised they'd meet at a later date when Tony would be the loser.

He stumbled away from the scowling security guard, whipped around, and rushed toward the hospital exit. Tony had promised Rhonda Norris he would retrieve her diary. He would honor that promise. He'd check on Victoria again. Then, he would go back to the fire station and discuss the situation with Eddy. The two of them might be able to make sense of Kevin's story.

Twelve

Victoria fumbled with inserting the key into her beach home's deadbolt lock. A gust of March breeze whipped in from the ocean and hurled a thatch of her wavy hair across her eyes. She grappled with shoving the apple-scented locks from her face while juggling an armload of garage sale bargains. The 50-cent lamp shade she'd snatched at the first yard sale slipped from her grasp and tumbled toward the steep wooden steps.

"Oh phooey!" Victoria pivoted to grab her treasure. But a swish of wind rolled the shade out of her grasp. The bargain scurried along the plank porch and hovered on the edge of the steps. Victoria deposited the less flighty bargains at the door and rushed toward the lamp shade. Yet when her fingers brushed the stiff linen, the shade toppled down the flight of stairs and crashed into the pearly sand.

"This is just great!" Victoria growled. She kicked off her slip-on sandals, lifted her ankle-length sundress, and chased her prize as it merrily jostled toward the azure ocean. By the time Victoria caught up with the escapee warm sand coated her toes.

She clutched the shade and dug her toes deeper into the fine sand. Savoring the smell of sea and surf, Victoria gazed upon an ocean that began as bright turquoise at the beach and gradually deepened to a rich sapphire that stretched toward the dazzling blue horizon. The steady rhythm of waves washing ashore blended with the swoosh of the spring breeze, and the trio of wind chimes hanging on the porch joined in nature's ensemble. Victoria recalled the day she and Tony decided to buy the house on the private beach, even though the place needed ample repairs.

"I can fix up the house," she'd claimed. "But I can't create this kind of scenery."

Tony had laughed, hauled her into his arms, and twirled her around. The newlyweds wound up tumbling onto the sand, and in that joyous moment their decision was made. The next day they signed the papers on the house and started working on the American dream.

Thoughts of Tony ushered in the remembrance of another dream they had experienced together — the dream that had been snatched away. She touched her lower abdomen and closed her eyes against the sting of tears. Time and time again she had imagined herself splashing in the ocean with a blond-headed toddler or chasing nocturnal sand crabs to the accompaniment of her child's delightful squeals. Victoria allowed her mind the luxury of wandering in that never-never land where she and her child frolicked in mutual love and fulfillment. She swallowed against the lump in her throat.

Yet in the midst of savoring that lost dream a haunting realization sneaked into the back of her mind and punctured the maternal paradise — a paradise with only *one* parent. Victoria's eyes popped open as a thought, disheartening yet revealing, swept aside her daydreams. Victoria never remembered a child-related fantasy that included Tony. In all her musings about her baby, Victoria had been alone.

With a frown she stared at the ocean's heaving surface splayed with the evening sun's silver glister.

"Well," she whispered, "he's at the fire station a third of the time anyway." *Actually, all the time now,* she added. After the miscarriage he had offered to take her home, but as things turned out Marilyn filled that gap. After Marilyn returned to Arkansas, Victoria's parents whisked her away to their home in Baton Rouge for two weeks of recovery. More than once Victoria had overheard her mother answering Tony's calls with something less than enthusiasm.

She dug her toes ever deeper into the warm sand and wondered if Tony might call today. Even though neither had discussed his moving back home during the month since the miscarriage, at least they had stopped yelling at each other. But in reviewing their polite telephone dialogue Victoria couldn't say the chat times were much more than that of distant acquaintances. With the tepid breeze tossing her wavy hair around her cheeks, Victoria examined the pristine sand and doubted even their most ecstatic moments. Indeed, she recalled the days after they signed the papers on the house. Even though both of them had shared the joy of the new venture, they soon fell back into the distant behavioral patterns — patterns now so entrenched in their relationship Victoria despaired that anything would ever change.

In an attempt to escape the disturbing thoughts, she uprooted her feet and scurried toward the steps. Yet she was only halfway up when she stopped. The front door, inlaid with beveled glass, loomed in her wake. A door behind which awaited an empty house. No husband. No baby. Just Victoria and her meticulously redecorated domain.

Her fingers flexed against the handrail. She propped her right foot atop the other, and sand tickled her arch.

"I want my husband back." She thought of that blank note from the flowers — a note still tucked inside her billfold. "I still want him back." Nevertheless, Victoria fell into the speculation that had been her bane during the last month. She wrestled with exactly what she would have to do to eliminate Tony's walls.

Although the phone's faint ring offered no answers it prodded Victoria to action. *Maybe that's Tony,* she thought and raced up the rest of the stairs. By the sixth ring Victoria dumped her bargains in one corner of the sofa and slumped into the other corner. She snapped up the receiver and blurted a greeting.

"Girlfriend, we'd about decided you forgot us!" Marilyn's cheerful greeting erupted over the line, and Victoria's shoulders drooped.

"Oh, it's you guys." She glanced at her watch and noted that seven o'clock had indeed arrived. Marilyn had called two days ago to set up a sister chat time, and Victoria had been so distracted she forgot it.

"Sheesh! You don't *have* to talk to us, you know," Jacquelyn Franklin said.

"You're a fine one to say something like that, Jac," Melissa Franklin chimed in, "you miss half the sister calls yourself."

"Ooooo, sister-in-law squabble!" Kim Lan injected. She then hissed and yowled like a cat.

A chorus of laughter broke over the line.

"Give me a break, will ya?" Jac defended. "You people act like I'm supposed to have your faces carved into my walls or something. I've got a full-blown career, you know! Criminals don't arrange their lives to suit your chat times. Besides, I'm a married woman now," she added with a sly twist. "I have to keep my husband happy."

"Exactly how happy *is* he?" Samantha Butler countered and the rest of the sisters chimed in with a teasing round of wolf whistles.

"Yeah well, *you're* the newlywed, Sammie," Jacquelyn replied, referring to the wedding that took place a couple of months before. Sammie and her new husband, R.J. Butler, wound up eloping and enjoying a Caribbean cruise for their honeymoon. "Maybe we should all be asking you how happy R.J. is!" Jac added.

"That's none of your bee's wax," Sam countered.

The whoops and yelps and laughter that followed sounded more in tune with a football game.

Victoria giggled and ran her finger along the couch's polished cotton seam. She marveled that Sam could speak of marital intimacy with such a light tone. After Sam's abusive husband was killed, Victoria and the other sisters wondered if she would ever be able to heal from his brutal wounds.

"Since we're on the subject," Kim Lan announced, "I can't stay on the phone too long tonight. Mick has been out of town and should be here in an hour. I arranged a babysitter so I can set a trap for him when he gets home."

"A trap?" Sonsee exclaimed.

"You bet! And Mick loves it, too!"

"I think we're on the verge of T.M.I.," Marilyn said, "too much information."

"You won't get another peep from me," Kim Lan countered with an artful giggle.

With the last of her chortles melting away Victoria started to tuck her feet under her legs yet remembered the sand. She grimaced and rested her toes against the oval oriental rug that featured a blend of pastels from sky blue to sea foam to the palest of taupe. Dubiously, she eyed the sprinkle of sand that had already settled upon the rug. Victoria glanced toward her electric broom propped in the corner of the kitchen, and she itched to whisk away the soil.

"Victoria? Are you still with us?" Sonsee Delaney's voice penetrated Victoria's housekeeping dilemma, and she wondered what she'd missed.

"Here and accounted for," she claimed.

"So, how are you?" Sammie Jones asked, and Victoria didn't know whether she imagined the undercurrent in Sam's voice or if she was being paranoid. She hoped that Sam had abided by her promise not to tell the other sisters about Victoria's shameful attraction to the choir director. Sam was the only one who knew, and she'd discovered the secret when she'd accidentally overheard a conversation between Victoria and Sam's mom a couple of month's ago.

A warm wash crept up Victoria's neck and cheeks. "I'm — I'm fine, I guess," Victoria said and wondered if she sounded as forlorn to her friends as she did to herself. They had all been so supportive after the miscarriage, and Victoria had cried on the phone with more than one of them — especially Marilyn. The silence that settled upon the fun-loving bunch momentarily comforted Victoria. Yet as the silence stretched, her comfort abated. Once again, she debated whether or not Sam had disclosed her secret.

Yet another worry descended upon her. Marilyn and she never discussed the fact that Marilyn called Tony after the miscarriage, even though Victoria asked her not to. *I wonder if Marilyn told the sisters about that as well.* She twined the phone cord around her fingers, and her worries escalated with every second. *So I haven't always done everything just right, but that doesn't warrant them comparing notes about me behind my back.*

Victoria shook her head. *Stop it!* she told herself. *Why are you always so paranoid? These women love you!*

"So . . . how 'bout them Red Sox," Melissa queried, and the group was hurled into a new round of laughter that erupted into another conversational volley.

Victoria stared at the couch cushion, the color of the Destin ocean on a clear summer's day. The cushion blurred into the backdrop of the oriental rug, and the faint scent of cinnamon candles ushered in memories of those horrid moments in Sam's kitchen when the two had discussed Victoria's wandering eye. Victoria squirmed and a new wave of anxiety made her wonder if Sam had revealed the secret from that January morning. They had shared a conversation about Victoria's marriage and Sammie candidly stated that she believed Victoria was as much to blame for her marital problems as was Tony. Despite the fact that Victoria had fought the rising irritation because Sam wasn't taking her side, the ire won; and Victoria stomped from the breakfast table to the kitchen sink. . . .

Victoria shoved the stopper into the bottom of the sink, slammed on the water, and squeezed the detergent bottle until a mountain of suds formed beneath the spout.

The clank of Sam's silverware against her plate preceded her presence at the sink.

"Thanks for doing the dishes last night," Sam finally said.

"Sure," Victoria mumbled and stirred the warm water with hands eager to scrub the plates laden with waffle syrup.

Sammie hovered nearby, and Victoria sensed she was about to speak again.

"I–I'm sorry," she finally stammered. "I didn't mean to upset you."

Victoria's shoulders shook, a broken sob erupted forth, and she gripped the edge of the damp sink until her knuckles shone white.

"Ah, Victoria," Sammie said, and placed a loving arm across her shoulders.

Without a word, Victoria hurled her arms around Sammie.

"I'm sorry," she choked out. "I shouldn't have gotten aggravated at you. It's just that — that — I — I thought you'd take my side. And I'm already so embarrassed over — over that other! It's all so shameful!"

Sammie didn't offer another word. Instead, she shut off the water, hugged her friend, and allowed her to cry against her wool blazer.

"It's okay. Really," Sammie finally said. "And just for the record, I'm not taking Tony's side any more than I'm taking your side. It's just that I think I can see two sides here, and —"

"Promise me you won't tell the other sisters, Sammie. Promise me." Victoria inched away then grasped for Sam's hands. "I would die of embarrassment if any of them found out I've been fighting an attraction for another man!" The heat in her cheeks attested to half the shame in her soul.

Sam gripped Victoria's shoulders. "I promise I won't tell any of them. But Victoria . . ." she shook her head, and her blue eyes shone with certainty, "I also promise not one of them would think any less of you. Just think about them. Between the six of us, we've experienced divorce, an affair, a near-murder, grudges, and abuse. And you know what I've been through, girlfriend." Sammie stabbed the center of her chest with her index finger, and a strand of her straight red hair fell from the clip at her neck. "I don't for one second want you to think that I am in any way judging you because I'm not. During all that torture Adam put me through, you better believe there were times when I'd look at other men who seemed, well, together, and sigh about my own fate."

"But — but — I've always been so — I don't know . . ." Victoria pulled away, snatched a tissue from her sweater pocket, and scrubbed at her cheeks, hot and damp.

"You're the epitome of everything I've ever wanted to be, actually," Sammie said and shook her head.

"What?" Victoria gasped and peered deeply into Sam's eyes for any hint of duplicity. Yet all Victoria perceived was pure honesty.

"You come from a solid Christian family that's functional, for cryin' out loud!" Sam raised her hand. "You guys get together for every holiday and actually *enjoy* each other.

Imagine that! Then, you're so ladylike and proper it just oozes out of your every pore. You're petite, and I'd stake my last laser jet cartridge that you don't have one trace of cellulite. And look at your complexion! Oh, please! It's flawless. Me? I've got freckles all over the place and zits, for cryin' out loud!" She stroked the bridge of her nose then touched a chin marred by a red pimple.

"And blue eyes most women would kill for," Victoria added, and her own hazel orbs seemed less-than-thrilling. "Plus, you've got a man of gold who'd *die* for you." The words floated around the kitchen as if they were some message straight from heaven. And Victoria couldn't remember ever sensing the I'm-all-yours-baby adoration from Tony that R.J. Butler displayed for Sam.

Victoria pressed the tissue against one eye and then another. "And really, I don't know if I've ever felt that from Tony," she admitted. "And — and now . . . now I've hauled off and offered to help Ricky decorate his house!" she bleated like a desperate lamb.

"Excuse me?" Sammie asked.

"Ricky!" Victoria explained, her eyes widening. "Ricky Christopher, the choir director!"

At last Sam nodded. "Oh!" she gasped. "You offered to help him decorate his house?"

"Yes! He came over just to pay a courtesy call about choir. He saw what I've done to my house and said he was desperate for some help with his home. His mom is coming for a visit and —" She waved her hand. "I won't bore you with the details."

"Do you think he was making a play for you?"

"No!" Victoria gasped and raised her brows. "It's the truth! He *does* need help with his house! The place is the pits!"

"So now you're committed to helping him?"

"Yessss," Victoria hissed, and the very admission made her feel like a wanton woman in the midst of a scandal. "And I don't need to be working that close to him! He's just too . . . I'm just too —" She pressed her lips together and grappled for the best euphemisms for the whole horrid ordeal.

"Well, why can't you just bow out?"

"Because he needs help! He doesn't have the money to hire a professional, and I *do* feel sorry for him. He's in a lurch. He's got his heart set on my helping him." She rubbed her forehead, leaned against the kitchen counter, and crossed her arms. "I also think he's clueless about how I'm feeling. Really, he's so upbeat and carefree and unsuspecting he'd probably fall over in a dead faint if he ever even suspected how I've been feeling."

Sammie ran the tip of her finger over the towering suds and Victoria watched as the fragrant bubbles popped in quick succession. "Would it help if I came to Florida for a few days and helped? I could be a buffer so you don't have to be with him alone."

"You'd do that?" Victoria squeaked.

"Of course." Sammie resumed her bubble popping. "I've got some vacation time coming, and Brett and I would enjoy the break."

Victoria covered her lips and shook her head.

"If you would do that, Sam, I'd be indebted to you for life!"

"Nah," Sammie said with a quick head shake. "That's what friends are for. Jac got me out of a tough spot. I'll do the same for you. End of discussion."

"Thanks!" Victoria grabbed Sammie for another tight hug. "You're the greatest."

Victoria shifted on the couch and eyed the claw-footed antique chair she'd recovered in polished blue stripes. Sammie had been as good as her word. Victoria wound up volunteering to keep Brett, Sam's son, while R.J. and Sam enjoyed their honeymoon. When Sammie and R.J. arrived after the cruise the two of them had pitched in to help Victoria with Ricky's home. Victoria hadn't talked to Ricky since the day he gave her a reimbursement check. Not only did she drop out of the choir but she also claimed a safe spot on the back pew — a spot that offered her ample opportunity to avoid the director. After word circulated about her miscarriage some of the choir members had expressed their condolences while others sent cards or remained respectfully silent. Thankfully, Ricky had chosen to send a card.

She rested her head on the back of the couch and stared up at the brass-trimmed ceiling fan's slow rotation. The sisterly chat gradually reentered her thought process in the midst of something Marilyn was saying.

". . . have a special announcement. I haven't said anything before now because I wanted to make certain it was really going to happen, but I believe that now it's going to be official." Marilyn's voice trilled with a note of expectancy, and Victoria raised her head from the back of the couch to stare out the wall-to-wall windows. A blazing ball of fire descended toward the western horizon and cast a golden sheen upon the azure waters.

"I know I mentioned a couple of months ago that Josh and I had decided that the Lord was leading us to adopt . . ." she started.

"And?" Jac Franklin prompted.

"Well, it looks like we've found our baby — or maybe *she* found us!"

A cascade of sisterly excitement chorused over the line. "Congratulations!" Victoria's toes dug into the rug. She moved to the edge of the cushion and stared hard at the molten sun that oozed bronze essence upon the heaving sea. Yet despite all her self-control her eyes misted, and the sun and sea blended into a blue-and-gold blur.

"Josh met her when he was on that mission trip to Los Angeles last month. We wound up offering assistance to the baby and her mother."

"Isn't this the gal you posted an e-mail about on our internet loop?" Sammie asked.

"Yes. I didn't say anything about the possibility of adoption because, well, we just didn't know whether or not it was even going to happen. Our desire was to help Camille get off the streets and *stay* off and help her get stable. Anyway, Camille and little Abigail have been staying here for a month now." Marilyn's voice grew wobbly. "As much as we tried to help Camille, she decided to go ahead and allow us to adopt Abigail."

"Is she still there with you guys?" Melissa asked.

"No." Marilyn sniffled. "Two nights ago she signed the papers releasing Abigail. The next morning she was gone." Her thick voice held a bittersweet edge. "We're consulting with a lawyer in our church who is waiving his fees even."

The sisters fell into a round of silence until Kim Lan broke in. "I guess I might as well confess that I knew all this was going down. Since Mick and Josh were on the same mission trip together, we had the inside scoop from the start. Anyway, Marilyn, I know this has got to be disappointing. I mean, it doesn't take a rocket scientist to figure out that Camille probably went back to the streets. But —"

"But maybe the Lord just put us in Abigail's life at the right time so we can give her what Camille never could," Marilyn finished.

"Exactly," Kim Lan agreed.

"I'm on the verge of tears here," Sonsee

admitted. "Just thought I'd share that."

"Oh, you're just an old ball bag," Jacquelyn teased.

"Yeah, and you're just trying to act tough," Sonsee shot back. "I bet if we could see you you're reaching for a tissue just like the rest of us."

"I know *I* am," Melissa said. "As a matter of fact I guess since this is share-and-care time I'll just go ahead and tell you guys that Kinkaide and I have been talking about starting a family soon."

"You and Kinkaide would make *great* parents!" Marilyn encouraged. "You could even be your own child's pediatrician." A baby's shrill cry reverberated over the line. "Oh . . . that's Abigail," Marilyn said, and a series of bumps and shuffles followed her claim. Victoria imagined what her life might have been like in a few more months if she hadn't miscarried. Abigail's persistent crying sent an unrequited longing through Victoria's soul — a longing that nearly broke her heart.

"You know what, guys?" Samantha injected. "Ten years ago we were young chicks ready to take on the world, but we're slowly turning into a bunch of mother hens."

Another round of laughter heightened the

sting in Victoria's eyes. As a trio of tears seeped from the corner of her eye Victoria pressed her tongue against the roof of her mouth and swallowed a sob. Without a word she reached for the phone's disconnect button, pushed it, and slipped the receiver back into the cradle. "You guys might be a bunch of mother hens," she whispered, "but not me."

The suppressed sob erupted from her spirit, and Victoria covered her face with her hands. When her palms were drenched, she staggered up the stairway that led to the bathroom. When she topped the stairs, Victoria stopped. She clung to the handrail and stared wide-eyed at a closed door as if she had never seen the room before. She had asked Marilyn to shut the nursery door when they came home from the hospital. Victoria had yet to open it. The doorknob seemed to bid her to turn it, yet Victoria possessed no strength to act upon the summons. Indeed, she was overtaken by the creamy smell of baby lotion, and she was certain her frenzied mind must be torturing her.

Instead of entering the nursery, she stumbled past the baby's room, raced into the bathroom, slammed the door, and locked it — as if by turning the lock she could somehow blot the tormenting loss from her mind. Yet the smell of baby lotion pursued her while a squeal and gurgle of infant delight echoed through the corridors of her mind. Victoria backed away from the door until she bumped into the claw-footed tub. She lowered herself to the tub's edge and then sank lower until her knees connected with the polished tile floor, the color of fresh peaches. Somehow Victoria managed to fumble through the decorative stack of plush washcloths tucked in a basket near the tub. She extracted one, turned on the tub's cold water tap, and immersed the cloth under the stream. Victoria sponged at her swelling eyes and splashed her face with the chilling water as the smell of fabric softener replaced the haunting scent of baby lotion.

Soon the emotional tide went back out to sea, and she steadied her ragged breathing. "I have got to get a grip," she whispered and longed for someone to talk to . . . someone who would understand her loss . . . someone who might offer the comfort she so longed for.

Tony. Her husband's name penetrated her frazzled emotions. She imagined his large hand wrapping around hers in comforting silence — just as he'd done at her grandfather's funeral. For the first time Victoria doubted her assumption that he wasn't as deeply affected by their loss as was she.

Victoria grabbed a thick towel from the rack near the tub and blotted at her damp face. When he failed to sign the card on the flowers Victoria assumed he hadn't cared enough to communicate. Looking back she now wondered if perhaps he really hadn't known what to say . . . or maybe he'd been so upset by the miscarriage he forgot to write on the card.

"Tony *has* called me every week since the miscarriage," she whispered, yet the memory of those strained conversations left her flat, to say the least. *Well, maybe it's time for me to call and see how* he's *doing,* she thought. Victoria wrinkled her brow and tried to trace the source of the thought. She had gone into her marriage believing that Tony was supposed to take care of her, that *he* was the one who should take initiative in every aspect of their marriage.

But it doesn't sound like that's what Kim Lan is doing! The thought offered itself as more than an observation. Indeed, Victoria began to wonder if she had somehow missed out on some nugget of wisdom that Kim Lan was privy to.

A muffled snort escaped her. "Yeah, right. The deal is that Kim Lan is about as free spirited as they come and I'm not!" She shrugged. "I'm not very spontaneous."

Victoria struggled to her feet and the grit between her toes reminded her she still hadn't cleaned up the sand from the rug downstairs. She eyed the tile that showed no signs of sand and wondered if there were areas in her marriage where she needed to do some housekeeping. In retrospect Victoria couldn't remember a recent conversation when she had taken responsibility for any part of their relationship. Indeed, she had been too busy hoisting blame upon Tony.

She gazed at the closed door and pondered the empty beach house that awaited her on the other side. "I still want my husband back," she restated the whispered claim that had overtaken her on the front porch. "And — and maybe Sammie was really right — maybe we're both to blame for this mess we're in."

Victoria stepped toward the free-standing sink that matched the tub. She draped the towel across the basin and looked into bloodshot hazel eyes full of sorrow — sorrow and a glimmer of speculation. And for a wrinkle in time Victoria wondered exactly what "set a trap" meant to Kim Lan, and how Tony might have reacted if she ever attempted such.

"He'd probably faint," Victoria said and nodded at her reflection. *And I'd probably faint if he ever did something really special for me,* she defended. Her eyes took on an edge, yet the sharpness slowly dulled as a snatch of scripture scurried to the forefront of her mind, "Do to others as you would have them do to you."

Victoria stepped back and shook her head. "But . . . but . . ." she stuttered. Her objections died before they left her lips. She marveled at her own reticence until at last she asked herself, *What is the one thing I want from Tony right now?*

Victoria nudged one large toe with the other and examined the floral wallpaper's perfectly matched seam. "I — I want him to call me," she admitted. "I'd like to talk about the baby." Victoria's voice cracked, and she covered her lips with the tips of her fingers.

Before she could second guess herself she spun toward the door, unlocked it, and strode past the nursery. Victoria entered her bedroom, crawled amid the mountain of overstuffed pillows, retrieved the cordless phone from the night stand, and pressed the on button.

Thirteen

Tony jogged along the beach's beaten path — a path he had often used before he and Victoria split up. A quartet of seagulls soared out over the ocean, the wind lifting their outstretched wings as they ducked and circled and sailed. Their high-pitched squawks mixed with the rush and slap of the ocean as it rolled into land and was sucked back out again. Only a third of the brilliant sun peaked along the western horizon, and the blue-green water was sprinkled with the shimmer of the evening's final rays. Tony's shoes pounded the hardened path. The chilled wind lifted his hair from his perspiring forehead, and the smells of salt and seaweed beckoned him to continue his journey.

During the last couple of weeks Tony committed himself to the jogging routine he had allowed himself to slip out of. Tonight, he wasn't certain whether his new drive to jog was propelled by his interest in physical fitness or because he was using the path near his home. Their beach house loomed in the distance. As with every night during

175

the last week, Tony debated whether or not he should stop in for a visit with Victoria. He hadn't seen her since right after the miscarriage, although he had made it a point to regularly call her. Never once had they shared what he would call a warm conversation, but at least they had stopped yelling at each other.

Tony winced when he recalled the ice in Victoria's mother's voice during the time his wife was staying with her parents. They never had thought he was good enough for their daughter, and Tony wasn't so sure they weren't right. Nevertheless, he didn't relish his mother-in-law's attitude.

He neared a trio of beach houses that were in as bad repair as his and Victoria's was when they bought it. Tony had often thought about checking into who owned them and trying to fix them up for leasing. Rental property had proven a lucrative business for his parents and offered them a steady flow into their retirement fund. However, his marriage problems and the miscarriage had kept him so off-balance lately that he hadn't given the idea much serious consideration.

During the last month he'd also been distracted by another incident — that upheaval with Kevin Norris at the hospital. Tony's brows drew together as he recalled the stressed conversation he'd shared with his partner, Eddy. After many days of consideration the two of them had decided Tony might be best served to keep his nose where it belonged — on his face and out of the Norrises' business. A couple of times he had even thought about calling Victoria's friend, Jacquelyn Franklin. As a detective she would certainly be a good person to consult. And in the midst of all his pondering Tony couldn't get away from the vindictive glare that heathen who attacked Kevin had given him before he hopped over the railing. A couple of times Eddy had suggested their going to the police, but then they hit a dead end. After all, the police *said* they had that ruffian in custody. But then there was Kevin Norris's warning about the local police and his conviction that his house's burning had been arson. The fire chief declared no foul play, but Tony knew as well as any firefighter that arson could be nearly impossible to prove.

So on this cool evening Tony resolved to do what he had done numerous times during the last month. He stopped dwelling upon Kevin Norris and all his problems. Instead, he turned his thoughts back to his wife.

When Tony drew parallel to the second dilapidated beach house he caught a glimpse of their railed porch. Victoria's white swing danced in the breeze. The brass wind chimes reflected the final rays of sunshine, and Tony strained to hear their merry jingle. All he could pick up were the squawks of those blasted seagulls. He increased his pace and strained toward his home.

The truth was, Tony missed his wife. After two months of separation he was beginning to wonder why they couldn't seem to get along. The miscarriage had certainly put some things into perspective for him. And he was beginning to suspect that maybe Victoria's perspective had also shifted to keeping their marriage together.

Tony checked off a mental list of all the reasons he shouldn't stop by to see her. His own foolish pride came in first and last and everything else was wrapped in between. After 20 more paces he deleted the first and last reasons and couldn't convince himself that any of the other petty rationales warranted his staying away. *So what if she thinks she was right,* he thought. *Maybe she was right on a point or two. I don't guess I'm the easiest guy to live with.* And Tony Roberts decided he should indeed pay his wife a visit. After all, he was still making payments on that house she was living in. He figured he was at least due a glass of cold water. Tony upped his speed and targeted the porch.

Buster Shae peered through the small yet powerful binoculars and swept from one side of the beach to the other until he spotted the blond runner.

"Right on time," he drawled.

The first time Buster spotted the guy was two evenings ago when he met that weak-kneed Kevin Norris, who had miraculously decided he needed to play their little game with no further resistance. Last month Kevin swore he had no idea what the blond man's name was. Even though Shae suspected Norris might be lying, he finally backed off. From there Shae had been left to his own devices in regard to finding the intruder. Finally, he assumed that the blond man was nothing more than a passerby whom he might never see again. After all, Pensacola was a big town, and Destin was a tourist attraction. Buster had conferred with the boss in Chicago. The two agreed it was best to manage the laundering project and forget the blond.

Until the day before yesterday.

Two days ago Darnell Hopkins had arranged for them to meet with Kevin Norris. The encounter happened inside the dilapidated beach house upon which Buster now leaned. For weeks now, the old house had proven to be the perfect meeting spot with the bank vice president. Nobody seemed to notice it tucked at the end of the beach.

Buster checked his watch and squinted toward the setting sun. The ocean breeze held but a hint of the cool front predicted to invade the coast before dawn. The smell of the salt-tinged air encouraged him to revel in the beloved game he was about to begin.

Now that they had picked up the blond's trail, Buster and the boss decided he shouldn't be ignored. After all, he saw Buster face-to-face, and Shae had been recently featured on "America's Most Wanted." When he spotted the blond two nights ago he'd told Darnell he was going to take the guy out as soon as was convenient. Hopkins went pale. After the meeting, Shae followed the intruder to the fire station on Crystal Beach Drive. As he drove by, Shae realized Kevin Norris had most likely *lied*. Chances were high that Norris knew of the fireman — especially after his house burned. Yesterday morning Shae and the boss decided Kevin couldn't live any longer.

He'd crossed them one too many times. Yet when Shae called the bank to discreetly discover Kevin's schedule, the secretary informed him that Kevin had taken a leave of absence and was traveling abroad. A quick phone call to the tele-banking network verified that Norris had nearly emptied the laundering account on his way out of the U.S. Add to that the massive funds they'd allowed him to place in a Swiss account, and Kevin Norris was nothing but a rich, laughing fool by now.

Shae released the binoculars, and they hung from the strap around his neck after bouncing against his barrel chest. His teeth ground into a blunt cigar. He sucked in one last draw and expelled the acrid smoke. The ocean wind whipped away the essence of his habit. Buster dropped the stub into the sand and ground his boot against it. *Too bad the stub isn't Norris's face,* he thought and blasted himself for ever pulling Norris into the deal. But the boss had needed key people in key places, and Norris proved too ready a participant. Shae should have recognized his instability from the start.

Buster gripped the binoculars, placed them against his eyes, and continued the game. Tony's lithe figure bobbed along the beach and proved a too-easy target. The temptation to take him out posed itself as a viable possibility. Yet Shae shook his head. Aside from the upheaval with Norris things had gotten a little boring. Lately, Buster found himself craving some excitement — anything to break the monotony. He enjoyed nothing more than stalking his prey, playing with them, terrifying them, and then killing them in his own good time. This time the murder would be especially delicious. By now Shae knew the man's name, his residence, and even his wife's name. The more intimate he became with his victims the greater his pleasure.

Yesterday afternoon, Hopkins used his city connections to run a check on the names and addresses of the firefighters who worked at the station on Crystal Beach Drive. The check produced a list of 31 men. According to the records only one of them lived on this stretch of private beach. It didn't take much more effort for Darnell to confirm the man's name: Tony Roberts. That was yesterday — the day Shae discovered Kevin Norris had tucked his tail and run.

Shae pressed a button on his cell phone and spoke into the speaker, "Got him in sight. Are you with me?"

"With you," the chief affirmed; his voice

held a hint of uncertainty.

Buster scowled and released the button. The thing he hated most about being on the front line was working with people who weren't professionals. When it came to murder, Darnell Hopkins was proving near useless. Yet even Darnell didn't know that tonight Shae was just beginning a process. A process of power. Power and domination. Domination and ultimate victory.

Shae's heart pounded beneath his Italian shirt in an excited tattoo. "Let the game begin," he whispered.

Buster lifted the rifle, propped it against his shoulder, peered into the scope, and placed the cross hairs upon the jogger. With a wicked grin, he rested his finger upon the trigger and relished the taste of playing havoc with Tony Roberts.

Tony reduced his gate to a hard walk and gradually slowed to a more leisurely stroll. He rested his hands behind his neck, tilted his head upward, and forced his breathing into an even rhythm. Tony had already run his two-mile quota for the evening and didn't feel the least bit guilty about walking the rest of the 200 yards toward his home.

Plus, he wanted to at least be breathing normally when he knocked on the door. *No sense in huffing and puffing at Victoria,* he thought. Tony crammed his hand into the top of his windblown hair and did an awkward job of finger-combing the mess. He looked down at his worn running gear and experienced the uncanny sensation of being a gauche 16-year-old on his first date. Tony shook his head, chuckled, and reminded himself he was going to talk to his *wife,* the woman he had lived with for more than six years. She'd seen his dirty socks and underwear and even the floppy running gear he now wore. But somehow this meeting loomed forth as if it were a pivotal moment.

"Maybe I'm just tired of fighting," he mumbled. "And I *know* I'm tired of living at the fire sta—"

Out of nowhere a tiny missile whizzed past Tony's arm and pelted the sand 20 feet in front of him. The ping and hiss stopped him in his tracks, and his stunned mind grappled for a logical explanation. As the incredible melded with reality a rigid terror raced from his feet to the top of his head. A series of frenzied thoughts bombarded his shocked mind. Like a squirrel caught in front of a car Tony debated which direction to dart. *Is someone shooting at me or was that a stray bullet?*

His frantic gaze darted around the beach

before a second bullet erupted from no-where and grazed the outside of his shoulder. An excruciating sting shot from the wound seconds before a warm gush trickled down his arm. And Tony's questions found answers. The bullets weren't strays — not by a long shot.

Tony raced toward the third dilapidated beach house as yet another bullet bit into the ground at his feet. Beads of sweat popped out along his forehead; and the ocean breeze, once inviting and assuring, now whispered that his life was over. A rush of tingles pricked his skin, and Tony surged into a fresh burst of speed. At last he slipped beside the vacated home. When a bullet splintered the porch's handrail Tony wondered if escaping was impossible.

He stumbled up the divide between the vacant house and the nicer home that was only three removed from his. Tony's feet crashed into the spindly grass sprouting in the thickening soil. As he neared the busy street stretching in front of the homes, Tony halted.

He pressed himself against the side of the house, now cloaked in shadows. The home's peeling paint pricked his palms, and Tony's fingers dug into the wood. Some 40 yards away vehicles roared up and down the

185

street. Yet a steady rhythm broke through the sounds of traffic. Despite the swishing breeze and the ocean's ever-present echo, the beat still persisted. *Somebody's chasing me!* he thought and imagined the gunman rushing him any second.

Tony glanced behind, leaned toward the road, and scrutinized the terrain to his right. *Nobody.* After another glimpse toward the ocean he sped to the left, in front of his two neighbor's homes, and toward the front entry he and Victoria seldom used. He orchestrated a long jump and skidded into the front door. The graze on his right shoulder screamed a protest, and Tony bit back a moan. He cradled his aching right arm and rammed his left hand into his shorts' right pocket. After seconds of digging, Tony pulled out a wad of keys and succeeded in fumbling so violently that he dropped them. Growling, Tony scooped them up and swiveled to examine his trail. He was still in the clear.

He inserted the key into the deadbolt and then the knob, whipped open the door, stepped inside, snapped the door shut and relocked it. Immediately, Tony moved toward the floral drapes and yanked on the cord. They danced shut with a graceful whisper and the darkened room remained perfectly still. Still and quiet. Quiet and eerie.

Only one image pressed itself upon Tony's mind — the image of a dark-haired man with the eyes of a black mamba. A man who silently swore that Tony hadn't seen the last of him. And Kevin Norris's final warning filled his gut with a dread as chilling as ice-laden rocks, *I'm telling you . . . if they decide you know too much they'll kill you.*

Fourteen

The second Victoria pressed the dial button for Tony's cell phone, the front door rattled. Footsteps floated from the formal living room. The door snapped shut; then more footsteps. Victoria's eyes widened. She rose to her knees in the middle of the bed. A swish and click sounded suspiciously like closing drapes. She examined the face of her cordless phone that announced her call to Tony was being connected. Her finger hovered over the "end" button. Victoria didn't need to call Tony. She needed to call the police!

A faint purr attested that Tony's cell phone was indeed ringing. Victoria raised the phone halfway to her ear and then decided to hang up and dial the authorities. Yet Tony's voice, cautious and soft, cut in halfway through the first ring.

"Tony?" she whispered.

"Victoria?" he hissed back. "Where are you?"

"I'm at home — in our bedroom." She swallowed the lump in her throat and lunged to action. Victoria scrambled from the bed, silently closed the door, and turned the lock. "I need to go," she continued. "I — I've got to call the police. S–somebody just came in through the front door, and —"

"Victoria, listen —"

"No! There's somebody —"

The heavy sound of footfalls reverberated up the stairway. Victoria clutched her throat and forced herself not to scream. "Tony, I need help!" she pleaded. "Somebody broke into our house!"

"It's me!" Tony whispered. "I'm at the top of the stairs. I'm right outside your door now."

"What?" The doorbell chimed in sequence with her exclamation.

A knock, gentle yet urgent, preceded Tony's next statement. "Open the bedroom door, Victoria. And don't worry about answering that door. Someone tried to shoot me just now."

Without another question Victoria unlocked the knob and tugged open the door. Eyes wide she gazed at her husband for a second before he hurried past her. Without a word, he snatched on the drape cord that hurled the curtains together with the whoosh of polished cotton. The brass lamp sitting atop the oak nightstand cast a warm glow upon the whole room — a glow far removed from the cold terror in Tony's eyes when he whirled to face her.

The doorbell chimed again; Victoria wasn't sure whether there really was an impatient edge in the bell's tone or if her imagination was overactive. Her thumb wandered to the cordless phone's off button. She pressed it, and the faint beep seemed as loud as a cacophonous gong. Likewise, Tony jabbed a button on his cell phone and tossed it onto the king-sized bed. He turned back to the window, inched open the striped curtains, and examined the front yard.

Victoria tiptoed to the window's other border and tugged aside the drapes in time to see a UPS truck pulling away from the curb.

"Thank goodness it was only the UPS guy!" Tony exclaimed.

"Tony, what is going on?" Victoria asked as the fog of suspicion seeped into her mind.

Tony covered his face with both hands and pressed his chin into the heels of his hands.

"Boy, oh boy, oh boy, oh boy," he muttered. "Have I gotten myself into it or what?"

"What's going on?" Victoria repeated, and was overcome with certainty that her husband must have gotten himself involved in something sinister. She crossed her arms and glared at her husband.

He lowered his hands and returned her scrutiny without a flinch. "Why is it you always assume the worst of me?" he demanded.

"Well, what am I supposed to think?" she charged.

"You might think that I'm innocent for a change!" Tony's words ran together in breathless staccato as a crimson flush tinged his tan. With an impatient growl he whipped around and headed for the doorway. "I don't know why I was even thinking about coming here," he snarled. "I must have been crazy."

Victoria clutched the cordless phone as Tony strode toward the hallway. For once in all their long list of disagreements Victoria doubted herself. During the last year she had been so bent upon defending her stance and proving her point she had fallen into a pattern of assuming Tony was always to blame. Yet this time she wondered if she had misspoken. Victoria wadded her peach-colored sundress against her trembling palm.

"Wait!" she called when he stepped into the hallway.

He didn't bother to heed her request.

"Tony . . . wait . . ." she ran behind him. "I'm — I'm sorry!" The words popped out and sounded foreign, even to her. Victoria couldn't remember a time when she'd ever apologized so readily.

He halted but didn't turn to face her.

The telephone screamed forth a demanding peal, and Victoria stared at the receiver as if it were a foreign object.

Her husband wheeled around to face her, his gaze riveting to the cordless.

"Should I answer?" she whispered.

"Yes. Go ahead. But if it's the authorities, tell them nothing."

"What do you mean — the authorities?" she asked.

"I mean the police are involved in whatever mess I've stepped into."

"The police?" she whispered. "But —"

"Just answer the phone, Victoria," Tony prompted.

She swallowed hard, pressed the button, and croaked out a wobbly greeting.

"Victoria, it's me — Melissa," the pediatrician rapped out with no-nonsense authority. "What's up? Are you okay? We were talking along, and all at once realized you weren't with us any more. Are you all right?"

"Uhhh . . ." Victoria eyed her husband. She shook her head and mouthed, *One of the sisters.*

He raised his brows and encouraged her to repeat. Tony never had been able to read her lips.

"Just a minute," she said into the phone and covered the mouthpiece. "It's my friend Melissa," she explained.

Victoria uncovered the mouthpiece and blurted out a swift message.

"Melissa, tell the sisters I'm fine. There's an emergency. Tony's here. Bye." She disconnected the call before Mel had time to respond. Without doubt, her friend would understand . . . eventually. Victoria stepped back into her bedroom and deposited the phone on the oak dresser.

When she neared Tony once more, his shoulders were drooping, his mouth in a tight line. That's when Victoria noticed the torn spot on his dark blue shirt and the trail of blood marring his sleeve. She also realized he cradled his right arm to his side as if it were hurting.

"What happened to your arm?" she asked.

"I told you, somebody shot at me!"

"But you didn't tell me they *got* you!" she exclaimed.

"It's just a graze on the side of my shoulder." Tony turned toward the stairway.

"Wait!" Victoria repeated her former request and reached out to him. "Tony, don't — don't go. *Please!*" she added and wondered if her entreaty would in any way puncture the man's stubborn soul.

Head hanging he stopped again.

Victoria hurried to her husband's side and placed a hand on his left shoulder. "Look, at least let me put a bandage on your shoulder," she insisted.

He cut her a glance out of the corners of his eyes, a glance that fused hope with suspicion.

"Besides, you can't just haul off and leave. Your cell phone is still on the bed." Victoria added a tiny smile to her dry remark. "You can't survive without your cell."

His eyes narrowed; his lips twitched at the edges.

"And what about the person who shot at you? Think he's still out there?"

Tony nodded and winced. "My shoulder *is* stinging." He touched the edge of his right shoulder. "I actually ran into the front door before I managed to get in."

"Exactly what happened?" Victoria

asked, nudging him toward the bathroom a few paces away. He didn't resist her prodding, and Victoria allowed him to enter the bathroom first.

"I was jogging along the beach," he explained, "and somebody started shooting at me. At first I thought it was a stray bullet or something. But when the bullets kept coming I knew there was nothing stray about any of them." He grimaced and lowered himself onto the toilet lid.

At last Tony's pain-filled words sank to the center of Victoria's heart. A tragic image sprang upon her mind — Tony's dead form sprawled upon the snowy-white shoreline. She wondered how she could have ever survived the loss of her child and the loss of her husband within a month of each other. Her knees wobbled; and Victoria focused upon his lanky legs protruding from those floppy old shorts she'd threatened to throw away at least a dozen times. She resisted the urge to fling herself into his lap and weep from relief and dread and fear. Whatever Tony had gotten involved in, the people on the other side were playing for keeps.

Victoria marveled at the situations her husband had a way of falling into. "I'm sorry I questioned you earlier. I . . . guess that's a bad habit I've gotten into lately."

Her attention slid to the damp mat of blood marring his right shoulder.

"It's okay," Tony said. "I'm sorry I blew up on you. I guess we both have some bad habits going here."

Victoria pressed her lips together. "Want me to take a look at the graze?" she asked.

He fidgeted with extracting his left arm from the T-shirt — yet another item Victoria had silently wished to haul off to Goodwill.

Victoria held up her hand. "Wait! I've got a solution." She stepped toward the cabinet and snapped open the door. The first aid scissors were right where she'd kept them ever since they moved here. She retrieved them from the basket and snatched up a bandage and some antibiotic ointment. Victoria deposited the ointment, washcloth, and bandage on the back of the toilet, lifted the right sleeve of his shirt, and prepared to cut away the material over the wound.

"Wait a minute!" Tony protested. "This is my favorite jogging shirt."

"Oh, it's just an old rag," she said.

"But it's *my* rag and I like it," he covered her hand with his and pulled the sleeve from her grasp. "Let me take it off instead," he said with stony resolve.

"But —" Victoria stormed into a mental

diatribe that would deprecate Tony's love for the decade-old shirt.

His lips hardened into a defensive line; his brows drew together. Victoria recognized the battle expression she had seen more often than not the weeks before they separated.

By some miracle Victoria managed to stop herself before the criticism left her mouth. After a deep breath she inched away, and from nowhere that snatch of a scripture from earlier penetrated her thoughts, *"Do to others as you would have them do to you."* On the trail of that she wondered how she would feel if Tony rummaged through her latest collection of garage sale treasures and tore into them with a pair of scissors. She recalled innumerable instances when she had demeaned something he loved because *she* didn't value it. Despite herself, Victoria recalled the day she cleaned out his closet without his permission and disposed of numerous items she perceived were of no worth. At the time Victoria couldn't understand why the man had gone spastic on her. But like a dark room immediately illuminated by a sudden blast of light, she now understood. She had declared *their* home *her* domain from the start of their marriage and had given her husband little room to be himself.

"Okay," she said, laying the scissors on the back of the toilet. "Let's take it off. I'll wash it. I'm sure you've got something here you can put on while it's in the laundry."

Tony leveled a gaze at her that bordered on astonished. "You mean you give up? Just like that!"

"There's nothing to give up. It's *your* shirt! If you want to wear it to your grave, then I guess that's your call."

A garbled chuckle erupted from Tony. "This has got to be some sort of historical moment. Are you on medication or something?" He wiggled his left arm out of the shirt and struggled with the other sleeve.

She shook her head. "No. But too many more statements like that and you might be *needing* some medication."

"I guess we can chalk up two points for you!" he shot back with a wicked grin.

Victoria rolled her eyes. "Here, let me help." She guided the shirt over his head and then gingerly slid the right sleeve down his arm.

Despite her attempts to focus upon his oozing wound her attention trailed to his torso, and she debated once again exactly *how* Kim Lan was setting a trap for Mick. Victoria had never really considered herself amorous, and for the first time she wondered how much her lack of interest had affected Tony.

"This doesn't look too bad," she said, forcing herself to examine his wound.

"Hmm," Tony responded in a way that sent goosebumps along her spine.

She grabbed the damp washcloth and started sponging away the excess blood. Only the faucet's drip broke the silence. The smell of peach potpourri mingled with the scent of floral soap and a nuance of Victoria's White Shoulders perfume.

She applied a measure more pressure to whisk away the final traces of excess blood. Tony grimaced.

"Watch it, woman," he groused. "You trying to kill me or something? How deep is it anyway?"

"Like I said, it's not that bad — really," Victoria said. "It could be way worse."

"Hurts like the dickens."

"I'm no expert but I figure the pain will subside after a few hours." She considered their options. "I guess we could let a doctor take a look," she said a bit dubiously.

"No way," Tony said with a swift shake of his head. "You know I hate needles. Just patch me up and we'll see how it heals."

"Why does that not surprise me?" she asked.

"Maybe you know me too well."

"I'm just glad it's only a graze, and they didn't hit you in the chest."

"I think that's what they were aiming for," Tony said.

"I wish you wouldn't even say that." Victoria's knees threatened to wobble again.

She sensed Tony's intense observation and squirmed under the heat of his scrutiny. Victoria snatched up the rolled bandage, tore it open, cut off a generous strip, and centered it upon the graze.

"Here, hold this," she commanded in a no-nonsense tone.

"Yes ma'am," he said through a smile.

Victoria stepped toward the closet and pulled out a roll of bandage tape. When she turned back toward her husband she noticed the unopened antibiotic ointment on the back of the toilet. "Oh phooey," she said. "I forgot the ointment."

"I guess I've just got you too rattled, huh?"

"In your dreams," she snorted with a teasing challenge.

"Maybe so." The tenor of his voice underscored his honesty.

"Tony —"

"Victoria —"

The two stopped to give the other space

to talk. When neither continued, Victoria tried to deny that her pulse was tapping along a little too fast for comfort. To cover her chagrin she grabbed the ointment and unscrewed the lid. After brushing aside her husband's fingers she removed the bandage and applied a generous amount of the medication. "Are you going to tell me why they were shooting at you?" she asked and hoped a change of subject might alter her wayward thoughts.

"You've got to promise you won't breathe a word to a living soul."

"Scout's honor."

"The day you had the — the day you were in the hospital —"

"Yes." That closed bedroom mere feet away seemed to echo her answer, and Victoria recalled the reason she was going to call Tony in the first place. She needed to talk about her loss.

"Well, that morning there was a fire up on the west beach. I rescued a woman and her son — Rhonda and Coty Norris. The father, his name is Kevin Norris, arrived right after we got out of the house. I saw him at the hospital later that day. He was on the fire escape. This gangster-looking guy had pulled a gun on him. And I, er, interfered."

Victoria laid the ointment on the back of

the toilet and replaced the bandage upon the wound. "How do you always manage to get yourself mixed up in this kind of stuff? First that convenience store robbery and now this."

"You tell me," Tony said.

She tore a strip of tape from the roll and applied it to the top of the bandage.

"Anyway, I wound up helping Kevin Norris escape. A security guard came on the scene and the gangster got away. After it was all over, Kevin told me that if I even so much as made a peep to the police or acted like I knew anything at all, I was dead meat. He said the police are involved —"

"In what?" Victoria stepped away and peered into her husband's eyes.

"I have no idea," he admitted with a shrug, and then he winced.

"Here — I've got some ibuprofen." Victoria pulled open the medicine cabinet and retrieved a blue-and-white bottle.

"You've always got everything together, don't you, Victoria?" Tony observed on an endearing note.

"Some days I feel like I get it all together and then can't remember where I put it," she said over a chuckle. Victoria opened the medicine bottle and dumped two amber-colored tablets into her palm. She extended the pills to Tony who reached to take them with his left hand. His fingers covered hers, and he didn't bother to retrieve the ibuprofen.

Victoria held her breath and met his gaze. For once, Tony let the wall slip and she saw to the bottom of his soul where she encountered uncertainty and loneliness. Loneliness and fear. Fear . . . and the embers of love.

"I've missed you, Victoria," he admitted.

A tremor raced from the pit of her stomach, and she gripped the medicine bottle until she was sure the thing would scream. "I — I've missed you, too," she squeaked out.

"How did we get to the point where all we ever did was fight?"

"I — I don't know." Victoria knitted her brows and shook her head. "I really don't. And — and I'm so glad you weren't — weren't killed," the last words hobbled out.

"Me, too." Tony loosened his grip on her hand.

She released the medicine into his palm, snapped the lid onto the bottle, pulled a disposable cup from the canister, and filled it with water.

"What are you going to do?" she asked and handed him the miniature cup. "If the police really *are* behind this —"

"They are." He tossed the tablets into his mouth, downed them with the water, and threw the cup into the wastebasket near the door.

"So if the police are involved, who do you report to?" Victoria asked. "I mean, won't they eventually find out about any report that's filed? And if they do —"

Tony sliced his index finger along the center of his neck, and the two of them shared an ominous silence. "If the police are involved then that would explain why the hospital security reported that the cops said not to question me."

"You've lost me now." Victoria leaned against the sink.

Tony filled in the story's missing details in succinct order.

"So, have you talked to Kevin Norris since?"

"Nope."

"Think you ought to?" Victoria asked.

"Maybe." Tony placed his elbow on his knee and rested his chin in his hand. "At first I thought maybe Eddy and I could come up with a plan but then I decided to just leave well enough alone. I figured since they hadn't come after me they had decided I wasn't a threat. I mean, all I could do is identify that guy who was after Kevin."

"But what if he's one of the big boys?" Victoria asked.

"Maybe he is — or he's playing with the big boys."

"And if the stakes are high."

"They must be. Kevin said they set fire to his house."

"Did the fire chief prove arson?"

"Nope, but arson can be tough to prove."

Silence settled between them. Victoria placed the tip of her thumbnail between her teeth. She never had been a nail biter but this was enough to make her want to chew off all ten of her French-manicured nails.

"You were calling me," Tony commented. "Is everything okay?"

Victoria squinted and grappled for his meaning.

"When I came into the house, my cell phone rang. You called me."

"Oh!" she exclaimed and touched her temple.

"Was there something you needed?" The concerned note in his voice matched the warmth of his eyes — a warmth she hadn't see in ages.

She examined the ibuprofen bottle, pivoted, and returned the medicine to its place. The faucet's monotonous drip seemed to beckon her to release her grief over the miscarriage in one huge gush. Instead, Victoria tightened the dripping faucet and took a cleansing breath.

"Victoria?" Tony prompted.

"I was just wanting to talk, I guess," she said to her own reflection. The woman who stared back looked as if she had it all together. *Oh, if only that were true!* Through the years Victoria had pinched every penny she could, but she purposed to always buy good cosmetics. The result was a polished look for which Tony used to compliment her. Only her wind-tossed hair attested to her recent chasing of the escaping lamp shade, yet the naturally wavy locks now appeared fuller, softer, more inviting. A stray thought suggested that Tony might agree.

The swish of his cotton shorts preceded his footsteps, and he stopped behind her. Victoria met his gaze in the mirror. The distress in his eyes stroked a chord in her heart and Victoria blinked against stinging eyes.

Fifteen

"You're really not okay, are you?" Tony asked and used mammoth self-control to stop himself from pulling her into his arms. The last thing he wanted to do was come across too strong. Besides, his blasted shoulder was killing him.

She placed trembling fingers over her lips and shook her head.

"I noticed the nursery is closed. Have you —"

"No," she interrupted, "I can't."

Tony nodded. "I don't want to either," he said and twined a lock of her hair around his finger. The wavy texture was as soft as he remembered on their wedding night, and the smell of green apples attested that she hadn't switched shampoos.

Victoria leaned into his touch, and Tony allowed his fingers to trail to the base of her neck. For once in his marriage Tony decided to be brutally honest. Somehow, he wasn't in the mood to hide behind walls tonight, especially not after that brush with death.

"That miscarriage almost knocked me flat," he admitted.

"Really?" she gasped.

"Oh, yes." He nodded.

"Why didn't you *tell* me?"

He swallowed, shook his head, and examined the brass-trimmed soap dispenser Victoria had found at a garage sale for a buck. She turned to face him, and his throat constricted with the intensity of his emotions. Oh, he'd cried himself to sleep a few nights since the miscarriage, but Victoria hadn't ever known it. Now that his admission was out in the open, Tony fought to keep himself under control. And for the first time in ages he sensed that the two of them were finally on the same page.

"Actually, that's the reason I was calling," she admitted. "I wanted to talk about it with somebody who, well, who I hoped might understand." She peered over his shoulder. Tony's gaze strayed to a decorative hat hanging on the wall beside her. The pale flowers and blue ribbon blended into puddles of splotchy colors. He couldn't ever remember crying in Victoria's presence, and the present threat proved more than he wanted to deal with.

"Really, I was hoping you'd call me," she added, "so I just —"

"So *you* called me?" He swept a stray fringe of hair away from her face and tried to rein in the pain in his heart.

"Yes."

"You *never* call me."

"I know." Victoria looked him in the eyes, and a glimmer of something indefinable sparkled back at Tony.

Whatever it was, he wanted more of it. Intimate fantasies bombarded him; yet his human frailty burst in upon his masculine musings. Tony balled his left hand and pulled his right arm closer. Fleetingly, he wondered how much agony he would've endured if the bullet had entered his body.

"You're hurting," she observed.

"Yes." Tony leaned against the side of the closet that held everything from linens to bandages. "For a graze, this thing is really talkin'."

"Look, why don't you lie down?" Victoria asked and started fussing around as if she were a mother hen. "I'll call Mel back. I think in cases like this it's okay for you to double up on the ibuprofen."

"Oh, so you want me to take four of those things?" he croaked.

"Well, I'll consult Mel first. She's a doctor, you know."

"Let's just stick to two for now. I don't like medicine. You know that."

"Yes, but if you start hurting enough,

you'll be glad to eat cow patties if you think they'd make it better."

"Not on your life."

"Look," she stepped into the hallway and pointed toward their bedroom, "go lie down on the bed. I'll fix you something — some chicken soup. You need to rest."

Tony followed her toward their room. "Heaven help us, woman, if you're going to cook, do something worth sinking my teeth into," he said with a wry smile.

"You're hungry," she stated with no hint of a question.

"I guess. At least, I was a little before I got shot."

"I've got some taco meat frozen. It won't take but a minute to thaw it out and whip together one of those Mexican salads you like."

"Now you're talking."

Victoria hurried him toward the bed, and Tony gladly sank to the edge. After he kicked off his shoes, his wife grabbed his legs and swung them upward. Tony waved her off. "Stop it, hon," he protested. "I'm not an invalid. It's my arm, not my legs."

"I know, I know," she said and her fingers knotted together. "I'm just nervous I guess. Sorry."

Tony placed his legs on the bed and relaxed against the pile of pillows she always insisted upon. For once he was thankful that his wife was forever organized. Her neat-freak tendencies had driven him crazy more times than he could remember. But tonight he was grateful she didn't have to run around the house looking for bandages and ointment and ibuprofen.

"Thanks for everything," he said and gave her fingers a squeeze. "I was just coming over for a chat. I didn't know you were going to have to play nurse."

"You were coming over anyway?" she asked.

"Yes." Tony closed his eyes, and the stress of the last couple of months seemed to crash in on him.

"Why?"

"I dunno," he said. "I just wanted to talk, I guess."

"Hmm." Victoria moved closer and stroked his temple.

Tony's eyes popped open. He looked up into those gorgeous hazel eyes that had captured his fancy the first time he saw her. She'd been staring at him from the church choir, and he caught her. Tony had attended that Sunday as a favor to a friend. From that point on he attended the church's singles group and made certain he sat in the same pew every Sunday until he worked up the courage to ask her out. The rest was history. But looking back Tony couldn't remember attending services with her in months. Even though he didn't quite understand the depths of her faith Tony still had respected her belief — at least until the last couple of years.

"I . . . guess we were both a little lonely tonight," she said at last.

"Yep." Tony nabbed her fingers in his left hand. He moved them to his lips and bestowed a gentle caress. Her softness reminded him of more intimate moments, and his wayward mind took him down the pathway of delight despite his stinging shoulder.

He firmly admonished himself to ask nothing of his wife — not tonight. Simultaneously, he wondered if a large part of their marital problems involved his always being the one who wanted to do the taking. Eddy, who'd been married 20 years, had dropped a couple of broad hints that had hit Tony smack between the eyes. Maybe the time had come for Tony to stop pointing his finger at Victoria and start taking Eddy's advice.

"I'm so sorry about the miscarriage," Tony said and squeezed her fingers. "It was like —" He stopped himself and marveled that he'd been about to say the miscarriage was like losing Toni all over again. His attention slid to the wicker settee in the room's corner, and he knitted his brow. That brush with death must have so rattled him that he was blabbering forth without a thought of the consequences. He and Victoria seemed to be making some progress. The last thing Tony needed to do was trot out a dark secret from his past.

"I felt like it was as bad as if we'd given birth and the baby died the next day."

"I know. That's exactly the way I felt, except we never even got to hold it." Victoria sank to the side of the bed. Her head's droop reminded him of a melancholic lily, and he wondered why he'd let her friend Marilyn take her home from the hospital. But looking back Tony had felt that maybe Victoria preferred that he kept his distance. Perhaps he'd been wrong.

"Well, I guess I need to go tackle project tacos," she said in a forced voice that seemed a little too bright.

Tony nodded and wished he could pull together some long string of meaningful words. As usual, nothing came. Nothing except the desire to hold his wife. She was hurting; he was hurting. Why in the world the two of them couldn't learn to cope with the other's weaknesses was beyond his comprehension.

"Come here," Tony said and brushed her arm with his left hand.

She tilted her head and observed him with a hint of suspicion that melted into grief. Then Victoria scooted to his side. Tony bustled to the middle of the bed and pulled her into the crook of his arm. He nudged his cell phone out of the way with his socked foot and stroked his wife's hair. He wouldn't have known she was crying if her body hadn't trembled against his. Not able to hold his emotions another second, Tony buried his face in her hair and allowed the hot tears to flow unchecked. The two of them clung together and weathered the waves of grief with each other.

While Victoria mourned but one loss, Tony mourned two. And he hoped for the sake of their marriage she never discovered the truth.

Sixteen

"Words cannot express to you what I am feeling at this moment." The college freshman's deep voice floated from the front of the classroom. A rigid dread covered E.T. Sinclaire. Her eyes widened. She clutched her organizer, whipped it open, and rammed her hand into the pocket where she'd stowed the letter from her birth father. Her fingers encountered the cool vinyl pocket and nothing else. She stared at the familiar piece of paper, yellowed around the edges, now in the clutches of Darien Colvin, the ham of the century.

"As I write you this message, I already love you, yet I've never even seen you." Darien looked up from the letter and made eye contact with his friend Matt. "He loves her, man!" Darien said as if they were watching a melodramatic movie.

Matt shook his head and rolled his eyes.

"Stop it," he growled as a tremor of giggles erupted from the back of the room. He glanced toward the feminine klatch and back at Darien. Matt's brow twitched. A flicker of scorn tilted the corners of his mouth and confirmed Evelyn's observation from the first of the semester. Matt Leavey was more mature than his friend Darien by a long shot.

"Whose is that anyway?" Matt challenged.

"I don't know," Darien admitted and cast another mischievous glance toward the trio of girls whose attention he'd grabbed.

A molten knot in her stomach threatened to engulf Evelyn. Her mother had suggested she take this college English class to get a jump on her credits in the fall. So far she had managed to keep a low profile in the back row while hauling in a solid A minus. The experience had been fairly uneventful yet pleasant — until now. Evelyn prayed that the guy would tire of his performance and drop the letter where he'd found it. She would then discreetly excuse herself for a trip to the restroom and retrieve the cherished note on her way out.

"The decision to release you was one of the hardest I have ever made. But, my baby, you must understand that I simply have no way to provide for you." The dude inserted a Shakespearean accent into his voice and the chortles from the back of the room encouraged him. He raised his hand as if he were Hamlet in his most dramatic moment.

Evelyn schooled her features into a resolved mask. She gathered her purse, book, and organizer. Without a hint of her purpose she slid from her desk and strode up the aisle.

"Please understand that a part of me will always be with you and that —"

When she drew parallel with the reading idiot, Evelyn snatched the letter, walked across the front of the room, and focused solely upon getting out of class before she exploded.

A wolf whistle from the back of the room attested to the presence of Peter Vancleave. He'd whistled at Evelyn every chance he got since January. For the life of her she couldn't figure out why the community college quarterback found her so appealing. She was far from a glamour girl in her jeans and T-shirt and ponytail. And right now the last thing she needed was another reason for the bustling students to focus upon her.

"Excuse me," a masculine voice interrupted her focused journey.

Evelyn looked up in time to sidestep the middle-aged professor before bumping into him.

"Everything okay, Sinclaire?" he asked.

"I'm not going to be able to stay for class," Evelyn mumbled and continued her escape.

She left the room in a hard stride and broke into a trot once she entered the hallway. The fury that raced through her veins demanded release, and she increased her pace to a dead run. Her ponytail swayed with every footfall, and the aged letter pricked her damp palm.

"Evelyn!" Matt's voice echoed from behind, yet Evelyn refused to respond. Instead, she topped the stairway and took the steps two at a time. The pounding of feet behind her suggested that Matt wasn't going to be put off. Once her sneakers touched the first floor she upped her speed to a pace that ensured her first place on the state track team.

Evelyn hit the glass doors with a boom and clack as the metal handle released the latch and the door flew open. The tepid March breeze rustling the palms urged her ever faster as the twilight embraced her in shadows.

"Stop, Evelyn!" Matt's words were punctuated by the bang of the door in her wake.

She bounded past a couple snuggling on a bench and her tennis shoes ate into the pavement as she neared the parking lot. Evelyn spotted her Volkswagen Beetle parked at the curb three cars away. The parking lot's light blinked on and bathed the yellow bug in a golden glow. She managed to make it to the car and was fumbling with her keys before Matt's hand descended upon her shoulder.

Evelyn stumbled from his grasp, turned, and lifted her hand. "Don't touch me!"

"Okay, okay!" Matt held up both hands and backed away. "I'm not trying anything funny." He shook his head and spread his fingers. "Honest."

Evelyn's rapid breathing matched his, yet his entreating green eyes reflected only concern.

"How could he?" The question exploded before she realized it was out. "That jerk!" Evelyn stomped her foot, and her teeth rattled with the strength of the impact.

Matt shook his head, gripped the back of his neck, and looked at the note still clutched in her hand.

"I know, I know. I'm sorry," he said. "That's why I chased you. I just wanted to tell you — I just wanted to see if you were okay."

"Okay?" Evelyn barked. "No, I'm not okay!" She inserted the key into her car and clicked the lock.

"You're madder than a hornet," Matt said. "Maybe you should calm down before you drive."

Evelyn forced her breathing into an even cadence and stared at her shaking fingers resting upon the door handle.

"Get lost," she growled and hoped her brusque tone hid the secret delight spawned by Matt's honest regard.

His silence inflicted a little guilt somewhere amid the irritation.

"Sorry," Evelyn said and darted a glance toward the basketball player who topped her six-foot-two by a good two inches. "I guess I shouldn't take it out on you." She focused upon her leather-bound steering wheel and debated the most graceful escape from this encounter.

"I'm Matt, by the way." He extended his hand. "Matt Leavey. You don't ever say much and . . . I guess we've never officially met."

Evelyn eyed his slender fingers, narrowed her eyes, and cast him a speculative glance. Dark brows quirked over guileless eyes, and she decided the guy must be about as decent as his friend was immature. Her breathing slowing to normal, she juggled the keys and letter, and then placed her hand in his.

"Allow me to apologize on behalf of my friend," Matt said as the handshake ended. "I've known him since junior high. He hasn't changed much." Matt shrugged.

"You can say *that* again," Evelyn injected.

A moth bobbed across the top of her car and rested on the hood. Evelyn stared at the insect's fluttering wings and wished she could fly away from the recent upheaval.

"I, uh, guess that dude must really love you." Matt's words were laced with a hint of caution.

Evelyn cut her gaze back to him, paused, and decided to live by the rule that guided her whole life — state the truth, the whole truth, and nothing but the truth. "The letter is from my birth father. He wrote it to me when he placed me for adoption. I found it a few weeks ago when we were cleaning out the attic."

A huff escaped Matt, he rubbed the corners of his mouth, and shook his head.

"Darien is an idiot!" Matt placed his hands on his hips and turned toward the scenic pond that appeared to be a pool of shiny ink in the dusk. His jaw flexed with the intensity of his emotions until at last he faced Evelyn once more. "I think I'll just flush him," he blurted.

"Flush him?"

"Down the toilet!"

A spontaneous chuckle gurgled from Evelyn, and Matt's rigid features softened into a smile. She decided she liked Matt

Leavey. He was more than decent. He was honorable — honorable and just plain nice.

"So . . ." he hesitated and angled a speculative gaze her way, "you're adopted?"

"Yes." The word tumbled out and Evelyn couldn't deny the tremor in her voice.

Matt edged the toe of his sneaker against a knot of loose gravel, and Evelyn groped for something to say. Yet no words came, only the tide of anxiety that made her feel like a ship without an anchor. Once again she was amazed at how the simple truth that she'd accepted her whole life was suddenly giving her so much grief.

From her earliest childhood, Evelyn's folks had been open about the way Evelyn came into their hearts. The fact that a couple of kids at church had also been adopted had underscored Evelyn's understanding that adoption was just another way God chose to give kids to couples. Then she'd found that letter . . . and the rattle . . . and her whole foundation seemed to be shaken. Never had she felt so disconnected from her family. Never had she so longed for a bond with her birth parents — especially with her father who admitted to being 17 when she was born. He was only a year younger than she was now. The note nearly tore her heart out every time she read it.

And she was scared to death her parents might learn the truth and be forever wounded.

"So was I." Matt's mumbled admission almost got lost amid the wisp of palms as the spring breeze ushered in the first glimpse of a full moon on the eastern horizon.

"Excuse me?" Evelyn prompted.

"I was adopted, too, sorta, I guess. I . . . my grandparents adopted me. My birth mom was an unwed mother." He crossed his arms, rocked back on his heels, and his jaw flexed again. "Nobody bothered to tell me until a few years back. I was a junior in high school before I found out my dear Aunt Olivia was really my mom and my mother and father were really my grandparents." Matt's full lips hardened around the edges.

"You mean they *lied* to you?" Evelyn gasped and recalled Johnna's candid remarks about her inability to hold her tongue.

Matt jerked on the neck of his Chicago Bulls T-shirt. "Not exactly," he said. "They just never bothered to tell me the truth."

"So how'd you find out?"

"I overheard a conversation at a family reunion between a couple of my aunts — I guess they're my great aunts actually. They were sitting on the edge of the crowd discreetly gossiping about my mom's latest boyfriend, and I came into the subject. They didn't know I was within earshot — right by the potato salad," he added with a goofy smile.

Evelyn smiled back but couldn't miss the sad flicker in his eyes. "Do your parents know you know?"

"Yep." He nodded and his dark bangs flopped over one brow. "I blew up all over the place. My birth mom was next." Matt rested his hands on his hips. "I'm not exactly proud of it, but that's what happened." He gazed past her. "Things haven't been quite the same since. I guess I'm still a little aggravated. I just wish they'd told me the truth, ya know?"

Evelyn shook her head. "Yes, I can understand."

"And what about you?" he prompted.

"Me?"

"How long have you known?"

"I've known ever since I can remember."

"Do you know your birth parents, then?"

Evelyn shook her head. "I'm thinking I'd like to find my father." Her fingers flexed against the letter she'd almost memorized.

"Me, too, actually." Matt stroked the length of one sideburn, and the breeze stirred a trace of citrusy male scent.

"So are you going to blast him, too?" Evelyn's words held a playful taunt.

A wave of mirth highlighted the golden flecks in Matt's eyes.

"Touché!" he exclaimed.

Evelyn leaned against her car and marveled at the sudden camaraderie that had sprung up between her and this Matt Leavey. It would appear the two of them had much in common. She cradled her books to her chest. Evelyn hadn't discussed her plight with anyone. The possibility of talking about her situation with someone who would indeed understand delivered a measure of ease to her frazzled nerves. Her snatch-of-a-prayer from last month sneaked into the forefront of her mind. That day Johnna found the rattle in the locker room Evelyn had beseeched the Lord to give her someone to talk to — anyone who'd understand and not ask too many questions. Johnna simply wasn't the ideal person. She had been on the verge of breaking into a sob session with the mere mention of the letter and rattle.

Maybe Darien's finding the letter was a God thing, she mused and examined Matt's sneakers, which were the size of small boats. The things were probably half again the size of hers, and she wore an eleven.

"Wantta go to the student center and get a Coke?" Matt prompted. "If nothing else, we could sit in silence and ponder our predicaments together."

Evelyn giggled. "You're crazy," she said and couldn't believe she was actually on the verge of agreeing to his request. Evelyn made a point of avoiding the guy thing. She and her parents were in agreement that she had too much going for her to get serious about a guy right now. But somehow Matt's request seemed less a method of flirtation and more an invitation for friendship.

"I guess I am a little crazy around the edges," he admitted after a thoughtful pause. "Then again, it's probably the only thing that's gotten me through the last couple of years."

"What about your books?" she questioned.

His brows rose, and he gazed at her as if she'd just trotted out a request in Russian.

"Your books — in the classroom," she added. "If we go to the student center now . . ." She pressed the light on her digital watch and noted they'd been talking for about ten minutes.

He waved his hand. "I'll just wait till class is over and get them then." He glanced at his leather-banded watch. "We've got over an hour."

"Okay, then," she agreed. "I guess we can get the class notes from Darien. He seems to have his act together."

Matt barked out a bold laugh. "Oh yeah, now that's a suggestion. Problem is — it's just not a *good* one!"

With another chortle Evelyn whipped open her door, dropped her books on the front passenger seat, and relocked her car. She stepped beside Matt, and they strode toward the student center on the east side of the small campus. If nothing else, she and Matt could brainstorm ways to find their birth fathers — and maybe in the midst of it all E.T. would get herself a new basketball buddy.

Seventeen

The low-slung sound of a quirky funk tune marched into the center of Tony's dream — a dream that involved a baby and Victoria and a gunman chasing them into a fire-ravaged building. The song continued, and Tony teetered between fantasy and reality until at last he crashed full force into consciousness. He opened his eyes and squinted against the brass lamp's soft glow. Victoria had painted the bedroom walls yellow last year, and the only thing Tony could think was just how much he detested yellow and why she hadn't heeded his suggestion of another color — any other color would have worked.

The funk tune prevailed, and Tony finally realized his cell phone was ringing. He stirred and struggled against the stiffness in his right shoulder. Obviously he and Victoria had drifted off to sleep. His growling stomach attested that the tacos never happened. A glance at the digital clock revealed he'd been with her most the night. Four-thirty blared back at him in red, and the cell phone continued on its third round of the same tune. If he didn't hurry, the voice mail would cut in after the third rendition.

He scurried to sit up, finally snagged the phone, and pressed the answer button. Even though he was officially off duty until tomorrow morning Tony fully expected the captain's voice to request his presence at a raging emergency. The familiar voice that responded to his gruff greeting was not the captain's.

"Is this Tony Roberts?"

"Yes." Tony tried to stifle a yawn but didn't succeed. He rubbed a hand over his whisker-roughened jaw and glanced back at Victoria, who continued to snooze in oblivion. In the midst of another yawn the familiar voice began to find a face in the catalog of his memory. A face with gray eyes full of terror. Eyes that insisted Tony would die if he made one wrong move.

"This is Kevin Norris," the man finally stated.

"Yes, I thought I recognized your voice." Tony rubbed his sagging lids and tried to make sense of the last nine hours.

"I'm out of the country," Norris explained.

"As in you've left the U.S.?" Tony asked.

"Yes," Kevin admitted with stony resolve.

Oh, well that's convenient, Tony thought. *You sucked me into some ungodly mess and left the country.* Instead, he said, "What about your wife and child?"

"They're with me."

"How'd you get my cell phone number?" Tony quizzed and didn't bother to analyze his muddled mind's flighty pattern.

"I called the fire station and told them this was an emergency — a matter of life and death — that I needed your number."

"They are *not* supposed to give out my phone number."

"They didn't. They let me talk to your best friend. He decided to give me your number."

"Do you know it's 4:30 here?" Tony asked.

"Yes. But I can't stand this anymore. We got here safe and sound a few hours ago, and I can't rest until I tell you. As soon as I could I found a public phone."

"Tell me *what?*" Tony prompted, and Victoria rolled over. He shifted his posture and cast another glance her way.

This time her hazy gaze met his.

"Everything okay?" she whispered.

Tony frowned and mouthed a definite no.

"What is it, Norris?" he rapped.

"They're going to kill you," he stated.

230

"You need to get out of the country — *now!* Don't think you can stay in the U.S. and get away from them. They will track you down."

"Who exactly is involved and what are they up to?" Tony demanded.

"What do you know about laundering money?"

Tony scooted to the edge of the bed and dropped his feet to the floor. His heels met the taupe-colored carpet with a thud. After standing, Tony paced to one side of the room and then the other. "Nothing. I don't know a thing." He raised his hand and at once was as awake as if he'd drank two cups of coffee. "I'm a law-abiding firefighter!" Tony exclaimed.

"And I'm a banker," Kevin explained, a heavy undertow in his voice.

Tony recalled Rhonda Norris's mentioning that her husband was a vice president with Continental Bank. "A pawn for covering dirty money," he uttered.

"Exactly."

"You got in over your head, and —"

"Listen to me," Kevin urged. "Not only are the local authorities involved, but there are key people in the FBI who are up to their necks in this. It's not some fly-by-night scheme that a few gangsters dreamed up over hot cocoa one night!"

Tony whistled. "The FBI? No way!"

"Yes! Can you get out of the U.S. by tonight?"

Shaking his head, Tony looked at Victoria, who sat up in bed and crossed her legs.

"N–no! I can't leave the country by tonight. Are you *crazy?*"

Victoria, dazed and yawning, focused upon him. Her shoulders went rigid. Her eyes widened. She clutched at the comforter.

"Listen to me," Kevin insisted, "would you rather be alive in Europe or dead in Florida?"

"I don't have the money to just —"

"I'll take care of it. I — I feel responsible. I can even arrange for a false ID so they can't trace your plane ticket."

Tony stopped pacing and stared at a vacant spot on the wall — a spot that once held their framed wedding portraits. He shoved the fact of their absence into a mental file for later discussion and forced himself to address the current crisis.

"So I'm assuming you must be financially secure by now?" he asked with but a thread of caution.

"We won't starve," Norris defended.

Tony's mind raced with the implications. "And how much of that money started out illegal and wound up in some foreign account?"

"Listen," Kevin growled, "I'm trying to save your life. This is no time for you to get picky about —"

"No, *you* listen!" Tony jabbed his right index finger into mid-air and a prick of pain whizzed down his arm. He bit back a moan and continued his argument. "In the first place, I don't run, and in the second place, I don't take dirty money!"

"Okay, fine then! Go ahead and *rot* in Florida for all I care!"

"Does your wife *know* why you left the country?" Tony lowered himself onto the end of the bed.

Dead silence permeated the line.

"She doesn't know, does she?"

"That's none of your business."

"Let me guess . . ." Tony looked up at the motionless ceiling fan, ". . . all she knows is that you have some investments that paid off, and now the two of you can afford to buy that little house out in the countryside who knows where and live happily ever after."

A click ushered in silence, and Tony stared at the floor until the implications of the phone call hit him smack between the eyes. After Tony had almost been murdered on the beach Kevin Norris offered him a way out — a pathway to safety — and he just turned it down.

"What was all that about?" Victoria's voice sounded like a winter's breeze amid a barren field of dying grass.

Tony covered the end button with his thumb and pressed. The cell beeped, and he placed it on the bed. After rubbing his gritty eyes, he swiveled to face his wife.

"That was Kevin Norris," Tony explained. "He left the country with his wife and child. He offered to pay my way out. He says they're going to kill me." The emotionless words fell into the room like bricks. Tony scowled. His left hand trailed to his wounded shoulder, and he wondered if he'd been crazy not to jump at Norris' offer.

"What are you going to do?" Victoria scooted to his side and laid a hand on his arm.

"Well, you probably figured it out — I turned him down."

"But *why?*" Victoria urged.

"The funds he was going to use to get me out were illegal — laundered! I can't take that money. It would be like putting my approval on what he did."

"But Tony, what if —"

He shook his head. "Don't say that. We've got to be able to do something."

"But what?"

"I have no earthly idea." Tony turned off the lamp and walked to the window. He pulled on the drape cord enough to form a narrow gap. The night's inky shadows waved with the shore breeze. As Tony's eyes grew accustomed to the darkness various pinpoints of light attested to the inhabitants of this small coastal town. A lone car purred down the road, and Tony stared at the red taillights until they were out of sight.

Victoria moved to his side and placed her hand in his.

"I'm scared," she wobbled out.

"You took down our wedding pictures," Tony commented and stroked the hollow of her hand with his thumb.

Her only answer was a piteous sniffle.

He cut her a glance out of the corners of his eyes.

"It was too painful." Victoria gazed downward and the streetlights cast a glow upon her translucent complexion.

"So it wasn't because you couldn't stand the sight of me one day longer?" He loosened his grip on her hand and nudged her chin upward.

"You know better than that," she whispered, and her attention riveted upon him as her eyes filled with unshed tears.

"Do I?" Tony prompted and didn't bother to mask his anguish.

"Do I?" she repeated and lifted her chin a centimeter. Tony recognized his own torment in Victoria's eyes.

He wrapped his good arm around her and pulled her close. "We've really done a number on each other, haven't we?"

At first Victoria remained stiff, yet soon her arms slipped around him and she rested in the warmth of his embrace. Despite himself Tony speculated that this might be their last hug . . . that he might not live to see another sunset.

He buried his face into her mussed hair and thoughts of his own mortality nearly drowned him. On the beach his only goal had been survival. But in the morning shadows his thoughts turned to what would have happened to him if he hadn't made it . . . if that bullet had gone through his heart . . . if he had to face eternity.

"Talk to me about Jesus, Victoria." The request tumbled out before Tony realized he had voiced it. Frankly, Tony didn't really need to know *about* Jesus. He'd been around the church most his life. What he needed to know was how to actually bring himself to believe that Jesus was God. That final step just never seemed to happen.

Victoria pulled away and looked up at him.

"You really don't know Him, do you?"

Tony shook his head. "Not the way you do."

Her brow wrinkled, and she tugged on a strip of hair. A ribbon of irritation played across her features, and Tony prepared to be blasted for misleading her when they got married. But the truth was, he hadn't lied to Victoria about any kind of a religious experience. He had simply never refuted her assumption that since he attended church he must know Christ.

"When we got married, I thought . . ."

"Yes, I know," Tony admitted. "I never lied to you, Victoria." *Not about that anyway,* he added to himself.

"No," she agreed, "you just let me believe." Victoria walked around the bed and retrieved the cordless phone from the dresser. Without a word she deposited the receiver into its cradle and kept her back to him, her shoulders hunched, her head down. "And it makes me wonder if there are other lies as well." Her breathless admission, soft yet powerful, nearly knocked Tony flat.

He stumbled away from her, and issues of his own mortality paled in the face of his need to hide the decaying duplicity. He whipped around and strode toward the hallway. Tony didn't know whether or not he should dare step into the morning, but the room's immediate chill drove him down the stairway. This time Victoria didn't come after him — not until he lunged off the last step.

"Tony, wait!" her panicked voice echoed from the top of the stairwell.

"I'm walking back to the station," he hurled over his shoulder and stepped through their home that bore Victoria's mark but precious little of his. "I don't think there's enough room here for me." He paused to take a spiteful kick at the chair she'd meticulously refinished. The antique's very presence provoked him to explode in a heated protest. His wife spent more time on inanimate objects than she'd ever spent with him. Ready to roar about his heaping disillusionment, he whirled around. Victoria was a few feet behind him, her face drenched in tears, her eyes desperate for some relief. Tony halted and backed away.

"I — I'm sorry," she said over a hiccup, and Tony blinked. He wasn't certain he'd witnessed Victoria using the "s" word twice in one year — let alone in one night.

"I don't know all the answers, and I don't understand everything that's going on between us. I r–really don't, Tony. But one thing I *do* know, you can't go back out there!" She pointed toward the doorway.

"I can't stay cooped up here forever!" he exclaimed. "I've got a job, you know!"

"I know, but — but —" She raised her hand, and then let it flop to her side. "You can at least lie low for a week or so, can't you?" She knotted her fingers before kneading her crumpled sundress. "You're supposed to have some vacation time built up. Perhaps now's the time to use it. And — and maybe we should call my friend Jac Franklin. She ought to have some sort of insight into what you can do. There's got to be *somebody* around here in law enforcement you can trust."

"I don't want to drag your friend into this. And Kevin Norris says the FBI is involved." He shook his head. "Who's left?" Tony tried to lift both hands but stopped when his right shoulder protested with a dull ache. He grimaced and slumped into the chair he'd just kicked. The soft folds provided a welcomed rest.

"You need more ibuprofen," Victoria

said and stepped toward the kitchen.

"The shoulder's a lot better," he said. "I *need* to live — that's what I need."

"What about the CIA or the Secret Service, or maybe there's somebody in Pensacola you could trust," she called over her shoulder. The creak of a cabinet opening preceded the water's rush, and Tony figured she'd placed her hands on the downstairs supply of ibuprofen.

"And how do you suggest I find this person?" he demanded. "Should I just go into every law enforcement office between here and Orlando and say, 'Hey! I've got the scoop on a money laundering scheme. They're trying to kill me. I'd like the help of anybody here who isn't involved!' "

Victoria approached him, her face flushed, her lips pressed together. The tears had stopped, and her twitching fingers gripped a blue-and-white pill bottle. "Don't be impossible, Tony! I think the smart thing here is that we *both* calm down and think this thing through. And . . ." her voice softened, ". . . would you *please* promise me you won't go tearing off in an uproar?" She handed him the glass of water and two pills.

Tony accepted the tablets, popped them in his mouth, and took the cool water. He downed the whole glass and replaced it into her outstretched hand. Glancing toward the drapes he'd recently closed, Tony wondered what horrors the dark morning might hold.

"You're right," he admitted. "I don't have any business walking out. But I guess you're well acquainted with my temper by now."

"Yep." She lowered herself to the claw-footed couch's arm. "You're famous for getting aggravated and storming off in all directions." Far from being a barb, Victoria's words held only sadness. Sadness and confusion. Confusion and longing.

Tony groped for something to say — anything — yet no words came. All he could do was sit and stare at her and relive the number of times during the last six years he'd stormed out on her. The last time had been when he moved into the fire station. Indeed, Tony could no longer deny that he had contributed a significant measure to their lack of unity. Nevertheless, he was at a loss how to restore what was lost or, perhaps, gain what they never had.

Start with the truth, the thought barged in upon him from nowhere, and Tony's spine went rigid. A dull ache radiated from his shoulder, and he wondered when the blasted thing would cease to protest with nearly every move. But the pain in his shoulder waned in comparison to the agony in his wife's eyes.

"I'm sorry," he muttered, and the words seemed far from adequate.

Victoria's mouth quivered, and Tony couldn't remember how many years had passed since he'd uttered those two significant words. He leaned toward her and stretched out his good arm. A cacophonous peal erupted from the den and sent a rigid dread through Tony's every fiber.

He looked at Victoria who held his gaze with wide-eyed terror.

"Who could be calling at this hour?" Tony stood and peered past the stairway, toward the phone.

"I have no idea." Victoria rose, set the tumbler on the brass end table, and stepped toward the den.

"Should I get it?" she asked, and began wadding her crumpled sundress all over again.

"I don't know," Tony blurted and shook his head. Those horrid minutes on the beach whipped through his mind like a murderous hurricane. *What should I do? Who can I contact? Since the police know everything, how long do I have to live?* Tony clutched the back of the chair and despaired that Victoria hadn't discussed Jesus with him.

"What if it's an emergency?" Victoria asked on the sixth ring and stepped toward the den.

"What if it isn't?"

She retreated to Tony's side and hovered like a hunted doe.

"What if it's *them?*" he added.

Eighteen

Marilyn stirred in the queen-sized bed and shivered. The last thing she remembered before drifting off to sleep was that she'd forgotten to flip the switch on the central heat. Yesterday's warmth had welcomed her to open the windows, but the Arkansas night had mocked the kiss of spring and ushered in a tinge of winter's chill. Marilyn snuggled toward Joshua's side of the bed and anticipated her husband's warmth. The man was like a furnace even during the bitterest snowstorm.

No matter how far Marilyn scooted she encountered only cool sheets. At last she cracked one eye open and examined Joshua's side of the bed. His rumpled pillow was vacant, the comforter, flat. Marilyn frowned and peered toward their digital clock; 5:01 glared back at her. She rolled to her back and gazed out the doorway. A golden light penetrated the hall's shadows. Assuming that Abigail must have awakened Joshua, Marilyn whipped back the covers, grabbed her terry cloth robe, and shrugged into it as she stumbled down the hallway.

But when she reached the modest living room, Marilyn encountered only Joshua. He was lying face down on the braided rug, his shoulders heaving. Marilyn stopped. She clutched her midsection as her muddled mind tried to comprehend the scene. The aroma of freshly brewed coffee tantalized her senses, and she noted the steaming cup on the table near Josh. Marilyn teetered between backing out of the room to give her husband his privacy or moving to his side.

Undoubtedly, he had been distracted the last few days. With Camille walking out on them and their trying to deal with a distraught two-year-old, Marilyn had figured they both were distracted, to say the least. Now she wondered if maybe there was something else going on with Joshua — perhaps his heart was being moved as was hers when she first learned of Camille. From the start of the whole frustrating ordeal, Marilyn thought about the hundreds of other "Camilles" on the streets. She wondered if anybody was there for them — anybody at all.

As she pondered her burden, Marilyn allowed her nose to dictate her next move. She padded into the white kitchen and fumbled for a cup in the overstuffed cabinet. A large Christmas mug fell from its precarious perch atop another mug and plopped against her palm. Marilyn figured any cup would do — the bigger the better. She filled the red-and-green mug full of Joshua's brew and wished the man didn't insist upon half-caffeinated. At five in the morning Marilyn could have used the jolt of full caffeine.

While she stirred in the cinnamon flavored creamer, the shuffle of socked feet against tile announced her husband's entry.

"Morning," he said.

Marilyn turned and look into his reddened eyes.

"Been praying?" she asked.

"I guess that's obvious," he said and took a long swallow of his coffee. "Either that or I was kissing the rug." He broke into a half-hearted grin that reminded Marilyn of the first time she'd ever met him. His Saint Bernard had just destroyed her garden, and Josh arrived upon the scene with his million-dollar smile. At the time Marilyn was still aching from her first husband's abandonment, and she had pledged to avoid Joshua Langham like the plague.

So much for that pledge, she thought.

Joshua came next to her, set his mug on the counter, and added a dollop of coffee to the black brew in his cup. Marilyn leaned against the counter, sipped her coffee, and examined her socked feet against the white kitchen tile. One toenail, spotted in red polish, peaked from the end of her sock. Marilyn wasn't sure what was more disgusting — that most of her "good" socks now had holes in them or that she hadn't repainted her toenails in two months.

"When I woke up and saw you were gone, I figured you were up with Abigail," Marilyn said.

"Actually, I was." Joshua edged closer to his wife and leaned against the counter beside her. He switched the mug to his left hand and encircled her shoulders with his right arm. "But I finally got her back to sleep and decided I might as well take advantage of the quiet house."

Welcoming Josh's warmth, Marilyn leaned into him and couldn't prevent the shiver that wracked her body.

"You're cold." Joshua tightened his grip on her.

"I woke up chilled." Placing the mug against her quivering lips, she partook of the steaming liquid.

"Well, we can fix that problem." Joshua walked toward the living room thermostat. He examined the small box, flipped a switch, and a click proceeded the rumble of the central heating unit.

Marilyn followed close behind him yet made a detour when she reached the plaid sofa. She clutched the robe around her waist and snuggled into the corner of the sofa.

"Here." Joshua grabbed a crocheted afghan from the recliner and tucked the folds around Marilyn. "Is that better?"

Marilyn nodded and the smell of fabric softener attested that she'd recently washed the afghan, which had been baptized in her daughter's chocolate milk last week.

As Joshua settled in beside her, she mustered her best morning smile and was thankful that her husband loved her for who she was, not for what she looked like in the morning. She was certain her hair must be going in a thousand directions. Marilyn eyed Joshua's spiky hair and chuckled.

"What?" he asked.

"Your hair."

"I figured it looked about as good as yours." He rubbed the top of his head and cast her a swollen-eyed wink. The crow's feet around his eyes crinkled with his smile.

"We're a pair, aren't we?"

"Yes, we are." Joshua nodded and rubbed the stubble along his chin. "We really are," he added on a more serious note.

"What have we gotten ourselves into?"

Marilyn asked and relived the last few weeks which culminated in their taking custody of an emotionally disturbed toddler who screamed half the night for her mother.

"We're either crazy or called," Joshua said.

"After the last few nights, I wonder which."

"You should have been up with her to-night." Josh propped his sock-clad feet upon the coffee table Marilyn had refinished. "She threw one fit after another and screamed so loud, I'm shocked she didn't wake you *and* Brooke."

"What did you do, Josh?" Marilyn asked and wanted to wail, *What are we going to do?*

"I just held her and rocked her," he said. "What else could I do?"

"Bless her heart. She's just so angry."

"I know . . . I know. And I can't say that I blame her."

"This isn't what we planned." Marilyn stated the obvious, and knew Joshua understood her need to vent. "Camille was supposed to stay another week at least, and she just — just left! How can a mother do that? I don't even think she said goodbye to Abigail." Marilyn's simmering exasperation tainted her words.

Joshua lifted her hand and pressed the palm against his lips. "And the streets of America are full of mothers and children and fathers just like her." Anguished conviction reverberated through his voice. "I know Camille didn't play fair, but I'm still glad we gave her a chance."

Marilyn stared into her coffee and then allowed her gaze to drift across the humble room. She and Josh didn't have much. They had pieced together the home's decor from secondhand shops and garage sale makeovers. Nevertheless, they had willingly opened their hearts and home to Camille who in turn left without so much as a thank you. While the prospect of becoming new parents certainly bred excitement, Marilyn couldn't deny that the situation was indeed a bittersweet ordeal.

Her attention settled back onto the coffee mug, and she eyed the diminutive solitaire near her wedding band. When Gregory divorced Marilyn she never dreamed she'd wear another wedding band. Yet God had brought beauty from that dreadful situation and restored her heart as well as her belief in unconditional love. She laid her head upon her husband's shoulder and reveled in the warmth that eased away the chill. Perhaps the disappointment over Camille was God's way of working yet another miracle.

"I just can't quit thinking of all those people I saw," Joshua finally said. "It's like they're ingrained on my mind. When I think of people living on the streets, I don't know. . . . I always envisioned them in a third world country, but —"

"Parts of the U.S. might as well *be* a third world country, as far as the homeless are concerned," Marilyn finished for him and never mentioned that this was at least the sixth time they'd shared this conversation during the last month.

"Exactly," Joshua said.

"Is that why you were praying?" she asked.

"Yes." He placed his feet on the floor, leaned forward, and deposited his coffee on the table. Joshua propped his elbows on his knees and rested his forehead against his palms. "There's got to be something we can do," he said at last.

Marilyn silently nodded. "Somehow, I knew you were going to finally get around to saying that."

Joshua lifted his head and peered at Marilyn as if her words didn't surprise him in the least. His eyes reflected the same burden that had weighed upon Marilyn the day she learned of Camille and Abigail. Marilyn clutched her coffee mug and didn't so much as blink.

"So what are we supposed to do now?" Josh whispered.

Nineteen

Victoria's phone stopped ringing on the seventh peal. She released Tony's hand and couldn't even remember grasping it. The two of them shared a wide-eyed stare, and she noted the spokes of blue that surfaced in Tony's light gray eyes when he was especially tired or angered. She figured the last ten hours had evoked innumerable emotions within her husband. Victoria herself felt as if she were riding a roller coaster, and she wasn't even the one who'd been shot at.

"Want to check to see if there's a voice mail?" Tony prompted.

"Y–yes, I guess I should." Victoria moved toward the den telephone and looked at the thing as if it were a venomous viper. Finally she snatched up the receiver and dialed the appropriate number. The impersonal voice on the other end announced that she did indeed have one voice mail. "There *is* a message," Victoria said on a breathless whisper and punched the number to retrieve it.

A familiar voice floated over the line, and Victoria wilted onto the couch. "Hi, Victoria, this is Eddy Graham."

"It's Eddy," she said.

Tony's face relaxed. He rubbed his jaw and expelled a long breath. "What does he want at this hour?"

"I, uh, hate to bother you so early," Eddy's message continued and Victoria kneaded the back of her tensed neck, "but I just got in from an emergency, and I'm on the verge of going to sleep here. And well, I can't sleep until I hear back from you. Tony left here yesterday evening about seven. I haven't seen him since. I just got a really weird call from a man who said it was a matter of life or death so I gave him Tony's cell number. I hope that's okay. I checked at Tony's boat, but he wasn't there. I tried to call his cell but he didn't answer. I hope he's with you. Do you mind giving me a ring here at the station?"

The voice mail announced the end of the message; Victoria deleted it and hung up. After standing, she leaned against the side of the couch and was so relieved she barely stopped herself from sinking to her knees. "He says they're worried about you down at the station," she explained. "Eddy checked your boat and called your cell. Did you hear it ring?"

Tony's brows knitted and he shook his

head. "Maybe the signal was lost. It happens to the best of us."

"Anyway, he was out on an emergency and can't sleep until he knows you're okay."

"Well, I guess he *would* be worried," Tony said and raised his hand. "The last he saw of me, I was going jogging yesterday evening."

"Why don't you call him?" Victoria suggested and her empty stomach longed for something warm and mellow. "While you're doing that, I'll make us some herbal tea. I've got cinnamon."

Tony cocked a brow. "Gotta Coke instead?"

Victoria chuckled. "What am I thinking? You never did care for herbal tea. I don't have Coke, though. What about ginger ale? That's about as strong as I buy."

"Beats cinnamon tea any day." He reached for the phone, paused, and eyed Victoria. "But then again, I'm so rattled, if you'd just put a cup of that herbal poison in my hand I'd probably have drank the stuff and never even realized what I was doing."

"In that case, I've even got lemon zinger."

"Oh, gag! Somebody spare me. The woman is going to kill me!" He clutched his throat. "Death by herbal tea!"

The two shared a chorus of companionable laughter, and Victoria caught her breath. She couldn't remember the last time they had fallen into the sporty banter that had characterized their engagement and early marriage. And she was once again engulfed in the warmth that filled her body when she was assisting him with his wound. Tony Roberts, tall, blond, and lithe, had probably caught more feminine fancies than Victoria would be comfortable knowing about. After weeks of separation she couldn't deny that she ached for the closeness of marital intimacy — not so much for the thrill as for the comfort of knowing she was cherished.

A flicker of hope ignited within her. And for the first time in months Victoria wondered if perhaps the two of them really could begin again. True, Tony's temper wasn't exactly tamed, and he did have his share of faults. Nevertheless, Victoria *needed* her husband. She needed him as never before.

As if he sensed her scrutiny, Tony looked up from dialing the station's number. "Something wrong?" he asked and placed the receiver against his ear.

"Uh . . . no — no, nothing," Victoria mumbled. She averted her gaze and edged into the kitchen.

Tony watched Victoria's retreat and would have sworn in court that the woman was thinking about him and her and their moving closer. He failed to remember how long it had been since they shared a bed for more than sleeping. He licked his lips, swallowed, and just about the time he decided Eddy could wait, Sal's voice broke over the line.

"Uh, Sal," Tony began and blasted his bad timing, "is Eddy close? He just left a voice mail for me. He said you all were worried about me."

"Yes, as a matter of fact we are," Sal said as if she were his bossy elder sister. "Nice of you to call and let us know you're alive."

"Actually, I'm here at home with Victoria." Tony strained to see into the pristine kitchen where his wife's sundress sashayed around her bare ankles as she prepared her tea and his soda.

"Aahh. That's what I told Eddy, but he was so hard-headed he wouldn't believe me."

"Well, he did leave a voice mail here for me," Tony said and hoped his voice hid his rising pulse rate.

"Maybe there's hope, yet. Some days I wonder if Eddy Graham listens to anybody.

Just a minute. I'm going to put you on hold, and I'll get him."

"Okay."

Victoria padded into the den with a tumbler full of fizzing ginger ale. He smiled his appreciation and wondered if his ravenous need was plastered all over his face. When Tony planned to visit Victoria yesterday evening he had no intentions of asking her for a thing. He simply missed her. But the flicker of hunger in her eyes sent him past all realms of reason. Many months had passed since he felt the heat from Victoria. Many indeed. And the very hint of her interest left him reeling.

Her brows arched in silent query.

"I'm waiting on Eddy," Tony supplied, and the microwave's bell dinged.

"That's my tea," she said and swiveled back toward the kitchen.

Tony reached to pull her down beside him but Eddy's voice boomed over the line.

"Whatcha need?" Tony's question came out more as a command than a request.

"Well, aren't you Mr. Congeniality this morning?" Eddy complained.

"Sorry." He propped his elbow on the couch's arm. "Getting shot at never did leave me in a good mood."

"What?" Eddy exploded.

Tony briefed his friend on all the latest details, ending with his call from Kevin Norris.

"I knew something was up!" Eddy vented. "But Sal was so dead certain you'd just meandered home for the evening. And I told her, 'No way! Those two are still miles apart!' "

Victoria padded back into the den sipping a mug of steaming tea. The smell of cinnamon tinged the air and Tony wondered if her mouth tasted of the tea. The thought of that herbal brew no longer repulsed him. His gaze followed her as she meandered around the room and then stopped at the end of the sofa.

"I'm going upstairs to take a shower," she whispered.

Tony's temperature escalated another notch. He knew Eddy was talking to him, but he didn't have one clue what the guy was saying. Instead, he watched his wife head toward the stairs while intimate fantasies rocketed through him.

As he strained for the last glimpse of Victoria, Tony became aware that his friend had stopped talking. He groped for something to say but all that came out was an awkward, "Uh . . ."

"What is the deal with you, man? Did you

even hear a word I said?" Eddy blurted.

"Uh . . ." Tony repeated and dragged his mind from the shower to the problem at hand. "Do you have any hot ideas on how to get me out of this mess?"

"That's what I was just telling you!" Eddy said. "But apparently your mind is elsewhere. Maybe Sal was more right than I know," he added on a sly note.

"Mind your own business," Tony said and tried to hide the telltale smile from his voice.

"Aahh. Say no more," Eddy said. "I'll keep this brief then."

"Please do."

"Or . . . it can wait a day or two if you like."

The temptation to wait proved almost too inviting, yet Tony's common sense kicked in.

"I don't think so," he shot back, "this is my *life* we're talking about here."

"Okay, then, my brother-in-law is a lawyer in the attorney general's office."

"Yes, you've mentioned that," Tony said. And a glimmer of light posed itself on the horizon of this dark situation. He momentarily forgot about the shower as his mind wandered toward the possibilities of Eddy's connection.

His friend smothered a snort. "To hear him tell it, the state of Florida can't get along without him."

"The two of you don't get along too well, do you?"

"That's a nice way of saying we pretty much can't stand the sight of each other."

"And here I thought you didn't have an enemy in the world, Eddy."

"I just never cared for the way he treats my sister. There've been a few times when kicking the stuffing out of him would have been too easy. His temper keeps her in line, let me tell you. But every time I try to tell her to stand up for herself she defends him." Eddy's words grew tense, his tone deep and forceful.

Tony cringed, and his fingers ate into the receiver. Eddy didn't know it but he'd just shoved a mirror in Tony's face. This brother-in-law wasn't the only one who'd blown up on his wife. And Tony couldn't deny that marching out on her two months ago had brought him no peace whatsoever — only emptiness. Eddy's silence interrupted his thoughts.

"Have you left me again?" he asked.

"Sorry, man, my mind keeps wandering. That's all."

"You've got it bad, don't you?"

"Why don't you just get back to whatever plan you're cooking up and keep your nose in your own marriage, okay?" Tony didn't bother to hide the smile this time.

"You're cold, man," Eddy said.

"I'm in over my head, that's what."

"Okay, then, I say we contact my brother-in-law and see how he can help us."

Tony leaned forward and stared at the oriental rug's pastel hues. A scattering of sand mingled in the pile and he wondered if Victoria was slipping in her house-keeping endeavors. A bump overhead attested to her presence in the bathroom. The shower was right over the living room. Tony stared at the neat pile of magazines stacked on the wicker coffee table and tried to remember where he'd left off the conversation.

"But I'm not sure I want to put myself in anybody's hands, even if he's in the AG's office — and he's related to you. How do I know there's not somebody in that office who's up to their necks in this? Kevin says there's even some people involved who are in the FBI." He raised his right arm and grimaced. The ibuprofen had helped some, but not enough.

"I know where you're coming from. But I will say that I believe in my brother-in-law's honesty. I'd rather eat a skunk than share Thanksgiving dinner with him, but he's straight when it comes to the law — straight as an arrow. When he was in private practice he actually turned down a few big cases because he believed the potential client was guilty."

"So *he's* honest," Tony said and gingerly used his right hand to retrieve his soda. "But what about the other guys in that office?" He swallowed a mouthful of the bubbling liquid, and welcomed the sting that hit the back of his throat.

"I don't think we have a choice," Eddy said. "He's the only contact we have. What else can you do? Sit around and wait until they *do* shoot you? Next time they might not miss!"

Tony sputtered as a droplet trickled down his windpipe. "You're right," he gasped and hacked against the ginger ale.

"This thing you've stumbled into is too big. It's going to take you under if we don't take some action."

"So what's the first step?" Tony asked and gulped another mouthful of soda.

"We call Brandon and tell him the problem. I'll see what he says, and we go from there. Agreed?"

Tony nodded. "Okay. But if anything

seems fishy you better run. We can't trust anybody, Eddy."

"I'm with you. Don't worry. I'll keep a low profile."

"Fine. And let's keep plenty of holes in the plan where I can disappear if I need to."

"Right." He paused a second. "It's 5:30. I'm going to shoot an e-mail to the jerk's office for him to call me, and then I'm hitting the sack. He'll probably get around to calling me 'bout ten or so I hope. He's not terribly prompt when it comes to family. Where do I reach you once I talk with him? Are you going to hang there for a while?"

"What is today?" Tony asked and deposited the tumbler on the oak end table near a framed photo. Tony examined the 5 x 7 of himself and Victoria, both sunburned and wind-tossed, standing near his sloop docked at Pug's Marina.

"Today's Friday," Eddy supplied.

"Yes. Right. Victoria has to go to the TV station this morning. Might be smart for me to get her to sneak me out to the marina. I can lie low in my boat for a while. Call me on my cell. I'll have it on."

"Will do."

"Oh, and Eddy, tell the captain I'm in the middle of an emergency, and I'll call him later today. Looks like it's a good thing I've got vacation time built up."

"Sure thing. I bet he'll be glad. You've been living here for two months. A break might do us all some good."

"Ah, shut up," Tony teased.

"Not a problem," Eddy shot back. "And . . . tell Victoria I said hi, will ya?"

The line clicked. With a smile Tony pulled the receiver from his ear and shook his head. "Eddy, you're as good as gold," he mumbled, "and as ornery as they come."

Tony hung up the phone and noted that a hint of cinnamon still lingered in the den. Victoria's influence was all over this house — and still all over his heart. He glanced toward the ceiling. Thoughts of his wife dashed aside his present problems. He checked his watch again and figured they had a good hour before the sun started creeping over the ocean. The longing cloaking Victoria's features bade him take his chances on moving up the stairway.

"Why did she bother to tell me she was in the shower," he whispered, "unless it was a hint for me to join her?" Tony's pulse began pounding anew; he was pulled under by the tidal wave of desire that refused suppression. With purpose in his step, Tony took the stairs two at a time and didn't care that his shoulder protested the jarring gait.

When he topped the steps he noted that the bathroom door was open by two inches. The first few years they were married an ajar door with her in the shower was a silent communication that Tony was welcome if he so chose. While Victoria had never been sexually assertive she had occasionally dropped some silent hints. The musings urged Tony forward yet he halted outside the door. *Or could it be that she's so used to living by herself she's forgotten the silent signal and she just accidentally left the door open.*

Tony gripped the door facing and tried to talk himself into going back downstairs. That was the rational thing to do. His common sense insisted Victoria wasn't about to be ready for anything physical between them. But the hunger raging through his blood reminded him of that glimmer of yearning he'd seen in her eyes.

He nudged open the door. The beige shower curtain around the antique tub billowed with rising steam. The smell of her apple shampoo made him want to lather her hair and whisper how much he'd missed her. With a defeated groan Tony entered the bathroom and clicked the door shut behind him.

"Hey, babe," he said and braced himself

for rejection, "is there room in there for me?"

She inched aside the shower curtain and her face appeared on the edge. Victoria's wet hair was plastered against her scalp and great droplets of water clung to her flawless complexion. Copious drops also clung to her weighted lashes, and her large hazel eyes observed him in a hauntingly seductive scrutiny. Tony, on the verge of smoldering, figured he'd awaken any minute to discover this was some erotic dream.

"What about your shoulder?" she whispered and her gaze trailed to the bandage.

"What shoulder?" he asked and offered the most provocative smile he could muster.

The corners of her mouth twitched and she tucked her trembling lower lip between her teeth. Her final answer was a timid nod, and Tony's fantasies melded with reality.

Twenty

"I don't like this, Tony." Victoria put her Toyota in park and perused the marina's parking lot. The predawn shadows, sinister and dank, invaded every nook. Light rain fell this Friday morning. Sometime during the night a front had invaded Choctawhatchee Bay and dropped the temperature into the 40s. Victoria squinted. Through the diminishing darkness she caught site of white caps pushing against the moorings at Pug's Marina. Even in this light the place's need of paint wasn't hidden. Victoria imagined the smell of singed grease that had accompanied her trips to Tony's haven, where he often listened to Pug Hampton's fishing fantasies.

Tony peered toward the long line of boats that were buoyed in the bay, his face tense. "Don't worry," he said, yet the words were hollow. And Victoria felt as if she could slice the air, fraught with anxiety.

"Okay," she responded and clicked the heater to low. "I won't. I'll just leave you here in the dark and hope that goon who tried to shoot you isn't hiding somewhere nearby." She tugged her long denim jacket around her torso and pinched a button. "How do I even know you'll make it to the boat without . . ."

Victoria examined the lifeless terrain surrounding them. Nothing seemed out of place. In the distance every boat bobbed in its usual position. Pug's framed home and store sported one porch light that the old man would probably soon snap off. Indeed, the approaching day promised to be like any other along the coast. Yet one gunshot could shatter that promise.

"I don't think they followed us." Tony took her hand. "Really." He pivoted in his seat, placed hands on both sides of her face, and peered into her eyes. His damp hair hung across his forehead and the smell of green apples attested that they had both used the same shampoo. The memory of their physical intimacy hung between them like a newly stated vow that perhaps they really could begin again. But even in the shadows Victoria observed something stirring in his soul — something unexplainable. The last few hours had brought them closer than they had been in months; nevertheless, she sensed that her husband still held something back. Victoria wondered if those impenetrable walls of his would ever completely crumble.

Without a word he planted his mouth against hers. The fires, still smoldering from their recent union, ignited anew. And Victoria clung to her husband as she hadn't in years. He'd insisted she take him to this God-forsaken place while she filmed the TV show this morning. Fifteen minutes ago the idea had sounded like a good one, yet now that Victoria was on the brink of leaving him she wondered if she'd been insane for agreeing.

Tony placed a trail of kisses along her cheek and rested his lips against her ear. "I'm going to be okay," he whispered. "Really."

"I hope so because I could never forgive myself if —"

"Don't even say it." Tony backed away and gripped her shoulders. "Eddy's going to call his brother-in-law and somehow we'll get through this." He scanned the bay and Victoria followed suit. The pale gray horizon promised dawn would arrive within the next few minutes. "I need to go ahead and get into the boat before the sun gets too bright," Tony said.

"Okay," Victoria croaked. "But . . ." She debated whether or not to reintroduce the idea of consulting her friend, Jac Franklin.

Tony had rejected the notion of getting one of her sisters involved, yet Victoria still clung to the hope that Jac might help. *The least she could do is give him some protection,* Victoria thought. Nevertheless, she couldn't imagine her husband allowing one of her friends to follow him everywhere he went. *Why does he have to know then?* Her mind whirled with the duplicity such an endeavor would entail. Furthermore, Victoria wasn't even certain Jacquelyn could fit the request into her burgeoning schedule. The woman was too busy for her own good.

"Well, this is it," Tony said.

As his lips touched hers for a final caress, her mind raced, wondering which direction to turn. She couldn't decide whether to mention Jac or not . . . whether it would be safer to beg him to stay with her or let him go. Caught in the midst of her deliberation Victoria remained helplessly mute. As if she were in front of a silent movie, she watched her husband slip from the Toyota, click the door shut, hunch his shoulders, and make a straight line toward the long row of boats. The wind whipped the sleeves of that tattered T-shirt, and Victoria wondered why they hadn't tried to find him some sweats.

Heart pounding, she gripped the steering wheel. Her lips trembled. A lone tear trickled beside her nose, and she dashed it aside.

"Oh, God, help us," she whispered.

E.T.'s eyes drooped open, and she gazed at the giant poster of two women professionals going for the ball at a basket's rim. The full-color testimonial of her obsession usually gave E.T. Sinclaire her wake-up boost. Today was different. Today, the poster was but a focal point upon which her ragged thoughts might rest. She shoved the confining covers from around her perspiring waist and welcomed the blast of the room's cool air. Like a woman who's teetering on the edge of a cliff, she struggled to drag her reeling mind from the precipice of nightmares and onto the firm path of reality.

The poster blurred into a meaningless blob as her muddled mind replayed the dreams that had accosted her fitful sleep. Garish mixtures of monstrous baby rattles, aged paternal notes, and a man in quicksand pleading to see his baby girl promised to shove E.T. into despondent depths yet unexplored. Her dad came through one nocturnal episode throwing silver trinkets into a crowd of cheering fans who refused to stop chanting Evelyn's initials. Her new friend Matt Leavey made his appearance after some idiot got on the PA system and started reading the letter from her birth father.

She turned onto her side and covered her face. Evelyn's jumbled mind promised that if she went back to sleep the illusions would cease and she could attain deep sleep. Yet when she dared peek at her bedside clock, it said 7:00 a.m. Her muscles said 3:30.

"Time to hit the showers," she moaned, and recalled all the times her father had said exactly that after a tough practice. Somehow E.T. dragged her body from the narrow bed and padded toward the corner bathroom that featured a tiny shower. She groaned through getting dressed and decided to act like her mother and drink a cup of coffee to start the day. School wasn't happening any other way.

The shower that promised rejuvenation did little to jolt her mind. At last, clad in jeans and a sweatshirt, she pulled her half-dried hair into a ponytail and wandered toward the sound of her mother's humming in the kitchen.

The smell of apple turnovers greeted her. Their golden retriever, Goldie, added her welcome with a companionable woof and a lick on the fingers. Evelyn scratched Goldie's ears and covered a yawn.

"Hi, Mom," she said and crawled up on a backless barstool.

In the knotty-pine kitchen Macy Sinclaire brushed back a drooping lock of copper-hued hair, leaving a touch of flour from the dough on the cutting board. Her face, classic yet pale, attested to her lack of makeup, and Evelyn was reminded that she hadn't bothered with cosmetics either. Some days just weren't magic.

"Hi, Sweetheart! The turnovers will be out in a minute." She glanced away and then back at her daughter. "You look like you've been playing basketball all night. Is Dad working you too hard?"

Evelyn hesitated and eyed the flattened dough at her mother's fingertips. Ever since that episode over the rattle and letter neither she nor her parents had brought up the topic of her birth father. Last night with Matt Leavey was the first time she'd openly shared her desire to find her father. He suggested she start looking for her father by surfing the internet, and E.T. debated whether her mother would be as supportive as Matt.

"I guess I just need a break," she mumbled. Evelyn reached for a paper plate from the stack near the salt and pepper shaker. Simultaneously, a ball of guilt smashed into her soul. E.T. didn't make a habit of with-holding things from her parents — espe-cially not her mother.

The bond of womanhood had been fused when E.T. told her mother about kissing Willis Wade in the sixth grade. Instead of admonishing her daughter against such "evils," Macy Sinclaire had told E.T. about pecking the cheek of a boy in grade school. That late-night exchange had been her first big venture into the mysteries of mother–daughter secrets. Sharing the onset of wom-anhood had made her feel secure in who she would become. Until today there was never a second thought about opening her life to her mother's confidence.

E.T. made a monumental task of posi-tioning the paper plate in front of her. She then slid from the bar stool and poured her-self a mug of coffee from the full pot. Her mother's surprised but accepting glance greeted Evelyn when she sat down again.

Silence crept across Evelyn's shoulders like a heavy burden that wouldn't be shaken. If Macy Sinclaire was anything, she was insightful. Evelyn wondered how long she could hide her desire to track down her birth father.

"I don't guess things have been the same between us since you found that silver rattle, have they?" Macy asked.

Evelyn stiffened. She stared at a snatch of her reflection in the coffee's glassy surface and groped for words to say. Nothing came. Nothing except the nuance of those horrid dreams.

The oven door creaked open, and a fresh waft of apple turnovers sent E.T.'s stomach into a rumbling fit. She sipped the hot coffee and grabbed a pot holder from the countertop. Glad for any diversion E.T. stood and assisted her mother in removing two baking sheets laden with the mouthwatering delicacies.

After snapping the oven door closed, Macy turned to Evelyn and grasped her free hand. "I've been thinking," she started. "If . . . if there ever came a time when you w–wanted to contact him . . ." Macy trailed off.

Evelyn's stomach twisted into a tight, nauseous knot, and she was almost certain her mother's blue eyes were begging her *not* to contact her birth father. All at once the apple turnovers repulsed her. E.T. filled her mouth with the hot, black coffee and plopped the mug on the bar.

"I don't ever want to do anything to hurt you and Dad," she mumbled, for lack of anything else coherent to say. "I'll catch a turnover tonight." She grabbed her back-pack and purse and blindly strode for the garage door.

"But . . ." Macy's broken word sent a spear through E.T.'s heart. Never had she been so torn. And she was beginning to think that Matt was right. The only way to track down her birth father was to find him secretly. Her parents need never know. Conversely, she would never experience the sorrow of hurting the two people who had unconditionally loved her from birth.

Twenty-One

Tony opened one eye just enough to encounter the weak light seeping in through a row of portholes along the top of the cabin. The gentle sway of the boat that had rocked him to sleep now proved an irritation. He snapped his eye closed and wondered if he had any coffee. The cupboard held a variety of precooked foods, and the little vessel had an auxiliary water system kept fresh by Destin's frequent rains. Tony recalled running out of coffee somewhere during the last week, but he couldn't remember if that was here or at the station. He decided to figure that out later and snuggled deeper into the sleeping bag. As his groggy mind wandered, Tony pondered exactly how long he'd been asleep. Once he'd secured the hatch at dawn and called Victoria on her cell phone to confirm he was safe, Tony dropped on one of the bunks forward of the mast and fell into a fitful sleep.

Frowning, he flopped to his back and his shoulder reminded him that it was still sore. This time, both eyes slid open. The muffled squawk of a seagull and an engine's rev blended with the slap of water against his boat. Tony lifted his wrist, stared at his watch, and widened his eyes. He'd been asleep nearly six hours. His stomach rumbled. Not only did the tacos not happen last night, neither did breakfast this morning.

"My wife really interfered with my eating," he mumbled and couldn't stop the satisfied smile from crawling across his face. "Yeah, she did," he added and felt as if things were more right in his world than they had been in months. He recalled the day he'd bought the boat three years ago. They had gone out in her together, anchored, and spent the night on the ocean. The moon was their nightlight; the sea's cadence, their music. Victoria willingly went into his arms and the two of them forgot the rest of the world — much like this morning.

Tony frowned. He couldn't remember a time in the last couple of years when Victoria had gone sailing with him. Once the new wore off she pursued her own interests. He sighed and wondered if the newness had worn off him, too. But maybe not. Maybe her response was an indicator of things to come. And while they still had some problems to work on at least they were acting like married people again.

Tony allowed his lazy gaze to meander

around the cabin of the 22-foot sloop he'd dubbed "The Recluse." Although she had age on most others, he kept her painted and polished. Like the fire truck he commanded, every piece of gear occupied a specific place and turned, slid, or rolled to their jobs like the parts of a well-oiled clock. In a few months she'd be paid off and all his.

"Now if I can just figure out if I have any coffee," he mumbled and tossed aside the sleeping bag. A blast of chilled air rippled along his arms and left behind a rash of goosebumps. He rubbed his hands together and reached for the tattered jacket lying on the other cot.

In a matter of seconds Tony had turned up the electric space heater, supported by the generator that also supplied electricity for the tiny stove in the corner. Accompanied by the generator's hum, he began rummaging through the overhead cupboard. By the time Tony got to the last shelf he'd thrown out a package of moldy bread, some stale crackers, and a tin of fruit that expired six months ago.

The sound of footsteps on the deck jolted Tony from his mission. In a flash he relived those heated seconds when that bullet grazed his arm. He touched the bandage on his right shoulder as his attention fell on the heavy wrench lying atop a roll of rope at the end of one cot. Tony bent, wrapped his fingers around the cold tool, and moved beside the steep steps. The trap door was locked, yet he couldn't be too careful.

The hatch vibrated with the force of a firm knock. Tony's every fiber tensed. He strained to see out a porthole for some clue of who might be on deck. He only glimpsed an aging yacht next to his sailboat and a snatch of gray sky. His breathing ragged, Tony prepared for the worst and hoped for the best.

"You in there, partner?" Eddy's voice accompanied another knock.

Tony relaxed his grip on the wrench and expelled a long breath. "I'm gonna kill him," he mumbled and shook his head. Tony dropped the wrench atop the sleeping bag, moved aft, and flipped the hatch's catch.

As he shoved the covering back, a blast of cold air bathed his chilled face and Eddy broke into a huge grin.

"Come on down." Tony rubbed his gritty eyes and reminded himself that his friend meant well. "I thought you said you were going to call. I wasn't expecting you in the flesh."

"Well, you know some days you just hit

the jackpot, and you get the real me," Eddy said as he began descending the ladder.

"That's a matter of opinion," Tony responded.

"Man, am I getting bigger or is this boat shrinking?" Eddy asked. "Every time I get in her, the hatch seems more narrow."

"The only thing about you that's getting bigger is your head." Tony strained at a chuckle.

"Touché!"

"No joke, this thing was built for people who like to be near each other. Some irony, huh! I would much rather have Victoria in here than you."

"So . . . things are better between you two?" Eddy's dark eyes, full of concern, penetrated Tony's mind.

"Yes, I guess you might say that," he drawled. His focus riveted upon the two white bags in Eddy's hand — bags that emitted a heavenly odor. Nothing beat Pug's grilled burgers with extra onions and mustard. Victoria, ever the nutritionist, called them grease burgers. Tony couldn't care less about the cholesterol level. They tasted great!

"We're dining in for lunch," Eddy announced and held up the bags.

"Let's get started then," Tony said. "I

haven't eaten a thing since the Snickers bar yesterday at four o'clock."

Eddy's black brows rose. "Sheesh. Did Victoria hold you prisoner and refuse to feed you or what?"

"No," Tony growled, and his stomach felt like a bottomless ravine. He snatched the bags. "Shut the hatch, will you?" After dropping onto one of the cots, he tore into the first bag and extracted two wrapped burgers. Tony tossed one onto the cot, unwrapped the other, and shoved it into his mouth. His tastebuds ached with the explosion of mustard and meat, lettuce and pickles.

The snap of the hatch accompanied his first swallow. Eddy's muffled exclamation accompanied his second bite. "Why don't you just inhale the thing?" he chided.

"I tol' you. I'm hungry," Tony said around a particularly juicy bit of onion.

Eddy opened the other bag sitting beside Tony, pulled out two large sodas, and extended one to his friend.

"Coke?" Tony muffled out.

"Yep."

"Good. All Victoria had was ginger ale."

"Hmmph. I'm surprised she didn't pour herbal tea down you."

"She tried." Tony rammed the hamburger back into his mouth and the two friends chuckled. Eddy settled onto the opposite cot, and Tony wasted no time downing every bite of his burger. He pulled two orders of fries from the bag and extended one to his friend.

Eddy eyed the offering and jerked on the neck of his Orlando Magic sweatshirt. "I'm afraid to take that. You might bite my hand off in the process."

"Oh, just take the fries will ya?" Tony shook his head. "How have I managed to survive 15 hours without you?"

"It's a modern miracle." Eddy accepted the fries and munched on a few. "Why don't you go ahead and eat the other burger," he said like a true sport and extended his hamburger to Tony. "I can order myself another one on the way outta here."

Tony swallowed a mouthful of salty fries, widened his eyes, and looked at his friend. "You must love me, man," he said and accepted the offering.

"Ah shut up and eat the hamburger before I cram it down your throat." Eddy took a long draw on his cola.

A slow creak came from the side of the boat, and Tony stopped in the middle of unwrapping hamburger number two. He and Eddy exchanged startled glances until the creak repeated itself at the precise moment the waves rocked the boat. Tony released his breath.

"I think it's just the boat pressing against the bumpers," Eddy said. He stood and peered through one of the portholes, and the limited sunshine highlighted the gray kinks in Eddy's short black hair. "I took special pains to make certain no one was following me," he added.

"I *hope* you did," Tony said. "If that assassin attacks with you here, I'm sure he'll get you, too."

"Thanks for the encouragement." Eddy settled back on the cot and resumed his eating.

Tony offered a reassuring smile to his friend, eyed the fresh hamburger, and then extended it. "Here," he said. "I think the fries will fill me up now. Really."

"You sure?" Eddy asked.

"Yeah." Tony's stomach rumbled, yet eating the hamburger suddenly seemed close to sacrilegious, especially after all Eddy was trying to do for him. His friend accepted the burger and tore into it with almost as much voracity as Tony.

"So, any news from your brother-in-law?" Tony asked and went back to munching the fries.

"Yes. As a matter of fact, that's part of the reason I came," Eddy said over a mouthful. "That, and to give you lunch."

"What's up then?" Tony asked and scooted to the edge of the cot.

"I talked to Brandon about an hour ago and laid out the whole story. He grilled me really good and I had to say 'I don't know' in a lot of places. I think in the end he was convinced something bad is coming down here in Santa Rosa County."

"So he *did* believe the part about the killer?"

"Yes, and he promised he would help. The thing that seemed to tip the scale in our favor was information he had received from the Field and Game people about an increased number of out-of-state boats in the bay. He's asking himself if there could be a connection with a money laundering ring."

Tony nodded as the boat lunged with the waves. A few of Tony's fries spilled onto the wooden floor, and he crammed his hand over the top of the carton. No sense in losing any more than he had to. "Did you set up a meeting?"

"Yep. At his office in Tallahassee, Monday, at three." Eddy paused before sinking his teeth into his burger. "Work for you?"

"I don't know. Let me check my calendar," Tony quipped.

Eddy snickered. Finally, he pronounced his judgment upon the approaching meeting. "I just hope you can stand him long enough to talk with him."

"Don't be so hard on the guy." Tony shook his head.

"We'll see what tune you're singing after you meet him." Eddy stopped chewing. His eyes widened, and he observed Tony as if he'd sprouted horns.

"What?" Tony took a long draw on his cola and relished the acidic fizz all the way to his stomach. *Ginger ale just doesn't cut it,* he thought.

"I almost forgot to tell you," Eddy garbled out over a bite of burger. He swallowed and continued, "Some woman called and left a message with Sal. She asked me to give you the note." He fished in the hip pocket of his jeans, pulled out a slip of paper, and handed it to Tony.

Distracted by his dangerous plight, he scanned the words. Sal had scribbled a phone number at the top with a message beneath. "Macy Sinclaire called. She would like to talk to you concerning a small silver object you gave to her daughter 18 years ago. She says she still has it and would like to meet you to discuss it." The words "silver" and "18 years ago" struck him between the eyes. Tony's attention riveted to the note. He reread the message to make sure he wasn't hallucinating. Curling his socked toes against the floor, he stopped himself from barking out an exclamation.

"You okay?" Eddy asked.

Tony looked up at his friend yet couldn't quite focus on him. His gaze roved back to the note. After the third read, he realized that he wasn't imagining a word. Somehow, some way, by some miracle, his baby girl's adoptive mother wanted contact. The probability of his assumption grew to mammoth proportions, and Tony's face chilled.

"You're going pale on me, man," Eddy said. "You okay?"

"Yeah, yeah, okay, I — I guess," Tony said in a daze and told himself grown men didn't cry over notes. Nevertheless, his eyes burned, and he kept them averted from Eddy. His friend had no way of knowing this slip of paper opened a wound that never healed. Tony's heart ached as it hadn't since the day he released his daughter. He ached to know her. He ached at the prospect of telling Victoria. If his daughter *did* enter his life, his wife would inevitably discover the truth.

Twenty-Two

Victoria pulled her Toyota around her home and scanned the drive that stopped where white sand started. She put the vehicle in park, turned off the engine, and scrutinized the vacated beach. No stalkers in sight. Victoria looked in her rearview mirror to check the space between her house and the neighbor's. Granted, the killer wasn't after her, but she could easily be bait to get Tony out in the open.

She grabbed the fast food bag that contained her salad, slipped from the car, double-checked the lock, and dashed up the back porch steps. Her hand trembled a moment as she slipped in the key. A quick shove on the knob and she slid through the door's opening. Her heel slammed it shut and she wasted no time securing the deadbolt. Four steps got her to the refinished striped chair in front of the TV where she fell in a heap.

This Friday's shoot was the toughest she'd ever encountered. Her worries about Tony spilled into her professional life. She even barked at Gaylord before the show this morning. Even though her apology quickly followed, the hurt lingered in his eyes as they signed off.

Victoria fumbled with her purse and pulled out her cell phone. She'd turned the ringer off during the shoot and forgot to turn it back on. With a glance she checked the message box to see if Jacquelyn had returned her call from the morning. No message indicator blinked.

"What does it take to get you to call back in the same day?" she grumbled and checked her watch. "A quarter of one," she whispered. "Tony's had time for a solid nap."

Even though Victoria had wanted to call him six times since she dropped him off at the marina she'd refrained. The minute he was secure in his boat he'd called. So she forced herself to think rationally and allow him some time to sleep. A yawn overtook her, and her early morning stress was demanding she take a nap. Yet Victoria squared her shoulders and refused.

Instead, she shrugged out of her fiery orange business jacket, gripped the cell phone, grabbed her salad, and marched into the kitchen. Her stomach reminded her she'd been too uptight for breakfast, and she wondered if the salad would be substantial enough. In the middle of rummaging through the refrigerator for the vinaigrette dressing, she pressed one of the cell phone's auto dial buttons. Tony picked up on the second ring.

"Hi," Victoria said, and the hours they'd just spent together rushed upon her. Certainly their morning had been a bit more exciting than she'd expected.

"Oh, hi," Tony said. "How are you?"

"*I'm* fine. The question is, how are you? And have you noticed anyone strange at the marina?"

"Uh, yes I have as a matter of fact," he quipped. "Some guy named Eddy Graham. He's stranger than strange."

Eddy's playful jeer jumbled with Tony's laughter.

Victoria nudged the refrigerator door shut and plopped the dressing next to the salad on the dining table. "So Eddy's with you? I'm relieved." Her shoulders relaxed. "At least you've got somebody there who can help if —"

"I'm okay, babe," he assured, "really."

"And your shoulder? How's it?"

"What shoulder?" he asked and Victoria broke into a slow smile.

"You are naughty," she teased.

"Hmmm . . . and you're nice. This

morning was great, by the way," he mumbled so softly she barely picked up the words.

Victoria figured Eddy hadn't heard. Nevertheless, her face grew warm, and she lowered herself into the wicker dining chair. Absently, she picked up the apple spice candle from the center of the glass-topped table, inhaled the homey fragrance, and closed her eyes. This morning had been more like a honeymoon flashback than anything else.

"Want to sneak back over tonight?" she asked and wouldn't have believed she'd been so bold if Tony hadn't answered.

"You bet." His voice, soft and sexy, sent shivers up her spine. "Why don't you come get me after dark?"

"Okay, that works. About nine then?"

"Nine it is," he confirmed. "Call me when you park at the marina. I'll be out in no time."

"Sure." Victoria set the candle down and ran her index finger across the top of the cool wax. She couldn't remember a time when she'd so anticipated seeing her husband. Something different was happening to their relationship — something she liked. Kim Lan's claim of setting a trap for Mick resurfaced in her mind. Perhaps the time had come to find out exactly what "setting a trap" meant.

"Is there anything I can bring?" he asked. "I've got a musty sleeping bag and an expired can of fruit."

Victoria giggled. "Sounds like I need to go shopping for you this afternoon. I'll try to pick up some groceries in a couple of hours. Is there anything particular you want?"

"No, just make sure you get coffee and some *real* Coke."

"Oh? No herbal tea?"

"Only if you'll drink out of my cup."

Victoria's fingernail ate into the wax. "Maybe we can just do that," she whispered.

Tony's poignant silence enveloped her, and Victoria felt as if she were being swept along by an unleashed force she hadn't encountered in ages.

A beep interrupted the call and Victoria muffled a frustrated growl. "I've got another call coming in," she said. "Let me see who it is."

"Okay," Tony agreed. "Look . . ." he added, "I . . . uh . . . need to return a call, too. So why don't we just plan to meet tonight. If anything comes up between now and then I'll call you."

"Okay," Victoria rushed as the phone

beeped once more.

After rushed farewells, she pressed the send button and encountered Jacquelyn's voice.

"What's the emergency?" she prompted without preamble.

"It's Tony." Victoria pressed the speaker button on her silver phone and laid it on the table, next to the salad.

"Why does that not surprise me?" Jac asked.

"Excuse me?" Victoria retrieved the salad from the white paper bag, placed it on the table, and snapped open the plastic top.

"I just checked my e-mail —"

"No way!" Victoria said as she shook the bottle of vinaigrette dressing.

"Don't give me any grief, Roberts," Jacquelyn chided. "I take enough off the other sisters without you taking shots at me, too."

"Oh, forgive me," Victoria mocked. "It's just that the last time I e-mailed you it took a month to get you to respond."

"Hey! I responded, didn't I? That's the main thing." Jac paused for a second. "Anyway, as I was saying before I was interrupted, I checked my e-mail and Melissa had posted on our sister loop. She said she called you last night and you said Tony was there and there was an emergency. She was asking if anyone had heard from you. I sent a response and told them you'd called me, and I was about to return the call."

Victoria's right brow arched. "I think Lawton must be really good for you. Not only have you returned my call but you even posted on the sister loop."

"Keep Lawton out of this," Jac shot back. "He's got his hands full like it is."

"Anybody married to you would have his hands full, Jac." Victoria laughed outright and poured a generous supply of dressing upon her salad.

"Well, aren't *we* in a good mood?" Jac questioned. "Care to share the details?"

"The details are that somebody shot at Tony on the beach yesterday evening."

"And you're glad about it?"

"No, no, no!" Victoria retrieved a plastic fork from the paper bag. "I'm not happy about that at all. That's the reason I called *you*."

"Needing legal advice?" Jac asked. "First, have you reported the incident to the police?"

"No," Victoria admitted and discreetly placed a small bite of the salad in her mouth. "Tony says the police are in on it," she said before chewing fast.

"What?"

She briefed Jac on all the details.

"Holy cow," Jacquelyn mumbled.

"And, well," Victoria continued and placed the fork on the table, "I was wondering if there was any way you might be free, you know, to fly out here and watch Tony for me and protect him. I'm scared to death."

"Well, off the top of my head I don't see a problem with that. I was planning . . . oh never mind. It should work. How long do you need me?"

"I have no idea," Victoria said. "And I'm willing to pay your going rate, Jac."

"I don't usually act as bodyguard, so I have no 'going' fees on that. Oops! Let's see right here. Yes, this price list says bodyguarding services are free the month of March. My only charge would be reimbursement for travel expenses."

Victoria picked up her fork and stabbed a generous clump of salad. "You're the greatest," she said.

"Looks like I can give you a week or so. I could even fly in tomorrow evening. Do you think that would work?"

"Really?" Victoria couldn't believe her good luck.

"Yep," Jacquelyn said. "Can I get back with you in about an hour or so to confirm? I need to talk with Lawton about this. You know, we always clear everything with each other."

"Okay," Victoria agreed and wondered what her marriage would have been like the last few years if she and Tony had cleared everything with each other. Instead, they had each made separate decisions concerning their separate interests. As a result they had begun living separate lives.

The realization struck her hard, and she paused with her fork midair. A clump of salad plopped back into the plastic dish as Victoria recognized that she hadn't cleared the decision to bring in Jac with Tony either. And it was a decision that directly concerned him.

But he wouldn't agree! Victoria argued. *I know he wouldn't!*

She shoved the doubts to the back of her mind as she and Jacquelyn chatted a bit. Before hanging up, Victoria posed a final request. "If you get the chance, please send an e-mail to the sisters and tell them that things are better between Tony and me but to pray for him. I'm not comfortable posting the details on the internet, but you know how to hint and make it sound serious."

"I'm the master of all serious hints," Jacquelyn claimed. "And I'll be glad to 'e' them for you. I'll call back in a few hours with a definite yes and the details of my flight."

"You're the greatest, Jac," Victoria repeated.

"You've already said that once. Stop it or I'm going to get a big head."

"Never," Victoria claimed. As they spoke their farewells, the tension drained from her. It would mean so much to know that wherever Tony was he would have a friend looking out for him. When Jacquelyn arrived she would explain that Tony didn't know Victoria had arranged a bodyguard. Jacquelyn would undoubtedly be willing to don a disguise to hide her identity.

Twenty-Three

By three o'clock Tony was on the verge of kindly asking Eddy to leave. The guy meant well, but the uneventful chess game was getting old and that note from Macy Sinclaire was getting hotter. As the sailboat gently rocked with the water's rhythm, he pressed the pocket of his floppy running shorts. The note crinkled under his touch. One side of Tony dared to hope his assumptions were correct — that the woman who called was indeed his daughter's adoptive mother. Yet a more rational side insisted this was an awkward time to bring his daughter into his life and the possibility of meeting her must be slim. Nevertheless, the message still burned in his mind.

Just about the time Tony was certain he would explode, Eddy stood up, stretched, and pulled on the neck of his sweatshirt. "I'm starting to sweat in this thing," he complained. "It felt good this morning but now it's getting a little warm."

He then cast a regretful glance toward his pal. "I hate to leave you, man, but I need to head on home. Barb and the kids will be home in about 30 minutes, and I'm sure she's got a honey-do list a mile long."

"Okay." Tony stood and nearly knocked the TV tray over. He steadied it, and the chess pieces toppled into a mixed heap.

"Are you sure you don't mind?"

"No — no, I don't mind — not in the least," Tony said and hoped he didn't sound *too* eager.

Eddy arched a brow, and his white teeth contrasted with his coffee-colored skin. "So . . . whazup?" he asked and crossed his arms. "All this time I thought I was doing you a favor — babysitting you — and now you act like —"

Tony socked his friend in the arm. "Babysitting!" he chided. "You were beating the socks off me in chess and enjoying every minute of it."

"Okay, okay." Eddy held up both hands. "I know when I'm not wanted. I guess I'll just take my burger bags and leave."

"Oh, for cryin' out loud, now you're climbing up miffed tree."

"No, I'm climbing up your ladder." Eddy retrieved the white bags from Tony's cot, wadded them in his broad hand, and reached to unlatch the hatch. Before ascending the steps, he looked Tony in the eyes. "Call me if anything weird happens. Understand?"

"Yep." Tony nodded and didn't even pretend to fool around on this point.

Eddy had taken only three steps when he looked down at his friend. "Should I get you another burger?" he asked.

The faint smell of onions still tinged the air, and Tony could indeed have gone for another burger. He started to accept but decided against it. Neither he nor Eddy were independently wealthy, and Eddy had a wife and two teenagers to support. Every dollar out of his pocket was probably a dollar he didn't need to spend.

"Nah," Tony said and shook his head. "I'll be okay. I've got some snacks in the cupboard. Besides, Victoria's coming —"

"Oooohhhhhh," Eddy said. "Now I know why you want me outta here."

"Oh, get a grip," Tony shot back. "She's not going to be here until after dark. I thought you heard us talking."

"No, I tuned you out. I'm too well-bred to eavesdrop."

"Yeah, right." Tony grabbed a wadded napkin and hurled it at his friend's nose.

Eddy ducked, caught the paper missile, and threw it back at Tony. "You stay put 'til she gets here. Understand?"

"I don't see that I have much choice," Tony said.

"Good. I'll keep my eyes peeled for anybody who matches the description of that man Norris says is after you."

"Right, and . . . call me as soon as you get home, will ya?" Tony asked. "I want to know you made it safely."

"No problem, man," Eddy said with a wink.

Seconds later the hatch snapped into place, and Tony secured the latch. He removed his cell phone from his waistband, pulled the note from his pocket, and deliberately punched in the Orlando number. A thin line of perspiration formed across his forehead. For over two hours he'd anticipated and dreaded this moment.

The phone started ringing, and with every peal his belly tensed a fraction more. While he debated what to say if he were required to leave a message, a warm feminine voice floated over the line with a greeting that reminded him of the ocean breeze on a summer's night.

"I'm calling for Macy Sinclaire," Tony said, forcing his tone to remain calm.

"This is she." The woman's voice held an expectant note.

"Hi. This is Tony Roberts." He dropped

to his cot, sat on the edge, and crumpled the note against his damp palm. "You left a message for me?"

"Yes . . ." She cleared her throat. "Are you the Tony Roberts who . . . placed a child for adoption 18 years ago?"

Tony closed his eyes and took a long, slow breath. "Yes."

"Mr. Roberts, I am the woman who adopted that child."

"I thought it was you." Tony propped his elbow on his knee and pressed his index finger upon the line between his brows.

"I'm sorry to have been so . . . sneaky . . . for lack of a better word," she said. "When I called the fire station I decided to leave a hint about who I was, rather than blurt out the whole story."

"I do appreciate your discretion, Mrs. Sin—"

"Call me Macy."

"Okay. And I'm Tony."

"Sure."

The boat's creaking coincided with a new fit of rocking. Certainly, that cool front had ushered in plenty of wind. "So, she still had my rattle with her when you got her?" he asked and marveled that something 18 years removed could seem so fresh in his memory.

"Oh, yes. That — and the note. I guess

she was taken straight from you to us."

"I guess so," Tony whispered and rubbed his index finger and thumb together as if he were caressing his daughter's velvet-soft hair.

"Evelyn found the note and rattle about two months ago," Macy explained.

"Evelyn?" Tony asked.

"Yes. We named her Evelyn Toni Sinclaire. A lot of her friends call her E.T."

"You kept my name?" Tony asked and chuckled at the nickname.

"Somehow, we couldn't get away from it," Macy explained.

"I'm glad."

A poignant silence engulfed him in bittersweet longing; his mind raced with questions. *Toni must be ready for college soon,* he thought. *Is this about a request for money?* Yet Macy's voice, sincere and confident, indicated no mercenary intent. *Perhaps there's some medical emergency and they need a donor!* Yet there was no urgency in her voice.

"Just so you know, when she was a baby Evelyn loved the rattle you left in her blanket. We kept it in a memory box along with your note, hoping to find the right time to give them to her as she grew up. Somehow the years drifted by and bringing everything back up scared her father and me." The woman's voice faltered for the first time. "Our daughter has known for years she was adopted, but I guess . . . we just thought that if she connected with the letter and rattle she'd somehow —"

"No need to explain. It's an awkward situation on all sides."

"Yes, well, as I mentioned earlier, we were doing some cleaning and sorting in the attic a few months back and Evelyn found both items."

An undeniable warmth oozed through Tony's veins. At long last his daughter had read his heart. "So, what was her reaction?" he dared ask.

"After a good cry, she was very peeved at us. She said we'd hidden the keepsakes from her, and they were rightfully hers." A sigh permeated the line. "And, well, we both said things we didn't mean. I guess the stress just overcame us. After a while we cried together and made up. But things have been strained ever since."

"I can imagine." Tony shook his head, stood, and paced the length of the short cabin. He paused beside one of the portholes and gazed onto the choppy sea bathed in sunshine that resembled crushed diamonds upon aqua carpet.

"Tony, I don't want to put you into an embarrassing situation," Macy continued. "I hope you aren't in any way irritated by my contacting you. Just so you know all the facts. I hired an investigator six weeks ago to find you because I knew the inevitable was about to happen — my daughter would want to meet the man who wrote that note. I've had your information for about a week-and-a-half now, but I haven't had the nerve to call before today."

"I understand," Tony affirmed. "But really, your contacting me doesn't bother me in the least. I've been hoping I'd meet my daughter someday."

"Good." Macy sighed. "I actually have your home number as well, but I called your work number so I wouldn't put you on the spot at home. According to our information, you've been married several years."

"Sheesh." Tony rubbed his forehead and shook his head. "I was easy to find, wasn't I?"

"I guess if you know how and where to look all our lives are essentially open books — especially given the internet."

Tony nodded and a vise of fear seemed to grip his neck. Undoubtedly, those who wanted him dead would soon discover everything they needed to know about him —

if they hadn't already. *Man, oh man,* he groaned to himself. *What a time for my birth daughter to be contacting me!*

"I — I guess we are all open books," he said instead and added, "I do appreciate your discretion. My wife — she doesn't know about the baby." *And what am I going to do when she finds out?* Tony thought and accepted that it was only a matter of time. "I guess it sounds funny to call Toni a baby," he added with a smile and marveled at how calm his voice sounded in light of the hurricane raging through him. "She's not a baby anymore." His agitated shrug irritated his sore shoulder. "My wife is a very religious person. I'm not sure she will understand."

"I see." She hesitated. "Our faith plays a big part in our lives, too," Macy said. "But please don't think I would ever use it as a platform to judge you." Her voice oozed with compassion, concern, and the verbal equivalent of what Tony remembered in Rhonda Norris's eyes. He had yet to see that elusive something in Victoria. Even though things were dramatically improving between them, Tony still wagered that his wife would be enraged when she learned of his indiscretion.

"I appreciate your attitude more than you

can ever know," he said, his voice thick. And Tony began pacing the length of the cabin like a caged lion ready to spring from prison.

"Anyway, the reason I called," Macy continued, "was to set up a meeting between us. My husband and I have agreed that we'd like at least one of us to meet you in person before we introduce you to Evelyn."

Tony stopped pacing. He stared at the half-open cupboard and allowed the implications to soak into his psyche. Apparently, it wasn't enough for the Sinclaires to know Tony was a hard-working citizen who lived a stable existence in Destin. These people wanted to check him out in person before allowing him into their daughter's life. The realization that initially irritated led to thanksgiving. Indeed, his little girl had been placed into the hands of great parents. Tony would probably have done the same thing if he were in their shoes.

"I don't think Evelyn is going to have peace until she meets you," Macy added.

Tony leaned against the refinished ladder and ran his fingertips along the rail. "What about her birth mother?" he questioned and wished the words didn't prick him with a melancholic pain. Once again, he wondered why Deloris O'Keefe's father hadn't kicked him off the planet.

"We have very little information on her at the present. But I'm sure one day . . ."

"Yes, I can only imagine." Tony nodded.

"Anyway, right now Evelyn needs to meet you. I guess it's because of the note —"

"And the rattle," Tony added. "The thing cost me a mint. It's sterling silver. Did you know?"

"Yes, we figured that out once it started tarnishing," Macy said with a wry twist of humor.

Tony laughed out loud.

"Anyway, I know this is all quite on the spur of the moment," Macy continued, "but I was wondering if you might have time in your schedule on Monday to meet with me. Perhaps lunch? I could even come to Destin."

Tony gripped the edged of the ladder, and a twinge of pain on his thumb witnessed a stray splinter. "Monday?" he croaked and imagined a calm meal at a local restaurant interrupted by gunfire. "Here?" His voice came out on a high note.

Awkward seconds ticked by, and he could only assume what Macy Sinclaire must be thinking. "I — I mean," he floundered. "Couldn't we meet in Pensacola instead?" Yet another important meeting loomed upon the edge of his mind — a meeting in Tallahassee with Eddy's brother-in-law. "Actually, I've already got a meeting that afternoon at three in Tallahassee," he explained.

"Oh, I see." Those three simple words held a lifetime of relief.

"Will you be driving in or flying?" Tony continued and hoped his no-nonsense tone covered his momentary panic.

"I had thought about taking a commuter flight."

A commuter flight, Tony mused. *That means she lives within driving distance.* Even though Macy Sinclaire probably knew everything about him but the size of his BVDs, Tony still knew nothing about her except that she loved his daughter. "Could we just meet at the airport then?" he rushed. "Say mid-morning? That would give me time to get to Tallahassee for my meeting."

"Of course," Macy agreed with no hint of caution. "I'll call you back with my flight number and the time of my arrival."

"Okay, good," Tony agreed. Victoria's promise to pick him up at nine echoed through his mind. Life was certainly getting complicated. "Do you think — would you mind calling me back before 8:30 this evening?" he asked and hoped he didn't sound too sneaky. The last thing Tony needed was for Macy Sinclaire to call him while he was with his wife.

"Better yet, you have my number here at home. Why don't you call me back?" she offered with a hint of a smile.

"Okay, thanks." Tony grinned. Not only did this woman love his daughter, she also possessed a wealth of insight.

"As soon as I get off the phone, I'll call and order my plane ticket. I should have my flight details within the hour."

After final adieus, Tony disconnected the call and stared at the cell phone until the keypad blurred. Some killer was after him. Kevin Norris suggested he leave the country. He was attempting to reconcile with a wife who had no idea of his past, at the same time his birth daughter might be entering his life. Tony sagged to the cot, stretched out, and propped his arm under his head.

"I don't know if I can make it through all this on my own," he whispered.

Certainly, his parents would be glad to talk with him. Now in their mid-sixties, they lived in Louisiana and would even offer their son a haven in which to stay. Yet Tony hated to drag them into danger, especially after dealing them the kind of grief he'd dished out during adolescence. When Evelyn was born, his girlfriend's parents were faced with a hefty insurance deductible; Tony's parents paid half. Once he matured into his adult years Tony had promised himself never to ask them for another thing. Somehow, he couldn't bring himself to break that vow.

Perhaps Jesus can help me. The thought penetrated his mind like a spear. Silently, Tony observed the low pine ceiling nicked by years of use. This morning when he'd been scared senseless, he'd asked Victoria about Jesus. That conversation had gone flat. Now Tony wondered why he hadn't requested help from Eddy. Over the years his friend had dropped enough broad hints about a relationship with Christ to sink an ocean liner. Tony had been around the church his whole life. And while he fully understood the process of accepting Christ as Savior, he didn't understand how to scrape together enough faith to actually believe Jesus was God.

The trip to Tallahassee loomed in his mind. He and Eddy would be together most of the day on Monday.

Maybe he will answer my questions then, Tony mused. *If I ever needed supernatural help, it's now.*

Twenty-Four

"This makes me really nervous," Victoria said. "I feel so devious."

"You'd be a basketcase if you worked with me," Jac responded with a chortle. "Sneaky is my business." She pulled the rental car into the last parking place, farthest from Pug's Marina and closest to a tangle of wiry brush. A clump of palm trees jutted into the parking lot and offered moderate protection from visibility while still allowing Victoria and Jac a clear view of the marina.

Jacquelyn lowered her window about three inches.

"Don't lower mine," Victoria said. "I'm just right and don't want to get chilled."

"I'm not hot now either, but it will probably get stuffy in here since we're both wearing jackets. We'll have a little ventilation anyway."

Across the bay to the west, the sun eased toward the horizon — a fiery orb sinking behind the bridge to Valparaiso. Seagulls squawked and circled the shore to the right, making their last try at a meal before dusk.

The sounds of waves lapping against the boats, the smell of Pug's greasy burgers, the fresh ocean breeze that trailed into the vehicle all quickened Victoria's senses. She tugged her hat low over her forehead and adjusted her sunglasses. The sunglasses, coupled with the approaching dusk, limited her visibility. She glanced at her friend whose bronze skin, full lips, and black hair made her appear particularly exotic beneath her own dark glasses and hat.

All Victoria could think was that Tony would not be happy if he knew she called in a bodyguard without his permission. Yesterday, Jac had arrived on the last flight from Denver. Since Tony spent all Friday night, all day Saturday, and Saturday night with Victoria, Jac had taken a taxi from the airport and booked a hotel room. Tony asked Victoria to drive him back to the boat this morning before sunup. She figured he needed a change of scenery more than anything else, and that gave her a chance to pick up Jac, attend Sunday morning services, and discuss a game plan with her friend. Now the night was quickly approaching, and Tony was expecting Victoria to pick him up by 9:00.

She gripped the door's armrest. The weekend, fraught with danger, clandestine meetings, and stolen kisses, had certainly been exhilarating. Nevertheless, the whole ordeal was growing more complicated by the day, and Victoria hoped Jac could do her job without being detected.

"I still can't believe you gave up your vacation for me," Victoria said. She reached across the Ford's gear shift to squeeze Jac's hand.

"Ah, it's nothing," she said and shrugged. "I was just going to hang out at the house anyway. As things turned out Lawton wound up having to go out of town most of next week too, so it worked out okay."

"Yes, but if I'd known when I asked you —"

"Don't worry about it." She turned a white-toothed smile toward her friend. "Truth is, Lawton and my secretary were the ones who made me take the time off. They say I work too hard."

"Hmm, wonder why?" Victoria asked.

"My thoughts exactly," Jac said with a no-nonsense nod. "I like my work. It's a part of who I am. If you want the truth, I was on the verge of going nuts just thinking about sitting home all next week. I was seriously thinking about going to the office anyway once Lawton left town."

"Sneaky, sneaky." Victoria stifled a smile.

She enjoyed nothing more than staying home and making a nest. Certainly, she and Jac had precious little in common — except that they'd been friends for ages and they *did* love each other.

"Now, let's get down to business." Jacquelyn's lips hardened around the edges and she observed the marina. "You said Tony's friend Eddy thinks he saw someone around the marina who might fit the description of that guy Tony attacked on the hospital fire escape."

"Y–yes." Victoria nodded and rubbed her hand down the length of her denim skirt. "The only difference is the man at the marina has a full beard."

"Means nothing. Beards can be bought," Jacquelyn said.

"But you know Eddy has never seen him. He's just going by Tony's description of the man."

"Right." Jac nodded. "And Eddy's supposed to be here now?"

"Yep. Tony said Eddy's just hanging out around the marina, in case that guy shows back up."

"Exactly what is our dear Eddy going to do if this man *does* show up?"

"You're asking me?" Victoria squeaked.

Jacquelyn rummaged through a small

leather backpack and pulled out a miniature digital camera.

"I've never seen such a small digital camera," Victoria said as the rental car's new smell blended with the aroma of sea and salt.

"Actually, it's not a camera. It's an infrared laser beamer disguised as a digital camera. When I push this button," she pointed to a tiny orange nob, "it will blow up the whole marina."

"Yeah, right, and I guess next you're going to tell me this car has machine guns behind the headlights and you're really 007 disguised as a woman."

Jacquelyn shook her head. "You're cold, Victoria," she teased.

The friends fell into companionable laughter and Victoria scanned the marina that docked about 50 boats. Most of the vessels received scant attention by their owners and the rate of traffic was marginal. Tony's 22-foot sloop, with *The Recluse* painted in dark blue on the stern, stood out among the rest. Indeed, Tony's extraordinary maintenance ensured that the vessel glimmered in the evening sun, even though it was docked in the distance.

"You might know his boat would be the one to stand out," Victoria complained.

"The Recluse, right?" Jac prompted.

"Yes. In living color."

Victoria picked up the binoculars that lay in the top of Jacquelyn's opened backpack.

"Watch out," Jac admonished. "If you turn the lenses those produce poisonous smoke that will kill you in three seconds."

"Oh, would you stop it!" Victoria shook her head. Yet the sight of Eddy banished her friend's banter. "There's Eddy," Victoria said and passed the binoculars to Jac. She removed her dark glasses and held the lenses to her eyes. "He's the black guy who just stepped out of Pug's place and is meandering along the dock," Victoria explained.

"Okay. I've got him." Jacquelyn acknowledged. "And you're *sure* you can trust him?"

"Who, Eddy?" Victoria arched her brows. "I'd trust him with my life. The man's as good as gold."

"Okay, if you say so."

"Why? You don't?"

"I didn't say I don't. I just don't know him. I'm a private eye — remember? After years of watching trusted people turn bad you get jaded."

"Well, you don't have to worry about Eddy," Victoria assured. "He and Tony are partners. They pull each other out of fires all the time. They've each saved the other's life. They've got some sort of male-bonding thing going —"

"Kinda like the seven sisters?"

"Exactly. Except there's just two of them."

"All right. You've convinced me." Jac lowered the binoculars and replaced her shades. "He's now officially strolling back into Pug's."

Victoria slumped into her seat and pulled her hat low while Jac burst into a round of constrained laughter. "You slay me," she said.

"What?" Victoria demanded.

"Keep hunkering down like that and pulling on your hat and everybody within a mile will be sure you're up to something."

"Well, what do you want me to do?" Victoria asked. "Get on top of the car and tap dance?"

"Try telling me what you think about that guy right there?" Jackie's voice had gone low and hard.

A chill raced up Victoria's spine. She riveted her attention back to Pug's, where a stocky, dark-haired man got out of a parked sedan the color of obsidian. His position obscured his face but his black overcoat made him look like an undertaker. Victoria shivered and tugged her denim jacket tighter around her torso. Her extremities flashed cold, yet her upper lip broke out in perspiration. A dark golfer's cap slid low over the man's forehead. As he turned toward Pug's, Victoria glimpsed a cigar butt protruding from stern lips surrounded by a heavy beard. He walked like he might step on anyone who got in his way, and she wondered if he packed a weapon beneath the overcoat.

"I got him," Jac said.

Victoria didn't realize Jac was snapping digital photos until she glanced back at her friend.

"You think he's the one?" Victoria asked and wadded her skirt in her dampening palm.

"He fits Tony's description. That's all I know, and . . ." Jac looked at her friend but a second and diverted her gaze.

"And?" Victoria prompted. "Don't keep stuff from me, Jackie."

The detective fished in the oversized pocket of her leather bomber jacket and pulled out a note pad. She extended the pad to Victoria. "See if you can read his license plate number."

"That's *not* what you were going to say and you know it." Victoria took the paper, tugged the shades down her nose, and strained to see the license plate. After about 30 seconds she gave up and tossed the pad back to her friend who was scrutinizing the car through the binoculars. Without another word Jac jotted down a series of numbers and nodded her satisfaction.

"Now tell me what else you know," Victoria demanded.

"My, my, my, aren't we feisty," Jac cooed. She laid her shades in the console and her inky eyes observed Victoria as if she were debating whether to tell all or keep her peace.

"This is my husband we're talking about," Victoria urged, and her voice caught.

"The guy looks like a poster boy, that's all," Jacquelyn admitted.

"A poster boy?"

"Yeah. You know — one of those guys who have 'wanted' plastered on their picture."

"Oh no," Victoria groaned and images of Tony's funeral bombarded her mind. "I don't know if I can take much more of this." Her stomach knotted.

"That's why I was holding back," Jac said and shook her head. "I should've kept my mouth shut."

Victoria ran her fingers under her glasses and pressed her damp eyes.

"Look." Jac squeezed her arm. "I can e-mail these photos to a friend — Len Scroggins — tonight. He's at the Colorado State Police Headquarters. In 24 hours he can probably give us a complete rundown on this guy — whether he's good, bad, or ugly. Len has access to data on every big-time fugitive — especially hit men."

"H–hit men?" Victoria wailed. "This is starting to sound like the mafia!"

"Maybe it is." Jac's words held the chill of an iceberg.

"What — what are we going to *dooooo?*" Victoria cried. "Oh, Jesus, help us!" she wailed through trembling lips.

"Stop it!" Jacquelyn clamped a hand hard over Victoria's mouth.

Her teeth ground into her lips and she swallowed against the anxiety surging up her throat.

"I'm going to release your mouth now," Jac breathed. "Don't make a peep, understand?"

Victoria gazed into her friend's steely eyes and helplessly nodded. Jac released her hold on Victoria, clicked the ignition switch, and pressed a switch inside the door. The window slid up and Jac turned the ignition switch back.

"Oh, I'm so sorry," Victoria wept and tore the glasses from her face. "I forgot you rolled down your window."

"If you're going to be with me, you've *got* to stay calm," Jac instructed. "It's a matter of life and death. Do you understand?"

"Y–yes." Victoria nodded and covered her face. "I'm just not used to this. I'm not tough like you."

Jacquelyn sighed. "I'm sorry. I didn't mean to get harsh on you, but you can't go hysterical on me."

"Okay," Victoria agreed and wanted to crawl under the floor mat. *I have no business spying on anyone,* she thought, *let alone my own husband.*

A classic tune reverberated from the folds of Victoria's purse. She looked at Jac, who gave her a nod. Victoria snatched the phone up and observed the tiny screen that announced Tony was the caller.

"Oh no! It's Tony!" Victoria gasped. "What am I going to tell him?"

"Why not tell him the truth?" Jac's dry words only added rancor to Victoria's agitation.

"Because he'll go nuts if he knows I called you in without his knowing it."

Jac expelled a long sigh. "You guys have problems, Victoria."

"I know — I know," she admitted and wasn't going to fool herself that their exhilarating weekend had taken care of all marital obstacles. She punched a button and took the call.

"Hey, babe," Tony said. "Still planning for me to come over tonight?"

"Of course," Victoria said in the most natural tones she could muster. The hint of danger coupled with their rekindled love life had turned the weekend into nothing short of an explosion. Nevertheless, her duplicity weighed heavily upon her conscience and curbed her anticipation of the evening.

"Well, you know I've got that meeting with Eddy's brother-in-law tomorrow?" he hedged.

"Y–yes?" Victoria answered as the dark stranger exited Pug's place. She turned a startled gaze to Jac whose silent intensity bade her remain calm.

"We were thinking we'd leave really early in the morning — before daylight — and stop at Eddy's mom's in Pensacola. We'll hang out there for a while then head on to Tallahassee in time for the meeting. So . . ."

"Oh, you mean — you're saying you'll just stay at the boat tonight?" she asked. The man in the dark coat stood near the ebony sedan, peered around the parking lot, and slid into the driver's seat.

"Yes. Would you be okay with that?"

"Oh — oh . . . of course," she stammered and tried not to sound relieved. Victoria never had been good at deception, and she feared if Tony saw her he'd perceive she was up to something underhanded.

"Well, that's fine then. I'll just plan to stay here. Eddy's going to stay, too, I think."

As if the mention of his name produced him, Eddy Graham stepped out of Pug's cafe and leaned against the building. While his posture indicated repose, his tense face revealed dread. He gazed after the departing sedan, pulled his cell phone from his belt, and pressed a number.

"Wait a minute, Victoria," Tony said. "Somebody's beeping in on me."

It's Eddy! she started to blurt but stopped herself. "Okay, I'll hold," she said instead. Victoria covered the phone's mouthpiece and looked at Jac. "Eddy's calling Tony now. He's going to tell him he saw the bad guy again." Victoria felt as if she were going to explode with the pressure of the situation. She pressed her loafers against the sloping floorboard and curled her toes.

Jacquelyn nodded. "Of course," she said

as if she were watching the rerun of some old movie.

The sun was taking its final peek over the horizon. The seagulls, tired of the hunt, had scattered. Even the wind seemed to be diminishing. Victoria felt as if she were witnessing the calm before a murderous hurricane.

What on earth are we going to do? she wailed inside and wished she and Tony could run. *Maybe running is the only answer. Maybe Kevin Norris was right!* Suddenly, the fact that his money wasn't clean seemed less important than getting out alive. Yet Victoria had no way of contacting the man.

She watched Eddy until he lowered his cell. She then placed her phone back to her ear and waited on her husband's inevitable urgency.

"Victoria, it's me again," Tony snapped. "Eddy's here at the marina. He's my watchdog."

"Yes, that's what you told me," she responded and felt that her placid tones were nothing short of fraudulent.

"Well, he just saw that guy again."

"No way!" Victoria exclaimed and guilt upon guilt dripped into her soul.

"I'm freaking out here!" Tony barked.

"They've tracked me here. They know I've got a boat here."

"How do you know —"

"Because Eddy saw him talking to Pug! You know Pug, Victoria. The man talks to everybody all the time. Eddy asked Pug. He said the old man told that person that I have a boat here."

"Oh no, Tony." Victoria gasped for every breath as her distress multiplied tenfold. "I don't know what to do!" Her voice rose with each word, and Jacquelyn squeezed her upper arm. The glare she cut Victoria reminded her of the scowl her mother had used in church when she was eight.

"I've got to get out of here!" Tony said as Eddy nonchalantly strode around the edge of the parking lot as if he didn't have a care.

"Wh–where are you going?"

"Eddy's going to hang out at the marina until dark and make sure the coast is clear. Then he wants to go ahead and drive me to his parents' home."

Yes, I see him, Victoria thought but held her tongue. "That sounds like the best plan. Will you call me when you get to Pensacola?"

"Yeah — I'll call," he said and hesitated. "And, baby?"

"Yes?" she whispered.

"If I don't see you again, I — I know I haven't done everything in our marriage just right. I *know* that, and I want you to know I love you. No matter what — I love you."

"Oh, Tony," Victoria wept and choked over a cough. "I love you, too. And — and —" His humble admission urged her to tell him about Jac's presence. After all, his knowing that she was watching might bring him peace. Yet admitting that Jac was here and they were both watching would reveal the lie she had lived rather than spoken. Victoria gripped the strap of her leather purse and teetered on the precipice of truth and deception. At last she decided to keep Jac's presence a secret. "And we're just going to have to trust that you'll get out of this okay," she finally said.

"Pray for me, honey," he pleaded.

"I — I will," Victoria agreed, and she couldn't remember a time when Tony had requested prayer for himself. "I will. And I'll call you every hour or so, just to make sure you're okay."

"Good. Do that."

After fervent farewells, Victoria disconnected the call and looked at her friend. She reported everything Tony said, ending with, "He and Eddy are leaving at dark to go to Eddy's parents' house in Pensacola. You know he has a meeting at the attorney general's office tomorrow."

"Yes, you said Eddy's brother-in-law is a lawyer there?"

"Right."

"Good. They're taking the right steps."

"But what if he doesn't get there?" Victoria squeaked.

"He will." Jac squinted as if she were certain.

"But that man —"

"That man is playing with him," the detective said. "I suspected, but this whole thing with Pug makes me certain."

"What do you mean 'playing with him'?" Victoria crammed her cell phone back into her purse, closed the flap, and toyed with the zipper.

"I mean," Jac peered straight into her friend's eyes, "he's playing cat and mouse."

Victoria gaped at Jacquelyn while the implications sank into her turbulent mind. Gradually, a foglike chill crept across her soul like a mist invading a cemetery. "You mean, he's t–trying to — to somehow terrify Tony and that's part of —"

"You catch on fast," Jac said. "I've seen it over and over. My estimation is that the man's a killer. But just taking down his prey isn't thrilling enough. He's probably in this for the power . . . and the sport."

"It's like he sees Tony as — as — like an animal?"

"Exactly."

Victoria's stomach threatened to unload its contents.

"That's the only explanation that makes sense," Jac continued. "Otherwise, Tony would be dead because poster boys don't miss when they shoot at people. They aim to kill. If he only grazed Tony then it was on purpose. And there's no reason for him to come prowling around this marina, asking about Tony unless he wants Tony to *know* he's found him. If he wanted to kill Tony right away, he'd just wait until dark, break into his boat, and shoot him."

Victoria covered her ears. "Stop it, stop it, stop it!" she begged. "I can't take this. It's like my worst nightmare come true."

With a sigh Jac propped her head on the seat's rest and closed her eyes. "This could get really nasty," she said.

And despite Victoria's wish not to hear the words they filtered into her spirit and heaped terror upon terror. A cloak of perspiration covered her body, and she longed for some reprieve.

"I think we'd better mosey along," Jac finally said. "Eddy's still on the prowl." She nodded toward him as he stepped back into the marina. "He'll be back out here in a few minutes — mark my word. At some point he's going to realize we're sitting over here and try to figure out what we're up to."

"Maybe I should just tell Tony —"

"Maybe so."

"But then he'll know that I —" Victoria stopped herself short of saying "lied to him" because technically she didn't *tell* a lie.

Jackie cranked the engine. "Suit yourself," she said. "But chances are high he's going to figure it all out at some point."

Twenty-Five

Buster Shae drove along the beach back to Destin and stroked the artificial beard. He hated wearing the thing because it always itched, but his professional satisfaction far outweighed the irritation. If his instincts weren't failing him, by now his victim was probably terrified.

Shae licked his lips and relished the hunt. The scent of the kill was wafting upon the winds of predatorial desire, bidding him to orchestrate the final blow — but tracking the prey was proving far too fulfilling. By now Tony Roberts was aware that Shae knew who he was and where he was. Buster's heart leaped. His festive spirit deserved celebration. Buster pressed a button on his CD player, and Bach flowed through the Oldsmobile's dark interior.

"The flight is next," Shae mused. His hooked fingers flexed upon the leather-bound steering wheel as he maneuvered a turn in the highway that stretched toward town. Without doubt Tony Roberts, like his numerous other victims, would soon arrange to run. Shae would trail him, as always. And just the time Tony thought he was free, Buster would move in for the kill.

One aggravation hung on the edge of his victory. According to that idiot Darnell Hopkins, no report had been filed after Buster shot at Tony on the beach. In the past his victims had immediately called the police. That always heightened Buster's satisfaction because it guaranteed his victims were in a state of panic. Tony's not notifying the authorities made Buster wonder at the cause.

He slowed as he passed the stretch of hotels that testified to Destin's popularity as a tourist retreat. Buster pinched his bottom lip, and a new insight barged into his mind.

"What if he knows the police are involved?" He frowned. "If he knows that, how did he find out?"

One name penetrated his bloodthirsty mind, *Kevin Norris.* He mulled the possibility over in his mind, examining it like an unusual shell he'd found on the beach. The longer he pondered the concept, the more it gained credence. The more it gained credence, the more angry he grew. By the time Buster pulled into the parking lot of the Seaside Inn he was ranting under his breath. If he found out Kevin Norris was botching any

333

of his plans he would hunt him down — wherever he was — and make him wish he'd died at birth.

Shae stepped from the Oldsmobile and slammed the door. He pulled his room key from his slacks' pocket and eyed the setting sun. He didn't have long before Tony Roberts tucked his tail and left town. Buster gave him until the ocean looked like ink against a blue-black horizon — just enough time for Shae to grab a shower, a bite to eat, and drive back to the marina.

Before heading into the lobby, Buster took a detour toward a taupe Taurus parked on the lot's east edge. He dug through his pocket for the set of keys the car rental clerk had provided. After double-checking the gas level, Buster was satisfied that he could drive all night if Tony so chose.

Marilyn Langham sat across from her husband at their oak dining room table. They each held a mug of hot cocoa with whipped cream on top. Neither had touched the favorite treat. Instead, they silently pondered their situation. This Sunday had started as any other: Josh rising early to prepare his sermon, Marilyn plopping a roast in the oven before dressing for church, Brooke struggling to find her shoes. Yet Marilyn and Josh also had to work together to help another little girl get dressed — Abigail, who had cried through the whole process.

After hours of talking through the difficulties, Marilyn had accepted the fact that Camille was gone for good and that Abigail would legally be theirs as soon as the paperwork was finalized. But then a knock on their front door halfway through lunch had changed everything.

Marilyn picked up her spoon, dipped the end in the whipped cream, and touched it to her tongue. The sweetness that invaded her tastebuds sent an ache through her glands. To appease her appetite, she cradled her mug, sipped the rich liquid, and looked over the top of her cup at Josh.

The dark circles under his eyes witnessed the late hour. Indeed, Brooke had long since fallen asleep. Joshua rubbed the base of his neck where his brown hair nearly touched his collar. Marilyn figured his exhaustion matched her own.

"Are you disappointed?" she asked and tugged on the end of a blond curl.

"A little," he said and reached for her hand. "And you?"

Marilyn placed her hand in his. "Not

really sure. I guess I'm more numb than anything else."

"Me, too."

"And the house sure was quiet after dinner," she added, observing the cheery sunflower border that seemed the antithesis of her spirits.

"No joke." Josh's melancholy gaze roved the kitchen. "I just hope Camille stays with the Stevensons and doesn't run off in the middle of the night or anything."

"I think she will." Marilyn shook her head and indulged in another swallow of hot cocoa. "She was pretty firm about making a change in her life, I think."

"I hope so — for Abigail's sake."

"Well, if it works, Abigail's better off with Camille anyway, Josh."

He expelled a long breath and shifted in his chair. "I know — I know. I guess that, despite the fact that she was giving us fits, I got sort of attached to the little gal."

"Me, too." Marilyn ran her finger across the inside of Joshua's palm, callused from his recent construction project — Brooke's playhouse. "But really, I never was at peace about Camille leaving her with us."

"Honest?" Joshua quirked his brows.

"Scout's honor." Marilyn lifted her hand. She shifted back in her chair and slipped off the flats she'd worn to church that night.

Joshua rubbed a hand across the front of his checked shirt and shook his head. "But I was so certain God was calling us —"

"Maybe God is calling us more to a process." As the words meandered forth Marilyn's heart warmed with the possibility. The day had been nothing but one stress after the other. First, Camille's surprise reappearance during lunch. Next, her willingness to stay with a church couple whose home was as big as their hearts. And then Josh and Marilyn's taking Camille and Abigail to the Stevensons. During all that turmoil Marilyn had simply tried to survive. Only now was some of the ordeal starting to make sense.

After a thoughtful reprieve, Joshua spoke, "What do you mean 'a process'?"

"I mean . . ." She leaned forward, pushed up the sleeves of her cotton sweater, and placed her elbows on the table. "Didn't you tell me when you were in L.A. that you wished you could help more of those street people?"

"Especially the mothers with children. They ripped my heart out."

"Well?" Marilyn queried. She widened her eyes and her head bobbed up and down.

His brow wrinkled as his index finger

tapped against the table.

"Don't you get it?" Marilyn asked. As the vision expanded in her mind so her excitement grew.

"Uh . . ." Joshua's eyes shifted. "I'm really tired, Mar," he admitted. "It's been a long, long day. I've preached twice, lost a daughter, and eaten too much supper." The smell of reheated roast underscored his claim.

"What would happen if we repeated the process?" she blurted without reserve. "Mick O'Donnel has the connections to street missions all over the U.S. What if we started a program for mothers and children where they could come here — to homes in our church and our community — and maybe they could have a chance to start over."

Joshua propped an elbow on the table and leaned forward. With a tired smile he reached for his wife's hand. "You know, Mar, I love you," he said, his heart in his eyes. "You never fail to catch my vision — and sometimes your visions are even better than my own."

"So you think it's a good idea?" she exclaimed.

"I think it's brilliant!" He doubled his fist and shook it. The haggard lines around his eyes crinkled with the prospect of hope. "I think it would work! We need to pray about it, of course," he added. "But —"

"Oh, of course," Marilyn agreed. "But still, it won't hurt to talk to Mick. He and Kim Lan already do so much for the under-privileged around the world, this probably would just be an extension of their ministry."

Joshua's eyes sparkled with the prospect, and a radiance began to cloak his features. "Once our congregation catches the vision, maybe it will spread to other churches."

"And maybe even to some other cities."

"Let's call Mick and Kim Lan tomorrow and see what they think!" he said and lowered his fist to the table. His mug shook with the vibration, and hot cocoa splattered to the table.

Marilyn snagged a paper napkin from the holder at the table's center and mopped at the liquid.

"Here, let me do that," Joshua said.

She released the napkin and gave her husband's hand a warm squeeze. "And maybe . . ." Marilyn hesitated and debated whether to mention the subject that she'd harbored in her heart for a year now. "Maybe there's something else for us to pray about as well."

Joshua's unwavering focus prompted her to share her other vision.

"Maybe we — we could actually have our own baby," she said with a whimsical smile. "I'm not saying I don't want to adopt. I think adoption is *wonderful!* And I'd still like for us to adopt, even if we have a child of our own. But still, I was hoping maybe one day we could . . ."

Joshua cocked one eyebrow. "You're saying you want to have *my* baby?"

"Well, yes," Marilyn admitted. "I — I love you like I've never loved before. And, well, I think it would be a wonderful expression of our love."

He lifted her fingers to his lips.

"I will pledge to do *my* part," Joshua promised with a wink and the fire in his eyes burned away any remaining stress.

"I guess you will," she taunted.

"Come here." Josh tugged on her hand and Marilyn stood. She rounded the table, settled in his lap, and reveled in the passionate kiss that threatened to overtake them.

The phone's persistent ring interrupted the tryst and Joshua growled. "If I weren't a pastor, I'd let the thing just ring," he mumbled as Marilyn slid from his lap.

"Let me get it," she said. "If it's not

urgent I'll have them call back in the morning."

"You talked me into it." Joshua stood, nuzzled her neck, and followed his wife toward the telephone.

As they trod across the braided rug, he wrapped an arm around her. When they arrived at the oak end table on which the phone sat, Joshua trailed a row of fiery kisses along her temple. Marilyn closed her eyes, leaned into his embrace, and reminded herself she needed to answer the phone. Yet when Marilyn picked up the receiver, the person on the other end was not a church member. It was Jacquelyn Franklin.

"Jac!" Marilyn exclaimed. "I wasn't expecting you. What's up?"

"Listen," Jacquelyn's voice, low and urgent, floated over the line. "Can you call all the sisters for me? Victoria's husband has stumbled into something big and deadly. We've *got* to pray."

"Uh . . ." Marilyn groped to piece together Jac's urgent mission.

"I'm hiding in the guest bathroom at their house so I can use my cell phone without Victoria knowing it. I'm trying to stay as calm as I can in front of her, but Tony's days are numbered if something doesn't change. Victoria's in the kitchen now. I'm not so sure she doesn't need a sedative or something. She's beside herself."

Marilyn stood erect and shared a concerned glance with Josh. "I read your post and Mel's post on our sister loop about an emergency. What's going on?"

As Jacquelyn supplied each detail of the blood-curdling drama, Marilyn eventually sank to the edge of the homey sofa. The whole thing reminded her too much of those dark days before she and Joshua were engaged. The days when she lived across the street as a single mother. The days when Clark McClure hunted Josh down and tried to kill him. Joshua still bore the bullet scar near his shoulder where Clark had shot him. And Marilyn still bore the images of that brave moment when she helped capture Clark.

"Victoria called me in as a bodyguard for Tony," Jac explained.

"So Tony's there with you guys now?"

Joshua sat down next to Marilyn and placed a hand on her knee.

"No, he doesn't even know I'm here," Jacquelyn said. "Victoria didn't ask his input on that decision because she was afraid he wouldn't want me around."

"Oh," Marilyn said on a blank note and recalled the day of the miscarriage when Victoria had told Marilyn not to notify Tony.

"I think they both have problems in this marriage, but I didn't say that," Jacquelyn said.

"Actually, Sammie hinted the same thing, and I figured it out while I was there as well."

"Yeah, well, I'm just glad Lawton and I started on a good foot, and we've stayed there. I'm picking up vibes that there's a lot of unresolved stuff under the surface between these two. It makes me tired just to think about it."

Marilyn glanced at her adoring husband. "I'm with you on that one," she said and twined her fingers in Joshua's.

"Fortunately, Tony has a close friend — Eddy Graham — who's also helping to watch his backside. Eddy's taking Tony to his parents' house in Pensacola tonight. They're leaving at 9:30."

Marilyn glanced at her Timex to see 9:00 swiftly approaching.

"I'm going to be following them tonight and tomorrow."

"What will you do if you see that — that hit man?" Marilyn asked.

"If he goes for Tony, I'll have to take him down," Jac said with stony resolve. *Pray!* Jac insisted. "And call all the sisters and have them pray as well."

Twenty-Six

The next morning Tony stepped into Pensacola Regional Airport with Eddy on his heels. They passed through the glass entryway and merged into the baggage claim area where Macy Sinclaire promised to meet them. Tony checked his watch and validated that Macy's flight should have landed 15 minutes ago. Traffic had been halted by a wreck, and Tony had never been so frustrated in his whole life. The hum and bustle of airport life engulfed them as they walked around knots of people awaiting luggage and others welcoming friends and family. Tony dashed a glance across the milling crowd and hoped he didn't spot a redheaded woman wearing a dark teal jacket. He would hate to keep Macy waiting.

"See her?" Tony asked.

"Nope." Eddy shook his head. "There's a redhead, but the jacket's brown."

"Good. She probably hasn't had time to get here."

"That's what I told you," Eddy said and gripped his friend's left shoulder. "Just calm down."

"Would you be calm if you were me?"

The two friends exchanged a contemplative gaze, and Tony recalled Eddy's astonishment last night when he sketched in the details of this meeting.

"No way." Eddy rubbed his freshly shaven jaw and ran a hand down the front of his striped sports shirt.

A smile pressed upon Tony's stiff face. "Enough said."

The smells of pretzels and burgers promised the presence of a food court upstairs, and Tony paused at the base of the escalators.

"Okay, okay, okay," he mumbled and drummed the escalator's moving hand rest. "Here we are. Am I nervous or what?"

Eddy crossed his arms, leaned back on his heels, and observed the crowd behind them.

"Notice anybody familiar?" Tony asked for the eighth time since they'd left Eddy's parents.

"Nope." Eddy shook his head. "Maybe we shook him this time."

"I hope." Tony squirmed in his sports coat and tugged at the neck of his freshly starched shirt. He'd asked Victoria to pack him a few nice things, and he'd thrown in his toiletry items at the fire station. He hoped his absence of a tie didn't offend

Macy. He wasn't exactly versed in the dress code for such meetings.

He scanned the sea of people coming down the escalator. Finally, Tony caught a glimpse of a teal jacket as a woman boarded the top step. Two men blocked Tony's complete view.

"Teal. I see teal," Eddy mumbled.

"Me, too. But she also mentioned wearing a cameo on the lapel."

Tony cast a fervid glance over his shoulder. The last thing he needed was for that fiend to take a shot at him while he was meeting Macy.

Eddy likewise scrutinized the crowd. "Somehow, I really think we've lost him this time. At least for a while anyway," he said as if he read Tony's thoughts.

After darting another glance around the airport, Tony focused upon the woman descending the escalator. At last, the angle was to his advantage and he spotted red hair and the telltale cameo. "She's the one," he said.

"Yep," Eddy affirmed. "Not bad either. Glad your wife isn't watching this."

"Oh, give me a break," Tony said. "She's older than I am."

"All I said was I'm glad Victoria isn't here," Eddy said. "She'd probably be asking questions. That's all I'm saying." He raised both hands palms outward.

"No comment," Tony shot back. "I'm too nervous to even think in that mode. I promise, if this was Cindy Crawford, it wouldn't matter."

"Now I *know* you're nervous," Eddy chided.

As she neared, the woman lifted her chin and riveted her attention upon the crowd beneath. Last night when they confirmed the time Tony had told her to watch for a navy sports coat and blond hair. Macy's gaze flitted to Tony, moved on, and dashed back.

He managed to smile, despite his wobbly knees. She smiled back and wiggled her fingers at him. Within five seconds she stood in front of him with an outstretched hand.

"Navy blazer, blond hair," she observed. "You must be Tony."

"Red hair, teal jacket, antique cameo," Tony answered. "You must be Macy."

They both laughed, and Tony relaxed as her soft hand embraced his for a brief handshake. He peered into eyes as blue as the Destin ocean and as welcoming as a warm hearth. In a flash, he recognized the same elusive something in Macy's eyes that he'd seen in Rhonda Norris's. And if he were really honest, he'd seen it in Eddy's eyes — except when the guy talked about his brother-in-law.

Tony motioned to Eddy. "This is my best friend, Eddy Graham. I hope you don't mind his being here."

"I'm just along for the ride, Mrs. Sinclaire," Eddy said. "I'm going to get a Coke here in a minute and make myself scarce."

"Oh, I don't mind your joining us," Macy graciously motioned toward the ascending escalators. "There's a food court upstairs. We could all get a Coke together."

Hedging, Tony looked at his friend. As much as he enjoyed Eddy's company, he preferred having this conversation alone.

"I think we better stick to plan A, don't you?" Eddy asked.

"Maybe so," Tony agreed.

"I'll walk with you guys upstairs," Eddy said, and Tony recognized the protective edge in his voice, even if Macy didn't.

"Sure." Macy's gracious voice once again reminded Tony of a mellow ocean breeze. Her makeup, meticulously applied, did make her appear closer to Tony's age than not. And he could no longer deny Eddy's immediate observation. This was one attractive lady. Yet the most important thing was the inner beauty that spilled from her radiant expression. His spirit soared. Macy Sinclaire had undoubtedly been a dynamite mother.

A bell penetrated Victoria's troubling dream — a nightmare in which she and Tony were trapped in his sailboat. That horrid bell, persistent and shrill, seemed to be predicting their demise. At last, she jumped to full consciousness and realized the bell wasn't a part of her dream at all. The phone was ringing. Victoria fumbled for the cordless on the nightstand and muttered out a gruff greeting.

"Did I wake you?" Jac's urgent voice penetrated the fog of her mind.

"Yes." Victoria yawned. "What time is it?" She peered at the nightstand and her eyes popped open. "Oh my word, it's a quarter to eleven."

"Right," Jac rapped out.

Victoria pushed her heavy hair away from her face and scooted up in bed. "I almost never went to sleep last night," she admitted. "I walked the floors until about four o'clock and then flopped on the bed from sheer exhaustion."

"Well, I dozed all night in a car," Jac returned.

"Okay, okay," Victoria said and stifled a yawn. "I know you had a hard night."

"It's not so much that as . . ." Jac hesitated. "I guess I'm a little confused here. I thought Tony told you he was going to meet Eddy's brother-in-law in Tallahassee."

"This afternoon at three." Victoria propped her head against the pile of pillows and gazed at the glittery speckles in the ceiling. The smell of laundry detergent attested that she'd decided to strip down her bed last night at midnight and change the sheets. Victoria had been so uptight she'd cleaned every room in the house — except the nursery.

"Did he say anything to you about meeting anyone else?" Jac asked and the caution in her voice made Victoria sit up.

"Uh, no. Why?" A long pause conjured up all manner of possibilities, and Victoria's mind whirled with questions. "Jac?" Victoria prompted. "What's going on?"

"I'm at the airport in Pensacola."

"At the airport. Is Tony there too?"

"Yep. Tony and Eddy and some red-headed chick who looks like she stepped out of the pages of *Better Homes and Gardens*. She definitely has the 'Stefanie Powers' look. Do you know this lady?"

"What?" Victoria tossed aside the covers

and swung her feet out. She stood; she sat down. She stood back up and gripped the phone. "No, I *don't* know her. Who would you say is meeting her — Eddy or — or —"

"I would guess Tony," Jac said on a flat note, "since it looked like he was making the introduction to Eddy."

"Do you have your camera with you?" Victoria demanded as a slow burn started in her stomach.

"Yep. Gotta go. They're heading up the escalator. I don't want to lose them. I'll keep you posted. Oh, and maybe it's a good thing he didn't know about me after all," Jac added. The phone went dead, and Victoria was left staring at the receiver in mute fury.

Eddy and Tony parted company when they reached The Propeller, a small diner that featured an extensive array of airplane artifacts and memorabilia. "I'll be waiting nearby," Eddy promised and gave Tony the thumbs up.

Tony nodded and allowed Macy to enter in front of him. Her floral perfume smelled a lot like Victoria's White Shoulders, and Tony wished he could be sharing this moment with his wife. Yet something inside him recoiled at the possibility. Instead of anticipation, he was once again engulfed in dread. *If Victoria finds out . . .* when *Victoria finds out . . .*

At Tony's request the hostess guided them to a table at the back of the large room that sported a miniature crop duster hanging from the ceiling. He assisted Macy with her chair and the two of them chatted along about nothing in particular. Indeed, Tony was so anxious to discuss his daughter he barely kept up with the conversational vein about weather.

After a waitress appeared, filled their coffee cups, and took orders for pumpkin pie, Macy smiled and looked Tony in the eyes.

"Now, where do we start?" she asked. The expression lines around her eyes crinkled, and at a closer range Tony would guess that Macy was closer to 50 than 40. Yet her tasteful clothing and full auburn hair lent her a timeless appeal.

Tony leaned forward, eager for any news of the child he'd named Toni.

"First, let me say that she looks a whole lot like you," Macy supplied.

"No way. Really?" he asked and beamed. The smell of their steaming coffee blotted out Macy's floral perfume, and Tony momentarily stopped worrying about Victoria.

"I have a lot of pictures," Macy began and

laid a flat travel bag on the table. She un-zipped the tote and extracted a stack of photo albums, some aged by the years. She started with a page that featured a blond infant in her arms. The baby faced the camera with a contented look that said, "I am loved. I am happy."

Tony stroked the album and swallowed a lump in his throat. For a wrinkle in time the baby in the photo became the child he and Victoria lost, and the sorrow was fresh again. The picture blurred, and Tony wondered when he and his wife would have the nerve to enter the closed nursery.

"She was three months old when her dad snapped this one," Macy explained.

The words "her dad" stabbed Tony like a rusty knife and ended the musings about the miscarriage. *I should have been taking that picture,* he thought. *What would it have felt like to touch those chubby cheeks each day and let her tiny fingers wrap around mine?*

Nevertheless, he respectfully flipped through the album while Macy described her excitement of having a new life in her care. "She cried so little, I worried about her," Macy said. "We finally realized she was just happy! My husband, Calvin, loved to rock her and my in-laws said he was spoiling her." Macy laughed. "He probably *did* spoil her some. He's still at it even now. Not only is he her dad, he's her coach."

"Coach?" Tony looked up from the baby pictures.

"Yes. She's nuts about basketball!"

"No way!" Tony gasped. "So am I. I played in high school even."

"That figures. She's nearly as tall as you are, by the way." Macy's eyes twinkled and she pointed to a photo of a chubby toddler. "Here's a shot when she was about 18 months old."

Tony grinned at a baby holding the edge of a coffee table. She looked back toward the camera with a shy grin as if to say, "I'm walking now. Guess how many things I can get into!" He caressed the picture's surface and wished he could feel the baby skin softness.

Next came a scene with Toni sitting in the kitchen sink amid a sea of bubbles. Soap coated Calvin Sinclaire's arms up to his elbows and frothy bubbles created a halo in Toni's blond curls. "Calvin and I took turns giving her a bath. He and she used to see who could splash out the most bubbles."

The tightness in Tony's throat almost cut off his breathing. He stared at the beautiful child now probably nearing two. *I bet he let her get soap in her eyes,* he mused, and immediately felt guilty for such a spiteful thought. He flipped through the album and stopped at a photo of Toni on a tricycle. Her cotton-blond hair had turned to a more golden hue. She had a teddy bear under one arm and a firm grip on the handle bar with the other.

For a moment Tony forgot the anguish of loss as the emptiness was replaced with a sense of pride. "Look at this," he said. "Does she look like me or what? I can't believe it."

"Just wait," Macy said and joined in Tony's laughter. "The older she gets the more like you she looks. If you had told me nothing of your appearance except that you were Evelyn's birth father I could have spotted you at the escalator with no problem whatsoever. It's amazing."

The waitress returned with their wedges of pumpkin pie.

"Thanks," Macy said. "Oh, and I noticed there's no sugar on the table."

The aging waitress, bone thin and tanned, nodded.

"I'll get you some."

Tony sipped his black coffee as Macy grinned sheepishly. "I like the hard stuff," she explained.

"Well, get in line," Tony said. "I passed

on the sugar substitute myself. If I'm going to do sweet, I like the real deal."

The waitress returned and placed a handful of sugar packets onto the table. Macy dumped two packets into her cup and slowly stirred the brew. Tony followed suit and took advantage of a break in the conversation to glance around the sparsely inhabited restaurant. A young couple leaned across a table, intent upon each other, oblivious to the world. A mother with twin toddlers struggled through what resembled an aerobic workout while eating a hamburger and keeping up with her children. A trio of businessmen sat at a center table, focused upon a discussion that must mean life or death, if their expressions were anything to go by. And a lone female with black, scraggly hair, a red hat and lipstick, and a pair of dark glasses claimed a booth parallel to them on the restaurant's other side. Something in the line of the woman's face struck Tony as familiar, yet he dismissed the notion.

The main thing was that no swarthy, hulking man was in the restaurant. Fleetingly, Tony wondered if Eddy were okay or if he'd flung his body in front of that gangster in an attempt to protect Tony. The guy meant well, but when it came to protecting his family and friends he could be somewhat rash.

Tony took an obligatory bite of his spicy pie, sipped his coffee, and reveled in the display of photos Macy continued to narrate. On they paraded through the albums until at last Evelyn Toni posed in her first varsity jacket. Tony touched this photo just as he had the one when she was a baby. And he wondered if she ached for him as he'd ached for her. Beyond doubt, the string of visual hammers left him emotionally drained.

Without preamble, Macy extended a single photo to him and Tony accepted it. "This one's yours," she said, and he gazed at a lovely young woman with long blond hair. Her gray eyes glowed with a serenity that touched him to the core. Although she still looked a lot like Tony, she had taken on an air of early womanhood; the lines of her jaw and nose had a grace like Victoria's.

In a moment of abandon Tony blurted, "She even looks a little like my wife!" No sooner had the words left his mouth than he felt like a complete buffoon. However, a deep longing within yearned to make an association between this person who was part of him and the wife he wanted to be all of him.

"Really? Is she blond too?"

"No. Her hair's a medium brown and curly." Tony shook his head. "There's really nothing distinct in their similarities. I really think maybe it's just the shape of their faces . . . or just wishful thinking," he added.

Macy's bronze-tinted lips tilted into a smile.

"I understand. Calvin has sworn Evelyn is a dead ringer for him since the day we got her, and he's got nearly black hair and dark-brown eyes. He's one-quarter Native American!"

The two fell into amicable laughter.

Tony looked at the picture again. With every stage of growth, Macy had reinforced her story through explanations of E.T.'s personality and character. One thread appeared over and over: the girl's Christian experience dominated her life. At first this concerned Tony because he feared that perhaps his daughter might somehow be as rule-oriented as his wife. Yet the compassion spilling from Macy's eyes suggested that their religion was more about love than law.

As he continued to gaze into Evelyn's eyes, the peace and assurance that cloaked her features affirmed the same love that her mother, Macy, emanated. While Victoria always looked calm and in control she seldom radiated the spirit of love that oozed from Macy. Even when Tony had asked her to talk to him about Jesus, she'd used the question as a means to vent frustration.

I've got to have that conversation with Eddy, he reminded himself. *Somebody's got to tell me how I can believe. It's just not happening.* And a nagging insecurity about his future suggested that talk needed to occur soon.

"Perhaps you can tell me something about yourself," Macy suggested. She observed him over the rim of her coffee cup.

Her request dropped Tony smack into the middle of stark reality. "Let's see, where do I start?" he began and hoped Macy didn't suspect that he was trying to think far enough past the threat on his life to gather the details of his existence. Simultaneously, he pondered the irony of being confronted with another situation where he dared not tell all the facts. Even the reason given for Eddy's presence wasn't the complete truth.

He peered across the restaurant and pretended to be grappling with the best starting point. Instead, he was skimming the tables once more to see if anyone new had arrived. The hair on the back of his neck prickled when he caught that woman with the scraggly hair looking back at him. Yet she casually stabbed her straw into her soda and acted as if she were simply passing time until the next flight.

That plane hanging from the ceiling posed itself as a momentarily logical escape, and Tony foolishly wondered if he could hop in it and zoom from the need to explain his life.

"Why not start with your childhood and go from there?" Macy prompted and touched his hand in a comforting gesture.

Tony smiled gratefully and wondered if the woman made an occupation of trying to put others at ease. Thankfully, his family of origin was a safe topic. Before Tony knew it he was describing his wonderful parents, elder sister, and a younger brother. From there, he eased into his experience at a Louisiana community college and talked about his love of being a fireman. Soon Macy had gently pulled out detail upon detail about his life. At last she sat back and nodded.

"You're as much a man of character as I assumed you were when we first read that letter. Not many teenage fathers would have opened their hearts so."

He coughed and stirred his coffee. "I guess that's probably about the last time I really opened it." The awkward admission flopped out onto the table, and Tony blinked at his own blunt honesty. He felt as if the words themselves cast a blinding light upon the fractures of his marriage. For the first time he wondered what might have happened if he'd just been honest with Victoria from the start. Maybe he'd misjudged her. Maybe she would have forgiven him, and they would have moved forward and grown together. Instead, they'd never grown together. They'd grown apart. Even after their weekend love affair Tony wondered if the newness might wear off once more.

"How would you feel about coming to Orlando in the next few days?" Macy asked on a decisive note.

"Excuse me?" Tony's eyes widened.

She nodded. "I really want you to meet our daughter. The time is *now*. She's hurting. She needs you." Macy leaned back and crossed her arms as if she meant business.

"Well, I . . . this week?" Tony repeated and wondered if his life could get any more complicated. He had a wild vision of meeting his daughter and the goon's gunfire missing him and hitting Toni.

"Is it not good timing?" she asked and touched her cheek. "I guess I *did* just spring that on you, didn't I?"

"Actually, I have some vacation time built up and arranged to take off this week anyway," he managed to say and didn't explain that he was actually in hiding. Still, Tony wondered if he could rent a car and sneak to Orlando. The possibilities began to increase his confidence. If he were successful, this might be an answer to his need to reduce visibility in Destin.

Twenty-Seven

Victoria snatched up the phone the second it rang. "Hello," she gasped into the receiver and scooted to the edge of the sofa. A garbled collection of cell phone static assaulted her ear, and Victoria knew this must be Jac. She had done nothing but wait on the detective's call for a solid hour. And in that hour she'd paced the floors, chewed up her perfectly manicured nails, and stared out to sea. She'd cried and screamed and even tried to pray. Nothing seemed to assuage her torment.

"Victoria? It's me." Jac's voice at last penetrated the static.

"Where are you now and what's he doing?" Victoria balled her robe's sash.

"First, let me tell you — I got some digital shots of Tony and that woman. But seriously, Victoria, I don't think this is an affair."

"Well, what else could it be?" Victoria demanded and resumed her pacing. "He's secretly meeting a redheaded siren! I'm sure they aren't playing checkers."

"Okay," Jacquelyn said with a calm aura

that chafed, "first, she's not a siren. Attractive, yes. A siren, no. I'd say she is a highly respectable woman in her mid to late forties. At first, I thought she was near Tony's age, but when you move in closer you can tell she's probably a good 10 years older than he is, maybe 12."

"Are you sure?" Victoria queried and fury mingled with uncertainty. She stopped pacing and gazed through the row of windows upon the azure ocean dotted by white caps.

"*Dead* sure. And second, they didn't play checkers, that's certain," Jacquelyn said. "They looked at photos."

"Photos?" Victoria asked and stroked her strained forehead. "As in — did you say — like, pictures."

"As in *snapshots,*" Jacquelyn enunciated every word.

Victoria rolled her eyes and flopped onto the couch. The room seemed to swirl into a blend of taupe and seafoam and blue. Her head ached. Victoria realized she'd skipped breakfast and now it was time for lunch. The aroma of the cinnamon tea she'd microwaved but never retrieved tantalized her empty stomach.

"Does he have any relatives that fit the description of that woman?" Jacquelyn queried.

"Oh, I don't know," Victoria whispered and hunched forward. "I've been so upset this last hour. I just knew —"

"You expected the worst, right?"

"Y–yes."

"Give the guy a break," Jackie said with a heavy dose of love.

"Well, you're the one who called and implied who knows what!"

"Oh," Jac said. "I guess you're right. But like I said yesterday when we were talking about Eddy — I guess I'm getting jaded in my old age."

"And you're sure they're not —"

"If those two are having an affair I'll eat this nasty wig I'm wearing," Jac claimed.

All anxiety drained from Victoria.

"What about the relative connection?" Jac asked.

"She might be a cousin or something," Victoria said and waved her hand. "I don't know. There's no one in his immediate family that fits that description, but his mother comes from a family of nine and he's got cousins I've never even met."

"Well, there you go," Jacquelyn said. "We'll chalk this one up to a family reunion for right now."

"Then why didn't he *tell* me?" Victoria asked.

"Maybe . . . maybe . . . I don't know." Jacquelyn continued, "Let's revisit this one later. But for now I'm following Tony and Eddy to Tallahassee and keeping an eye out for lover boy."

"Who?"

"Our poster boy," Jac supplied. "Have you checked your e-mail today?"

"N–no, not yet."

"Please do," Jac requested. "Len should have gotten those digital photos I e-mailed him last night. As soon as we hear from him, we'll hopefully know who we're dealing with. Call me on my cell if you hear anything. I might need you to fax me the information."

"Can you receive faxes?"

"Of course. I'm a virtual walking office. I've got a briefcase full of stuff. I've even got a new wireless device that just hit the market. It allows me to receive faxes on the road. All I have to do is turn it on and it's a done deal."

"No way," Victoria said and seriously doubted her friend's claims.

"You oughtta get out in the real world a little more often," Jac teased. "This time I'm serious," Jac insisted. "This isn't about deadly laser beams and poisonous smoke. It's for real. As a matter of fact, if I'd been thinking, I should have just told Len to fax the information directly to me. But some days I just don't have it all together. Anyway, if the e-mail comes through and I need the data on the road, I'll set up and give you my number. Okay?"

"Right," Victoria agreed and felt as if she were drowning in Jac's high-tech world. Not only had she been up half the night, she'd been jolted awake by the assumption that her husband was having an affair. Presently, Victoria had gone from livid to flat — *really flat.*

"Oh, and Victoria?" Jac added.

"Yes?"

"I'm sorry. I should have waited to call you. But I just had this gut feeling Tony was up to something sneaky. I don't know what happened. My instincts are usually on. This time —" Jacquelyn expelled a long breath. "Sorry," she repeated.

Victoria tugged on a ribbon of hair until her scalp protested. She wrapped the strand around her finger and tried to find the words to hide the sudden onslaught of aggravation for one of her dearest friends.

"Not a problem," she said as brightly as possible, but the words sounded brittle. "I guess I need to hit the shower. It's after noon, and I'm still in my gown here."

"Oh, all right," Jacquelyn mumbled. "Go

ahead and have me for lunch, why don't you?"

"Well, I just wish you'd have waited before —"

"I said I was sorry. What more do you want?"

"Oh, I don't know." Victoria grabbed the throw pillow that was resting on the sofa's arm. The edge hit a basket of apple-scented potpourri, and the contents tumbled upon the oriental rug. The aroma of apple pie accompanied a new surge of tears. "I'm sorry too, Jac," Victoria admitted. "I'm just so strung up over —"

"Holy Toledo," Jacquelyn's hardened voice broke through Victoria's apology.

"What's — what's the matter?" she stammered.

"Uh . . ."

"Don't hedge on me, Jackie!"

"The last time you said something like that, you wound up going into hysterics," Jacquelyn said in measured tones.

"It's something bad, isn't it? I know it is!"

"Just calm down," Jac advised. "I'm not sure. I'll get back to you."

"Tell me!" Victoria urged, but the phone line went dead.

"Talk to me about Jesus, Eddy." Tony

crossed his arms, examined the oak-covered hills along the freeway, and awaited his friend's response. He'd thought about posing the question ever since they left Pensacola. Finally, Tony just laid it out and hoped for the best.

Eddy, at the wheel of his Suburban, cut a look at Tony and then back to the highway that would take them into Tallahassee. After the meeting with Macy they had been driving an hour. They had another hour to go.

"You've been acting weird ever since we left Pensacola."

"Weird? Acting weird?" Tony placed his elbow on the truck's windowsill. "I haven't said a word, and now —"

"That's the whole point, you've been sitting over there like a zombie."

"I've been thinking."

"Like I said, that's weird for you, man." Eddy threw in a cocky wink.

"You know what, Eddy Graham, one day I'm going to take you down and nobody's going to even ask why." Tony rolled his eyes. "If this wasn't your truck I'd just throw you out."

"Yow! Why don't you get vindictive?"

"A fine one you are to talk about . . ." Tony trailed off. Maybe after all this time

Eddy really wasn't comfortable with such a direct question, despite his years of hints.

"Jesus?" Eddy finished.

"Yeah."

"Now we're talking about my *best* friend," Eddy admitted. "Frankly, I didn't think this day would ever come."

"What do you mean?"

"I mean when you'd finally ask."

A brotherly silence penetrated the Suburban's cab, and Eddy switched off the soft hits station. "What can I tell you that you don't already know?" he finally asked. "You've been in the church your whole life."

Tony peered into the side-view mirror — no dark sedans.

"Tell me how you overcame —" He stopped himself and studied Eddy's profile. His straight nose, strong brow, and gentle smile underscored his spiritual stability. Eddy was a man who kept his word. A man Tony wished to emulate. "I guess I've just never made that step because it's hard for me to believe that a *person* who lived more than 2000 years ago really was God in the flesh. I mean, Jesus Christ was a *man* just like you and me."

"Right. But He was born of a virgin," Eddy replied.

"But do you *really* believe that?" Tony scrubbed his thumb along his jawline. "I mean *really?*"

"Yeah, man." Eddy increased the vent's velocity and pointed a stream of air toward himself. "I've believed since I was a child. I was 12 when I accepted Him as Savior."

"And what happened to you?"

"He came into my heart. I know He did. I remember the place and time when He moved in. Ever since, I've felt His presence with me. It's incredible."

"And you're sure you're not . . ."

"Imagining things?" Eddy supplied with a wry grin.

"Well, yeah." Tony toyed with the door's electric lock and flipped it to the down position. The door clicked, and he glanced in the side-view mirror again.

"Not a chance, not a chance." He cut a calculating glance toward Tony. "Remember last year when I knocked you out from beneath the burning doorway that showed no signs of collapsing, but did anyway?"

"Yes," Tony responded and tried to knit together the connection.

"I'll believe until I die that Jesus Himself spoke to my mind and told me to shove you out of the way. I didn't ask questions. I just did it. Sure enough, 20 seconds later, the whole thing came down."

"Why didn't you *tell* me?"

"I tried!" Eddy gazed at his friend with the glow of determination. "But you said I was trying to get out of taking credit. It was like you wanted to make me some hero, but I figure Jesus was the hero. I just did what He showed me."

Tony made a monumental job of rustling through the canvas bag of snacks Eddy's mom had packed for them. The gray-haired lady had put everything in the bag from bananas to chocolate chip cookies. Tony extracted a cookie, smelled it, and decided the thing needed to be eaten. He hadn't eaten breakfast and that single wedge of pumpkin pie was wearing thin.

"You know what?" he said, his mouth full of moist chocolate and crumbs. "I *want* to believe. I really do. And if there really is a heaven — and only God knows if I'll live or die in the next few days — then I'd like to know that's where I'm going. And really, Eddy," Tony waved the cookie, "I don't have problems believing in God. I mean — just look at the world and how it's all put together. Any idiot can see there's a God. But my deal is actually being able to believe that Jesus was *Him!* It's almost like flying reindeer. I figured out there wasn't a Santa early on because all I could think was 'reindeer can't fly.' "

Eddy barked out a single laugh then sobered. "Actually, it sounds like you don't want to talk *about* Jesus so much as you want to know how to have the faith to believe."

Tony crammed the final bit of cookie into his mouth, and propped his head on the seat's headrest.

"Well, yes, I guess," he said after a hard swallow. Tony observed the rows of oaks swaying beneath a cloudless sky. The cool front had finally moved out by last night; the morning began a warming trend that hinted at the need for air conditioning. He pointed a vent toward his face and enjoyed the fresh bath of outside air.

" 'Faith comes by hearing, and hearing by the Word of God,' " Eddy quoted.

"Explain that." Tony pivoted to face his friend and propped his knee on the seat.

"That's a verse found in Romans — Romans 10:17 to be exact. I guess it means that if you're having trouble believing, get out the Bible and start reading it. Read that book cover to cover. Start with Matthew, Mark, Luke, and John. Those are the books that major on Jesus. Start there and listen for God's voice." Eddy tapped his blunt fingernail against the leather-wrapped steering wheel.

"Got one with you?" Tony asked.

"What?" Eddy glanced in the rearview mirror and back at the road.

"A Bible. Got a Bible with you?"

"There's one in my suitcase," Eddy said and darted a surprised look at his partner. "You're serious, aren't you?"

"Would I be wasting my breath if I weren't?" Tony asked and swiveled to see if he could spot his friend's overnight bag.

"All right, man." Eddy applied the brakes and the vehicle began to slow. He clicked on his right blinker and pointed the Suburban toward a fast-food joint. "I'm hungry, and I'm tired of watching you eat up my cookies," he said. "Let's go in and eat. We've got time. It'll also give me the chance to get the book out."

"Deal," Tony agreed and fell into contemplative silence once more. Regardless of his weak faith, he had finally recognized that he needed a friend — someone who could go with him even when Eddy couldn't. Someone to protect him and hold him up. Someone who would do all the things that those who knew Jesus claimed He did.

Not only was Tony running from some

mobster who was christened by the law, he was also facing this meeting with his daughter on Wednesday. He and Macy had left on the best of terms with Tony holding the instructions to the Sinclaires' residence. He fingered his pants pocket and felt the note's presence. The void in his soul begged him to irrevocably believe in Jesus and find the strength to face the next few days.

Twenty-Eight

Shae wove in and out of traffic and kept the Taurus at a safe distance behind the Suburban. He had predicted his victim's fleeing, and his prediction was correct. For a few minutes Buster had considered letting the coward leave town without him. Tony would eventually come back when he felt safe. They all did. And then the killer would end the game for good — when his victim expected it least. Shae gripped the steering wheel and could nearly taste the need to kill.

But after some thought, Buster had decided he needed to track Tony. Something about all this didn't add up. And the more he thought about the plausibility of Kevin Norris having squealed to Tony the more it made sense. So Buster followed. He'd trailed them to that second-class neighborhood in Pensacola and stayed half the night in a ratty hotel. By sunup, he positioned himself in the alley behind the house and watched for Tony's exit. Shae took a chance on their heading back to the main highway. The gamble paid off. From there, he'd stayed a safe distance back.

For the first time since the sporting started, Buster's confidence was shaken. He fleetingly wished he'd just taken Roberts down on the beach and gotten rid of him. While playing with his victim had certainly produced some thrills, something unusual was up, something he sensed he might not like.

And he wasn't so sure that the scraggly haired woman in that sporty gray Ford he'd passed wasn't a part of the picture. He'd noticed a similar car sitting down the road last night, but couldn't validate that it was the same one. Then, when he parked at the airport and waited on Tony and that friend of his, he may have seen someone who resembled that dame. Problem was, Shae was so focused on his victim he'd failed to connect with his surroundings as intently as he normally did. Nevertheless, not much got past Buster, even at the height of his murderous game. So if the dame were tracking Tony . . . or him . . . Shae figured she was good. And that made him doubt the veracity of her following. Not many people could track someone with such finesse.

Her presence still nagged at Buster. He simply couldn't pin her. When he passed her a few miles back she'd done more than cast him a passing glance. Shae looked in his rearview mirror to see her still in the distance. He wasn't young enough or virile enough to have women gaping at him anymore. All at once, he doubted that he was still on top in this hunt.

Shae pressed the CD player's power button, and Bach floated forth. This time the music did nothing to calm his increasing irritation. He snatched a thin cigar from the case in the console, clamped it between his teeth, and chewed the bittersweet tobacco. While the act relieved some pressure it did precious little to ease his mind.

Victoria stepped from the restroom and fidgeted with her damp hair, slung into a side ponytail. She debated whether or not to call Jacquelyn back and demand to know exactly what "holy Toledo" meant to her. Her intuition suggested Jac didn't want to tell her she'd seen that poster boy person on Tony's trail.

For the third time she adjusted the Capri pants that hung loosely around her waist. With a shake of her head, Victoria acknowledged she'd lost a few pounds since the last time she wore this cotton suit — pounds she had no need to loose. *But I was pregnant the last time I wore this,* she thought. While most of her clothing had hidden the slight bulge in her abdomen, her closer fitting pantsuits had proven snug.

Victoria paused in the hallway and stared at the closed nursery. For once, she wasn't overcome with a sense of loss. Sure, thinking of the miscarriage did hurt, but at least she didn't feel the need to burst into tears. Victoria stepped forward and rested her unsteady hand on the doorknob. The last time she'd had a good cry over the baby was Friday night when she and Tony mourned the loss together. Indeed, Tony wept nearly as hard as Victoria, and she was astounded that he could have hidden the agony so well. Or perhaps she had been so blind that she hadn't seen he was hurting as much as she.

Somehow, pooling their pain had ushered in a balm to Victoria's spirit. And now an impulse insisted she open the door. She stared at the gold-toned knob and wondered if perhaps she was so stressed over Tony's situation she was acting rashly. Yet the urge to open the door remained. So Victoria held her breath, turned the knob, and pushed on the door. As it glided open Victoria possessed no fortitude to gaze upon the contents. Instead, she rushed into her bedroom. By the time she stopped near the corner computer, the nursery door lightly thumped the bumper behind it.

Victoria released her breath and then stepped back to her bedroom door. She snapped it shut. She also decided not to analyze her behavior — essentially because she didn't know if she could come to any rational conclusions. Instead, she blocked out the spontaneous act and focused upon the computer. Jac had requested that she check her e-mail. Before Victoria hopped into the shower she had clicked the "Get Mail Now" icon on her e-mail account and left it in progress. Now she bent over the keyboard, rested her hand upon the mouse, and scrolled down the list of messages.

Numerous subject lines indicated that the Seven Sisters e-mail loop had been active since the last time she checked her e-mail. A couple of subject lines even mentioned her name.

Victoria curbed her curiosity and continued the perusal for a message from Len Scroggins. She had nearly given up hope that Len had responded when her attention was riveted upon the next-to-last e-mail titled "Poster Boy."

She nudged the rolling chair away from the desk, dropped into it, and clicked on Len's message. As Victoria read the revealing lines her grip on the mouse increased tenfold.

Hi, Jac. Good to hear from you. What have you gotten yourself into now? This poster boy is a dandy. I took your photos and ran them through our data bank. Yes, you've gotten on the trail of the real deal here. See attached photos and data files. This one plays for keeps. You'll notice his links to the mafia. He has five aliases, by the way, and we're not even sure, at this point, of his real name. His specialties are money laundering . . . and murder. Oh, and I'd say your assumptions are correct. I figure he's playing some sort of hunting game. He's so hardened, simple murder isn't a big enough thrill anymore. This kind of person likes the power that comes with terrifying his victims first. Once you read his data, you'll understand. If he missed your friend on the beach, like you said, I'm with you. It had to be on purpose. My guess is the license plate you gave me is one they've stolen. Be really careful this time.

Len.

A slow tremble began in Victoria's torso and radiated to her extremities. She opened the files one by one. As much as she attempted not to look at the man caught in different settings, her traitorous gaze scrutinized each print. And in each one he had altered his appearance. When she caught sight of one with a beard, her empty stomach knotted. She didn't bother to read the data. Len had told her more than she wanted to know. She printed off the e-mail files. Then she stomped toward her cordless phone, picked up the receiver, and dialed Jac's cell.

"Jac here." The no-nonsense greeting told Victoria more than she wanted to know.

"You saw that man on Tony's trail, didn't you?" She voiced the worry that nagged her since she last talked with her friend. "That's why you said 'holy Toledo' and hung up on me. You saw him and —"

"I can't talk right now," Jac shot back.

"I just printed off the files," Victoria stated as if she were a female version of Sherlock Holmes. Her inflexible tone nearly made her laugh from hysteria. She was starting to sound as much like a hardened detective as Jac. The wild urge to laugh spawned by stress passed as quickly as it came, and the trembling began anew.

"Okay," Jac replied. "What do they say?"

"You were — were right. Len says he's mean — really mean. He's got five aliases.

Five!" She lifted the papers toward the ceiling and dug her bare toes into the short pile carpet. "I didn't read all the facts, and I don't want to. I know enough to put me six feet under like it is."

"Right. Look, Tony and Eddy are pulling over at a fast-food place. I'm going to pass them and stop at a gas station so I can keep an eye on their vehicle. I *need* you to fax the info to me. I'm working on a plan. We're going to have to hurry. I don't think they'll be still for long. I'll set up and get ready for your fax."

"But I don't have a fax machine here! And I still don't have your fax number!" Victoria gazed around her brightly decorated room as if to find a machine miraculously tucked in a corner.

"Call me when you find a machine." After reciting her fax number, Jac declared, "Now go!" and disconnected the call.

Stunned, Victoria hung up the phone, grabbed a pen, and scribbled the number atop the printed e-mails. Once through, she blankly stared at her reflection in the oak dresser mirror. The wan face that gazed back was free of cosmetics and sported dark circles under the eyes. Indeed, the woman in the mirror looked as stressed as Victoria felt. There had been a few times through the years when Victoria imagined Jac's life as a private detective was somehow glamorous and exciting. Suddenly Victoria had tasted more of Jac's excitement than she ever wanted to, and she couldn't find a trace of anything glamorous.

At last she broke free of the momentary trance and bolted. She zoomed down the hallway, snatched her purse and cell phone, and ran toward her car. They had a fax machine at the fire station. She was sure Sal would give her access.

Twenty-Nine

Victoria hovered over the fax machine until the last paper crept through the rollers and out the front. The gray-haired secretary, surrounded by an office full of clutter, sat at her desk and filed her nails. The whole time Victoria felt as if Sal were straining for any clue as to what she was faxing. After every paper had slid out Victoria snatched them up and cradled them to her chest.

"Well, thanks," she said on a breathless note and hoped to make a gracious escape before the "queen of double knit" began her interrogation routine. "This was an emergency and I'm so glad —"

"Think nothing of it, dear." Sal laid her file atop a folder and gazed up at Victoria. While her smile indicated friendship, her brown eyes raged with curiosity. "How's Tony?" she asked. Her musk perfume grew more stifling with every passing minute.

"Oh, he's just fine," Victoria said and hoped she was telling the truth. Jac had yet to affirm that the poster boy was following Tony, and Victoria imagined the worst.

The large clock hanging over a photo of a

raging fire clicked off the seconds, and each second was one Victoria wanted to be on her way out. Jac might call any minute, and she didn't want to take the call with an audience.

As if Victoria's worries instigated the call, her cell phone began a classic tune from the folds of her leather purse. "Well, I guess I'll go, now," she said and edged toward the door. Before Sal could speak another word Victoria pushed on the glass door and marched into the sunshine.

The weekend's cool front was no more, and a thin film of sweat beaded her upper lip as she fumbled for the phone. At last she answered it while keeping the papers intact.

"Got it," Jac stated without greeting. "This is ugly."

"That's what I was telling you." Victoria scanned the city block past a scenic fountain near a park. A police car sat near the curb, and the very sight urged her toward her vehicle. She had no idea whom she could trust. A wisp of a breeze stirred the clump of palms near the red-trimmed station — a breeze that seemed to whisper, "Trust no one."

"I need Tony's cell number," Jac demanded.

"What?" Victoria gasped. She struggled

between maintaining her hold on the cell and gripping the papers while groping through her bag for her keys. She was certain she'd misunderstood her friend.

"I said," Jacquelyn repeated, "I need Tony's cell phone number."

"But why?" Victoria asked. "He's not supposed to know —"

"I've *got* to call him, Victoria." The edge in Jac's voice reminded her of jagged rocks at the bottom of a monstrous waterfall — a waterfall over which Victoria was falling. Everything was going fast — much too fast — and Victoria wasn't so sure she wouldn't be pulled under.

While she processed the new request, she managed to open her white Toyota, drop into the driver's seat, put the papers down, slam the door, and lock it. "If you call him, Jac, he'll know!" she protested.

"I need to tell him he's being followed."

"I knew it!" Victoria declared and clutched her keys until they pricked her palm.

"Don't go crazy on me," Jac said.

"I — I'm not," Victoria whimpered as she slung her keys into the passenger seat.

"I've got a plan to get this thug arrested, but I'm going to need Tony's help. I don't have a lot of time. I need to go into the bathroom to change so I've got different hair and clothes."

"You even travel with different disguises?" Victoria queried and thanked heaven for her normally uncomplicated life.

"It's part of the business," Jac said. "Now come on, Victoria, tell me his cell number. I'm running out of time here."

Victoria propped her forehead on the top of the steering wheel, closed her eyes, and spoke the numbers without a hint of emotion. Perhaps when she explained her duplicity Tony would understand that her intent was honorable and, therefore, he might extend some grace.

His stomach full of tacos, Tony buckled his seat belt and settled in for the rest of the ride to Tallahassee. He and Eddy had kept a close watch all during lunch for any sign of the stalker. As Tony opened Eddy's Bible, his mind wandered to that woman who'd sat across from him at the airport restaurant. He debated once again whether she might have been there watching him. Tony shook his head and told himself he was being paranoid. Besides, the time had come to change his focus for awhile. Eddy said he needed to read, so read he would.

Tony had barely delved into Matthew

when his cell phone began playing that low-slung funk tune that usually drove Eddy nuts. "I thought you said you were going to change that!" Eddy squawked as Tony pulled the phone from the belt holster.

"Oh, get a life." Tony snickered and examined the screen for who might be calling. The words "unknown caller" left him rigid, and he pondered the possibilities of this being Kevin Norris again. When he spoke a greeting the voice that answered was feminine.

"Tony, this is Jac Franklin," she said with a hint of caution. "Victoria's friend."

"Oh, hi!" Tony said and wondered if Jacquelyn was trying to reach Victoria.

The ominous pause that followed dashed away his doubts.

"I've got good news and bad news," she began.

"All right." Tony snapped the Bible shut. "Is something wrong with Victoria?" he asked and relived those awful moments when Marilyn called to confirm the miscarriage.

"No. This isn't about Victoria. It's about *you*."

"Me?"

"The good news is I'm right behind you."

Tony darted a glimpse into the side-view

mirror and noticed a Ford 20 feet behind them. A thousand questions tumbled through his mind.

"The gray sedan?"

"Yep. Victoria explained your situation to me, and then she asked me to protect you. I got here Saturday night, and I've been with you for the most part ever since."

"She arranged this?"

"Yes."

"Why didn't she *tell* me?" Tony strained a look into the mirror again and picked up the faint image of a woman holding a phone.

"She thought you wouldn't agree."

"She did mention calling you, and I told her not to." He reached for his Styrofoam cup and took a deep draw of the sweet cola. The smell of fast food still clung to the cup.

"Well, there you have it."

Tony groaned. *When is my wife going to realize I can take care of myself?* he wanted to scream. "Eddy's been guarding me just fine," Tony said, stifling a frustrated growl.

"Oh, *has* he?" Jacquelyn asked on a cunning note.

"What's that supposed to mean?" Tony inserted the cola back into the console holder.

"Does Eddy know that Buster Shae is following you as we speak?"

"What?" Tony sat straight up.

"Yes. The man at the marina, Tony. He's now on your trail. Did you know?"

"No!" Tony pivoted in the seat and glared out the back window. No sign of a black sedan. "I don't see him. If it's the guy at the marina, he's driving a black car."

"Not today," Jacquelyn purred. "Today, he's in a taupe Taurus." She paused. "Best I can tell, about three cars behind me."

With a hiss Tony spotted the Taurus, turned around, and hunkered down in the seat.

"What is it?" Eddy demanded and shot a glance at his friend.

"He's behind us!" Tony croaked and felt like a helpless fox cornered by hounds.

"How? I've kept a close watch," Eddy hollered, and his panicked gaze shot to the rearview mirror.

"How should I know!" Tony exploded.

"I'll tell you how," Jacquelyn said. "He's a professional. He's good. He means business. Today there's not a beard and the hair's solid gray. According to the data I have, he's a master at disguise. He has five aliases."

"Data? You mean you even have *data* on him?" All of a sudden the tacos weren't sitting so well.

"Yes. I took some digital photos of him last night when he was at the marina. I e-mailed the pictures to a friend at the Colorado State Police. Victoria just got his response and faxed it to me on my portable fax while you and Eddy were eating lunch."

"Victoria got the information?" Tony asked and felt as if his wife had become a master of trickery. All weekend he was with her, and she never said a word — not one word! *If she decided to go ahead and call Jac — fine! But did she have to live a lie?* A slow irritation pricked his mind. Just when Tony was ready to hold his concerns for later discussion, he thought of the lie he'd been living all these years. The truth of his own deceit smacked him between the eyes, and he pinched his lower lip.

Thoughts of his past ushered in that hour when he was talking to Macy Sinclaire. Across the restaurant sat a woman who struck him as somehow familiar. "That woman in the restaurant — that was you!"

Jacquelyn offered no response.

Tony pressed his forefinger and thumb against his eyes and was hurled into a sea of repercussions. If Jac knew he had coffee with Macy Sinclaire then Victoria's knowledge was inevitable. That klatch of seven women were as close as he and Eddy were.

What one knew, they shared with the others. "I guess you've already told her about Macy," he said with conviction. "Am I right?"

"The redhead who looked like Stefanie Powers?"

"Yes."

"She knows."

"Oh, great." Tony sighed and glared at the gray Ford.

"But I *did* tell her I didn't see any signs that you were having an affair," Jac said without a hitch of doubt.

"Oh, well, that was kind of you," Tony shot back with a sarcastic edge.

"Look —"

"Sorry," he added yet his tone hadn't changed, "but I've never enjoyed being spied on during a private conversation."

"Whatever you were talking about is *your* business."

"You'd better believe it's *my* business," he commanded. Simultaneously, he imagined Victoria awaiting an explanation.

"Look," Jacquelyn continued. "This isn't about the redhead. Let's drop that. It's about this man who's following you. I have a plan. If Buster Shae cooperates, we might very well nab him if we work together."

Thirty

Buster Shae glowered until his head ached. He'd been glowering since they took the exit for Tallahassee. Now, his first instincts were proving valid. Tony Roberts wasn't just running. He and that fool friend of his were going toward the state capital. They turned into the all-too-familiar route surrounded by shrubs and buildings and pedestrians.

Uttering a long stream of oaths, Shae grabbed his cell phone and scrolled down a list of names in his phone book. He pressed send when he reached the desired number. A masculine voice floated over the line — the voice of deception.

"It's Shae," Buster barked.

"Yes?"

"I'm tracking a couple of idiots who might know more than I think. Looks like they're heading toward you. They should be there in about five minutes. As soon as I'm certain they're heading into the capital, I'll call you back. Wherever they head, you need to plan to move fast and meet me at the front door. We need to deal with them."

"We can't just take them down in broad daylight!"

"We can't let them get past the ground floor either, especially if they're targeting the attorney general's office," Shae insisted. "If they have information and it lands in the right hands, the boss will kill us both. Understand?" Buster squirmed beneath the warming sunshine pouring through his window. A flash of his own form in a casket sent a twist of desperation through his bones.

"Yes, I understand, but —"

"No buts!"

"Do you have a piece?" the informer asked.

"You know I do." Shae eyed his overcoat draped across the passenger seat and dreaded the smothering folds. If he was packing a gun he needed the extra coverage. "Plan to meet me in front. Between the two of us, we can convince them to walk back to this God-forsaken wreck I rented. If by some chance they happen to get inside, I'll discard the gun. It won't get through the metal detectors. What about yours? Didn't you pay someone to look the other way and sneak it into your office?"

"Yes. But the whole point is that I can't exit with it. The detectors will go off."

"Hold tight and wait until I call back!" Buster commanded. "If they wind up in your building there won't be a problem. We can take them from the inside if we have to. Your piece has a silencer?" He pressed the brake and slowed for an intersection.

"Yes, as always."

"Good. Get rid of your secretary for an hour. If we can't take them outside, we'll force them into your office and kill them."

"And what are we supposed to do with the bodies?"

"We'll stuff them into your closet until tonight and then hide them in the basement and let housekeeping deal with them!" Shae snarled and a stab of pain pierced his temple. "Whatever! Let's just get the main part over."

"Tell me what they look like."

"One tall blond guy and a shorter, stocky black guy."

"I'll be waiting," the informer promised.

"Don't blow this," Buster snapped. "If you do, you're dead!" He jabbed his finger against the end button and slammed the phone into the passenger seat. It bounced onto the floor and Shae pounded the steering wheel with his fist.

"I should have shot Roberts when I had the chance," he roared.

After Jac detailed her plan, Tony repeatedly attempted to connect with Eddy's brother-in-law, but to no avail. He'd left three messages with Quinn's secretary and one on his cell phone.

The steady hum of the Suburban slowed as Eddy neared a stop sign. They had followed a trail of signs toward the state capital. The domed building stood like a silent sentinel one block away. Tony turned around and peered behind him. After their phone conversation Jac had sped ahead toward the capital to prepare the setup. As they cruised the vicinity, Tony spotted the gray Ford at the end of a corner. A tired looking bag lady with tattered blond hair was propped against a nearby tree.

"There she is." He nodded toward the bag lady. Tony hunkered down in the seat and looked into the side-view mirror. A taupe Taurus followed two cars behind.

"This is the thing I can't stand about my brother-in-law," Eddy grumbled. "Sometimes it's days before he returns my wife's calls. I guess if there were some emergency . . ." He trailed off.

"I think we could validate this as an emergency," Tony snapped, and his cell rang.

He went erect in his seat and pressed the

answer button. "Tony Roberts," he said.

"Roberts? Brandon Quinn."

"Listen," Tony started, "we're here outside the capital. We've got a criminal on our trail, and we've got a plan to nab him. We need your help."

"Excuse me?" Brandon questioned with a trace of disbelief.

Tony expelled a slow breath. "Buster Shae. Does that name ring a bell?"

"No. Not in the least," Brandon said, an aloof meter to his words.

"Well, he's a wanted mafia hit man. His specialties are murder and money laundering. He's part of the ring of people we're coming to discuss with you."

"About that —" Quinn began.

"No!" Tony gripped the base of his neck. "Let's take care of Shae before we discuss the other stuff I know. He's followed us all the way from Destin, and I think he's probably the one who shot at me."

"I'm sorry, but if you don't supply me with more pertinent details I have no idea where to begin."

Tony glared at Eddy, who rolled his eyes.

"He's impossible," he mumbled. "What'd I tell you? He's impossible. I don't know how my sister puts up with him."

"I realize your concerns, Mr. Roberts,"

Quinn continued in a controlled tone. "But have you considered that you might be jumping to conclusions here? At this point, you're probably figuring the bad guys can come from any direction. I find it highly unlikely that —"

"Listen to me!" Tony hollered.

Eddy leaned toward the window and covered his right ear.

"I am listening to you. And I assure you my only interest is protecting Florida's banks from crooks like the people Eddy said are on your tail. However, this is not the time or place to panic."

Tony's blunt fingernails ate into the leather seat.

"You might as well tell him what he wants to know first, man," Eddy mumbled and shook his head. "His head is harder than a mule's."

"What details do you need first?" Tony bit out and raised his hand. His palm slapped against his slacks with a crack.

"First understand that we will need to validate most of what you tell me. As I told Eddy there has been increased boating traffic in the coast and we are beginning to wonder if there's a connection. But first, we'll need to do some investigating. Then, if everything looks like we need to pursue this, we'll bring you back in to help us make the case."

"Meanwhile, we just cruise around with the murderer on our tails? We could drive around out here for weeks!" Tony yelled.

"Look," Quinn purred, "why don't you just come on into my office as planned —"

"Because there's a killer following us! Didn't you *hear* me?"

"Yes, but are you *certain?*" Quinn asked with a jeer.

"If I weren't certain, why would I be telling you all this? Haven't you listened to a word I've said!?"

Quinn went silent. Cold and silent.

"The problem is, he doesn't respect *me,*" Eddy mumbled. "And he never has. I'm beginning to wonder if I was crazy to even think he'd cooperate. Crazy, crazy, crazy!"

"Look," Tony said on a last effort, "there's also a private eye involved right now. She's sitting on the front lawn of the state capitol, dressed like a street woman. She's leaning against a tree. Can you see her?"

The faint sound of footsteps preceded Quinn's response. "Yes, I see her," he admitted and his voice took on a thoughtful nuance.

"She's got the scoop on this idiot behind

us. When he steps onto the walkway, she's going to bump into him and place details about his criminal history in his pocket, along with a stapler."

"A stapler?"

"It's a *metal* stapler. We're going to run toward the state capitol's main entrance in hopes he'll follow us in. When he does —"

"And exactly what part do I play?" Quinn questioned.

"Would you at least be willing to alert security?" Tony demanded.

"And what happens if he doesn't play along?" Quinn asked.

"Then I'll tell you what I know and try to find somebody else who'll listen to me!"

"That's tellin' him," Eddy taunted.

Tony slammed his fist against his thigh, and his injured shoulder complained with a tiny prick. The graze hadn't hurt him in hours, and the very reminder sent an icy chill through his heart. If Shae was the one who shot at him, he probably would mean business the next time.

"Okay. I'll call security," Quinn acquiesced.

"Thank you! We'll be in there as soon as we can find a parking place."

Thirty-One

The parking place came easy. Eddy pulled into a vacant spot not far from the capitol's main lawn, so close that Tony made eye contact with Jac before her gaze listlessly slid away. Tony unlatched his seat belt and darted Eddy a wide-eyed stare.

"This is it," he said.

"We've got to be crazy." Eddy shook his head and rubbed his jaw with stubby fingers. "I've got a wife and two teenagers at home —"

"You don't have to do this," Tony said. "You really don't. As a matter of fact —"

"No." Eddy raised his hand. "I won't let you go in alone. We're partners. Remember? We work together." Eddy lifted his palm, and Tony slapped it. "There's no guarantee that idiot will even follow us in," he added.

"In a way, I hope you're right." Tony scanned the parking area and stopped on a Taurus. "I see taupe." He glanced down at the Bible he'd never read. After Jacquelyn called Tony had been too distracted to think about anything other than their mission.

"Let's go then," Eddy said.

"Wait!" Tony grabbed his friend's arm as if it were his lifeline. "Pray," he demanded. "Pray for me — that I'll have faith. I — I can't go into this without Him."

"Man," Eddy said, "if you want Him that bad, just tell Him. He'll give you the faith."

So Tony told Him. In a wrinkle in time he reached out to Christ and pleaded for protection. Protection and guidance. Guidance and grace. Blindly he exited the vehicle and strode next to Eddy as they calmly walked toward the capitol's main entrance. They passed Jac. They passed pedestrians. They passed a fountain sparkling in the afternoon sunshine.

Tony couldn't say that he saw rockets or stars or heard a heavenly choir, but something unusual happened to him. All his tremors disappeared, and he was engulfed in an inexplicable peace.

The rhythm of heavy footfalls fell in behind them. Although the skin crept along his spine, Tony didn't dare turn around. Instead, he prayed. He prayed like he'd never prayed in his life. Eventually, he heard a surprised "uumph" followed by cursing and a feminine whimper that preceded an apology.

Eddy was the one who glanced back.

Tony refrained. "She made contact," he mumbled.

"Let's speed up," Tony whispered and the two friends hustled toward the broad steps.

The heavy footsteps grew nearer, and Tony felt as if he were trapped in a beautiful garden with a deadly serpent. The smell of freshly mown grass reminded him more of a cemetery than the onset of spring. The more he pondered that cemetery, the faster he walked, the harder he prayed.

When they finally reached the front doors, Tony banged the bar against the glass and trotted past the metal detector. He searched the milling crowd for the man Eddy had described as his brother-in-law — a tall black guy, a good-looking devil, with wire-rimmed glasses, close-cut hair, long nose, and square jaw. Brandon Quinn stepped from near a stairway to the right. Arms folded, he tilted his head to one side in a scoffing gesture.

Tony, now sweating profusely, swerved toward him.

"I never thought I'd ever say this," Eddy mumbled. "But I'm glad to see the jerk."

Another man, blond and short, approached them from across the marble hallway. As he whisked past a trio of alert security guards his icy blue eyes — the eyes of a soulless shark — focused on Tony.

Tony grabbed Eddy's arm. A creeping suspicion socked him in the gut. He feared perhaps *they* were the ones who'd been trapped and imagined the man's mouth full of pointy teeth, ready to tear flesh.

The sudden shriek of a metal detector diverted the shark's attention; he stopped and peered toward the entryway. His face impassive, he ignored Tony, turned, and took the stairs two at a time. Tony released Eddy's arm and pivoted to face their stalker. Apparently the shark was his imagination.

Buster Shae casually smiled toward the trio of security guards as if he didn't have one worry about his culpability.

Someone who smelled of some froufrou men's stuff moved beside Tony. He glanced toward Quinn, whose brows were arched in a stupefied expression that nearly made Tony laugh out loud.

Eddy wasn't suave enough to stifle his satisfied chuckle. Quinn scowled down at his brother-in-law, and Eddy didn't bother to stop laughing.

Deciding to forget the in-law conflict, Tony focused upon Shae, who shrugged out of his overcoat and allowed the guards to explore his pockets. The dark-eyed gangster scanned the relaxed crowd who appeared to assume that the detector was dysfunctioning again. Tony wanted to shrink into the wall when Buster's gaze nearly encountered him. One of the guards shoved a meaty hand into Shae's overcoat and pulled out a sheaf of papers, and the mobster quit examining the crowd.

The officer's exclamation was lost in the bustle of people. The stapler that fell from the guard's grasp went unnoticed. Instead, all attention riveted upon the data.

Shae's lips hardened. His nostrils widened. A deep line formed between his brows. He cast a mystified glance over his shoulder. Without warning, Shae bolted toward the doorway, but two of the guards were onto him. The struggle that ensued snared the attention of the milling crowd, yet Tony had seen all he wanted to see. And he sure didn't want Shae to notice *him*. While Buster's days in prison were certain, criminals had a way of getting parole.

"I've seen enough," Tony mumbled toward Quinn. "Can we go to your office?" He felt as if his feet were leaden, his arms as heavy as logs. The whole weekend had been nothing short of one blast of stress after another.

"Of — of course," Quinn babbled. He adjusted his glasses, yanked on his scarlet tie, and gaped at his brother-in-law. "I'm sure they'll want a statement from both of you, though."

"Fine," Tony agreed. "Call the head of security when we get to your office. We'll talk as soon as they need us."

"You want me to *kill* them — *both* of them?" Darnell Hopkins gasped and immediately lowered his voice. The hum and rap of a busy police station filtered through his office door. The last thing he needed was someone on the other side hearing this conversation. The day had gone as usual. Nothing much to report but a minor car accident and a couple of petty thefts. Certainly, he hadn't planned on murder.

"Yes, that's exactly what I'm telling you," the boss snarled. "The informer at the state capitol says they somehow trapped Shae." A weighted pause filled Hopkins with images of the boss puffing a fat cigar while he stroked the toy poodle that was snuggled in the crook of his arm. That's the way Hopkins met him — the one and only time he'd seen him.

Chief Hopkins sank to his leather chair, worn shiny by years of use. He looked at the east wall, lined with the merits of achievement gained over his decade of tenure. He'd planned to retire next year. That's when his contract expired with the boss. Then, Hopkins was going to sail into the Gulf of Mexico with a fat checking account and a yacht filled with as many women as he could buy. He never imagined his contract would lead him to murder.

"I'm not a murderer," Hopkins pleaded. He fumbled in his pocket for a Camel and stuck the cigarette between his lips. "I didn't get into this to kill anyone." The smell of tobacco bade him light up.

"I don't remember giving you a choice." The boss' steely voice sent images of tombstones through Darnell. "Maybe I should make this more clear," he said on a final note. "Either you kill Tony Roberts and his friend Eddy or we'll kill *you*. You've got 24 hours." The line clicked.

Darnell, hands trembling, floundered for a lighter and realized he was already holding one. He flicked the flame into existence, sucked on his cigarette, and waited for the smoke to calm him. This time, no release came. Instead, he imagined himself lying on a mortician's slab and nobody giving a flip that he was dead — especially not the head honcho in Chicago.

Once the cigarette was just a butt, he

started another one, then another. After pacing the stuffy office and smoking and debating his options, Darnell came to the conclusion that he'd rather be alive than let Tony Roberts and his friend live. The boss said they probably knew too much. Darnell halted in midstride and stared toward the row of windows behind his desk.

Maybe they even know about me, he thought. The desire to murder started as a hot splinter of fear in the center of his chest. Yet the splinter dissolved into a pool of terror. On one side he had a boss who threatened to kill him; on the other, a couple of local yokels with too much information. At last, Hopkins was consumed with the knowledge that he had precious little choice but to end their lives.

Thirty-Two

Tony steered his Chevy pickup alongside his home and noted that the gray Ford was parked by Victoria's Toyota. He sighed. Victoria wasn't alone after all. The day had been a long one. After delivering an exhaustive report to Quinn and the state police, Eddy and he arrived at the fire station half an hour ago. Now the final shafts of sunlight surged past the horizon to create a bejeweled sky laced with smoky gray clouds.

Tony glanced in his rearview mirror and noted that no strange vehicles followed him. Quinn made a point of Kevin Norris's stating the local authorities were involved as well as key people in the FBI. Brandon Quinn promised they would indeed begin an aggressive investigation they hoped would culminate in rooting out all key people. Now, Tony couldn't shake the conviction that in nabbing Shae they'd only just begun. Quinn seemed to think Kevin Norris might call Tony again, and he encouraged Tony to keep his cool and glean any information he could. As things turned out Brandon Quinn did his job and did it well.

Too bad his attitude has to stink in the process, Tony thought.

He put his truck into park, shut off the engine, and clutched the steering wheel. On the seat beside him lay Eddy's Bible. His friend had insisted Tony take it with him until he could get one of his own. "I've got every version ever printed at home," Eddy had claimed. Thankful for such a loyal friend, Tony laid his hand upon the word of God and paused to marvel at the sunset's beauty. Indeed, no human artist could ever blend together such a perfect array of hues and textures: the turquoise deep sprinkled with foamy caps; the pearly sand stretching as far as the eye could see; the streaks of clouds near the horizon that had changed from gray to rich purple.

Tony gripped the Bible and marveled in the God that created the splendor of nature, the God that had come in the form of a man to die on a cross for him. He nodded and reveled in the newfound peace that hadn't waned since he climbed the steps of the state capitol. In the midst of desperation, the Father had extended to him the faith to believe. Now Tony clung to his faith — a faith he wanted to share with his wife.

"We have a lot to talk about," he said and pulled E.T.'s photo from the front of the

Bible. He examined his daughter's youthful image and debated whether or not to take the picture in. After several uncertain minutes Tony decided to leave the photo for later. "First, the confession," he said and placed the image back into the Bible.

Tony stepped onto the grit of sand on concrete. The smell of the sea, the wisp of a spring breeze seemed to assure him that all would be well.

He double checked his truck's door lock and then trotted up the back porch steps. This was the house he and Victoria had once committed to turning into a home. Maybe now they really could.

Yes, with Christ as the foundation, Tony thought. He started to open the door and step inside but thought better of it. Even though he'd called Victoria when they made it back into town, he still didn't want to startle her. If Jac and she happened to be upstairs and they heard him prowling around, no telling what they might think.

He raised his fist and prepared to rap on the wooden door that featured beveled and etched glass inserts. Yet he stopped as unpleasant memories bombarded him. The times they fought seemed as numberless as the needles on the twisted pine standing nearby. Tony dashed aside the negative and focused upon his newfound hope — a hope kindled by his faith. After all these years, he could present himself to Victoria as an honorable man — an honor he found in Christ.

Summoning his courage Tony rapped on the door and then twisted the knob. The door was locked.

"Good going," he mumbled and attempted to look through the glass. Two figures appeared on the other side and halted.

"Who is it?" Victoria asked, her voice tense.

"It's me, baby," Tony said. "Everything's fine."

The door whipped open. Victoria stood inside, her face strained, her eyes brimming with unshed tears. She wore a snazzy Capri pant set with a pair of strappy sandals. As far as Tony was concerned she looked as good as if she'd been dressed for a ball.

"Hey! What's the deal with the tears?" Tony asked. He brushed at a warm droplet that plopped on her cheek, and she flung herself into his arms.

"I've been so — so worried," she coughed.

"But I called you the minute we left Tallahassee and the minute we got into town."

"I — I know, but — but — oh Tony, I'm so sorry!"

"About what?" Tony buried his face in her wavy hair and stroked the length of it to her waist. The sweet smell of her White Shoulders perfume rocked him with memories of their weekend. Tony pulled her slender form closer and felt as if he was falling in love all over again. While the weekend had certainly been nice he never remembered feeling the incredible love he now experienced for his wife.

"About not — not telling you about Jac," she said and eased her embrace.

"Even though you didn't tell me, I think it was still a good thing you called her in. She was great today." Tony backed away and sneaked a peek into the den in time to see Jac trotting up the stairs. Thoughts of the private eye conjured that restaurant scene. Although the meeting with Macy had taken place only this morning, Tony felt as if a lifetime had occurred since then. He also knew the time had come to be completely honest with his wife. The holy presence filling his heart nudged him toward telling all.

"Let's sit down," he said. "We need to talk."

Victoria twined her fingers in his. After securing the door they walked arm in arm to the couch. Now on the brink of confession

Tony could nearly taste the freedom from his prison of deception. Before settling on the couch beside Victoria he nudged aside one of the closed blinds, glanced outside, and hoped the attorney general acted as swiftly as Brandon Quinn promised.

Tony approached his wife once more and settled beside her on the couch, the color of Destin's seascape. He looked around the room and took in the ambiance of her creation. The careful balance of pastels wove together with her touches of art to create a room with heart. The heart of a princess. Indeed, his wife was a master homemaker. The last few years he'd spent so much time resenting the energies she poured into her talents that he'd stopped appreciating the core of who she was. A tense conviction insisted he express his overdue appreciation.

"You know, honey, what you can do with a room is phenomenal," he said and was glad the awe oozed from his words.

"Do you really think so?" she asked.

"Oh, yes. I don't think most women can do this. You're gifted." He waved his hand and observed the painted lamp shade. "Just like that lamp shade. I mean, who'd have thought of painting our ocean view onto a lamp?"

"You mean you *like* it?" she marveled.

"Of course. It's exquisite." Tony rested his weary head against the cushions. He lifted Victoria's fingers to his lips and allowed them to linger until his senses were full of her sweet perfume.

"There's something different about you, Tony," she said and he turned his face toward her.

"You noticed?" he said.

"Yes. It's in your eyes." Victoria peered deeply into his soul.

This time Tony didn't feel the need to hide behind his walls. Instead, he allowed her to see to the bottom of himself — all the way to the void that Christ's presence now filled. Tony searched Victoria's spirit for some sign of the unconditional acceptance he so longed to see. Yet a part of him shivered at the hard glint he still encountered. A temptation, swift and nearly irresistible, bade him keep his secrets, to make up some story about a relative or friend that would cover that meeting with Macy.

Tony tugged on the collar of the T-shirt he'd changed into at the fire station. Ironically he'd told Eddy he wanted to get out of the dress clothes and go home in comfort. But right now, he felt anything but comfortable despite the worn jeans that were like a second skin. He rubbed his hands together and tried to find the best place to start. No words came. Finally, he decided to begin with his recent decision.

"I guess the reason I seem different," Tony explained, "is because I asked Christ into my heart today. And well, I know for a fact that He came in."

Victoria, silent and still, didn't move. The antique clock sitting atop the console TV ticked away the time while Tony rubbed his thumbnail along the edge of the wicker coffee table.

"Tony, that's wonderful," she finally said and laid a supportive hand on his shoulder.

The graze, now simply tender, recognized the added weight. "I'm glad you think so," he said and covered her hand with his. "And I hope you think it's still great after what I have to tell you." He picked up a copy of *Good Housekeeping*, fanned the pages, laid it back down.

"It's about that redheaded woman, isn't it?" Victoria asked.

Tony snapped his attention to her and didn't break eye contact. "What did Jac tell you?" he asked, groping for a starting place.

"Just that you met with her and that you guys looked at photos." Her face tensed. "What was that all about, Tony?" She sniffled and dabbed the end of her upturned nose with a tissue.

Tony stroked her hair and despised himself for the truth he now must admit. "I lied to you, Victoria," he said.

Her shoulders stiffened. Her fingers dug into the couch's arm. Her hazel eyes, wide as a startled doe's, spilled forth a lifetime of heartache. And Tony felt like the cad of the century.

"Then you *are* having an affair with that —"

"No." He raised his hand and shook his head. "I've never broken our wedding vows," he affirmed. "Not in the sexual sense anyway. I guess I've probably broken that part about cherishing you, though." He stroked her cheeks with the back of his fingers. "And while there was never another woman after we were married . . ." He balled his fist against his knee and chose to focus on the spread of magazines.

"There was before?" she whispered.

Tony swallowed hard and nodded.

"When we were engaged?" she asked on a shrill note.

"No, before I ever even met you." Tony raked his thumb along the edge of his jaw. Now the taste of freedom held a twist of pain. He met Victoria's scrutiny again and was tempted to erect the old walls, say something abrasive, and stomp out. Yet a voice deep within suggested that mode of operation was part of the old Tony. The new Tony far preferred to please Christ.

"Was it that — that redhead?" she prodded. The flush on her cheeks was only matched by the heightened accusation in her voice.

"*No*, Victoria." Tony stood and paced toward the long line of windows whose shades were securely down. "I already told you. I am not, nor have I ever had an affair with her."

"Okay then, who is she?" Victoria stood and clamped her hands at her sides.

A snatch of classical orchestra music floated from upstairs. Tony figured a crashing hard rock tune would better fit the boiling emotions playing across his wife's face.

"She is . . ." Tony paused and wracked his brain for any possible means to tell his story without losing honor in Victoria's eyes. At last he figured he'd never had a silver tongue anyway, and there was no way around the brutal truth. "She is the woman who adopted my daughter," he explained and shoved his fingertips into the tops of his jeans pockets.

Victoria gaped.

"Your — your *daughter?*" she finally asked. "You mean you gave away a baby for —"

"I didn't *give* her away!" Tony's voice came out sharper than he intended, and he struggled against the bile boiling within his spirit. "My girlfriend and I decided that she would be better off with a family who was ready for children. We were only seventeen."

Victoria hugged herself and observed Tony in stunned silence.

"The adoptive mother contacted me just last week. We arranged a meeting this morning." He shrugged. "I guess she needed to make sure she wants me in her daughter's life." After pacing toward the beveled glass door he faced Victoria. "I'm going to meet Toni for the first time on Wednesday."

"Toni?"

"Yes. That's my birth daughter's name. Evelyn Toni Sinclaire." A trace of delight sparkled amid the stress. "From what I understand her friends call her E.T." His lips curled into a half smile. "That nickname just *slays* me. Anyway, she's tall like me," he added with pride, "and plays basketball on her high school team." A new thought bombarded Tony, and he wondered if perhaps Victoria might even go with him to meet her.

"You are going to meet her the day after tomorrow?" All color drained from Victoria's face. Only twin splotches of rouge remained. Tony recalled her pallid features during the TV show right before her miscarriage.

"Wednesday," he supplied. "I'm driving to Orlando."

"And all these years —"

"All these years, I guess . . ." He crammed a hand into the hip pocket of his cotton-soft jeans. "I guess you could say I was living a lie."

"You *lied* to me about knowing Jesus and you *lied* to me about this — this illegitimate child!" Victoria's face twisted in fury.

"Don't talk about her like that," Tony said. He crossed his arms and backed away. "She can't help it because —"

"So now you're defending your sin!" she blasted.

Her accusatory tone made him feel as if he'd been punched in the gut. He reeled with the mounting tension. Something inside suggested the time had come to blow up and retreat, as he'd done for six years. Yet a calm presence within bade him hold steady. "No, I'm not defending my sin," he explained. "I'm just saying that Toni didn't have a choice in this matter. We can't blame her —"

"You lied to me!" she yelled and stomped her foot.

The stomping got to him. He hated it when she stomped at him because she made him feel like a disobedient child.

"Okay, I lied to you," he exploded. "And you lied to me about calling Jac!" Despite his attempt to stay calm he tromped across the living room as if he were heading into battle.

Victoria lifted her chin and glared at him through teary eyes. "It's not the same," she said with a hard twist to her lips. "That was for your best interest, and —"

"Oh, and you think my lie *wasn't* for my best interest?" Tony demanded. "Obviously it was because you're about as compassionate as a rabid bulldog!" He waved his arm and hit the edge of the painted lamp shade. The thing toppled off the table and crashed to the floor. The ping of broken glass accompanied hundreds of light bulb slivers. Dead silence permeated the room. Tony gazed at the lamp, a creation he'd praised minutes before.

With a broken sob Victoria lunged toward the stairway.

"Victoria!" Tony called and raced after her. "Don't do this!" he demanded. "I'm not through."

She stopped halfway up the stairs and pivoted to face him. "Well I am!" she screamed, her face contorting in fury.

Thirty-Three

As soon as the bedroom door slammed, Tony rushed after Victoria. However, he stopped the second he crested the top of the stairway. The baby's room was open. Tony peered into the shadows. Victoria's touches were undeniable. The white crib. The rocking horse border near the ceiling. An oversized teddy bear in the corner. A pile of disposable diapers were stacked on the changing table. When Victoria started preparing, she left nothing out.

Tony closed his eyes and leaned into the handrail. The last few months had been nothing but one upheaval after another. Their separation . . . the loss of the baby . . . this tangled web he'd fallen into. Now Victoria had to deal with the added pain of her husband confessing a monumental lie.

He opened his eyes, observed the baby's room, and decided to extend to Victoria what God had extended to him: an ample supply of grace.

The bathroom door opened, and Jacquelyn stepped out. Dressed in jogging shorts and a baggy T-shirt she toweled her hair dry. When she saw Tony she stopped. They hadn't spoken since they each gave a report at the attorney general's office. He didn't delude himself into believing that she hadn't heard her friend's volatile retreat. He fully expected to be the brunt of Jac's aggravation. Those seven friends were more apt to defend each other than not.

Instead of censure Jacquelyn offered a smile. Her eyes, dark and observant, evoked kindness rather than judgment.

"Want to share some herbal tea?" she asked and darted a glance toward Victoria's bedroom.

"Sure," Tony said, "but I'll rummage around for some Coke. I think Victoria got some over the weekend." He started down the stairway, paused, and glanced back at the bedroom.

Jacquelyn, close behind, patted him on shoulder. "Maybe all she needs is some time to cool off," she explained, yet her voice held little conviction.

Tony quirked an eyebrow and examined Jac's expression. He wouldn't vow that she approved of Victoria at this moment. The realization shocked him into mumbling a placid okay and continuing on his journey to the kitchen.

Soon, he and Jacquelyn found the beverages of their choice and settled at the dining room table. Jac held her herbal tea to her lips, paused, and looked at Tony over the rim.

"I have a confession to make," she said.

"Oh?" Tony pushed an ice cube into the depths of his Coke. It bobbed down and popped back up. Absently he wondered how long he should give Victoria while trying to offer Jac at least the semblance of his attention.

"I heard much of what was said down here," she admitted.

Tony rubbed his thumb along his jaw. "Well, that figures," he said. "We weren't exactly trying to keep it down."

"I just want to tell you that —" She stopped and toyed with the wick of an apple spice candle sitting in the middle of the table. Tony leaned forward and tried to read her expression. Her short black hair, tousled from the towel, hung around her face and shadowed her features. Tony had never spent a lot of time with Jac, but he was learning that she didn't play games.

"Let's see." She looked upward. "I think Victoria has a few problems."

"Oh, so you aren't, like, taking her side?" Tony asked, his forehead wrinkled.

"Let's see," she said again and worried

the charred wick. "How do I say this . . . uh . . . I think maybe Victoria — maybe Victoria has some *spiritual* problems."

"As in . . ." Tony prompted and wished he could reach into her mind and pull out her complete thoughts. He casually sipped his soda and tried to harbor his impatience.

"Understand that I love her. She's my friend. All seven of us have been through a lot together. . . ."

Tony leaned back in the seat and shook his head. "I thought you gals all thought I was the scum of the earth by now."

"Nope." Jac propped her chin in her hand and her full lips tilted at the corners. "We love each other *to death.* There's nothing we wouldn't do for each other. But, well, by this point we've been friends so long we know each other's faults." She picked up a salt shaker and tapped a few grains on the table. "We've just decided to love each other despite our faults," Jac finished.

"So, uh, define spiritual problems," Tony said.

"It's all about rules for Victoria." Jacquelyn leaned back in her chair and cleared her throat. "I probably don't need to say anymore," she admitted with a sheepish grin. "She'll be yelling at me before the night's over. I guess I just wanted to let you know that, well, I hope it all works out between you two. And I'm going to be praying for you. Actually, all the sisters are, for that matter."

"Thanks," Tony said and drank half the glass of soda. When he deposited the tumbler back on the table, his cell phone began playing Eddy's favorite tune.

Tony clicked the phone from the holster, examined the screen and encountered the words "unknown caller." Still distracted with Victoria he pressed the answer button without a thought for who the caller might be.

Tony spoke the obligatory greeting and waited for a return. No answer came. He glanced at the screen to see if perhaps the call had been disconnected, yet the display showed a long number and the "connected" indicator. *Maybe it's some sort of a solicitation,* he thought.

"Hello," Tony repeated with intent to disconnect the call if no one spoke.

"Is this Tony Roberts?" A familiar voice, tense and hard, blasted his ear.

"Yes." Tony tried to place the voice as Jac retrieved an apple from the refrigerator. The snap of the refrigerator's door seemed to usher in recognition. *Kevin Norris!*

"This is Kevin Norris." His response

echoed Tony's thoughts.

"I recognized your voice," Tony responded and attempted to keep his tone even. Brandon Quinn insisted that Tony not aggravate the banker if he called again. *Try to get as much out of him as you can!* Quinn insisted. *Don't anger him again. The longer you can keep him talking the better. The longer he talks, the more he'll probably tell you.*

"Good. I'm glad you're still alive," Kevin said and his voice drained of all tension.

"Well, things have been a little, er, hectic, since I last talked to you."

"Hectic?"

"Yes. Scary." Tony and Jac made eye contact and held it.

"They've been after you?"

"Buster Shae. Know him?"

Silence was his only answer.

"We managed to take him down at the state capital today."

"The state capital?"

"Yes, my friend has connections with the attorney general's office. To make a long story short, Shae is in jail tonight."

"But he's not the only one!" Norris insisted.

"I know." Tony leaned forward and scooted the chair back against ceramic tile.

"You should have taken my offer and gotten out of there."

Tony bit back a retort about dirty money.

"I don't have long to talk," Kevin said.

"Why are you calling again?" Tony asked, and motioned for Jacquelyn to hand him the note pad and pen lying on the counter.

"What I have for you this time will clean up the problem," Norris said, his voice strained.

Jacquelyn plopped the note pad on the table and placed the pen in Tony's hand. He wrote, "Kevin Norris!!" on the pad and shoved it back to Jac.

When she read the note, her inky eyes sharpened.

"What are you offering?" Tony asked and was astounded that his voice didn't reflect the rapid tattoo of his heart.

"Facts, names, places. You interested?"

"As in . . ."

"As in the whole scoop on the money-laundering setup."

"Why?" Tony asked.

"You saved the lives of my wife and child. In spite of what you might think of me, I still love my family more than life. I just can't let them kill you. I can't! I've had the most miserable weekend of my life. I've been so down Rhonda even thinks I'm sick."

Maybe he does *have a conscience,* Tony thought and regretted his rudeness during the last call.

"When I saved your family it was all in a day's work," Tony said. "But I'll take the info any way you want to hand it out. We're talking about my neck here!" He gulped a deep swallow of cola, stood, and began pacing the kitchen. The white cabinets and cheery flowers seemed an ironic backdrop for such dark schemes.

"O.K. Here's the deal. Every bit of information is in a safety deposit box at the bank. Once I realized the magnitude of what I was involved in I started keeping records."

"Uh huh."

"There are two keys to the deposit box. I have one. My mom has the other."

"Your mom?" Tony imagined a little old lady in an apron being held hostage by gangsters after that key.

"Yes. All she knows is that it's an extra key to a deposit box that holds important paperwork. I'm placing a call to her as soon as I hang up. I'll give you instructions to her house. You call the attorney general's office. Have them send some protection for you. Go get the key, go to the bank, and hand everything over to the attorney general."

"What all is in this box?" Tony questioned.

"A list of names — from the biggest guys in the laundering scheme down to the guy over me. Some are foreign but not out of reach. Transaction numbers on most of the deposits. Drop spots. Corporations that are involved. People paid off to look the other way. That includes people in the FBI. This list also includes the chief of police in Destin — Darnell Hopkins."

Tony stopped pacing and whirled to face Jac. She stood erect, as if ready to go to battle.

"The chief of police is in on this?"

"Yes."

He surged toward the table, grabbed the pen and pad, and scribbled, "Darnell Hopkins, chief of police — Destin." Jacquelyn read the inscription and whistled.

"Who else is involved locally?" Tony demanded. "I'm thinking I really ought to get out of town and *stay* out for awhile."

"No one else locally," Norris said. "But there is a mole in the attorney general's office."

"Holy cow!" Tony shook his head and collapsed into the chair Jac had vacated. He covered the mouthpiece and looked at the detective. "He says there's a mole in the attorney general's office."

She never flinched.

"Care to tell me his name?"

"It's all at the bank."

"Is it by chance Brandon Quinn?"

"No. That name doesn't ring a bell. I'm almost certain there's no Quinn involved," Norris said.

"Thank goodness," Tony breathed, "that's who we reported to today."

"Got a pen and paper?" Norris asked. "I want to give you my mother's contact information and her number. I'll tell her you're coming. It's after dark there, right?"

"Right."

"Go to my mom's tonight while it's dark. Also, call your contact at the attorney general's office. Can you call him now and have him meet you there in the morning?"

"Uh . . . their offices are closed," Tony began and stopped himself. "Wait, my friend can call his brother-in-law at home."

"Good. Here's Mom's information."

Tony scribbled to keep up with Kevin's rapid rendition of his mother's street address and phone number.

"Now, give me ten minutes to call my mom and tell her you're coming and then get over there and back as quickly as you can. I'll call you back in an hour to make

sure everything went smoothly. Understand?"

"Yes. Of course," Tony said. "But —" He
stopped himself and debated the wisdom of
posing the question that had popped into
his mind.

"Was there something else?" Norris
asked.

"I . . . was just wondering why you waited
to give me this information," he said and
couldn't deny the thread of irritation in his
voice.

"That wasn't my original plan." Norris'
tone dared Tony to doubt his wisdom. "My
original plan was to offer you a way out of
the U.S. If you declined I was going to tell
you about the files. But you made me mad,
Roberts, really mad," Norris said, a tinge of
hostility lacing his words. "Before I knew it
I'd hung up on you. And I wasn't in the
mood to chitchat anymore!"

"Why didn't you just offer the files in the
first place?" Tony asked and raised his
hand.

"Listen to me," Norris ground out. "Get
it through your thick skull. You are *still* in
danger. Just because you know the location
of the files and you're planning to give them
to the authorities doesn't mean they won't
kill you! In my opinion, your best bet is still

to *leave* the country!" his voice crescendoed on a high note.

"Okay, okay," Tony said and lifted his hand palm outward. "I — I understand."

Once darkness claimed the ocean, Darnell Hopkins crept through the shadows beside the Roberts' residence. A hunting knife strapped to his belt proved his only weapon. A black shirt and slacks helped him mingle with the shadows. The bitter smell of geraniums tainted the air and he noticed a clay pot full of the flowers near the driveway.

The continued swoosh of the ocean rushing inland seemed to whisper, "Murder, murder, murder. Murder him now."

Darnell, his blood hot, had worked himself up into a frenzied state of despair. He had watched the fire station most of the evening until Tony and Eddy arrived. The whole time the boss' final words left Hopkins no choice. Absolutely none. It was either Tony's life or his. And after Tony, Eddy Graham.

He stroked the knife's slender handle, whose blade was in the sheath on his belt. After thinking all afternoon he'd finally come to the conclusion that he shouldn't use a gun. Bullets could be traced. But if he stabbed Tony in the heart he could take the knife with him. No one would ever suspect that the chief of police was the criminal. He could continue with his profitable games for another year as planned.

Now all Darnell needed was the opportunity. If Roberts didn't exit his home this evening, Darnell would be forced to go inside.

Thirty-Four

Victoria sat in the middle of her bed, legs crossed, and stared at the far wall. The framed wedding photos now claimed their rightful spot. She had rehung them in an attempt to please Tony. When he noticed, his ready smile was all the answer she needed. Now she felt as if their whole marriage had been nothing but a charade.

Numb from the shock of his news she relived their wedding night. Both of them had been nervous — especially Victoria. And Tony had pretended to discover the ecstasies of marital union for the first time. He told her he never gave himself to another woman. He'd lied about his past and turned their present into nothing but one gaping falsehood.

Victoria began to gently rock. No tears came. Only the hollow loneliness of a soul that has been betrayed. One thing that Victoria had always said, "If I'm going to save myself for my husband then I want a husband who has done the same." Victoria had never accepted double standards. *Never!* Tony's lack of a sexual past was one of the things that helped her decide to marry him.

"And the whole thing was a lie," she whispered. "Our whole marriage has been a lie."

She frowned at the wedding photos until she could stand them no more. On an impulse Victoria stood and removed them one at a time. She placed the smaller ones atop the largest and then scooted them under the bed. Once they were out of sight she experienced the conviction that perhaps she should extend Tony the grace she would have wished he extend to her. Her fingernails ate into her palms and she wondered if there was any way to erase the pain he'd inflicted. Finally, she shook her head. No, the pain wouldn't ease. Victoria couldn't help the way she felt, and right now her emotions were all negative.

She walked to the window and leaned against the frame. Pressing her lips together, Victoria tried to absorb the news that her husband had an 18-year-old daughter somewhere. A girl whom she'd never met. A girl who probably resembled Tony's girlfriend. A wave of blind jealousy nearly knocked her flat. And Victoria wondered if she would have been any less devastated if Tony were having an affair now.

As Victoria rested her forehead against the cool windowpane, she stared upon the

Destin evening. The lamp's glow prohibited her from seeing many details, only the street lamps and headlights of passing vehicles. The moonless night might as well have been the landscape of her soul.

A gentle knock vibrated against the door, and Victoria hunched her shoulders.

"Victoria?" Tony's voice, low and urgent, beseeched her. "Can we talk?"

"There's nothing left t–to talk about." Her eyes began to sting, and she pressed them with a wadded tissue. *Doesn't he understand I can't talk right now?*

"I just wish you'd let me apologize."

"I'm listening," she choked out and wished she could hide the evidence of her tears.

"Are you going to make me talk through the door?"

Dead silence pervaded the room.

"Victoria?" he repeated.

Darting a prayer toward heaven Tony tried the knob. The hinge produced a muted creak as he eased open the door. Victoria stood near the window, her back to him. The lamp's gauzy glow outlined the slender curves of her body. In times past, that alone would have stirred Tony's emotions, yet this time her forlorn appearance touched other places in his being. She was an integral part of him because of the mystical bond that made them one. Victoria — God's creation — was to be cared for and nourished and protected.

"Victoria?" he repeated.

When she didn't answer or turn to him Tony recognized the old flames of resentment creeping into his mind. He managed to extinguish them with a renewed vow to keep his cool.

"You know," he began and tried to choose his words well, "I'm not a great theologian. But I *do* know that when I reached out to Christ today He was there. He didn't accuse me. He forgave me. And I — I guess that's what I need from you right now. Forgiveness . . . and maybe a little grace." Tony stepped toward her and stopped about five feet away. He rested his weight on one leg and placed a hand on his hip.

"Well, how would *you* feel?" she asked, her voice rigid, accusing.

The question felt like a slap. Tony winced. A slow anger began to simmer at the bottom of his soul, and he didn't try to extinguish it this time.

She whirled to face him, her eyes swollen and red, her hands balled at her side.

"Well?" she demanded. "Would you be all roses and kindness and understanding if *you* found out I had a child out of wedlock — that I'd — I'd lied to you about all these years? Wouldn't it somehow affect the way you felt toward me?"

"You *did* lie to me," Tony snapped. "You went behind my back and got Jac here and then pretended like she wasn't here!" He raised his hand.

"I already told you. That's different." She jerked on the hem of her blouse as if to underscore her claim.

"No, it's not." Each word resonated with deliberate emphasis.

Her eyes blazed with unquenchable fury and she blasted him with a silent glare.

"All I wanted was to ask you to forgive me. I guess I have my answer," he snarled and didn't attempt to keep the disdain from his voice.

"We've been married six years, Tony," she snarled right back. "I've forgiven you so much already — more than most women ever would."

"Oh, so now you're through forgiving?" Tony swept his palms together as if he were dusting them. Jac's comments about Victoria's religion being rule-based resounded with the rhythm of his hands.

"Look, Tony, I've had enough of this. All you can see is *your* side! That's the way it's been from the start. You're always more interested in what *you* want and what you think than in meeting my needs."

"Well, what about this past weekend?" he demanded, his voice rising with every comment. "I thought that was something special — at least you *said* it was!"

She ignored him. "All these years I've looked over the hurt and kept trying, but you *lied* to me about something *so important!*" Her cheeks flamed scarlet.

His lips turned down at the corners, and he was engulfed in a momentary wave of confusion. Tony wasn't a Christian with years of experience. On the contrary, he was just beginning. But from the second he connected with Christ — *really connected* — he'd experienced an overwhelming sense of being loved, of being forgiven. And that forgiveness spanned so much that Tony had no desire to hold a grudge against another person. Even when Victoria confessed to having deceived him, he had readily released any bitterness.

"You just don't get it, do you?" he finally asked.

"Get what?" She shook her head a bit.

"You know, if I didn't know any better —"

He stopped himself short of stating the unexpected thought.

"What?" she asked and leaned toward him, as if by getting closer she could read his mind. Victoria never had been able to tolerate someone not completing thoughts with her. It usually drove her crazy.

But this thought was so unexpected and so debatable that Tony dared not state it. As mad as she was now, he figured voicing these words would turn her into a ball of fire. "Never mind," he said and headed for the door before this got any uglier.

"Tony Roberts!" she snapped and a thud attested to her stomp. "Don't do this to me! Don't start something and not finish it!"

The urge to speak his mind overtook him. The stomping was what got to him. He whirled back to face her, and the words began spilling from his mouth before he could stop himself.

"Okay, I'll finish then, if that's what you want!" He pointed a finger at her. "If I didn't know any better, I'd say you don't even *know* Christ, Victoria!"

Her mouth fell open. Her eyes widened. She balled a fist and punched it against her palm. "How *dare* you!" she shrieked.

"I dare because you preach one thing and live another!" he yelled. "All these years,

Victoria, all these years you've acted like you're just a little too good for me because I'm not in church every time the doors are opened."

Her mute fury pooled in shattered eyes and spilled onto her cheeks.

"You're doing the exact same thing now! You think it's just horrific that I lied to you, but you think your lie wasn't as bad! I don't know a lot about walking with Christ, but one thing I *do* know is that a lie is a lie! And the second He forgave me today I knew I couldn't hold your lie against you because He has forgiven me of so much, I —"

"Get *out* of here!" she bellowed. "I don't need your sermons!"

"No, *you need Jesus!*" Tony accused. Before she could utter another word he marched toward the doorway. Once on the threshold he whipped back around. "You know *about* Him, Victoria. You've known about Him your whole life! But I want to know if you really, *really* know Him?"

Tony slammed the bedroom door and rushed toward the stairs. He didn't stop to even say goodbye to Jac, still sitting at the kitchen table.

"Tony!" Jac called.

He gripped the doorknob and kept his back to her.

"Don't forget about Kevin Norris's mother," she admonished.

With a growl he crammed a hand into the top of his hair. "I *did* completely forget! How could I have forgotten?"

"Er, I think we could say you're under a lit–tle stress here." Her nearing voice accompanied the pat of bare feet on tile. "Here's the directions."

He pivoted and took the piece of paper. "Thanks."

"You bet," she said and silently retreated.

Head hanging he opened the door and stepped into the fragrant night. The ocean's ever-present roar seemed to mock him. Out of habit Tony inserted his key into the deadbolt and clicked the lock into place. Never had he been in such turmoil — not even when he'd said goodbye to his daughter.

He moved to the first step and stood between the handrails. Looking at the myriad stars glistening above, he sensed God's presence. *Despite how badly I blew it, You're still with me,* he marveled and couldn't deny that his aggravation with Victoria was far from extinguished. A tempting voice, strong and unyielding, suggested that he hold a grudge against Victoria for her lack of ready forgiveness. The struggle within refused to relent as he descended the steps and stepped to the left.

A rustling from behind insisted Tony stop. In a split second his concerns over his marriage were replaced with the potential for peril. He wanted to dismiss the noise and move toward the truck. He wanted to, but he couldn't.

Before Tony could turn, a lean arm circled his neck, ate into his Adam's apple, and sent a wad of pain to the back of his throat. As the word "murder" breached his mind, the flash of a blade moved toward his chest. The metal went through his T-shirt and entered the muscles. A searing pain zipped from his chest, and he released a muffled cry.

Tony bent his knees and rolled forward. His attacker toppled over his back and landed in front of him with an "umph" and a thud. Panting, Tony rose and staggered back into the railing by the steps. The aging wood groaned and cracked beneath his weight.

A rivulet, warm and oozing, streamed toward his waist. Gripping the railing he touched his chest. When Tony drew his fingers away they were coated in blood. The tall redheaded man now facing him inched forward. He moved the knife from hand to hand as if he were preparing to carve meat. The man looked quite familiar — someone he'd seen around town but in the present panic he couldn't place a name with the flushed face.

"Jacquelyn!" he yelled and hoped Victoria's claim about her friend's blackbelt was not hype. Tony had never shrunk from defending himself, yet he was unarmed, facing a knife, and already injured. The knife wound pulsed with his every heartbeat and Tony resisted the urge to sink to his knees and nurse the injury.

The assailant, panting and determined, rushed in. He feinted a move to the right. Tony went with the move. The knife flew to the man's opposite hand and bore in from the left. Tony's knee hit the ground with a burn as the knife entered again; this time, tearing deeper into protesting flesh.

"Aaaahhhh!" Tony hollered and his fingers ached with the struggle to break the knife from the maniac's hand.

The assailant's hot breath, laden with the scent of tobacco, fanned Tony's cheeks and sent raw repulsion through his veins. The attacker was about to strike a third time when the door banged open. The man swiveled to face the intruder. His crazed blue eyes were soon smudged by a sarcastic smirk. Somehow a wad of grit had claimed Tony's mouth. He grimaced against the taste of earth and welcomed the sight of Jacquelyn. She stood at the top of the steps, replete in her jogging shorts and loose T-shirt.

Face impassive, eyes afire, she moved down the steps toward the man. When Jacquelyn arrived within kicking distance she stopped, crouched, and balled her fists. A battle cry splitting the night, the assailant lunged. A kick of her right foot sent the knife flying into the distant sand. That only added fuel to the animal's vengeance. He screamed like a rabid bear and rushed her anew. A deft whirl placed her heel in his ribcage with a smack and her grunt. He doubled over in breathless agony, yet Jac didn't stop. Her face crumpled into a warrior's mask, and she kicked the man's right knee. Her victory roar accompanied tearing ligaments.

"No more. Oh, please stop," the man begged as he crashed to the ground like a writhing Goliath. And in that moment Tony remembered where he'd seen this heathen — behind the wheel of a police car. A car with "Chief of Police" written on the side.

"Darnell Hopkins!" Tony panted.

Jacquelyn jumped to Tony's side, and he

pulled himself to a sitting position. His left hand clutched his chest as copious blood oozed onto his palm.

"I'll call an ambulance," Jacquelyn said.

"No — no!" Tony shook his head. "The key. Somebody needs to get the key. And — and call the p–p — call the police."

"But how do we know they'll help?"

"He's the only one, Jacquelyn," Tony explained.

"Oh somebody help me." The spring breeze lifted Darnell's panicked cries toward the heaving ocean.

"Fine, that's fine." Jacquelyn said and shoved her disheveled hair out of her face. "I'll call the police. But we need some EMTs here for *you*."

"Oh, help me," Tony groaned as Jacquelyn's face wobbled in and out of focus. "I can't s–stand EMTs. B–bossy." He struggled against the gray mist creeping across his vision. "They're too — too b–bossy."

Victoria paced the emergency room waiting area. Presently Destin's small clinic wasn't very crowded, and Victoria thanked God that half the town wasn't going to see her sobbing. She mopped her drenched face and did her best to contain her emotions, yet the task seemed an impossibility.

A concerned R.N. approached and laid a hand on her shoulder. "I really believe he's going to be okay, ma'am," the young man said. "The doctor is bandaging him now, and he's come back to consciousness. I thought the doctor told you the wounds weren't as deep as they originally thought."

"Oh, I know, I know!" She waved her hand. "It's not just about that. I'll —" She hiccuped. "I'll be okay."

"Are you sure?" The R.N.'s concerned gaze roved her face. "May I get you some coffee or a soda?"

"N–no." Victoria sniffled. Despite the fact that he meant well, she wished he'd move along. *"Really!"* she added. He finally took the hint and meandered back to his post.

The first Victoria knew of the emergency was when Jacquelyn used Tony's cell phone to call her. She had immediately rushed downstairs and knelt at Tony's side as he floated in and out of consciousness. Seeing his shirt covered in blood, the gray tinge of his cheeks, the limp tilt of his neck had nearly sent Victoria into hysterics.

The ambulance descended upon the home seconds before the police. Soon, Victoria crawled into the ambulance beside Tony's gurney. The last Victoria saw of

Jacquelyn she was detailing a full report to a couple of astounded policemen who were preparing to arrest their injured chief. He, of course, was now doing time in the emergency clinic before doing time in jail. Through it all Victoria somehow contained herself. Her composure only lasted until they arrived at the clinic and Tony was wheeled into a room.

A new wail burst upon her, and she covered her face. A young couple entered the clinic with a screaming child, and their attention immediately rested upon her. With a mortified groan she stumbled toward the ladies' room and shoved open the door. A quick check validated she was alone.

Victoria stepped toward the sink, turned on the cold water, and bathed her face. The shock of the chill took her breath but enabled her to bite back a renewed round of tears. She fumbled for a paper towel, scrubbed her face dry, and looked at her reflection in the mirror.

A swollen-eyed woman stared back at her — a woman who needed to radically encounter the love of Christ.

"You have been s–so wrong," she whispered and shook her head. The thing that distressed Victoria the most was the picture of her own ragged, filthy self-righteousness in the face of Tony's newborn purity. "He was right," she told her reflection. The fire of conviction ravaged her spirit.

Tony's direct comments had shoved Victoria to an edge of a precipice she'd never encountered. For the first time in her life Victoria came face to face with her need of a Savior. She had always attended church. She had talked like a Christian. She had lived like a Christian. She even called the name of Jesus in her infrequent prayers. But deep in her heart Victoria used her righteous lifestyle as a platform for elevating herself. Her swollen face chilled as she realized she was looking in the face of a Pharisee — someone who kept the letter of the law but was missing the heart of Christ.

Victoria moaned anew, leaned against the wall, and slid to the tile floor. "Oh Jesus," she groaned, "save me. I am a sinner. I need You. Oh, Jesus, forgive me." She pulled her knees to her chest, rested her forehead on her knees, and heaved against the contrition surging through her spirit. For the first time in her life, Victoria recognized that nothing she ever did was good enough. *Nothing.* Only by God's grace could she stand complete before the Lord. Only by His mercy. Only by His love.

"And I have no business railing at Tony

about lying to me when I lied to him, too," she confessed. Speaking of Tony's indiscretion conjured images of a daughter he'd never even met. A renewed current of negativity threatened to suck her back into the grips of jealousy and resentment and self-righteousness. "Oh, God, help me," she whispered, "I was *horrible* to him."

She thought of that pending meeting with his daughter, and a certain awareness surged through her. Despite her struggles with her vacillating emotions, Victoria whispered a broken admission, "I can't let him go meet her alone." She rested her cheek on her knees. Absently, Victoria stared at the tiny gray tiles that merged as one to cover the floor. A single thought, like a firefly at dusk that refused to be extinguished, flew into her mind: *You're his wife. Go with him!* She hiccuped. *I will.*

On the heels of this decision a supernatural presence flowed through her soul like a pristine ocean, holy and pure, filling a dark and wretched cavern. As the heavenly waters rushed her spirit they brought deliverance and healing and hope. Hope that she and Tony really *could* begin again. This time, with Christ in the center of *both* their lives.

Thirty-Five

Tony awoke to a gentle shaking that jostled him to the edge of sleep and sent a stab of pain through his chest. At first he thought he was still in the hospital. In his hazy state he'd been dreaming that the doctor was trying to stop him from making the trip to meet his daughter. A pair of bossy EMTs appeared with the intent to trap him in rehab and hold him hostage. The shaking continued, and Tony attempted to wave off the EMTs.

Yet when his eyes slid open Victoria's face was inches from his — no EMTs in sight.

"We're here," she said, her concerned gaze penetrating his.

Tony plunged into an alert state. He dashed an excited glance around the Sinclaires' neighborhood. The houses along Magnolia Lane were stamped with a neat but classic design. Clearly this was a neighborhood that had been upscale 50 years ago but now graciously served the middle incomers. Next door an American flag flowed in the summerish Orlando breeze while the Sinclaires' meticulous yard resembled the work of a master landscaper. Tony pivoted in his seat. The trees along the sidewalk provided a canopy of thick limbs over Magnolia Lane. The neighborhood's general ambiance indicated a haven of peace.

"I like it," he said and smiled.

"Yes, it's a nice neighborhood." Victoria smiled back, and Tony reveled in the love spilling from her eyes.

He brushed her cheek with the backs of his fingers and snagged her hand in his. "I love you so much," he whispered, and his chest muscles protested with the movement. He tried to hide a grimace and resisted touching the stab wounds. When the doctor released him yesterday morning he'd frowned on Tony getting the key from Norris's mother and retrieving the incriminating paperwork for the attorney general's office.

If the physician knew I made this trip he'd probably slam me back into the hospital. Tony figured that crazy dream sprang from the doctor's injunction that he stay home for a few days.

"Are you going to be okay?" Victoria questioned. "I've got more ibuprofen."

"Woman," he gruffly teased, "you're going to fill me full of that stuff."

"If you wouldn't be so ornery about it and

take the full dose the doctor said to, I'm sure it would help."

"I'm okay," he confirmed and touched the thin bandages covering his chest.

"You look a little pale, that's all." She fidgeted with her purse and keys. "I just hope this doesn't so wear you out —"

"Nervous?" he asked.

Victoria's fingers rested on the top of her purse. She sighed and helplessly gazed at him. "Can you tell?"

"Yep." Tony conjured his most reassuring smile. "I'm supposed to be the one who's nervous here."

Her eyes filled with unshed tears. "I guess part of the reason I'm so nervous is because I . . ." She trailed off and looked out the opposite window.

"Don't do that." Tony tapped her on her shoulder. "You know Victoria can't stand it when you don't finish your sentences."

A snicker escaped her and she faced him once more. "I just hope I don't disappoint you. And well, I'm so — so sorry about that explosion the other night," she added and shook her head. Simmering tears dotted her lashes.

"Ah, honey." Tony leaned toward her and gently tugged her head toward his shoulder. "You've already apologized. We *both* said some things that —"

Before her head touched his shoulder Victoria pulled away. "I know, but the deal is, Tony, you were *right*. All these years I've blamed you for our marriage problems — all these years. And I was just as carnal as —" She bit her bottom lip and lowered her gaze.

"As I was?"

"I didn't say that."

"But it's the truth." Tony shook his head and chuckled. "I blamed you. You blamed me. And —"

"I guess we were both up to our eyeballs in our*selves*."

Tony shifted in his seat and focused solely upon his wife. "Well, hopefully we're both up to our eyeballs in Jesus now," he said.

"I hope so." Victoria placed her hand on the side of his face. The warmth from her palm seeped all the way to his soul as Tony finally saw in her eyes what he'd seen in the eyes of Rhonda Norris and Marilyn Langham — grace. No blame. No accusation. No questions. Nothing but acceptance. Acceptance and love. Love and forgiveness.

"Thanks for coming today." Tony kissed the inside of her palm. "It really means a lot."

"I wouldn't miss it for the world." Victoria darted a glance toward the house. "If she's important to you, she's important to me."

Tony cupped her face in his hand and bestowed a gentle kiss upon lips as soft as satin. He never dreamed marriage could be so good.

E.T. sat in the rocking chair in the corner of a bedroom that resembled a checkerboard of posters and pinups. In one hand she held the silver rattle. In the other, she held the cherished letter. Her birth father was scheduled to arrive any minute, and Evelyn analyzed a dozen different ways she should greet him. None seemed right.

Her fingers shaking, she tucked a curtain of freshly washed hair behind her ear. She'd chosen a pantsuit the color of her eyes, and her dad told her she looked beautiful. He'd always said she was the prettiest girl in the world. As a little girl she really believed that must be true. When she aged into a young woman Evelyn realized her father was biased — but that made his endearments all the more precious.

She stood up, walked around her bed, stepped back to the rocker, and sat down. Evelyn checked her watch. Four o'clock was a minute away. Her parents told her his name was Tony Roberts and that he was married to a lady named Victoria. They had no children. Her mother also said Tony looked just like E.T.

"What should I call him?" she'd asked her mom over last night's dinner.

"Why not try Tony," she'd said and dashed an uncertain glance toward Evelyn's dad.

E.T. had looked at him and recognized a trace of insecurity in his vulnerable brown eyes. *He* had always been her dad. E.T. decided to reserve the cherished word only for him. "Yes, I think I should just call him Tony," she agreed and somehow sensed that her birth father would understand.

She fidgeted with the note again and decided to go spray on some of the light floral perfume her mother had given her for her eighteenth birthday. With that task complete, Evelyn debated whether to remain in her room or wait in the living room. Either way she was dying with impatience.

She shook that tiny silver rattle, and it glistened in the overhead lighting. E.T. pondered the note, and an inner voice suggested she should read it one more time. Settling back into the rocking chair, Evelyn opened the letter and began rereading the lines that had changed her life.

My dearest Toni,

Words cannot express to you what I am feeling at this moment. As I write you this message, I already love you yet I've never even seen you. The decision to release you was one of the hardest I have ever made. But, my baby, you must understand that I have no way to provide for you. Please understand that a part of me will always be with you and that one day perhaps you and I will be reunited. Please believe me when I tell you, if there was any other way, I would choose not to release you. But I honestly believe I have no choice. My only hope is that you can one day grow into a beautiful, strong woman who will have the courage and strength to forgive me. I will always love you.

Your First Daddy

Evelyn's eyes stung, yet she stopped herself from relinquishing the tears. She'd cried enough. Today was a season for rejoicing. Matthew Leavey was even coming for dinner. When Evelyn told him she'd found her birth father, he was so awed that the natural thing was to invite him to help celebrate the reunion. And she hoped that if his birth mother would cooperate they might be able to find *his* father as well.

The doorbell rang. E.T. curled her toes and glanced toward her bedroom door. "This is it," she whispered and moved into the hallway that smelled of her mom's peach cobbler. The journey down the corridor felt like the pathway to a new dimension of her life.

By the time Evelyn stepped into the classic living room, replete with her trophy case, her parents were already at the door greeting a tall man with blond hair. Tony turned to introduce his petite wife. Her slender curves and relaxed smile made E.T. feel gangly and at a loss for words. Yet her attention was drawn back to her father whose facial features so resembled her own. Pale eyebrows, gray eyes, a prominent nose, square jaw. His navy blazer and gray dress pants emphasized his slender height. He wasn't what Evelyn would call handsome in the classic sense, but his demeanor spoke of a man of character. A man she wanted to know.

Her pulse pounding, Evelyn stepped forward. For the first time, she thanked her mother for the ballet lessons. She would rely on that training to maintain a poised and gracious response.

Her movement must have caught Tony's

eye for he focused solely upon Evelyn. Her palms moistened as everyone else in the room faded from existence.

"So you're E.T.?" he asked as he neared. His jovial smile said he loved the nickname and was trying to make the best of an awkward situation. The twitch of his eye suggested he was as nervous as she.

"Yes," she whispered and couldn't seem to find any more of her voice.

Tony stopped a few feet away. His expressive eyes brimmed with all the love that letter expressed, yet he acted as if he didn't have a clue what to say.

Neither did Evelyn. So she grasped onto the only link they shared — the rattle still in her hand. "I, uh, I — I think you left something with me the last time we were together." She raised the rattle.

Just the mention of the silver piece hurled Evelyn back to that day weeks ago when she'd found it in the attic. She'd cried half the night and spent most of Saturday in her room. Her eyes watered despite her desire to maintain her composure.

Tony reached for the silver rattle. She didn't understand why he stared at it so long until he looked back at her. His eyes were misty as well. "I meant for you to keep it for life." He placed the memento in the palm of her hand, closed her fingers over it, and wrapped his larger hand around hers. "Because I don't want you to ever forget me."

The feel of Tony's hand upon hers made Evelyn crave the assurance of his arms around her. Before she realized she was stepping toward him, E.T. found herself encircled in long arms that held her tight in warmth and security. His muffled sob against her ear instigated a flood of her own tears. After pressing her knuckles against trembling lips, she closed her eyes, rested her cheek against his chest, and clung to the father she would call Tony.

Epilogue

Victoria stepped into the nursery for the first time since she'd flung open the door that desperate spring day. She paused on the threshold and absorbed the ambiance of a room she had so meticulously planned. From March until June Victoria passed the nursery and glanced inside. Week after week of seeing the baby's room uninhabited had served as a healing balm for her. Finally, she conjured the courage to enter the infant's haven which smelled of baby powder. She deposited a blue department store bag on the changing table. She'd gone to the store to purchase two bags of chips and some hamburger buns for the Seven Sisters semi-annual bash. While in the store Victoria had also picked up a pregnancy test along with a tiny pair of baby shoes — just in case.

She stroked the stack of receiving blankets meticulously folded nearby. The soft down reminded her of the day she'd purchased the blankets at the department store — the day she learned of her first pregnancy. Victoria laid the used pregnancy test wand on the changing table and removed the baby shoes from the store bag. She looked down at the short plastic wand that had come in the test box. The instructions said two red stripes in the indicator window meant she was pregnant. As she had hoped, two red stripes presented themselves for the world to see.

"Yes!" she said for the sixth time in three minutes. She examined her coral-colored shorts set and was now thrilled that the waistband was a little snug. This morning Victoria had worried that perhaps she was starting to expand for the wrong reasons.

She giggled as she recalled the last few months. While Victoria couldn't call herself the queen of romance, she had taken some wise and exciting pointers from Kim Lan. Now, she knew exactly how to "set a trap" for Tony, and he *did* love it!

Victoria proudly picked up the test wand. Moving to the nursery window she gazed down upon the beach party in full swing. Her six closest friends had decided to descend on Victoria and Tony this June for their reunion. The brilliant sun, unmarred by clouds, christened the event with a warmth and beauty that were mere reflections of the bond the seven friends enjoyed. Tony and the guys were cooking hamburgers. While the men stood around an oversized grill and talked about manly stuff the ladies enjoyed the surf and sand — everyone except Kim Lan, Marilyn, and their husbands.

From the start of the reunion those four had focused on plans for putting together a ministry network to help get people off the streets and back into society. Kim Lan, elegant and lithe, leaned back in her chair and flopped her shiny black hair over one shoulder. She said something with that cocky little smile of hers, and Marilyn nearly fell out of her seat laughing. Joshua and Mick were both acting like whatever Kim said was the corniest crack of the century.

"They'll be great together," Victoria whispered and wished them the best of blessings. With the money Kim Lan earned as a supermodel, Mick's international ministry connections, and Marilyn and Joshua's grass-roots contacts, Victoria could only imagine the good God could bring.

A frisbee sailed straight for Joshua's head and he ducked before the thing hit him smack between the eyes. He called something toward Sammie Jones who was attempting to teach her son, Brett, how to throw a frisbee. Brett, at the ripe age of four, preferred to aim at people rather than space.

Sammie, her red hair flying in the ocean breeze, ran after her son, who zoomed straight into the arms of his father, R.J. Butler.

Their big news of the day had been the adoption papers R.J. proudly displayed as he informed everyone that he was now legally a father. Brett, as red-headed as his mom, had responded with a hug and a wet kiss. The sisters and their husbands had cheered.

Now, R.J. turned his son upside down and tickled him. The biker righted Brett, walked toward Sammie, placed an arm around her, and forgot the guys. The couple strode toward the water's edge and looked upon the azure sea. Victoria recalled Sam's abusive first marriage and was thrilled that God had given Sam a man of gold.

Jac, cell phone plastered to her ear, walked past Sam and R.J. and headed toward the driveway. All morning she'd been interrupted by intermittent calls and had promised the sisters she'd turn off her cell. Somehow that wasn't happening.

Why does that not surprise me? Victoria thought. Jac called to Lawton, ever the adoring husband, and allowed him to place his arm in hers. Jacquelyn removed the phone from her ear and started chatting with him as she led him away from the crowd. The man who was born blind didn't seem to mind that his pint-sized wife had brought part of her work on this trip. And Victoria remembered the early days of their relationship when Lawton fell — and fell hard. She never doubted for a minute that Jac didn't neglect Lawton. Both of them were independent to a fault. Both of them traveled in their careers. And both of them unconditionally accepted each other.

Melissa Franklin ran past Jac and Lawton with Marilyn's daughter and Kim Lan's son on either side of her. She'd done nothing but play with those two for the last hour. Her husband, Kinkaide, saw them coming, scooped Brooke up into his strong arms, and twirled her around. She squealed, and Khan Ahn reached up for his turn. Melissa leaned her head toward her husband. The two people who almost didn't get married were a striking couple. As they focused upon the children, Victoria recognized the symptoms that had gripped her a year ago — they had the baby bug. She recalled Mel saying that she and Kinkaide were thinking of starting a family, and Victoria calculated that might become a reality in the next couple of years. Whether they adopted or gave birth, she believed they would be exceptional parents.

Sonsee Delaney, already a mom, sat on the edge of the ocean with her 18-month-old son, Donny, in her lap. The older the child grew the more he resembled Taylor, in every way except his auburn hair, so like Sonsee's. Her hair plastered to her head, Sonsee flopped into the sand every time a wave washed ashore. Donny squealed with laughter and hung onto his mother's neck. Sonsee's husband Taylor ran toward his wife and son and plopped beside them. He grabbed his son and ran into the rolling ocean. Little Donny's laughter, although blocked by the window, filled Victoria's heart.

And she imagined Tony and her in the ocean with their own toddler in a couple of years. She examined the test wand once more and giggled again. Without another moment's hesitation Victoria stepped into her bedroom, retrieved the cordless phone, and dialed Tony's cell number. By the time she got back to the window, he had reached for his phone and was examining the screen for who might be calling.

With a smile he placed the cell to his ear and said, "Hi, honey."

"Hi," Victoria responded. "I'm in the nursery," she said. "I'm looking out the window at you as we speak."

He turned from the grill and gazed up at her. She wiggled her fingers and he waved in return.

"Come on up," she invited. "I've got a surprise."

"Oh?"

"Yes. You're *not* going to believe it!"

"Uhhh, okay," he said. "Let me give my spatula to one of the guys, and I'll be right up."

"Great. See you in a minute."

As they disconnected the call Tony was shrugging out of his apron. He dropped it into Joshua's lap and handed him the spatula. Mick, Marilyn, and Kim Lan listened while Tony explained his mission. When the three of them looked up at Victoria, she waved and they all returned her sentiment.

Victoria then rushed back into the restroom to retrieve the instructions that came with the pregnancy test. She folded the paper in half and half again which left one important section easy to read. By the time she got back to the nursery Tony was coming up the stairs.

"What's up, babe?" He paused on the nursery's threshold and tucked a fold of his shirttail back into his pleated shorts. "I'm thinking about changing into my swimsuit and hitting the surf," he complained. "It's hot out there, and I'm sweating like a sow."

Beaming, Victoria ignored his complaints about the heat and handed him the pregnancy test instructions. "Read this section right here," she said and pointed to the specified text.

"Okay. If one pink line shows on the wand as indicated above, no pregnancy has occurred. If two pink lines show on the wand as indicated above, then that *does* indicate a pregnancy."

Victoria shoved her wand between his face and the paper. For a breathless second Tony said nothing. He just stared at the indicator as if he were trying to piece together the situation. Finally, he whooped and grabbed his wife. Laughter gurgling in her throat, Victoria returned his embrace and the two rocked in each other's arms.

"So *that's* why you're in the nursery," he said at last.

Victoria pulled away. "Yes. And look." She reached for the new baby shoes on the changing table. "Aren't they cute?"

"I love 'em!" he declared. The two of them popped open the plastic box and Tony extracted a shoe. "Look," he said, "it fits my two fingers perfectly."

"Oh you," Victoria said and the two fell into the laughter of lovers.

Tony hugged his wife once more and Victoria reveled in the difference Christ had made in their marriage. His love forever promised the hope of tomorrow amid the joys of the present.

"Let's go tell everyone," Tony whispered.

"Okay," Victoria agreed and gazed around the nursery. Even though she'd already done a lot of work much still needed to be prepared. And she sensed a deep inner peace that this time she really would get to hold her baby.

Author's Note

Dear Friend,

I hope you have enjoyed reading the Seven Sisters series as much as I have enjoyed writing it. *Let's Begin Again* has been especially dear to me because I featured some themes from my popular book *Romancing Your Husband.*

I have learned that while many couples might not physically separate, as did Tony and Victoria, they are separated in their hearts. Often we applaud couples who stay together through the years, when in reality there has been an emotional divorce. The result is two people living together but living separate lives. What a tragedy.

When Christ is the center, foundation, and substance of a marriage, our homes become like heaven on earth. Because of the principles featured in *Romancing Your Husband*, my husband and I are tasting the essence of heaven in our home. While neither of us is perfect by any means, we have learned to unconditionally love and accept each other without the nagging need to change the person we vowed to honor and respect.

This kind of peaceful home life is *only* possible when spouses first have a radical encounter with Jesus Christ. There are many people in churches like Victoria who *think* they know Jesus, but in reality they only know *about* Him.

Do you *know* Jesus or just know about Him? Has there ever been a time when you recognized that you are not holy or righteous or worthy in your own power? Do you spend chunks of time ever week romancing the Lord, being still before Him, and reading the words of Christ? If not, I hope you will begin the journey to a deep-down, heart-cleansing relationship with Christ and encounter His radical love.

In Christ,

Debra White Smith

About the Author

Debra White Smith continues to impact and entertain readers with her life-changing books, including *Romancing Your Husband*; *The Harder I Laugh, the Deeper I Hurt*; *More than Rubies: Becoming a Woman of Godly Influence*; and the popular *Seven Sisters* fiction series. She has 31 book sales to her credit and, since 1997, has been blessed with more than 635,000 books in print. The founder of Real Life Ministries, Debra touches lives through the written and spoken word by presenting real truth for real life and ministering to people where they are. Debra speaks for events across the nation and sings with her husband and children. She has been featured on TV and radio shows, including "The 700 Club," "At Home Live," "Getting Together," "Moody Broadcasting Network," "USA Radio Network News," and "Midday Connection." Debra holds an M.A. in English and is working on a master of divinity through Trinity Seminary. She lives in small-town America with her husband of 20 years, two children, and a herd of cats.

To write Debra or contact her for speaking engagements, check out her website:

www.debrawhitesmith.com

or send mail to:

Real Life Ministries
Debra White Smith
P.O. Box 1482
Jacksonville, TX 75766